LISA CASSIDY

# RISE OF THE
# SHADOWCOUNCIL

HEIR TO THE DARKMAGE - BOOK 4

Tate House

 A catalogue record for this
book is available from the
National Library of Australia

**National Library of Australia Cataloguing-in-Publication entry**

Creator: Cassidy, Lisa, 2022 - author.

Title: Rise of the Shadowcouncil

ISBN (ebook): 978-1-922533-08-1

ISBN (print): 978-1-922533-09-8

Subjects: Young Adult fantasy

Series: Heir to the Darkmage

First published2022 by Tate House

Cover artwork and design by Jeff Brown Graphics

Map artwork by Chaim Holtjer

This one is for the English teachers.

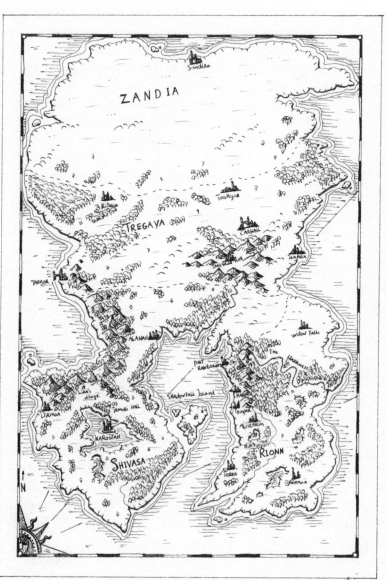

# CHAPTER I

Salty spray flew into the air as the ship plunged into a trough, the icy droplets spraying Lira's face and dancing with her water magic. A picturesque sunrise had turned into a golden morning, specks of sunlight glittering like gold dust across the turquoise ocean, the breeze soft and cool. The creaks and groans of a ship at sea sounded behind her, mixed with the occasional call of one crew member to another.

It made her feel oddly content. The simple beauty of the day sank into her skin, easing some of the hard edges of the past two years, reminding her that not all was darkness. And for once she let that peace settle over her.

It was going to be impossible to find again in the months to come.

Their ship plunged into another trough and sent seawater flying high. Lira blinked and swiped at her face with the sleeve of her shirt. Enough admiring the sunrise. There was still much planning to be done.

She hadn't moved from her spot at the prow since exchanging combative words with Alyx Egalion as they sailed steadily away from Rotherburn. Egalion hadn't returned, and none of the others on board had come to speak to Lira either. She wasn't surprised—no doubt Egalion had filled them in on the deal Lira had made with Lucinda, and they would be predictably furious with her. And Tarion ... well, he was likely devastated about his father, whose survival seemed unlikely as soon as Lucinda learned Egalion was reneging on her word.

She was glad they'd left her alone. It had given her the time she needed to think. Even now, ignoring stiffened muscles from standing too long and the creeping fog of exhaustion at the edges of her thoughts, she remained. The water surrounding the ship soothed her, a gentle susurration against her magical senses as she worked through her situation for the hundredth time since Egalion had walked off, trying to figure the right path forward.

She hadn't had any luck yet.

Lira was once again dancing to Lucinda's tune, agreeing to do what the woman wanted. Lucinda's instructions to Lira and Egalion had been clear enough. Bring the Mage Council under their control. Use that power to subdue the kingdoms and any resistance they might summon. Then allow Lucinda's people to resettle on their continent. Do that, and Ahrin Vensis and Dashan Caverlock, whom Lucinda currently held hostage back in Rotherburn, would be returned to them.

What had gone unsaid was that Lucinda would then expect to take that absolute power *from* Lira and Egalion. Presumably she'd have some other leverage to force them to hand it over.

Lira suspected that had *always* been the woman's end goal: to rule the continent herself. Her country's desperate need to save themselves from the mercilessly encroaching hordes of razak and nerik merely provided the justification she needed to take control of the Seven and use what was left of Rotherburn's resources to reach that goal.

But Egalion had already decided to sacrifice her husband and ignore Lucinda's orders. Which meant Lira not only had to accomplish the task alone, but with the most powerful mage in the world opposing her.

If she failed, Lucinda would kill Ahrin.

*"You are a fool. Sacrificing everything to save the thing most dangerous to you."* Lucinda's words echoed through Lira's memory, sharp with the same contempt that had been written all over Lucinda's face. *"She will destroy you, Lira."*

Lira lifted a weary hand to rub at aching temples. She'd spent days thinking Ahrin was gone, the Darkhand's death hitting her so hard it had felt like walking around with a severe concussion. And then to see her, alive, chained up in Lucinda's cage, rigid with panic. Captured for leverage. The relief had been so profound, combined so inextricably with horror and anger ... even now, she shook when she thought about the blind terror on Ahrin's face.

Yet Lucinda's parting words wouldn't let her go. Lira's hands curled into fists, the violet light flickering around her forearms betraying her deep agitation. With an effort, she slowly wrestled all the emotion away. She couldn't afford it. Her words to Ahrin back in Rotherburn had been truer than any she'd ever spoken.

She would do whatever Lucinda wanted if it meant getting Ahrin out of that cage. Yet Ahrin Vensis was no damsel in distress. She was more capable than anyone Lira had ever met. She'd get herself out. Lira just had to buy her the time to do it.

Which brought her back to doing Lucinda's bidding.

Lira took a deep breath, spent a moment checking and reinforcing her mental shields—no doubt Egalion would be regularly attempting to read her thoughts—then refocused her mind.

Every time Lira had gone up against Lucinda and tried to outwit her, she'd failed. She hadn't even come *close* to winning. It would be beyond stupid to think she could try again and succeed this time.

Since the first moment she'd met the Seventh, Lira had been juggling too much—her desperate need to belong in the Mage Council's world against an equally strong desire for vengeance against Underground for her kidnapping and torture. Her mistrust of, and deep love for, Ahrin. The yearning to accept the hand of friendship that her fellow students at Temari had extended, despite the fact their privileged lives represented everything she hated. Her fury at the Mage Council for locking her away for life. Her desperate desire to be both like and unlike her notorious grandfather—a desire that hid the aching emptiness where her mother's love had once been.

Lira's fists tightened again, but with a deep breath she loosened them. Behind her, a sailor shouted something to a fellow crewmember, who whistled in response, triggering more whistles along the length of the ship. Moments later, wood groaned as another sail unfurled, catching the stiffening breeze. The sounds helped re-orient Lira in the present.

She'd already let go of her need to belong. Maybe it was time to let the overriding desire for vengeance go, too. At least for now. It certainly hadn't gotten her anywhere but inside another noose of Lucinda's making.

She still didn't have a workable plan for carrying out Lucinda's task. Even after hours of thinking. Not even the beginnings of one. But she knew one thing for certain: taking down the Mage Council single-handedly was something her grandfather had failed at twice despite having an entire army behind him and far more magical power than Lira ever would. She wasn't going to succeed where he failed unless she approached the problem a different way.

Footsteps sounded behind her, moving quickly, and she turned, magic rising. But it was just one of the sailors crossing the foredeck.

The sight was a relief, but also … disappointing. She'd half-hoped it had been one of them coming to talk to her. Tarion Caverlock. His cousin, Garan. Their fellow mages Fari and Lorin. Unexpectedly, the thought of them had her shoulders relaxing, the rolling deck under her feet suddenly steadier. A lot more had happened in Rotherburn than Ahrin almost dying and Lucinda successfully manipulating them again.

Her companions had stayed at her side in the tunnels under the ravine city even when despair and magic overuse had made her a burden. They'd tried to find Ahrin, someone they feared and distrusted, because they knew how much Lira loved her. And after they'd found Egalion, they'd stood up to her on Lira's behalf.

They'd done all that because they called themselves her friends. Even when she'd refused to accept it, refused to trust them, had been *unable* to do any of those things. When she'd thrown it back in their faces repeatedly.

*A different way.*

That thought came back to her again, nudging at her, not letting her ignore it. Following it through, Lira ignored her need for vengeance, on *anyone*, and focused on what she wanted most.

Ahrin's safety. That answer was clear as a ringing bell inside her mind. But after that … when she pushed everything else aside and allowed herself to admit it … Lira let out a slow breath. Not just Ahrin's safety, but Tarion's and Garan's and Fari's and Lorin's too. Those five people. Her friends.

Apart from her own survival, that's all Lira Astor cared about in this world.

When she framed it that way, it was oddly easy to admit. And it felt astonishingly good … to *know* something about herself, to know it clearly, without any doubt or hesitation. There was fear, too, in knowing she had more to lose than just Ahrin. But, even so, her shoulders loosened even further. And a different path came to her.

It was a tiny thread of an idea, one the old Lira would *never* have considered, would have laughed out of the room. Even now, every instinct she had rebelled against it. But it would buy her the time Ahrin needed, and shift the chances of success from zero to marginal.

What if she did something *nobody* would see coming? Not what Lucinda wanted *or* what the Darkmage would do. What if Lira Astor ran a con on everyone, one that turned the world on its head and, in doing so, put herself in a position to finally end Lucinda and her Seven?

A chuckle broke out of her at the craziness of the idea. At how heady it made her feel. She'd have to carry this out very carefully, one piece at a time, revealing her true intentions to nobody. Everyone would have to believe she was carrying out Lucinda's orders. There could be no doubt in anyone's mind or Lucinda's spies would ferret it out and Ahrin would die.

Could she do it?

Hope unfurled like a tiny new seedling, one she quickly but gently put away. There was no place for hope *or* vengeance if she was to carry this out. She had to be focused, clear-thinking, like Ahrin had taught her.

She turned, thoughtful gaze taking in the narrow steps leading down into the ship's hold where Egalion and her companions must be.

Lira turned back, resettled against the railing, and soaked in the sunshine's warmth on her face.

Lucinda thought she knew Lira so well.

But maybe she didn't know her at all.

# CHAPTER 2

I t was dusk when Lira finally emerged from her thoughts, blinking, and registered that the sun was setting on the horizon. Her back and legs ached, her cracked ribs also registered a sharp complaint. Her head throbbed, both from her still-healing head injury and the effort and focus required to maintain her mental shields; Alyx Egalion could not catch wind of her strategising.

She'd spent the entire day at the prow of the boat. She was half-surprised nobody had come out to capture her and lock her away in a cabin. Maybe they'd thought it unnecessary as they were in the middle of the ocean and Lira had nowhere to run. But it meant Lira had had the time and space she'd needed to properly think through her next steps in enough detail to reduce the chances of failure. Just like Ahrin had taught her.

She gave herself a gentle shake, loosening cramped muscles, and took a few deep breaths to calm her weary mind and restore focus. Then, one final time, she ran the steps through her mind. Made sure she'd tested the holes, that she knew the details inside and out.

It was only once she was done, finally satisfied, that she realised how exhausted and filthy she was. But she couldn't rest just yet. She needed to set the first steps in motion now.

Turning away from the prow, Lira crossed the deck and found her way to the tiny cabin she'd been shown to when first boarding, which, in addition to a narrow bunk, contained a tiny table holding a basin of cold water. Her pack sat on the bunk, bow and quiver of arrows beside it. Everything looked untouched. Leaving it there, she stripped down and washed as best she could.

Every movement made her wince. Standing for hours on end hadn't done much for her injuries, and the multitude of cuts and bruises all over her body stung fiercely at the touch of water. Still, the wash gave her a little burst of energy. Enough to dispel the doubt she was already feeling about the sanity of her plan.

Her hand settled on the doorknob, and she hesitated before leaving the cabin. Maybe it would just be easier to ... no. She let out a long breath. Deep down she knew that doing things the way she would have in the past wasn't going to work, not against Lucinda. The plan she'd come up with might be crazy in its scope, and it might have a miniscule chance of success, but it at least *had* a chance. If only because nobody would see it coming.

And with Ahrin's life in the balance, she would choose the plan offering the greatest odds of survival, no matter what that meant for Lira personally. She didn't linger on the awareness that something deep inside, barely acknowledged, felt *good* about it in a way she never had before.

Resolve hardened, she opened the door and stepped out, making sure her mind was focused and shielded and her expression clear of anything that might give her away.

Time to put the first steps of the plan into play.

She found the others sitting in the galley, silent and grim, despite the cosy orange glow filling the small space from a stove burning in the corner. A kettle bubbled, untended, over it. The remains of a meal littered the narrow table.

Alyx Egalion wasn't among them, and neither was Athira. That made things much easier ... she wasn't sure whether to be buoyed by the fact that the first step in her plan was going so well, or suspicious. Either way, there was nothing for it but to forge ahead.

They all looked up at Lira's entrance, and while none of them said anything straight away, they watched her closely. Doubt and suspicion filled the room, palpable in its intensity. They didn't know what to expect from her.

"Athira's not here?" she asked, simply to break the silence, to try and judge exactly how furious they were at her.

"No." Garan spoke but didn't elaborate. The dark shadows under his eyes were enhanced by the firelight, highlighting the stubble on his jaw, the unkempt appearance of his usually perfectly messy hair.

"And Egalion?"

"Obviously not here either." There was an edge to Garan's voice this time. "Did you just drop by to ask us stupid questions?"

Inwardly, she winced. So ... pretty mad then.

She returned their stares for a moment, then found a spare stool, dragged it over to the table, and sat down. She opened her mouth to start talking, but before she could say anything, Garan cut her off.

"Before you start with whatever lie you're planning on telling us, I have a question. Ahrin's alive, isn't she?"

Lira scowled. "I—"

"Don't lie. We already know the answer," Fari said.

Lira might have been annoyed by the interruptions if she wasn't so damned tired. Instead, she merely let out a sigh and decided to let them get whatever they needed to off their chests. It would be quicker than arguing. "How did you know? Egalion told you, I presume?"

Garan blinked, clearly surprised by her lack of denial.

"No, it's just obvious. After you thought she died, you..." Fari took a breath. "You were depressed, severely so. The magic overuse and your injuries contributed to that as well, but ... I was really worried about you, Spider. Tarion said you didn't even attempt to keep yourself alive when fighting the razak queen. But now, since your secret little meeting with Lucinda, the depression is gone. While you're obviously exhausted and sore, you're back to normal Lira ... scowling and simmering away with anger a hairsbreadth under the surface."

Lira couldn't help it. She smiled, huffed an amused breath. "Normal Lira is 'scowling and simmering with anger'? How poetic. I don't hate the description though."

More blinks of surprise. This time it was Tarion who forged ahead. "Lucinda has Ahrin, we take it, and is now using her as leverage over you?" He sounded more curious than angry at her. Lira would have once been surprised by that. Now ... she knew that he trusted her. And she him.

"Correct." She settled more fully on the stool, hiding a wince as her aching ribs protested the movement. "And before you cut me off just now, I was about to explain all of that to you. No more secrets," she said.

"Just like that?" Fari scoffed.

"Secrets between us didn't turn out so well last time, did they?" She held Fari's gaze, then shifted to each of them in turn, waiting for the slight signs of acknowledgement in each expression.

"You were right." Lira shrugged. "If I hadn't lied to you all about spying on Underground for the council, about having new magical abilities, maybe things would be different now," Lira said, ignoring the sting of knowing that to succeed, she was going to have to lie to them again, even if it was for their own good. "I'm not ignorant of what you all did for me back in Rotherburn, how you stood by me. Not to mention saving me from spending the rest of my life in prison. I am ... grateful." Whatever else happened next, they all deserved to hear that much.

They shared glances, some—like Lorin—looking less dubious than the others about her sincerity. But after a moment, Garan spoke. "If that's true, then why don't you start with telling us what Lucinda wanted with you and my aunt, and why she's holding Ahrin as leverage?"

Lira looked up, startled. "Wait, Egalion didn't tell you *anything* about what happened when we met with her?"

A series of shaking heads.

Another stroke of luck. Egalion hadn't been in here already telling her side of the story. What had the woman been *thinking*? "You can't be serious. What did she say when you asked her?"

"She promised she'd share everything once we were safely home," Garan said, but a flicker on his face told her this wasn't the full truth. The son of Ladan Egalion was not a good liar. That was okay. After everything, maybe Lira needed to earn their trust back too.

"You don't need to wait. I'll tell you everything I know." Lira looked between them. "Lucinda doesn't just have Ahrin. She has your father, too, Tarion."

Tarion looked as shocked as the others at Lira's words, but it quickly dissolved into confusion. "Mama would have told me if that were the case."

"It's true. I saw him with Ahrin, both of them chained up in a box."

He leaned forward, eyes bright with a combination of hope and fear. "Was he hurt?"

"He's a prisoner, but apart from some cuts and bruises, he and Ahrin were both alive and mostly well when we saw them."

Garan shook his head stubbornly. "Aunt Alyx would never leave Uncle Dash behind."

Lira gave them the pure and unvarnished truth. "Lucinda threatened to kill both Ahrin and Caverlock unless Egalion and I agreed to return home, take control of the Mage Council, and use that control to subdue the kingdoms and allow the Seven and the people of Rotherburn to make a home in our countries."

Thick, shocked silence filled the room. It was obvious they didn't know whether to believe her. The moment drew out for several heartbeats before it snapped, and everyone moved to talk at once.

"Hang on, what—"

"You're not saying—"

"There's no *way*—"

"One at a time." Garan held up a hand to quiet them, then looked at Lira. "If Lucinda wanted to move her people to our continent, why didn't she just petition the kingdoms to be allowed in as refugees? Their circumstances are genuine, and King Cayr wouldn't refuse them, even if other monarchs did."

Lira snorted. "Think about what you know of this woman. Do you really think she'd be content to move to Rionn as a refugee and live out a quiet farming life? No, she wants ultimate power gathered into a single set of reins that she can take hold of when she arrives. She's always wanted it, and she has slowly and steadily been working on the Seven until she had them fully under her control. Our failure to kill all the razak queens delivered her that control—she's manipulated them into believing there is literally no other option for them. There's nothing holding her back now."

He huffed in disbelief. "And the Seven just let her do that?"

"I don't have all the answers, Garan. I suspect in the beginning the Seven thought they could manage the monster problem themselves. But by the time the realisation set in that they were losing … Lucinda pounced. She used their fear against them. She's a master of manipulation, and she's terrifyingly intelligent. Everything she does is planned out to the final detail."

Garan opened his mouth, sighed, then closed it, rubbing one hand tiredly against his forehead. "Tell us everything."

Lira did. She didn't hesitate, didn't prevaricate, and it was obvious how her honest account affected them by the expressions on their faces. "That's it, the whole exchange with Lucinda," she said, trailing to a halt, "as best as I can remember."

There was another drawn-out silence. They believed her. Garan seemed momentarily defeated, but Tarion's gaze was narrowed in thought, mind clearly racing to put pieces together. Fari's expression indicated she didn't know where to even begin with what she'd just heard. Lorin was quiet, processing in his own dignified way, content to wait for everyone else's thoughts.

It was Tarion who broke the silence. His voice was firm, no trace of his usual shyness. "Mama would never agree to such a thing, even for Da."

"She didn't. She won't." Lira shrugged, again not hesitating. "She's going to try and stop me."

For Lira's true plan to succeed, Lucinda *had* to believe Lira was doing exactly as ordered. Which meant everyone around Lira had to believe it too. At least for now, until she could get a better grasp on who Lucinda had watching her. So she kept her shoulders straight and voice confident, not giving any reason for them to suspect she might have other intentions.

"Wait, you *did* agree?" Garan sat up on his stool, looking at her in horror.

"Why wouldn't I?" Lira lifted an eyebrow. "I certainly don't care a rotted toss about the Mage Council after what they did to me. If I do what Lucinda wants, then Ahrin gets to live. That's all I care about."

Lorin frowned, speaking for the first time. "I can see why you'd feel that way, Lira, but I don't understand why you're so willing to tell us all of this."

"Like I said, I don't want to keep secrets from you anymore. But also, if I'm going to succeed, I'll need help." Lira pointed at Tarion. "You're the mage heir to the most powerful council member alive." Then at Garan. "You're the heir to Rionn's lord-mage and lord-Taliath." Then at Fari. "You're the only heir to the powerful and influential Dirsk family."

"And me?" Lorin asked quietly.

She met his gaze. Held it. "I'm going to need fighters."

Those things were all true, and using truth as much as possible was always the best way to succeed at running a con.

"You've gone insane. Literally mad." Garan was shaking his head in disbelief. "Are you asking us to *join* you in taking over the Mage Council? I don't care a fig's toss for Ahrin Vensis, and I'm certainly not going to help you overthrow the council for her."

"What about for your uncle?" She lifted an eyebrow.

"I..." He hesitated, unable to meet her gaze. His jaw worked, genuine pain in his voice as he spoke. "My aunt knows what his choice would be, and she honours that. I can do no less."

"I will help you," Lorin announced calmly.

She bit back a smile of triumph. That—

"As will I," Fari said quietly.

"Me too." Tarion held her gaze with quiet certainty.

Stunned, Lira opened her mouth but wasn't sure what to say. She'd thought only one of them would agree so readily. She'd hoped to convince the others after significant persuasion, but part of her plan had relied upon a quick capitulation from one person.

Before she *could* say anything, Garan rounded on his cousin, the force of his turn so great his hip knocked the table and made all the dishes rattle loudly. "Tar, you can't!"

"I understand the choice Mama made," he said steadily, "and I respect it. It's the right decision, no matter how difficult, and I know it's what Da would choose. But I'm making a different choice."

Garan stared at him. "Why?"

"Do you think Lira would be choosing this now if we'd stood by her last time she was accused of being a traitor, if the council had believed in her?" He was looking at his cousin as he spoke, voice ringing with conviction. "Lira is not the Darkmage. I know this for certain. This time I choose to stand with her, like I should have last time."

Something leaped in Lira's chest at his words. It was live and warm and so much *steadier* than the heady thrill she felt each time she did something reckless.

"You want to stand with her to destroy the council and take over the kingdoms?" Garan's voice went up an octave. "Tarion, you've gone mad too."

"I don't have a place in that council anymore, not with this monstrous power of mine." Tarion's voice turned dark. "But it's not just that, Garan. I know that one day, Lira is going to burn Lucinda and her people to the ground. And I want that just as badly as she does."

Garan let out an incredulous breath, swinging to Fari and Lorin. "And you two?"

"Lira saved my life and my place as a mage warrior." Lorin spoke in his haughty Shiven way. "I still owe that debt."

"My reasons are my own," Fari said simply, then looked at Lira, challenge in her dark eyes. "You'll just have to trust me."

Lira held her gaze for a moment, trying to judge her sincerity, then looked at Lorin. "You fulfilled your debt when you helped me escape prison and ruined your career as a mage warrior doing it. You owe me nothing anymore. If you join Egalion's side now, you can get your life as a mage warrior back. You know that's true."

He was silent a moment. "I don't see it that way. But even if it *were* true, I agree with everything Tarion just said."

Garan ran an agitated hand through his hair. "How do you even know Lucinda won't kill Ahrin *and* my uncle once she finds out that Aunt Alyx isn't doing what she's supposed to? And you know she *will* find out; she clearly has spies everywhere."

"A gamble we'll have to take," Lira said crisply, eyes narrowing slightly at the mention of spies. "I'm going to make it very obvious to anyone watching me that I'm doing what I'm supposed to."

Garan pounded his hand onto the table, making Fari jump. "You have *no* way of knowing what Lucinda does to Ahrin while you're thousands of miles away starting a war on her behalf."

"True," Lira said. "But now that she knows holding Ahrin as leverage over me works, do you truly think she'll kill her? Lucinda is a rational strategist, a pragmatist. She knows as soon as she loses her leverage over me, she has a problem on her hands." She lifted an eyebrow. "No, Lucinda would be foolish beyond belief to harm Ahrin while I'm obeying orders. And Lucinda doesn't do foolish."

"So my uncle dies while the Darkhand gets to live, and no matter what my aunt does Lucinda gets what she wants?" Garan bit out the words. "Aunt Alyx will fight to oppose you, Lira. And she *will* win. Lucinda won't get what she wants—Uncle Dash won't die in vain."

"He won't die at all," Lira snapped. She couldn't help but feel intensely irritated by Garan's casual confidence that she couldn't defeat Egalion, despite how accurate it probably was. "Given she is getting what she wants from *me*, Lucinda will see Caverlock as more useful to her alive. She doesn't discard potential leverage for no reason. While it might not have worked on Egalion, I bet it would on Tarion or Caria."

Tarion looked at her, catching her gaze. "That's a big gamble to make."

"And one I wouldn't be prepared to make on Ahrin's life," she said, wanting to be honest with him.

His mouth quirked in a sad smile. "I happen to think you're right, though."

Fari glanced at Lira, eyes narrowing. Lorin stayed quiet.

Garan let out a long breath and sat back in his chair. "You don't know that for certain, Tar. You're agreeing to help Lira start a war," he said flatly. "People will die. I know you too well to think you'll be okay with killing innocents."

"Stop being so rotted black and white, Garan!" Lira snapped. "I—"

"Garan, do you truly believe, deep down, that Lira will act like her grandfather did?" Tarion turned in his chair, seeking and catching his cousin's gaze.

There was a pause, but not a long one, before Garan murmured, "No. No, I don't."

Lira reeled, eyes widening despite herself.

"But that doesn't mean this is the right thing to do," he continued. "People will be hurt, no matter what her intentions."

"All this is moot anyway." Fari rose suddenly, going over to the bubbling kettle and lifting it to pour steaming water into a chipped mug. She stirred a handful of unidentified leaves into the water, then carried it over to place it in front of Lira. The others watched her in silence.

As Fari returned to her seat, she held Lira's gaze. "It's time for us to be honest with you, Lira. Councillor Egalion left the ship hours ago, flying back to Dirinan. She took Athira with her. There'll be a welcome party waiting for you when this ship docks, and the council isn't going to let you out of their grasp this time."

Lira shifted on her stool, tired and sore, lifting a hand to rub it over her face as she tried to summon the energy she needed to finish this. Giving herself a moment to think, she reached out for the mug, taking a sip of floral-tasting tea. "This whole time you knew that and didn't tell me?"

Garan gave Fari a mutinous look. "Aunt Alyx gave us direct orders not to."

"After telling us absolutely nothing about what was going on." Lorin scowled at him. "She didn't even tell us about your uncle. Or how and why Athira suddenly showed up in Rotherburn. We didn't even get a chance to talk to her."

"She was trying to keep us safe, to protect Tarion for as long as possible from the pain of her decision," Garan said.

"I'm a grown man. As are you," Tarion said quietly. "I love, trust, and respect Mama. But that doesn't mean I must always choose the same path as her. She can't fight for Da, but *I* can."

Lira tried not to roll her eyes at the sentiment and sought to bring the conversation back to relevant information. "What *did* she say, exactly, before she left?"

"That we were to keep a close eye on you until we arrived in Dirinan, and that no matter what had happened in Rotherburn, you remained a traitor to the council," Fari said. "Which all turns out to be true, incidentally."

She let out a sigh. Doing any of this suddenly seemed impossibly difficult. Then she thought of Ahrin, confined to that cage, eyes dark with panicked terror. And her resolve hardened to granite.

Tarion leaned forward. "Athira wouldn't talk either. Lira, do *you* know anything else about why she's here, what happened to her?"

"I'm sorry, I only know what I've already told you, from our conversation with Lucinda," she said honestly. "All I'm certain of is that she is now Lucinda's creature, and we have to treat her as such."

Silence greeted her words. It felt as bone-weary as she did.

Lira lifted a hand. "Before you decide to walk out of this cabin on my side, Egalion made things clear. You choose me, and you're betraying your beloved council. Any goodwill you won back by rescuing Egalion will be gone. You'll lose that nice blue cloak and the trust of your friends and family. You might be captured and placed in prison, or worse."

Garan stood immediately, chair screeching on the uneven floor. "I won't help you, Lira. I'm going home to Alistriem and I'm going to help protect my king from whatever the fallout is of this insane fight you're about to start."

She held his gaze, remaining seated. "I understand and respect your decision, Garan. Thank you for hearing me out."

For a moment, Garan seemed to search for the right words to say. Finally, he whispered, "Please don't do this."

"I have no choice." Tears welled in her eyes. The last thing she wanted to do was refuse his entreaty to be worthy of the faith he'd always placed in her. But she couldn't explain that to him now. Ahrin's life depended on swift, ruthless progress. "But I understand that you don't either. We part as friends, Garan Egalion."

"I wish that were true," he said sadly, casting a lingering glance at the others before adding, "Goodbye, Lira."

He left the galley without another word. Lira took another sip of her tea, then regarded the others, all remaining in their seats rather than following Garan. "Are you sure this is what you want?" She looked at each of them in turn, no give in her voice or glance. "Because once this starts, there will be no turning back. Your one and only chance of being re-instated by the council is to walk out now and join Garan."

"I understand," Lorin said gravely. "I stay with you."

Fari let out a sigh. "Don't make me say it again, Spider. I'm still sitting here, aren't I?"

Tarion gave her a little smile. "I stay too."

She nodded at them and stood up, the legs of the stool screeching. "I'm going to get some sleep. You should all do the same. Tomorrow, we'll discuss what happens once we arrive at Dirinan."

"What if we just change the ship's course now?" Tarion suggested. "After all, the captain is Rotherburnian, and he has a vested interest in you succeeding, Lira. If we made port farther north in Tregaya, or even Zandia, you could avoid Mama's waiting party."

"It's a good idea—but unfortunately the most important thing right now is that Lucinda believes I'm doing what she asked. For both Ahrin's and your father's sakes. So I'll need to put on a nice show in Dirinan, where we know she has spies. Athira will be there too, and she will be writing regular messages to Lucinda. We can't be sure Lucinda will learn that I'm doing as ordered if we go anywhere else."

Fari looked dubious. "You think you can escape Councillor Egalion and whatever mages and Taliath she's managed to gather in Dirinan?"

"I'm going to have to." Lira smiled suddenly, seeking to lighten the mood. "Don't worry, we'll come up with a suitably devious plan. And don't forget Dirinan is home territory for me."

She left them in thoughtful silence, brisk strides carrying her away from the galley. Anxiety tightened her shoulder blades. She hadn't quite expected that discussion to turn out the way it did, and the easy win she'd thought she would be able to start with hadn't materialised. As good as it was to know that Fari, Tarion, and Lorin had chosen to stand with her, she was soon going to have to make a difficult judgement call.

And if she got it wrong, her plan would be a failure before it had even started.

# CHAPTER 3

The first thing Lira did the next morning was seek out the ship's captain. He was a lean, wiry man with a furtive gaze that held a gleam of fanaticism Lira recognised all too well. There had been signs in Rotherburn of division among the country's soldiers, some holding loyalty to particular members of the Seven over others. Given he was the one chosen to captain them back, she had to assume he was aligned with Lucinda. The Seventh didn't leave things to chance.

"Something you need?" He eyed her from his position at the ship's wheel beside the navigator.

She held his stare. "I assume you noticed that two of your passengers disembarked early?"

For a moment he didn't respond, but then he stepped away from the navigator, nodding sharply towards the railing. Interesting; he didn't want the navigator to hear their conversation. "Ship's watch told me. Amazing ability that—flying."

"Indeed," Lira said dryly. "We're going to face an ambush in Dirinan. Can you ensure we approach after dark? You'll have to let us off then raise anchor and get clear before anyone realises we're there."

"Appreciate the warning." He glanced up at the sky, squinted, then shrugged. "If the winds stay as they are, we're due to make port late afternoon, but slowing up is easy enough."

"Good. Please do so." She went to leave, but curiosity had her turning back. "Are your orders to return straight to the ravine city once you've dropped us off?"

"Aye. We'll be heading straight back." The words were casual, but a quick shift of his eyes told her it was a lie.

"You don't think there's a better way of doing this?"

"Doing what?"

She swept her hands in an expansive gesture. "Going to these complicated lengths to save yourselves. I'm not sure I understand why any of you are listening to Lucinda."

"There's no explanation I can give that you would understand." He gave her a sharp look. "Not unless you, too, had spent your entire life hiding in the dark, watching friends and family being picked off one by one."

"So why not ask for help decades ago?"

"That is none of your business." He spat over the side.

"You mean you don't know," she needled.

His mouth twisted in scorn. "You think you've had a difficult life, but it's nothing on mine. So don't stand there and ask your ignorant questions like you have any right to ask them. I have a ship to run—was there anything else you needed?"

A similar scorn rose in her—he knew nothing of her life either—but there was no utility in antagonising him further. "No, that's all."

"Good." He left without another word.

Watching the man walk off with the rolling gate particular to sailors, her gaze fell on Garan, standing on the opposite side of the deck. He was in shirtsleeves and looked like he'd been practicing sparring manoeuvres with his staff.

She'd almost taken a step towards him—the urge to go and make things right burning in her—when she stopped herself, turning away instead and heading for the galley in search of breakfast.

No matter how much she wanted to, she couldn't avoid people being hurt.

As requested, their ship made its final approach to Dirinan just after the sun set over the horizon, shadowing the port in darkness. The captain showed no hesitance about sailing straight into the harbour under a merchant flag. It made Lira wonder how frequently ships from Rotherburn had sailed in and out of Shiven—or other—ports over the years without anyone realising who they were. They spoke the same language after all, despite a difference in accent, and sailors, always a motley group to begin with, were never scrutinised particularly closely.

Even so, Lira suspected it wasn't often. From what she'd seen in the ravine city, Rotherburn had little to trade with and a limited number of seaworthy ships—or at least no safe access to a harbour to maintain or keep any ships they had. The one they travelled on now had been the only one bobbing at anchor when they'd boarded it just west of the ravine city, and it had been a slow and laborious journey upriver to the ocean in challenging waters.

Lira glanced over to where Garan and Tarion were having an animated conversation a short distance off. Presumably Garan was making a last-ditch effort to change his cousin's mind. Tarion's hunched shoulders and downcast gaze told her Garan was failing—he always got uncomfortable disagreeing with others, particularly those he loved.

Garan had been a silent, brooding presence the remainder of their journey, but while making his disapproval clear, he hadn't sought to intrude on or otherwise interfere with their planning. And there had been *a lot* of planning—long days shut in the galley together, talking and debating about how to deal with the ambush awaiting them.

She would always be grateful to him for giving her that.

Apart from assuring them she had planned for their next steps should they successfully evade Egalion and the council, Lira hadn't revealed any details to them. The con she was putting into play would look very much like she *was* taking down the Mage Council, which meant she couldn't afford the council learning the details of her next steps any more than she could afford Lucinda learning of her true intentions. And she now knew that Lucinda had at least one telepath at her disposal in Rotherburn, in addition to the powerful telepathic abilities of Alyx Egalion and Dawn A'ndreas that were now arrayed against her.

Surprisingly, Fari, Tarion, and Lorin hadn't made much of a fuss over Lira not explaining everything. In fact, they'd already considered the threat posed by mage telepaths.

"We've decided to trust you, Lira," Lorin had said pragmatically, Tarion and Fari nodding beside him. "There are no half measures in doing that given what we've signed on for. That means I choose to trust that you will tell us what we need to know as soon as you can."

A little smile came unbidden. It was nice not having to do everything alone. It was a feeling she was hesitant to trust, for fear of it being ripped away again, but for once she didn't try and deny it.

One of the crew called out to the captain, who bellowed something back about tacking to port. Their voices hid the sound of Fari approaching, and Lira turned as the healer appeared suddenly at her shoulder. "I know you're suspicious about why I agree to help you," she said without preamble.

Lira didn't pretend to disagree. "I don't trust anyone whose motivations I don't understand. But you know that already."

"I do, and neither do I, when it comes to it."

"And yet you're here standing with me." Lira eyed her curiously, still unsure. Maybe this conversation might help her make the decision she was eventually going to be forced to make. Part of her quailed at what that would mean, though, even though she didn't shy from the inevitability of it.

Fari smiled a little. "Do you remember, years ago, talking about my family? When I told you I was afraid I'd be expelled from Temari Hall and they'd throw me out of the household as a result. You thought I was being dramatic."

"I remember," Lira said, softening despite herself. "But you changed my mind. It was the first time I realised that someone could be wealthy and privileged and still be trapped."

"In the end, what I feared most *did* end up happening. I became a disgrace. I failed my Trials, I haven't distinguished myself in any other way, and I'll never give them the blood heir they so desperately want." A hint of bitterness coloured her voice. "Although that will all change the moment I help unseat a Tylender from his spot as Magor-lier of the Mage Council."

Lira started in surprise. "Is *that* why you're doing this?"

Fari laughed. "No, I stopped worrying about impressing my family a long time ago. It will be a nice side benefit, though, proving to them that I'm not actually useless. Not that I will ever understand why the Tylenders and Dirsks hate each other so much. Zandian rivalry is as much a part of our makeup as our fiercely hot deserts, but it's really not productive."

Movement flickered in Lira's peripheral vision, distracting her. Across the deck, Lorin joined Tarion and Garan, but it didn't look like they were talking anymore. All three stared out at the lights of the approaching harbour.

A shiver of unease ran through her at the grim expressions on all their faces. She was about to face Alyx Egalion, and if she didn't walk away from that confrontation, she'd be back in prison, trapped again for the rest of her life. Or worse. Fear and dread squeezed her chest so fiercely that for a moment her breath froze.

Fari shifted at her side and Lira buried her fear. "Then why join me?"

"When I told you that I'd failed my Trials, that Councillor Egalion had been the only one to argue for me to pass, you never said anything—it was during your brooding and aloof hating-us phase—but what did you think?"

Lira frowned, not needing to think about her answer. "That the council were just as foolish and ignorant as I'd always thought they were and that not giving you a mage cloak had to be one of the stupidest decisions they'd ever made."

Fari's smile was bright and blinding. "You've never thought I was useless. Not for a second, not even when you barely knew me, not even when I was failing half my classes at Temari."

"That's because you're *not* useless. You're far from it." Lira cocked her head in puzzlement when Fari merely continued to smile at her. "I don't think I understand."

"People generally look at me, note my propensity for jokes, my air of general cheeriness, my lack of stiff honour, and they forget I'm Zandian. A Dirsk." A hard look closed over Fari's face then, one Lira had never seen. "Lira, you might be the reincarnation of Shakar Astor. You might be worse. You could even turn out to be something none of us ever imagined. Whichever it is, *I* choose the leader that sees my value. The one that looks at me and sees my strengths, not my failings. The one that respects me for who I truly am."

"I'm no leader." Lira huffed out an incredulous breath at the thought.

Fari put her hands on her hips. "Then you'd best call all of this off right now, because how else are you going to take control of the Mage Council and make Lucinda let Ahrin and Caverlock go? You're the one with the name, the influential heritage. *I* can't do it. You're going to have to headline this fight, Lira Astor, heir to the Darkmage."

Fari was right. Lira had *known* that for what she planned to do she would have to fully assume the mantle of Shakar's heir, no halfway measures. But until it had been said aloud, she hadn't quite faced it. She hadn't wanted to. Mainly because she wasn't sure she *could*. Lira was an outsider, one who walked her own path, free of encumbrances. She'd never had any interest in being responsible for others. Or worse, being responsible *to* them.

Her hands curled white-knuckled around the railing. "I'm not him." The words came out without thinking. But the realisation rocked her to her core. Because it was the opposite of everything she'd always feared. What she'd decided to stop fighting within herself.

Where had those words come from?

She was *like* Shakar in many ways. Cool, arrogant, self-interested, determined. But he hadn't just been those things. He'd been a man with a vision, a clever strategic mind, and a charismatic ability to achieve his vision by drawing others to it, imposing his will on them. Lira didn't have any of those attributes. It was why doing what Lucinda wanted felt so impossible, why she'd known for a fact she couldn't do it alone.

Fari gave her a knowing look, as if she could read the thoughts tumbling through Lira's mind. "It's always been so black and white with you. You veer between terror of being the Darkmage, and terror of *not* being the Darkmage. Lira, you are not him." She paused. "I know this for two reasons."

She let out a shaky breath. "And what are those?"

"First, and most importantly, people aren't born a certain unchangeable way. We are who we are based on the choices we make along the way. You may choose the same things he did, or you may choose a different path, but your choices are your own."

"And?" Fari's words rang true, but they also made everything so much more complicated. So much less clear. If she wasn't him, what was she?

"Second, he tried to destroy the world when the Mage Council murdered the woman he loved." Fari gave her a sad smile. "When you thought the woman *you* loved had died, you were barely capable of putting one foot in front of the other, let alone destroying the world."

"When I thought she was dead, nothing mattered anymore," Lira mumbled, remembering those dark hours. "There was no point in vengeance."

Fari spoke gently, "Lira, you're not just *his* granddaughter. You're your mother's daughter, your father's daughter, your grandmothers' granddaughter, and so on."

But they *always* saw him. They looked at her and they saw him. "I don't know how to be anything else when that's what they always see." She regretted the words the moment they were out of her mouth, her instinctive fear of being too vulnerable, of showing weakness, rising to close her throat over.

But Fari only shifted closer, one hand touching Lira's forearm. "That's not what *I* see. It's not what Tarion or Lorin or Garan see either. We haven't for a very long time, you know?"

She did know. She might not have ever been able to trust it, but she knew, deep down. Lira let out a long breath. "But if I'm not him, how can I..."

"Don't worry." Fari squeezed her arm with a conspiratorial smile. "I've been around pompous leaders all my life. I can help you fake it. First, we're going to have to change your look. Rats' nest hair and raggedy clothing isn't going to inspire anyone to take over the world."

"I—"

"And then, maybe you should put aside all your anger and fear about what everyone *else* thinks you are and start thinking about who you *actually* are." Fari beamed. "I think I've got a pretty good idea, so once you've worked it out, let's sit down and talk and see how right I am."

Lira stared at her. She didn't even know where to begin with that. Yet … this plan she'd come up with. Her true plan. Wasn't that evidence that maybe Fari was right, that Lira could forge a different path for herself than the ones set out for her by the council, or by her grandfather's notoriety?

"Are we ready?" Lorin approached, Tarion trailing behind him. Garan had disappeared. The lights of Dirinan harbour had come even closer while she and Fari had talked.

Lira stared at them, still lost in her thoughts, but Fari pinched her arm lightly and she shook her head. What came next needed all her focus. She could let Fari's words sink in later when she had time to process them properly. "You're all clear on what to do. No final questions?" A series of shaking heads followed. "Good. Make sure you follow the instructions I gave you to the letter. Then you wait. Someone will find you at the meeting point."

They didn't know where she was going, a safety precaution in case one of them was captured by the council. Lira couldn't afford a telepath reading her location from one of their minds.

With a final hopeful glance around the deck fading to disappointment—she would have liked to say goodbye to Garan properly—she gave them a little wave, and then climbed up onto the railing. There she paused for a moment, taking a deep breath. It was time to set into motion her grand and sweeping world-changing plan. A con to end all cons.

First step—face down the world's most powerful mage and live to tell about it.

The thrill stirred in the pit of her stomach, hot and heady, and an anticipatory smile spread across her face.

Lira readied her magic and dived off the side of the ship.

# CHAPTER 4

T he icy waters of Dirinan harbour closed over Lira's head as she hit the surface. Her mental shields were focused, impregnable, and she'd made sure to dive off the side of the ship not visible to anyone watching their approach from the docks.

The ocean sang to her water magic, giving her a feeling of comfort despite the strong current and dangerously cold temperature. She wore a knife at her belt, but given the distance she had to swim, she was barefoot, wearing only light breeches and a sleeveless shirt. With winter fast approaching, it wasn't the ideal time of year for a swim in the ocean along Shivasa's coastline, but there was no other way off the ship. She would have to hope the exertion of swimming kept her from hypothermia.

Using a touch of magic to speed her progress, she swam underwater until her lungs clamoured for air, before breaching the surface and floating there, sucking in deep lungfuls of air. Lifting a hand to push back sopping hair from her eyes, she took a good look around, letting her body flow with the current. The night sky above was clear, no clouds, the stars bright and shining. The opposite of what Lira had hoped for.

Still, a scan of the surrounding ocean revealed nothing unexpected. Only ships rocking distantly at anchor, the lights of Dirinan to the east. The cold was already sinking into her bones, making her teeth chatter, so she kicked out, beginning the long swim to shore.

By the time she approached the northernmost jetties—hundreds of them stretched out into the harbour along the curving shoreline—her arms trembled with exhaustion and her lungs were burning. It hadn't taken long before her swimming had turned laborious, and it felt like she breathed in as much seawater as air with every breath.

The moment she was underneath one of the wooden constructs, she carefully braced her palms against a barnacle-covered support beam and sagged in utter weariness. Seawater lapped against her shoulders while she caught her breath and tried to recover some of her strength.

As soon as she stopped moving, though, the cold began to creep inexorably through her. Her breath frosted, causing a brief surge of panic that a razak might be around, and already her extremities were turning numb. Her teeth chattered.

Gathering her resolve, she forced herself back into movement, pushing off the pillar and swimming underneath the jetty until the water turned to shallows and she could stumble up onto the embankment.

Soaked to the skin, shivering, she sank down on the grainy sand where the shadows were deepest and gave herself a few more moments to rest and catch her breath. But too soon, the tendrils of icy air began digging deeper into bone and sinew. If she didn't move now, wet through and ill-dressed as she was, she'd be in serious trouble.

So she stood, steadied herself, then scrambled up the embankment to the main road leading along this part of the docks. It was as familiar as if she'd been there only yesterday—right in the middle of the harbour district, where she'd once run the streets as part of Ahrin's crew.

"Nice swim?"

The familiar voice rang clearly through the silence of the night. Lira stilled as a cloaked woman emerged from the shadows on the opposite side of the road, then let out a breath. It frosted in front of her face, and she tried to stop her teeth from chattering.

She'd hoped to get a little farther before Egalion found her ... but this was better than the woman not finding her at all.

In the next second, Egalion's magic yanked Lira off her feet and sent her flying through the air. She laughed, feeling her magic spread through her veins, lighting her up, setting her skin aflame with power. She wrapped herself in her own telekinetic magic, halted her flight, and dropped gracefully to the ground, one palm slapping against the ground for balance.

A concussion burst came at her next, its green light blinding as it flew directly at Lira. She dived to the side, rolled with her momentum along cobblestones, then covered her ears just before the electric roar exploded right where she'd been standing. The concussive energy squeezed her chest hard enough to send a stabbing pain through her ribs, before vanishing as quickly as it had come.

Lira let out a shocked breath. Egalion wasn't messing around. That burst would have killed her if it had hit.

"So it's kill me then, not capture?" Without waiting for a reply, Lira shot to her feet and ran. Two steps closer to Egalion and she sent her telekinetic magic out like a whip, wrapping it around the woman's mage staff—still hanging down her back—and throwing it high into the sky.

It was a move calculated to annoy rather than do any damage. Lira was realistic about her chances of truly hurting her opponent, but she'd seen how attached Egalion was to that staff—the woman's only remaining tie to Cario Duneskal, the best friend who'd died for her.

That was how she'd keep herself alive. Defeat via distraction.

Unguarded anger flashed over Egalion's face, and the path of the staff halted abruptly as she threw her own telekinetic magic after Lira's to try and take it back.

At that moment, Lira learned two things.

Egalion's magic was stronger, *far* stronger, than her own, an endless well of strength that made Lira quail. But her ability to wield it was either rusty after years of not fighting, or it wasn't equal to Lira's. She could use that. Lean on her skill rather than sheer strength.

So, concentrating fiercely, she battled Egalion for control of the staff at the same time as she began using telekinesis to rip buttons from the woman's shirt, untie the laces of her boots, and yank the knife from her belt. In seconds, those items were whizzing through the air around Egalion's face, distracting her focus.

Egalion faltered, something unnameable replacing the anger and focus that had been written all over her face. Shock maybe. Or despair. Whatever it was, Lira ignored it, not allowing her own focus to slip.

And she won the battle for the staff.

It flew towards her, landing firmly in her outstretched left hand. Her fingers curled around the wood. It was warm in her palm, welcoming, its magic sliding against hers like they fit together. For a long moment she and Egalion only stared at each other, the councillor's eyes wide with stunned shock, like she realised something she'd long feared.

Then Lira ran at Egalion, swinging the staff in a powerful blow at her head. Yet she'd forgotten one crucial thing.

Alyx Egalion was a mage of the higher order who'd absorbed not only her Taliath husband's immunity to magic but also his fighting ability. She didn't need a weapon to fight.

She ducked under Lira's swing with contemptuous ease, slammed a fist into her ribs, and followed up with a second blow to Lira's jaw. Lira stumbled backwards with the force of the punch, landing hard on the cobblestones, the breath rushing from her lungs. The staff flew from her hands and clattered across the ground. Her vision blurred. Pain exploded through her face, her jaw broken, or maybe her nose, or an eye socket. Or all three. And those still-healing ribs of hers were most definitely re-cracked.

But pain had never kept Lira down before.

Grunting with the effort, she called the staff back to her hand, got to her feet, and lunged again. Egalion knocked aside her second attempt with equal ease, and then a booted foot landed in Lira's chest, sending her back to the ground, hard.

Rotted carcasses. She was going to have to end this soon or Egalion would have her. Lira wavered, unsure if the display so far had been enough. But she was down, Egalion so close to catching her, and suddenly all Lira could see was that cell. The bars. The narrow window. The clank of the manacles that the guards locked around her ankles every single day.

Her chest closed over, breathing becoming too quick, panic threatening. Shit. She had to go. She just had to hope she'd made enough of a display for any observers. Surely getting beaten to a pulp by Egalion would prove Lira was doing as Lucinda had asked. For now, at least.

Time to withdraw.

Lira rolled away, dragged herself back to her feet, and let out a cry of effort. Magic poured from her, violet flame roaring to life as she wrapped Egalion's clothes in fire. Or tried to. A shimmering shield dropped into place around the mage, stopping Lira's fire before it could take hold of her clothes.

Rotted hells. Lira's flame could breach immunity but not a magical shield.

Something like regret flashed over Egalion's face then, and she lifted her hand, tossing another concussion burst straight at Lira. Lira dodged away and it ploughed into the wall of a building nearby. The boom it let off shook the ground under their feet.

Lira kept running, knowing more attacks would be coming. She forced her legs to run faster, building momentum, speed, heading straight for the building on the eastern side of the street. Another concussive burst exploded so close it almost knocked her off her feet, the staff flying from her grip as she fought to right herself. Regretfully, she let it go, continuing onwards.

As she got within a few paces of the wall, Lira wrapped herself in her telekinetic magic and threw herself upwards. It was a technique that used a lot of power and had taken her a long time to master—but master it she had.

She landed almost perfectly on the roof just as another bright green burst ploughed into the wall below, where she'd been seconds earlier. Stone splintered, the magic powerful enough to gouge out a deep chunk of it. Yet something told Lira that Egalion wasn't even scraping the surface of her magical strength.

The roof rocked under Lira's feet, and a small part of her focused on keeping her balance while the rest gathered more magic, pulled everything she could into her grasp, holding it until the last moment.

Then she used the ability she was best at.

She stepped up to the edge of the roof, spread her arms wide, and let out another roar of effort. Her telekinetic magic exploded outwards, encompassing the entire square, ripping doors from hinges, shutters from windows, gratings from gutters, and drainpipes from walls. Any debris on the ground rose into the air with everything else.

Her breath came fast, sweat dripping from her, blood like fire in her veins. Sunk deep into her magic, she stirred everything into a whirling storm and flung it at Egalion. It crashed against her shield, one thing after another after another. That shield had to be a serious drain on her magic, but it held.

Lira hadn't expected it to break. But she used the distraction to pick the woman's fallen staff off the ground, unnoticed amidst everything else flying through the air, and bring it to rest at her feet.

Before her magic could drain entirely, Lira let the telekinesis go. Everything clattered to the ground, and a tense silence fell over the square. The place now looked like several explosions had gone off inside it.

Lira stood on the roof's edge, chest heaving, shoulders straight.

Egalion let her shield drop, staring up at Lira. The woman hadn't broken a sweat, wasn't even breathing hard. "You are no heir to the Darkmage, Lira Astor."

Lira sucked in quick, gasping breaths around the stabbing pain from re-broken ribs—not to mention her broken face—and managed a smile, thinking about Fari's words earlier. "No. I'm something different entirely."

"I don't want to kill you," Egalion said. "That's never been what I wanted."

Lira barked a laugh, regretted it as hot pain stabbed through her jaw and chest, making her voice loud and clear for anyone around to hear. "But you'd like to lock me up again for the rest of my life. I'm not letting you kill me or imprison me. Never again. I'm going to save Ahrin, and you're not going to stop me. Your compassion is going to be your downfall, Egalion. You would have caught me tonight if you'd brought an army with you."

Exasperation flashed over the mage's face. "You know you can't survive me, not forever. I will find you."

"You keep on believing that," Lira said, then with a quick flick of her fingers, she lifted Egalion's staff back to her left hand. The wood was warm, solid, under her skin—it steadied her racing heart and weary limbs. "I've needed a new staff for a while now, and this was never yours, was it? I think it will do nicely. See you around, Egalion."

And she turned and ran.

# CHAPTER 5

Egalion came after her, of course.

Her flying magic lifted her into the sky, and within seconds she was chasing Lira across the rooftops of Dirinan's harbour district.

Ignoring weariness and pain with practised skill, Lira sped quick and light-footed over the paths she still knew like the back of her hand. She kept her stolen staff ready, in case of a waiting ambush, but nothing materialised. Even so, she moved warily, ready to react to anything that came at her.

The occasional concussion burst hit the ground perilously close, Lira saved by dodging and weaving as best she could, but none were large enough to do serious damage to property. Telekinesis wrapped around her occasionally too—but Lira brushed that off with contemptuous ease. And green fire, once, though again it was clear Egalion wanted to avoid setting anything alight. In this rundown part of the city, an uncontrolled fire could decimate multiple blocks of homes and businesses before it was brought under control.

Her compassion. That was what Lira had gambled on to get out of this.

Twice, the mage of the higher order dropped to the roofs behind Lira, almost close enough to reach out and grab her, but on the ground, Lira was too fleet-footed, too agile, too familiar with all the nooks and crannies of the area she traversed. Each time Egalion was forced back into the sky to keep up with her.

Relief took some of the edge off Lira's weariness, giving her an extra burst of energy as she reached her target—a neighbourhood of roofs lined with poorly constructed overhanging eaves that formed narrow corridors invisible to anyone looking down from above ... an area Lira had once relied on to survive pursuit when living as a child alone in the city. Better yet, there was no street lighting and even on a moonlit night like this, the warren of pathways remained deep in shadow.

Egalion must have realised she couldn't track Lira from the sky through this area, because the sound of her boots landing on wood sounded distantly. It was exactly what Lira had wanted. She ducked left into an overhang between two roofs, then cut through a tiny corridor leading off one of them.

Silence and darkness enclosed her, rich with the rotting scent of leaves and other debris that the wind blew in to marinate with the damp of rain and melting snow. Her chilled bare feet plunged into sludgy muck, her arms brushing the moulding and spider-infested roofs either side of her. It was disgusting but so familiar she welcomed it.

The sound of boots slapping against wood and similar muck sounded in the distance, but these narrow crawlspaces distorted sound. It was impossible to know how close Egalion was. Lira wasn't too worried. The much taller woman would struggle to move quickly in such tight spaces, even if she knew where she was going.

Lira traversed two more blocks via the dark crawlspaces before emerging from a gap between two roofs and clambering down a rusted drainpipe onto a dark alley. There she paused a moment, body aching, to siphon what little energy she had left into shoring up her mental shield and taking stock of her surroundings.

Silence filled the night, broken only by the rustling of rats through the refuse nearby and a distant slamming door.

Lira finally began to feel confident that she might win free of pursuit.

Relying on Egalion not bringing any backup to capture Lira had been a gamble. One she hadn't liked but hadn't had much choice in. She would have been relieved, triumphant, if her chest and face weren't on fire with agony. If her legs weren't threatening to crumple under her from exhaustion.

And she wasn't clear yet.

She glanced up, gaze searching, until ... there ... Egalion was back in the sky searching for her. Even as Lira glanced up, the woman spotted her, a dark spot framed against the moonlight, turning to arrow towards her, but she was a good distance away. Lira had won herself enough separation for what she needed to completely shake free.

She took off at a run down the street, keeping to the shadows before pushing through a narrow door set into a tall building. The door clicked closed behind her, and she sagged against the wall beside it for a moment, breath wheezing, biting her lip through the increasing pain. She was almost there. She just had to force herself through this next bit and she'd be okay. Her opponent might be the most powerful mage alive, but she didn't know these streets and buildings like Lira did.

She'd grown up here. This was her home. It would protect her.

She took a few steadying breaths and started up the steps, pushing her body back into a run. Either Egalion would follow her into the building, or she'd hover in the skies above and wait for her to emerge somewhere. It didn't matter to Lira which. She'd lose her either way.

On the third floor, she paused on the landing, simultaneously catching her breath, waiting for the pain to subside to bearable levels, and listening for the sound of footsteps on the stairs behind her.

Everything inside was silent. Still. So Egalion was waiting in the skies for her to emerge somewhere. Smart move—better not to walk herself into a potential ambush when she had more of an advantage out in the open.

Lira forced her aching body down the long hallway until reaching the apartment at the end. There, she pushed through into the abandoned rooms beyond and crossed to the tiny balcony jutting out from the side of the building.

The gap between this building and the one next to it was so narrow the roofs above practically touched. Which made it dark. Which meant that nobody watching from the sky above could see as Lira clambered onto the balcony railing, then jumped the gap to grab the drainpipe running down the outside of the next building.

Pain spiked through her chest so fiercely she had to swallow down a cry. She hung blindly to the pipe for several moments, tears sliding down her cheeks. Even breathing felt close to impossible until the agony finally faded enough that she could move again.

She climbed down as far as the nearest window, picked the lock, and climbed through. The inhabitants of the tiny apartment were asleep on a pile of blankets on the floor, and she crept silently past them, slipping out of their front door. From there she padded along the hallway and down the main stairwell. A narrow corridor at the bottom exited into the alley behind the building.

A powerful stench of waste hit her nostrils, and she took a few shallow breaths until her senses adjusted. She pressed back against the wall, staring up at the sky. There was no trace of her pursuer. The surrounding alley was still, silent, dark.

One arm cradling her ribs, she pushed away from the wall and set off down the alley, careful now of *anyone* seeing her—in this area, the mage no doubt still searching the skies for her wasn't the greatest threat to Lira.

This was Gutter Rat territory.

It took another long hour, Lira staggering from alley, to building, to rooftop, to dark street, but eventually she was confident that she'd lost Egalion.

Once she was sure of that, she headed for her old hunting ground, back to the harbour district run by the Revel Kings, the powerful criminal gang that Ahrin had so recently taken control of. Thinking of the Darkhand hit Lira like a punch to her newly cracked ribs, and she let out a pained breath. Then, she used her fear for Ahrin to bolster her determination rather than drain her strength further.

A welcome sense of reassurance washed over her as she padded into familiar territory, the ever-present tightness in her chest dissipating. This had never been a safe place, but she understood and appreciated the rules of this world. It hadn't ever pretended to be something it wasn't, and Lira had clung to that. She still did.

The gambling hall—headquarters of the Revel Kings' boss—was quieter than the night Lira had arrived after escaping jail in Carhall, though the interior was still brightly lit and there were enough people inside to indicate that business was doing well.

Lira paused across the street, considering. She'd mostly dried off from her ocean swim, but her face was bloody, her feet and arms bruised, scratched, and filthy, her shirt torn. If she walked in the front door like this, she'd be marked as prey instantly—if she even got through the door without being tossed back into the street.

Her gaze roved the outside of the building. She thought of the night she and Ahrin had robbed it and considered the best way of getting in.

Magic ready just in case someone spotted her—she had just enough left to defend herself against an opportunistic criminal—she worked her way around the block and made her approach through the alley to the left of the gambling hall, coming to a stop far below a lit window on the higher levels.

Suddenly, so close to her goal, all the weariness and pain crashed down over her. Climbing up to where she needed to go seemed an impossible task. She swayed forward, her forehead pressing against the wall, palms following suit. Everything hurt. She couldn't even stand up straight from the pain in her chest. She had no strength in her arms for climbing, even if she had been able to move them properly.

Lira took a deep, shuddering breath. She thought of Ahrin in that cage. Then she stepped away, curled her hands around the icy metal of the pipe, and began to climb.

She barely made it, only sheer will getting her the last few metres to the window ledge. Her trembling arms were so exhausted by then that all she could do was shove the window up with a touch of magic and then fall through the gap onto the thick carpet below.

For a moment she lay there, her entire body a ball of hot pain. Then her presence of mind reasserted itself and she forced herself to sit up and drag herself to a standing position. The room was small, warm from the fire crackling in the grate at her back, and the man she was looking for sat behind the desk opposite the hearth.

His feet rested on the surface—clad in gold satin slippers that gleamed against his dark Zandian skin—and he leaned back in the chair as far as it was possible to go. Smoke curled from the cigar in his mouth; cloudweed, by the sweet scent drifting through the room.

He'd frozen, mouth half-open, features set in utter bemusement at the sight of her falling through his window. But then his groggy gaze sharpened, his eyebrows shot skyward, and he swung his legs off the desk. "Lira? Is that really you?"

She managed a smile and staggered a step forward, one arm cradling her ribs. "Hello, Yanzi. Good to see you again."

He blinked, stared at the cigar in his hand as if wondering whether the drug had developed hallucinatory properties, then glanced at her. "You are real, yes?"

"Correct." She winced as her nod sent pain throbbing through her skull. An odd vertigo was niggling at her, her legs beginning to shake alarmingly.

"Well." He stood up, stabbed his cigar into the ashtray near his hand. "You look rather awful if you don't mind me saying. And that stench coming off you ... what brings you by?"

"Ahrin sent me." She got the words out, then her vision spotted, and she promptly passed out. The last thing she felt was the sharp pain throughout her body as she collapsed, and then everything turned to delightful blackness.

# CHAPTER 6

Not much time seemed to have passed when Lira roused back to consciousness. Certainly, none of the pain had faded. She was lying on a soft couch, still in Yanzi's office, while an older woman with her hair tied back in a severe bun hovered over her. Her expression rivalled Ahrin's at its most unimpressed.

Yanzi stood at the end of the couch, his gaze shifting between amused and curious. Lira studied his perfectly tailored silk shirt, sleeves rolled up to the elbows, and loose Zandian trousers ... business *was* going well.

"She's got two cracked ribs, a concussion, and a broken nose. I think the jaw's just badly bruised," the woman listed out like she was ordering food from an inn. "Her pulse is slower than I'd like, but that could be a result of too much magic use. I have no expertise in that."

Lira slapped the woman's hand away—it was currently pressing annoyingly into her neck. "I'm fine."

The fingers returned, digging harder this time. Lira levelled her most intimidating scowl at the woman. She remained unfazed. Several moments later, when *she* felt like it, the healer removed her hand. "It's improving. Slightly."

"Does she need anything to prevent her dying?" Yanzi asked.

"She shouldn't sleep for another few hours in case the concussion worsens. And if she pushes those cracked ribs too hard before they heal, they could snap and puncture a lung. Not much I can do for her if that happens. Otherwise she should be fine with proper rest."

"Thanks, Irina. You can go."

Lira gave Yanzi a hard look. "Nobody can know I'm here."

"Irina is as discreet as they come." Yanzi waved a hand, then rolled his eyes when Lira's expression didn't change. "I'm not killing our best healer for you. Ahrin would murder me. And she's far scarier than you, so it's not even a contest."

"Nobody will hear about you from me." Irina sniffed in offence, clearly far more bothered by the implication she might be indiscreet than that Yanzi might have her killed. "I know my job, and I get paid well for my silence. It would be bad for business to start blabbing all over the place about my clients." With that, she swept out of the room, shoulders stiffened in affront.

Yanzi dragged a chair beside the couch. He seemed more clear-eyed than he had been, presumably the cloudweed wearing off.

Lira tried to rise, gave up when her body protested that far too fiercely, and tried to settle back into a comfortable position. To mask the pain, she muttered, "Ahrin would slit your throat if she knew you smoked that stuff while running her operations."

"Maybe that would scare me if I were actually running anything. While she officially left me in charge, I'm little more than a figurehead. Her little private army of frighteningly capable Shiven warriors make sure nobody comes at us." He stretched out his long legs, looking perfectly content at this arrangement. "I'm guessing that rather dramatic ruckus down on the harbour earlier was you? I've been getting a constant stream of messages from our runners about Councillor Alyx Egalion going toe-to-toe with some rogue mage in an epic battle. I thought maybe the entire district was smoking cloudweed until you fell through my window."

"Don't worry, I didn't lead her here. I made sure I was well clear before heading this way," Lira said.

He shook his head in reluctant admiration. "Only you would willingly go up against the world's most powerful mage. But despite your precautions, Egalion's presence in the city draws more heat than is safe for us, especially if she's looking for you. I don't like you being here, Astor."

"The council has no idea which crew I used to run with, nor any knowledge of these streets or how things work here. I was clear of pursuit before I stepped foot in your district. I've got it covered; I promise. You're protected."

"And their telepaths?" he inquired.

"You keep the circle of knowledge about my presence here to yourself and Ahrin's Shiven fighters, and we'll be fine. I won't stay longer than I need to."

He looked unconvinced. "Does your sudden appearance mean Vensis will make a return at some point in the near future?"

An ache rippled through her—she was too tired to ignore how badly she wished Ahrin was with her right now—but for Yanzi she managed a brusque, "Not yet. She's busy."

"Oh? Busy doing what, exactly?"

"Nothing you need concern yourself with. She sent me here on her behalf."

"Oh, she did, did she?" Yanzi lifted a thoroughly dubious eyebrow. "Last time I saw you, she was ushering you and your council friends off our territory while warning you to never come back. And the time before that, you were a scrawny fifteen-year-old who fled to the fancy mage school in Karonan. How do I know that you being here has *anything* to do with Vensis?"

"Do I really have to jump through these hoops with you?" Lira ignored the pain this time, forcing herself to sit up. "I'm sure she told you she was leaving with me last month."

He shrugged. "She just said she'd be gone for a while and to take care of things until she was back."

Damn. "Well, she *did* leave with me, and she's sent me back on her behalf. She has instructions for you."

"Back from where?"

"Can't say."

"Maybe you're telling the truth." He shrugged again. "But even if you are, what makes you think any of us care what she wants anymore?

She's been gone for weeks. In crew boss time, that's an eternity. That's effectively abdicating your position."

Lira smirked, beginning to enjoy this little game despite herself. It was comforting in its familiarity. "Yanzi, you act as if I've forgotten how terrified everyone is of Ahrin. And why. She hasn't been gone long enough yet for that fear to have dissipated sufficiently for anyone to make a serious move. Besides, I know more about her little army than you think. There's no way they'd ever turn on her, no matter how long she was gone."

He threw his hands up in the air, letting out a chuckle. "Fine. Consider yourself vetted. I don't have the smarts to go more rounds with you, Lira."

Lira glanced around. "Timin here too?"

"No. He's a Silver Lord these days, and I have a new flavour of the month. He's much prettier."

"Good."

Yanzi laughed at the satisfaction in her voice, then gave her a fond look. "I'd forgotten how much you two hated each other. Are you back for good, Lira? Decided the mage life wasn't all it was cracked up to be?"

Lira hesitated, oddly struck by his question. By the instinctive response that welled up inside her. Maybe it was the concussion, but she found herself admitting, "I wish I was, but no."

"That's a shame. I miss having you around." He took a breath, voice turning businesslike. "I take it Ahrin has instructions for the crew, then. Lay it on me."

She settled back against the cushions. "We've got big plans, Yanzi. She says you're to do whatever I need." Ahrin hadn't, not really, but Lira wasn't above using her name to get what she needed. After all, she was doing it to save Ahrin's life.

As long as her crew, and more importantly, the rival crews, never learned Ahrin Vensis was a prisoner locked up far away in Rotherburn, then everything would be fine.

Lira was confident Ahrin would get herself out. She was far *less* confident that she could maintain the ruse long enough for Ahrin to do it.

"Big plans, huh? No doubt these plans have something to do with why you were lighting up the harbour district with Egalion earlier. I feel like I'm going to need another cloudweed cigar for this," he said mournfully.

"First, provided they don't get lost on their way here, you're going to get some mage visitors crossing into your territory around dawn. Two young men, one Shiven, and a young Zandian woman. They might look like entitled, arrogant nobles with sticks up their behinds ... but don't kill them. When the runners spot them entering, bring them to me, but keep them out of everyone else's sight and tell the runners to keep their mouths shut."

"Easy enough. Next?"

"As you already know, Egalion is in Dirinan, no doubt with a contingent of mages and Taliath. More will be on their way. She's holding a prisoner, a mage named Athira. I need to know where she is, and I need to know fast. Egalion could move her out of the city any moment."

His gaze narrowed. "Your business seems to have a lot to do with mages, Lira. Not a subject Ahrin has ever particularly cared about."

She levelled him with a look. He sighed. "Fine."

Lira watched as he rose to his feet and went to the door. She glimpsed a tall woman with blond dreadlocks and tattoos twining down both arms waiting outside, before Yanzi angled his body so that she couldn't look inside to see Lira. "Ordra, the runners were right. Councillor Egalion is in our fine city. She's holding a prisoner—a female mage. I need the prisoner's location yesterday."

Lira didn't hear a response, but presumably Ordra agreed, because soft footsteps headed off down the hall. He closed it behind her, lifted his eyebrows. "Anything else?"

"Yes." Lira's gaze roved over his fine clothing. "Have you got more silk where that came from?"

He snorted. "You? Silks? You want to try brushing your hair first? Or maybe cleaning the blood off your face."

"You're hilarious. Also, I want to speak with Shiasta as soon as possible."

"How about you take a bath, wash off all that blood and grime, and get into clean clothes?" He waved off her protest and continued, "Third door on the left down the hall. While you do that, I'll make sure nobody wanders into this area of the building, fetch Shiasta for you, and let the local runners know to look out for your visitors. Deal?"

"Deal." Lira hauled herself off the couch, grunted at the pain, then limped towards the doorway. She opened it and glanced back. "Yanzi?"

"Hmm?"

"No more cloudweed. I catch you with that stuff again and you'll be a runner on the smelliest street of the district for the next ten years."

She saw the hesitation, the moment where he wavered on whether he was willing to take orders from Lira rather than Ahrin. She held his gaze, not backing down.

He was the first to break. "What you've asked so far, it's easy work for us, and I've no concerns keeping you protected here for old times' sake. But I sense something off with the boss's absence. I hope you haven't forgotten how ... sharp ... we can be, us crew folk. How we tend to know when we're being double crossed."

"How convenient for me that I'm not here to double cross you, then," she said evenly.

A small hesitation, then, "The cloudweed will stay gone. For now."

"Glad to hear it." Her shoulders relaxed as she limped down the hall outside, a bath sounding increasingly tempting. Fari might have been right. She just needed to fake this leadership thing.

Maybe that would be enough for now.

# CHAPTER 7

The warm bathwater soothed some of Lira's aching muscles, but weariness and the sharp pain in her ribs and nose still weighed heavily on her shoulders. Still, she brightened at the sight of Shiasta waiting in the hall outside after she finished. The Shiven Hunter stood straight and unnaturally still against the wall, dressed simply, weapons strapped around his body.

Genuine pleasure filled her, despite the discomfort she felt at the void of magic shimmering around him caused by the medallion hanging around his neck. "Hello, Shiasta."

"Lady Astor." He bowed gracefully.

"Is there somewhere I can sit down, maybe get something to eat and drink while I wait for my friends to arrive?"

He gestured left, down the hall. "A room has been prepared. I've sent my two best trackers to find your companions and make sure they arrive safely. Yanzi informed me they were important to you, and that their arrival here was to be as discreet as possible, so I hope you forgive my presumption."

She swallowed, eyes inexplicably filling with tears. What was wrong with her? It must be exhaustion lowering all her usual defences. "It's really good to see you, Shiasta."

He didn't smile, not quite, but she thought there was a softening in his expression at her words. "I am glad to see you as well." He hesitated. "Commander Vensis didn't return with you?"

"No, I'm sorry," she said carefully. "She sent me with her authority though ... is that all right?"

"We ultimately serve you, Lady Astor," he said simply.

And although those were the words she wanted, *needed*, to hear if she was going to succeed in her plan, they caused a sharp spike of guilt in her chest. Shiasta and his warriors had never been given a choice in serving her or Ahrin. And while Lira hated that, she was also going to use it for her own ends. What did that say about who she was?

Ugh. She rubbed at her eyes. She was too exhausted for introspective thought, and the night was far from over. *Focus, Lira.*

Shiasta opened a door farther down the hall and stepped aside for her to enter first. A fire flickered warmly in the hearth, and a steaming pot of tea stood on a table in the middle of a grouping of several chairs. Beside the teapot sat a plate of sandwiches.

"Before you go," she said to Shiasta, when he made to close the door behind her and step out into the hall, "is my understanding that you are Ahrin's lieutenant correct?"

He inclined his head. "She usually passes orders to my warriors through me, Lady Astor."

She wanted to ask why him, why they all followed Ahrin, and whether it had to do with the tattoo on his wrist—on Ahrin's wrist too—but those questions had always caused such pain in Ahrin, and she didn't want to inflict the same upon Shiasta. The answers would come, and she'd get them without causing any additional pain for her Hunters. "In that case, you'll stay and join my planning discussions."

Without a word, he moved to sit gracefully in one of the other chairs.

"How many Hunters came with you to join Ahrin?" she asked.

"My full unit. Twenty-five warriors."

"And what happened to all the other Hunter units after Underground disbanded?"

"I don't know, Lady Astor."

She'd mostly expected that answer, but his lack of knowledge was going to make things more difficult. "Do you know what happened to Underground, where they fled, what their true purpose was?" she asked carefully.

"I do not." He stopped there, but when she raised an eyebrow, he added, "They conditioned us to obey, not to ask questions or take action into our own hands. All I can tell you is that Commander Vensis countermanded Lucinda's orders to kill her and then ordered my unit and I to assist her in escaping Shadowfall Island."

"So Ahrin's orders superseded any that Lucinda or her mages gave you?"

"That is correct, Lady Astor. We cannot disobey Commander Vensis unless *you* overrule her."

She opened her mouth to ask why, but then noticed how rigid his shoulders had become, how his eyes had gone a shade darker. So instead she simply said, "I am ... sorry, Shiasta, for what happened to you."

He frowned. "I don't understand."

"I know you don't." Her heart clenched. "But I'm going to make it right one day, I promise you that."

He was silent a moment, then ventured, "It feels ... calm. To be near you. Like there's nothing inside my head tugging me in another direction."

"I'm going to fix that too," she promised. "As soon as I'm done with what I need to do, your life will be your own."

The confusion on his face only deepened, and regret welled up in her again, but a sharp knock came at the door before she could say any more. Shiasta was on his feet in a blink, hand on his knife as he crossed to open it a crack and peer out. Whatever he saw beyond had him stepping away and opening the door wider.

Fari stepped through first, her glance sweeping admiringly over Shiasta's tall form. "You found Ahrin's big scary Shiven guards, I see." Standing as close as she was to Shiasta, she must have felt the dissonance from his medallion, because a frown crossed her face.

Lira stood with a smile, drawing her attention away. "Fari, this is Shiasta. Shiasta, Fari Dirsk. And with her, Tarion Caverlock and Lorin Hester."

Tarion gave Shiasta a friendly nod and a smile—the two young men were of a similar height and build, with a similar grace to their movements—while Lorin looked more reserved, as if unsure of the big Hunter.

Tarion's gaze lingered for a moment on Shiasta's neck—he'd learned back in Rotherburn what Ahrin was, and Lira watched as he put the pieces together and quickly worked out that Shiasta, too, was a Hunter. He didn't say anything, though, merely flicked a glance in Lira's direction before sitting down. Shiasta spoke briefly to the Hunter outside before closing the door and joining them.

"Any troubles getting here?" she asked them as they settled in chairs and helped themselves to tea and sandwiches.

"None." Fari smiled. "Your plan went smoothly—as soon as we saw the lights from your battle with Egalion, we used the distraction to slip into one of the ship's boats and row ashore. The welcoming party waiting at the docks was no doubt disappointed when the only person to walk off the ship when it anchored was Garan."

"Shiasta's warriors found us soon after." Tarion nodded acknowledgement at him. "Which helped us get here much faster. What about you?"

"As you can see, I survived the run-in with your mother." Lira glanced at Tarion. "She's fine, don't worry. But it will have been clear to any Underground spies watching that I'm doing exactly what Lucinda wants."

"Good. What's next?" Lorin asked. "Surely we can't afford to be here much longer ... the council forces will find us sooner rather than later."

Lira finished a bite of the sandwich before answering. "I agree we can't linger too long, but we *do* need to be here. I'll need resources to pull this off, and Ahrin's crew provides all that and more. Yanzi is her official deputy, and I've convinced him I'm acting on Ahrin's authority. So not a word about where she really is, clear?"

Before any of them could reply, the door opened and Yanzi stepped in. "I was told our guests had arrived." He gave them a quick, speculative glance. "We're diving straight in, then? No rest for the wicked."

"Have you found out where Athira is being kept?" Lira asked.

"I expect Ordra to report back at any moment."

Lira waved him to a seat and explained to the others. "Egalion told me she was holding Athira prisoner."

"That's unfortunate." Lorin frowned a little. "It could be a significant obstacle to what we need to achieve."

Fari shot him a look and opened her mouth, but then seemed to realise Yanzi was in the room and closed it.

Yanzi didn't miss that, of course. "Maybe now that we're all gathered, you'll enlighten me on what exactly it is you're doing?" He sprawled, idly, in his chair. "What do mage guests and mage prisoners have to do with your orders from Vensis, Lira?"

"It's simple. I'm going to succeed where Shakar Astor, and then Underground and the Shadowcouncil, failed," Lira told him. "And you're all going to help me do it."

Yanzi stared at her, eyes going wide as saucers. "You're talking about the group Vensis worked with after leaving Dirinan? The one that venerated your grandfather and wanted to take over the world."

"That's the one."

"The Shadowcouncil didn't really fail, though." Tarion spoke as Yanzi continued gaping at her in incredulity. "Lucinda learned Lira and Ahrin had effectively penetrated her group, meaning the Mage Council understood too much about her operations. So she cut loose those that didn't have any value to her, removed Lira from the picture, and made a strategic withdrawal."

"I'm sorry, who is Lucinda?" Yanzi cut in.

Lorin ignored him, casting Tarion a sidelong look. "Well, what actually happened is that the Seven ordered Lucinda back to Rotherburn. They were afraid the council would learn where she was from and come after them."

"Lira, explain this now or I'm walking," Yanzi said tightly, the good humour vanished from his face. "Who is Lucinda, what is the Seven, and what does Ahrin Vensis care for taking over the world in Shakar Astor's name?"

"Ahrin wants power, you know that," Lira said, once more keeping to the truth as much as possible. It would be easier if she could tell Yanzi the entire tale, but as much as he wore his amiable persona like a cloak, he was a hardened criminal who had no principles other than money and power. If he knew Ahrin was out of the picture, contained and imprisoned ... she couldn't trust that he would still give her what she needed. "That's why she joined Underground. That's why she's helping them, *me*, now. If we achieve what I want, she'll have much more power than being crew boss in Dirinan."

He didn't look convinced. "And this Lucinda person? The Seven?"

"It turns out the Shadowcouncil wasn't from around here." Lira explained the Rotherburn story as quickly and succinctly as she could. Yanzi's eyes grew rounder and rounder the longer she talked.

Eventually, he sank back in his chair, looking confused. "Why did this Lucinda person wait two years to kidnap Egalion and Caverlock to enact an entire charade of sending them after razak that she already knew were too numerous to wipe out?"

"The answer to that is the Seven." Fari crossed her arms. "Lucinda was only one vote of many, and I'll bet you a thousand gold pieces the rest of the Seven didn't want to risk a war they couldn't win. It took her time to convince them they had no other choice but kidnapping Egalion and her husband."

"I still don't understand why she thought one mage could be the answer to their problems—powerful as Mama is, the razak are still immune to her magic," Tarion murmured.

Lira shot a glance his way. It was a good question, and one she didn't like not knowing the answer to. A memory niggled at her ... Lucinda threatening Egalion with a secret she held, something that had genuinely panicked Egalion. Could that have something to do with it?

She shook her head—something to figure out later. "Whatever the reason, Lucinda wanted Caverlock just as much, so that she could use him as leverage over your mother. This way she gets control of the council without having to risk any Rotherburnian lives. And Egalion's failure to kill the razak only put the Seven further under Lucinda's influence. Their desperation has them agreeing to whatever she suggests."

"Except you just said Egalion isn't going to do what Lucinda wants," Yanzi clarified.

"No."

Yanzi let out a low whistle of understanding. "So you and Ahrin are running a con on this Lucinda and her Seven ... using their desperation to take over the world before you discard them and keep that power for yourselves?"

"Something like that, yes." Lira hedged. "Lucinda has a lot of infrastructure here, not to mention direct contacts into my grandfather's network. We need that to win, Yanzi, and as long as she thinks we're on her side, we don't have to worry about her as a threat. Be under no illusions that if we cross her before we've gathered enough power, she can and will destroy us."

Across from them, Tarion shifted in his chair, clearly uncomfortable with the lies. Lira had to fight the urge to glower at him. Luckily, Yanzi was too focused on what she'd just said. "So you're essentially holding her at bay until you can build enough power here to turn on her. What happens if you *do* succeed, and Lucinda shows up here expecting to be allowed entry?"

Lira didn't have to feign the ice-cold tone of her voice when she replied. "She finds out how much of a fool she's been."

Yanzi's face turned bloodless. "Do you have any idea what you're dragging us into? Our crew is powerful, unassailable almost, *here in Dirinan.* You go at the Mage Council and fail, and nothing will protect us from a swarming horde of angry mages and Taliath burning us to the ground."

"These are Ahrin's orders, Yanzi," Lira added a thread of steel to her voice.

"Given on your behalf. And I only have your word that she's part of this." His face turned hard. "I'm inclined to draw the line here, before her crew is demolished and I'm dead or blamed for it."

"And how is your crew going to fare without Shiasta and his warriors?" Lira challenged. As much as she liked Yanzi, thought of their past together with genuine warmth, there was no room for any of that here. Strength was the only way to win loyalty. "Because one word from me and they walk away. I think we both know that without them or Ahrin the Revel Kings will be swallowed up within a month."

Yanzi's gaze switched to Shiasta, who merely nodded. Fari and Lorin looked between Lira and Shiasta in surprise. Yanzi let out a long breath and sagged back in his chair. "Damn you, Astor. You'd better not be playing me."

"I'm not."

He still looked hesitant. Sighing, he rubbed a hand over his face. "What exactly do you want from me?"

"I want the full weight of your wealth, your logistics network, and you."

He lifted an eyebrow.

"A Darkmage needs an impressive retinue." She waved to the others. "Mages, of course, but a powerful crime boss will help too. I can't do anything if people don't take me seriously."

"The operative word there being *crime* boss. What do me and the crew get out of this? Vensis orders or not, I'm sure as hell not going to help you and risk my entire operation, not to mention my life, because I'm a believer in the cause."

"You'll get reimbursed for your help; I promise you."

He huffed a laugh. "And I guess I'm just supposed to trust you on that?"

"We were crew once," she said quietly. "I never crossed you then, and I won't now. If you help me, I'll make sure I repay what's owed. There will be enough gold to satisfy even your taste for shiny coins, Yanzi." At least, if she succeeded, there would be.

He thought on that for a moment, then he leaned forward, holding her gaze. "Is Vensis really a part of this?"

Lira let out a breath but didn't make the mistake of looking away. "I tell you this truly—she knows what I'm doing here, and she supports it."

"Is she coming back to us?"

"Yes," Lira answered without doubt or hesitation. "You can trust that if you trust nothing else I say."

He held her gaze for a moment longer, then shrugged and sat back in his chair. "Right, let's take over the world. I know Shiasta, of course, but will you properly introduce me to your fellow conspirators? If we're going to be taking down the Mage Council together, I'd like to at least know their names."

Fari lifted a hand. "Fari Dirsk. Healer mage. Family outcast."

"Tarion Caverlock. Mage-Taliath, the first of my kind." His mouth quirked. "Probably also now the family outcast."

"Lorin Hester. Concussive mage." He spoke in his dignified way, then cracked a small smile. "My family still counts me among them."

Lira settled back in her chair, a little smile lighting up her face. "I hereby announce the establishment of the new Shadowcouncil."

# CHAPTER 8

B y the time a knock sounded at the door, Lira was completely exhausted. All she wanted was to crawl into bed and sleep for a month. But Egalion could move Athira at any time, and they needed to get to her before that happened. So she forced her drooping eyelids to stay open and took another sip of tea in the hopes it would help keep her awake.

Shiasta went out into the hall to talk to whomever it was, but it wasn't long before he returned and closed it carefully behind him. His gaze was on Lira as he spoke. "Ordra and my scouts report the city is crawling with soldiers, city guards, and mages looking for you, Lady Astor. None of the searchers are focused on the harbour district yet—the city guard won't want to get tangled up with us unless they must—but they'll come here eventually."

Yanzi waved a dismissive hand. "At which point they'll have the usual luck that soldiers and city guards do when they come looking for people inside crew territory. We won't be in trouble until the mages and Taliath come. What of the imprisoned mage?"

"She's being held at the city guard barracks," Shiasta reported. "The usual guard presence on the cells has been doubled, and there are two blue-cloaked mages there too."

Yanzi looked at Lira. "The barracks are well out of crew territory. What do you need this mage for?"

"She's a key part of Underground and a member of my Shadowcouncil. We need her with us if we're going to succeed, and there's a time imperative. If we don't grab her soon, this all might be over before it even starts."

"My warriors can get her out," Shiasta spoke softly. "We'll have her back here before dawn."

"With all due respect for your fighting skill, those will be warrior mages guarding the woman," Yanzi said.

Shiasta shifted his gaze to Lira, one eyebrow lifted in question.

After only a brief hesitation, she gave him a nod. Revealing who Shiasta was, who his warriors were, felt like a betrayal to them. But she'd decided to be as honest as possible with her friends, and it felt right that her Shadowcouncil know the full truth about their fellow council member. Not to mention, it was information Lucinda and her people already knew.

"Magic can't touch us," Shiasta told Yanzi.

Yanzi blinked. "Oh..."

"I'm sorry, what does that mean?" Fari asked.

Lira didn't look away from her. "Shakar's network kept the Hunter program going after his death. Ahrin was one of them—only she escaped as a child before her training was finished. I don't know how or why; she can't tell me." Lira took a breath. "But a lot *did* finish their training, and Lucinda managed to get her hands on them."

A brief, horrified, silence filled the room. Yanzi just seemed confused, but the mages were clearly shocked. Lorin's features had turned hard, and Fari lifted a hand to her mouth.

Tarion looked nothing but horrified, even though this wasn't a complete surprise to him. "There's an *army* of them?"

Lorin's grim look faded, and he sat forward in his chair, almost eager. "How many of you are there, Shiasta?"

"I was never given that information."

Lira jumped in to forestall all the questions blooming on their faces. "I don't know a lot about the program, but I do know there was some kind of mental conditioning involved. Pestering Shiasta won't help. We will get answers, but we will have to do it ourselves."

"*Hunters* out in the world?" Fari crossed then uncrossed her legs, and she shook her head as she spoke. "If the council had known about this..."

"Luckily they didn't," Lira said, "and we now have an asset at our disposal the council knows nothing about." *If* she could track down the others. That was high on the list, but she needed other pieces in place first, not to mention any clue as to where to start looking for them.

"Back to your mage prisoner." Yanzi looked at Lira. "If we break her out, the search will only intensify. It may reach the point where we're unable to keep you hidden here—you won't be able to hide from telepaths indefinitely."

"There actually aren't that many telepaths in the council," Lorin pointed out. "A handful at most."

"Yes, but we know Egalion is already here, and you can bet Lord-Mage A'ndreas will be on her way," Fari said.

"I'm not talking about council mages." Yanzi gave them a mildly scornful look. "The bigger, nastier, crews in Dirinan have their own pet mages, and I know of at least one with a telepath. The reward money for you will be irresistible."

"There is a way to counteract that, which I'll explain in a minute, but I agree we need to leave soon," Lira said thoughtfully. "I think the best plan will be to coincide breaking Athira free with our departure from the city."

"Where will we go?" Fari asked.

Lira looked at Shiasta. "Can you tell us who Lucinda's contact in Shakar's old network was? I'm sure you must have accompanied her to a meeting or two as her bodyguard."

"Yes, Lady Astor, but there was only one I was aware of. If there were more, Lucinda kept that knowledge from me. He was a Shiven lord. I believe his estate is in the north."

"His name?"

"I only knew him as Lord Anler. That's all I can tell you—I was never part of Lucinda's meetings with him. My responsibility was only to escort her to meetings when he came to Dirinan."

*Anler.* That name reverberated through Lira like a shot, and she frowned, trying to chase down why.

"Lira, is something wrong?" Fari asked.

"That name ... I feel like I've heard it before." She frowned, shook her head. "But I can't recall. Shiasta, can you lead us to Anler's estate?"

"I'm sorry, no. I was never informed of its location."

Yanzi waved a hand. "The crew can get that information in a matter of hours."

Lira shrugged. "Good. Then that's where we're going next." That would be the best starting point for re-engaging Shakar's network and resources, but there might also be other answers to be found among those people too. Answers she wanted badly.

"All of us?" Tarion asked.

"No." She hesitated. "Yanzi, Fari, Shiasta, and Tarion will come with me—Athira too, once she's out. Lorin, you'll stay here to oversee Ahrin's network and be our point of contact in Dirinan. Shiasta, you'll nominate one of your warriors to take your place here and help Lorin."

Yanzi looked mournful. "I see. You trust your little mage friend more than you trust me."

She grinned. "You're a Dirinan street criminal, Yanzi. I'll never trust you completely. Plus, you're so much prettier than Lorin. I need an impressive retinue, remember?"

Lorin looked proud, his shoulders straightening. "I won't fail you, Lira."

"I know you won't." She held his eyes, gave him a little smile, then her voice turned businesslike. "Okay, counteracting telepaths. From this moment on, I want four of Shiasta's warriors shadowing us at all times when we're together. When we separate, we take two Hunters each with us too. A concentration of Hunter medallions creates a bubble that mage magic can't penetrate—including telepathic magic. Any questions?"

There weren't any.

"We all need sleep. While we're resting, Shiasta, you'll prepare your warriors to hit the guard barracks to grab Athira. Yanzi, you'll organise to have horses and supplies waiting for us outside the city. We move tomorrow morning if we can—I assume one of the smuggling boats can get us out of the harbour and up the coast to rendezvous with the horses?"

"That will be the easiest part of this whole crazy plan," Yanzi said morosely. "Although don't you think the middle of a busy day is a poor time to stage a jailbreak and daring city escape?"

"It is. But you and Shiasta need a few hours at least to prepare what's needed, and if we wait until tomorrow night, Egalion might have moved Athira out of the city already," Lira said. "I'd rather not risk lingering here either. Once we're clear of Dirinan, I think we have a real chance of staying free long enough to carry this plan out, or at least enough of it that when they do catch up, we'll be in a position to fight back."

They broke up without further comment. Shiasta and Yanzi headed out to take care of their assignments while another Hunter showed Lira, Tarion, Fari, and Lorin to rooms where they could rest.

The sounds of the gambling hall—laughter, shouting, clapping, hooting—drifted through the thin walls, but the corridors they took were empty of Yanzi's people. None of them would know that Lira and her council were inside their headquarters.

The familiar sounds made her exhaustion an even heavier weight, though. A large part of her wished she could give up on all this and go back to the life she'd once had with Ahrin and Yanzi and their crew. A dangerous life, but a good one. One with simple joys. But the heir to Shakar Astor would never be allowed that freedom.

By the time they reached a cluster of rooms on the third level, right in the back corner of the property, four more of Shiasta's warriors had joined them. The moment they were close enough, her access to her telekinesis magic vanished, with a sharp popping sensation in her chest. Lorin winced, Fari made a face, and Tarion sighed. Lira touched her flame magic, just to reassure herself it was still there.

At Lira's instruction, the Hunters took up positions in a square-like formation around their rooms. She then walked in each direction down the hall and inside each room to check where the bubble ended. It was large enough.

"It's like a weird emptiness." Fari kept shaking her head. "Or not being able to get quite enough breath in my lungs."

"You'll get used to it." Lira had, when staying with them on Shadowfall Island. "Now get some sleep." She opened the nearest door. "We're going to need it."

# CHAPTER 9

L ira had just laid down with relief on her small bed, eyes sliding closed, when her door clicked open and Tarion entered. As soon as he was inside, he closed it behind him, softly enough that it made no sound.

"Something wrong?" she asked, instantly sitting up.

"Could be." He glanced around, as if to ensure the room was empty, then came to sit beside her on the bed, close enough that he only had to murmur for her to hear him. "When Athira boarded the ship in Rotherburn, she was carrying a bulky pack, almost as big as she was. I didn't pay a huge amount of attention to it, apart from to wonder why she needed so many supplies for a short ship journey. But then when she left the ship with Mama, she didn't take the pack with her."

Lira's gaze narrowed. "Okay."

"That *did* make me curious, so I went looking for it when none of the crew was paying attention to me. It wasn't in her bunk room. I couldn't find it anywhere that I could get to without being seen."

"You think she tossed it overboard before leaving the ship?"

He shook his head. "Tonight, when we were boarding the ship's boat to row into the harbour, I saw one of the crew carrying it up on deck. I asked Lorin to slow down on the oars and used my magic to transport back to the ship ... staying out of sight. The crewman loaded the pack onto another ship boat with two rowers, then lowered it from the opposite side of the ship to keep it hidden from our view. I kept watching as we rowed ashore—it was dark, so I can't be certain, but

I think I glimpsed the other boat heading towards the southern end of the harbour."

She straightened, tiredness momentarily draining from her. "Where exactly?"

"It was impossible to tell—there were so many ships at anchor tonight, and the boat I saw could have been heading to another one. But..."

"You think they were delivering Athira's pack to someone in Dirinan?"

"I do."

"Rotted carcasses." Lira swore under her breath. "Lucinda has something else up her sleeve, doesn't she?"

"It makes sense, right? The task she set you has a high level of difficulty ... she must know that. Not to mention she won't be trusting for a second that you'll do as she says for long. She'll have contingencies in place."

Lira nodded slowly. "A plan for if I fail or go rogue. Another way to achieve her ends."

"I wouldn't be surprised if all of this is just another ruse covering her actual goal."

Lira covered her face with her hands, weariness returning to weigh unbearably on her. Tarion was right. It was bitter knowledge to think Lira could be doing all of this for nothing. Still ... what if she *did* manage to succeed? She would have the power to do a lot then, enough to thwart whatever else it was that Lucinda had going on. Much more than if she just followed Lucinda's orders.

That thought brought a spark of hope to her chest, despite her aching weariness. Maybe she'd made the right call with the path she was taking. Just as long as Lucinda didn't see it coming...

Tarion's voice jerked her from her haze. "How do we find out what it is?"

"Get Yanzi's people to do a board and search of the ship we came on first thing tomorrow. If they find anything, maybe it will help us figure out what's going on. If not, we'll get Lorin to investigate while we're away."

He nodded thoughtfully. "You're right that the gang here gives us resources we don't have on our own. And leaving Lorin here was another smart move."

She snorted. "I'm glad you approve. Now, Yanzi's runners would have spotted someone coming ashore tonight and marked them—and as strangers, a runner would have followed them. Wait here a moment."

Lira rose and went to the door, summoning one of the silent Hunters in the hall outside. She immediately came forward. "Lady Astor?"

"I have some instructions for Shiasta." Lira relayed them. "Come straight back here when you're done."

She bowed her head and was gone.

Lira went back into her room, dropping with a sigh beside Tarion. He had a small frown on his face as he said, "I suppose we can try asking Athira once we break her out too, though I don't like our chances of her telling us anything. What do you think happened to her?"

"Knowing Athira as I did … it's hard to see her willingly joining Lucinda's cause." Lira shrugged.

"She was tortured and experimented on like us, and for longer. That kind of trauma can irreversibly change a person."

"You knew Athira better than I did," she said. "Can you think of a good reason she would have switched her allegiance to Lucinda … and so completely that the woman is comfortable enough in Athira's loyalty to let her roam free of her control?"

"I've been thinking about it over and over. Mostly because I feel so guilty that this happened to her. But no." Tarion sat up a little straighter. "Although if it's a result of trauma, that might be something Aunt Dawn and Uncle Finn together could heal, with time."

"Yes, but for that we'd need to let your mother take her to Carhall, which we can't afford. Lucinda needs to believe we're doing what she asks, and that means bringing Athira along with us so she can tell Lucinda about it. And even though Lucinda has other spies watching us, if Athira suddenly stops reporting in, she'll know something has gone wrong."

"I think it could be a greater win for us if the council helped Athira ... then she could tell Lucinda anything we wanted her to, not to mention tell us what she brought from Rotherburn in that pack and what she knows of Lucinda's plans."

"Are you confident that it *is* just trauma, and that your aunt and uncle could heal her quickly enough—before she misses whatever timeframe she's supposed to report to Lucinda by?" Lira asked.

He let out a long sigh. "No. That kind of healing would take time and patience."

"Then we don't have any choice." Lira hesitated at the look on Tarion's face. Letting out a small sigh, she said, "Maybe Fari can help her—I'm willing to try it as long as we don't push too hard and risk making Athira suspicious."

"Okay," he said, brightening a little. "That's a good idea."

Lira ran a weary hand through her hair, eyelids drooping of their own accord now. "Why tell me this now, in private?"

He gave her a look that told her that her plans might not be so secret as she thought, at least from him. "There's a reason that you're not telling us anything about *how* you're going to take down the council." He hesitated. "You think there's a spy close to you."

"I—"

He lifted a hand to cut her off. "Lucinda basically proclaimed to you and Mama that Athira is her spy. That means she's not the only one ... there's someone else out there. Maybe more than one. I know you've figured that out too."

Lira simply nodded.

"You know what that tells me?" His voice dropped so low that she barely heard him. "You're not planning to do what Lucinda wants. If you were, you wouldn't care if her spy knew the specifics of your plans." He must have seen the panic that flashed across her face because he quickly reached out to take her hand. "You don't have to say a word about it and we'll never discuss it again. Just know that I trust you and have faith in you, Lira Astor, and whatever your plans, I will stand by your side."

She had to wipe away tears. "I'm so glad you're with me, Tarion."

He blinked, clearly surprised by her admission, but then smiled. "I'm glad too. Now, do you mind if I sleep on the floor in here? Just in case, if I change into the monster…"

He didn't have to say it—he trusted her to talk him down. "You can't change," she said gently. "The Hunters outside, remember?"

"I know… but…" He stared at the floor. "I'm so worried about Da, and Mama too, and scared about what comes next. And tired to my bones. I just think I'll sleep better near a friend."

"Oh." She blinked. Then realised with a start of surprise that she would sleep easier knowing Tarion was nearby too. "Don't snore. Do that and you'll be sleeping out in the draughty hallway."

His grin was bright and real. "Thanks, Lira."

She tossed him one of the two blankets from the bed, and he laid out on the floor beside it while she curled up, then blew out the lamp. After a few moments of listening to his steady breathing, her mind turned restlessly, sticking on the idea of spies.

It was a nagging suspicion that had been at the back of her mind since her imprisonment. Lucinda had *always* been one step ahead of her. She'd had watchers in Underground, of course, but it was more than that. At some point she'd learned that Lira was a traitor to Underground, that she was spying on them for the council.

Lira had had a lot of time in her prison cell to think about how that had happened.

The obvious answer was that the Magor-lier had told her. The date of the letter that Lira and Ahrin found in Lucinda's office on Shadowfall indicated that Tarrick Tylender had been replaced—presumably killed, since he'd stayed gone ever since an imposter took over his life— probably around the same time Lucinda found out about Lira being a spy. And the head of the Mage Council had been one of only a handful briefed on Lira's mission infiltrating Underground.

But it wasn't the *right* answer, for one key reason. Lucinda hadn't just known about Lira being a spy. She'd known Ahrin was working with her. The night Lira had escaped Shadowfall, Lucinda had issued orders to kill Ahrin too.

And *nobody* in the Mage Council had known about Lira and Ahrin's relationship, their love for each other. In fact, there was a *very* short list of people who either knew outright or knew enough to suspect.

During those long, long, hours in that prison cell, Lira had started to wonder. The Mage Council had accused Lira of joining Temari Hall as a spy for Underground. It wasn't true, but that didn't mean Underground hadn't done something very similar with another person. Placed someone in Lira's inner circle, someone who would be in a position to spy on her every move. It was just the sort of complex and long-term plotting Lucinda was best at.

The shortlist: Lorin Hester, Fari Dirsk, Tarion Caverlock, and Garan Egalion. Or had Lucinda acted even earlier, placing Yanzi in her life, her crew, there and ready to activate if she ever returned to Dirinan?

Now, she had all but Garan gathered close by her. A double-edged blade, of course. For now, she was following the steps of Lucinda's orders, so they could know everything she was doing. But eventually she would need to decide, about which of them she *could* trust with her real plans. And if she got that wrong ... it would all be over before it began. Lucinda would come, and Lira would be back in prison or dead.

She turned, restless, eyes falling on Tarion's sleeping form. Rationally, the only member of her Shadowcouncil she could truly trust was Shiasta. But now she mentally added Tarion to that list.

And by walking away, refusing to join her, Garan Egalion had unknowingly exonerated himself, making her list even smaller.

Fari. Yanzi. Lorin.

It *was* one of them. She knew it in her bones.

# CHAPTER 10

"The ship that carried you here raised anchor and left on the pre-dawn tide, before we could get to it," Shiasta reported to Lira and Tarion over breakfast the next morning. It was painfully early, the sun barely emerging on the horizon, and he'd just returned from scouting the Dirinan prison. They'd left Lorin and Fari sleeping a while longer. "Ordra reported that it was tacking to the north."

Lira sighed. "It could have gone in any direction once it was out of sight of the shore."

"I also spoke to the runners on duty last night," Shiasta continued. "There *was* a sighting of an unfamiliar ship's boat coming ashore. As per usual procedure, the man who disembarked was tracked through Revel Kings' territory. He didn't stop anywhere and didn't speak with anyone, and he crossed into Silver Lord territory without incident, so they left him alone. An hour later, he crossed back into our patch, this time from Gutter Rat territory, returned to his boat, and he and his companion rowed out to the ship that brought you here."

"Was he carrying anything?" Tarion asked.

"A bulky pack when he got off the boat, nearly as big as he was. The runner following him thought it must have been heavy—the man was moving slowly and huffing a lot. He was very careful with it too, which they thought odd." Shiasta said. "The bag was gone when he came back through our territory."

"Careful how?" Tarion asked.

"Like he didn't want to touch it, and he made sure it didn't brush against anything when he walked," Shiasta said. "He was sweating, too, despite the chilly night, though that could have been exertion if the bag was so heavy."

"Any chance we can find out where he took the bag?" Lira asked the Hunter.

"It will be difficult, Lady Astor. I can send my Hunters searching the streets, but Dirinan is large, and we have no starting point to begin. The man was outside our territory for an hour—he could have gone to many places in the city and back within that time."

"No, we need your Hunters to focus on getting Athira out. We'll have to let this go for now." Lira didn't like it, but she didn't see any other choice. "How's that coming along?"

Before he could reply, Yanzi swung through the door. Although he probably hadn't slept yet, he seemed alert and cheerful. "Your daring escape from Dirinan is all set, Darkmage. Don't let anyone say I'm not upholding my part of being a dangerously suave and effective Shadowcouncil member."

"Perhaps you could elaborate," Lira said dryly.

He dropped into a chair, picked up her cup of tea, and took a long, blissful swallow. "One of my trusted smugglers is ready and waiting to take you out this morning. I'd like to time your departure for when Shiasta and his warriors hit the jail to break out Athira. That way the authorities' attention will be directed there."

Tarion frowned. "I assume your smuggler has no idea who we are? There will be substantial rewards offered for our location."

Yanzi waved a dismissive hand. "She thinks she's moving crewmembers who bloodied up the wrong merchant's son in a bar fight and need to get out of the city for a while."

Any unease Lira felt about getting herself out of the city faded entirely. She trusted this part of the plan more than any other. The Shiven government and its forces, Mage Council included, had no foothold in, or control over, the harbour district. The Revel Kings made sure that trade continued in and out of the port without incident—giving the authorities no reason to try to regain their authority over the area—and everyone coexisted mostly happily.

Moving things illegally was the crew's livelihood, and they would get her out. Shiasta though … she feared for him and his warriors going up against council mages and Taliath. Not to mention the consequences of such a clash—her first direct attack on the Mage Council. Before she could ask, though, Shiasta spoke.

"Lady Astor, my warriors and I have scouted the prison and we have a plan in place for Athira's extraction. We can move on your order."

"And your escape from Dirinan once you have her?" she asked.

"Our medallions prevent detection by mages, and we already have an exit route from the city. It's standard procedure from our training to have one in place, and it was established when we first settled here. We'll meet up with you at the rendezvous point Yanzi has organised."

"Where there will be horses and supplies waiting," Yanzi finished. "They're already on their way."

Shiasta's confidence eased some of her fear. "Thank you," Lira said to both men, genuinely grateful. "You've done excellent work, as always."

Yanzi smiled and tipped his non-existent hat at her. "I live to serve."

She chuckled and rose. "Tarion and I will go wake the others and prepare to leave, and you'd better do the same, Yanzi. Shiasta—we'll aim to be aboard this smuggler's boat in two hours. You can be in place and ready to launch your assault by then?"

"We can, Lady Astor. My warriors are preparing as we speak."

Yanzi rubbed his hands together with glee. "How exciting all this cloak and dagger taking over the world business is! It's been a long time since I've left Dirinan for distant and exotic shores."

"I think you'll find where we're going is far from exotic," Lira said dryly.

"Not once I arrive." He beamed, far from deterred. "You said dress to impress, yes?"

Normally this would have coaxed a smile from Lira, but her thoughts were preoccupied. She felt safe here in Dirinan, confident of her advantage. But once she left … Alyx Egalion was going to throw everything she had at finding Lira. Fear bubbled under her mask of confidence.

Her shoulders straightened. She was the Darkmage, and she had a Shadowcouncil now.

Let them come.

The smuggler's boat sailed out of the harbour and up the coast without incident, clearly a trip this seasoned crew had made many times moving illicit cargo in and out of the port city. It was a cramped journey, though, all seven of them shoved together in a secret hold belowdecks, with no room to stand. Lira, seated with Tarion pressed against her on one side and Fari on the other, took the opportunity to get some more sleep, lulled by the rocking of the boat.

When she woke to find her head resting on Tarion's shoulder, she didn't jerk away in annoyance at herself like she once would have done. Instead, she smiled a little to see him sleeping too. Soft snores rose from Fari to her left.

Without moving, she shifted her gaze until it fell on her three Hunters. They sat awake and alert, ready in case their charge came under threat. "Thank you for keeping watch," she said softly.

"Vensis would never thank them for doing their jobs," Yanzi remarked from the shadows on the other side of the hold, where he sat.

"No, she wouldn't. You doing okay over there?" The tall Zandian couldn't be comfortable. Neither he nor Tarion had enough space to stretch out their long legs.

"I really need to pee," he said plaintively.

She chuckled. "You and me both."

"It's good to be working with you again, Lira," he said after a moment. "I mean, I think you've gone completely crazy, thinking you and Vensis can take down the Mage Council … but it was never the same after you left. Even when Ahrin came back. It didn't feel the same without you."

She fought back a smile. "That's a lot of sentiment for a hardened crew leader."

"You know what I mean. Vensis was the most ruthless boss I've ever come across. There was little softness. We were often hungry, and we were always looking over our shoulders." He met her gaze. "But it felt like home."

This time she let the soft smile escape, memory soothing her. "That's exactly what it was."

Neither of them said anything more, but the silence in the small space grew appreciably warmer. Lira stayed resting against Tarion's shoulder, thinking. It had felt like Yanzi truly meant those words. And if they were true, could he really be the spy?

Yanzi the silver-tongued. It was what they'd all called him. He could make anyone believe anything, and he'd been the crucial factor in every confidence scam they'd run.

Lira sighed, closed her eyes again. She didn't have to make that decision yet.

They waded onto the isolated sandy shore under the glow of the setting sun, groaning and muttering as cramped limbs asserted their complaints and ice-cold seawater soaked them to their waists.

Once out of the water, Lira took a deep breath of fresh ocean air, tried to stand up straight through the protesting of her healing ribs, then looked around. A narrow track led into thick woods directly ahead of her. Nothing else was around apart from unbroken shoreline in both directions. The light was quickly fading.

"We'll go first, Lady Astor," one Hunter spoke as she moved towards the track. Tarion followed her, one hand on the hilt of *Darksong*.

"So protective," Fari murmured appreciatively. "How does one get some Hunters for themselves, Lira? As a Shadowcouncil member, it would only be fitting."

"You don't want that." Lira said shortly.

"I can't see why not," Yanzi said airily. "Trained attack dogs are useful in my line of work."

"That's not what they are," Lira snapped, irritation growing.

Silence fell after that, and they headed along the trail, pace quickening as stiffened limbs loosened up. Eventually they emerged into a clearing where several horses, all carrying bulging saddlebags, waited for them, heads down as they grazed contentedly.

Shiasta was there too, alone, with Athira standing at his side. Lira could have hugged him—as skilled and clever as her Hunters were, she hadn't been sure it was possible to get Athira out amidst all the mages and Taliath around.

"Lady Astor." He bowed. "We retrieved your friend without significant incident. There was a bit of a scuffle getting away, but no Hunters were injured, and no mages either."

"And you're sure they didn't follow you?"

"Certain." He paused. "However, I am confident at least one mage noticed our medallions and the stifling effect it had on their magic. It is possible they will guess what we are."

She winced. She would have liked to hold that trump card a while longer but getting Athira free had been worth the price. Her gaze shifted to Athira. "Welcome. And apologies for Egalion's rather blunt tactics."

Athira lifted an eyebrow. "I can't say I'm surprised she reneged on her word—honourable to a fault that one. I *am* pleased that you seem to be keeping yours."

"I went to substantial effort to set you free." Lira pointed to one of the Hunters that had come with her. "Adara here will take whatever message or sign you have for Lucinda back to Dirinan with him. I'm sure you have a prearranged signal to let the Seventh know that I'm doing as she ordered?"

Athira crossed her arms over her chest. "And if I do that, then what happens?"

Lira shrugged. "I intend to take up my grandfather's mantle, Athira Walden, and I will succeed where he failed. You'll get a front-row seat to all of it."

Athira hesitated for a long moment, but then eventually nodded. "Do you have parchment?"

Adara immediately stepped towards her, tugging a folded piece of parchment, quill, and pot of ink from his tunic.

Athira scribbled some quick words, blew on the ink to dry it, then folded it and handed it back to Adara. "Take it to the inn called 'Rustic Broom' and give it to the barkeeper named Ronan. Nobody else."

"That's in the wealthy district," Yanzi murmured in Lira's ear.

She nodded. An inn not in crew territory ... interesting.

"Ronan has no link to Lucinda, just in case you were wondering." Athira smiled. "Tailing him or his communications won't help you intercept mine."

Lira huffed a breath. "Ah, so the words on the parchment don't matter? It's a signal only—someone will be watching for Ronan to get a message. Clever."

Adara looked at Lira. "Lady Astor?"

Aware of Athira's assessing gaze on her, Lira made a quick decision not to attempt passing any messages back. Adara would report the inn and barman's name to Lorin, and she could trust his initiative to investigate that lead. "Go on, Adara. Hand the message over and then return to Revel Kings' headquarters. Lorin will be your superior until either myself or Yanzi return."

He bowed, turned, and loped off into the trees. Athira didn't turn to watch him go—instead she eyed Lira with something approaching a challenge. Lira held her gaze. She couldn't see much of the entitled but brave pureblood mage who'd once looked out of those blue eyes. Who was this Athira, the one who'd been held hostage for years and presumably tortured via experiments for a good portion of that time? She thought about how over two years of imprisonment had changed *her*, hardened her. Made her unable to trust.

Athira was an unknown quantity now, a dangerous one until Lira understood *why* she was acting so decidedly on Lucinda's behalf. But she had time to do that. Lira shifted her gaze from Athira and regarded her party. Four Hunters, three mages, and a crew boss.

Not a terrible start. Not a terrible start at all.

She straightened her shoulders and moved for the horses. "Shall we get on with taking over the world, then?"

# CHAPTER 11

I t was a bitingly cold autumn day in northwest Shivasa. In the days since departing Dirinan, they'd followed the coastline north towards their quarry, sticking to it as it veered northwest, revealing a part of the country Lira had never seen before.

Today the air was still, the previous night's snowfall covering everything in a carpet of stark white. It reminded Lira of those fuzzy memories she had of the time before her mother died, when they'd lived in that tiny cabin in a remote rural village. Years later, fully grown, and she still hadn't lost that faint sense of never being quite warm enough. Or full enough.

What would her mother think of her now?

The thought came unbidden. Lira didn't remember specific details about what her mother had been like. She didn't know how her mother had felt about being Shakar's daughter, or what she'd hoped for her own daughter's future. These questions had always been there, at the back of Lira's mind, but other things had always been more important, more demanding of her attention. And she'd let them stay hidden. She'd had enough pain to deal with already.

But now ... Lira wanted some of those answers.

Her whole life she'd been focused on who she was because of the man her grandfather had been, but her recent conversation with Fari had made her realise for the first time how skewed that view was. Because Fari had been right—Lira was also a product of her mother. The woman who had loved and wanted her. Just because she wasn't infamous didn't mean she wasn't just as important, if not more so, to who Lira would become.

Lucinda had promised her the identity of her father if she carried out her plan successfully, but Lira had dismissed the offer, too horrified at the sight of Ahrin trapped in a cage before her to care about information so useless. But while Lira didn't care a rotted toss for him, he might have some answers she sought on her mother. He'd known her, after all, well enough to bed her, get her pregnant. He should have memories of her. But Lira had no idea where to even begin looking for him, and the last thing she would do was take Lucinda's word on who her father was.

Hence riding deep into northern Shivasa. Yes, finding Lucinda's contact in Shakar's old network was the obvious first step in putting together what Lira needed to keep up the appearance of taking down the Mage Council ... but these people had also known her mother. Shakar's daughter had been part of her father's network during the war, and she had retained links to it afterward.

Lira's horse swung his head around as a fly crawled along his nose, attempting to use her boot as a convenient scratching post. She grinned. Yanzi had acquired her a handsome dark brown horse—fleet and strong and well trained, as were the horses of all her companions. Despite his size and impressive appearance though, Alfie was a gentle soul who remained patient with an inexperienced rider. She'd begun to look forward to seeing him in the mornings when they saddled up to keep moving.

There had been no trace of pursuit from Dirinan. They'd presumably figured out by now that Lira had left the city, but not where she'd gone. The Mage Council had no clue of the resources now at Lira's disposal, which was exactly how she liked it. She needed to stay ahead of them until she'd assembled all the pieces she needed.

But so much had to go right for that to happen.

Lira huffed a breath and dispelled the useless worries from her thoughts. This was the problem with long hours of travel ... it left too much time to get stuck in her thoughts. She widened her awareness to take in her surroundings.

They'd spent the previous night in the coastal town of Kharan before riding out along the northern road not long after dawn. If they'd continued along that road, it would have eventually led them over the border into Tregaya and all the way to its southern port city of Tarnor.

But less than a half hour out of Kharan, Shiasta had turned them off the road onto a narrower local thoroughfare heading east. It wasn't a cobbled road, but its muddy surface appeared well maintained, and it had been cleared from snow despite a heavy fall the day and night before. Deep drifts of it were stacked on the verges. This told Lira that wherever this road led—presumably the estate they were looking for—it was owned by somebody powerful, or rich, or both.

"I assume you noticed the attitude of the townsfolk back in Kharan?" Fari asked, her horse moving up alongside Alfie. "And in Ralan, the night before."

Lira couldn't help but smile. "Welcome to rural Shivasa, Zandian mage pureblood."

Fari made a face. "You mean they're all like that?"

"You laugh at her, but most of the looks were directed at Fari and me," Yanzi said pointedly, turning to glare over his shoulder. Farther ahead, Tarion and Athira rode behind Shiasta, silent, lost in their own worlds. At the rear came the three Hunters—Therob, Laun, and Pestra—whose medallions prevented a telepath mage from finding them.

"Oh, I've been subjected to those looks too. I didn't look Shiven enough to fit in when I first arrived in Dirinan. Shiven don't like strangers." Lira shrugged off how isolating, terrifying that had been, especially after being expelled from her home village. "It's better in the big cities like Karonan and Dirinan, where there are larger numbers of Tregayans, Rionnans, and Zandians. But out here, anything that looks different marks you as a stranger."

"Why do Shiven hate strangers so much?" Fari wanted to know.

"I don't actually know," Lira said.

"Beats me," Yanzi said with Fari's gaze shifted to him.

"How did you end up in Shivasa, Yanzi?" Fari asked.

"Much the same way Lira did. My mother was a sailor on a Zandian merchant ship. She liked a good time—drinking and lots of cloudweed. One time while they were on shore leave, she got blind drunk at the inns and lost track of me ... at least, I like to think that's what happened. She never seemed to come looking for me, though." He shrugged. "So there I was, seven years old, stuck in a foreign city, all alone. I learned how to survive—it was that or die. By the time Ahrin recruited me, I was one of the best pickpockets on the docks."

Fari opened her mouth as if to say something, but then closed it. Maybe she realised there was nothing she could really contribute to that story. Instead, after a moment, she changed the subject. "You know, we're actually two short."

"What?" Lira blinked, confused by the segue.

"If we're the new Shadowcouncil ... then we need eight council members to match the Mage Council. There's only six of us."

Lira chuckled. "We have eight members. Ahrin and Athira make up the final two."

"I really don't enjoy being on the same team as Athira." Fari sighed.

"Actually." Lira hesitated, then pressed forward. She had promised Tarion, after all. "Do you think you could try talking to her? See if you can use your healing abilities to get a sense of why she might have joined Lucinda's side?"

Fari glanced ahead. "You mean, if she was traumatised from the experiments to the extent that Lucinda was able to manipulate her into believing we're the enemy?"

"Something like that, yes."

"I can try, but if that were the case, I suspect it wouldn't manifest physically in a way I could heal. I think you'd need a combination of someone with Master A'ndreas' knowledge of healing lore and a skilled telepath."

"You're probably right." Lira's heart sank a little. Part of her had been hoping that Fari could bring the old Athira back to them. She'd even take a constant stream of uppity, ignorant comments over the stone-faced disciple of Lucinda's Athira had been since joining them. It made her uneasy, on edge.

Fari gave her a considering look. "It's worth giving it a go anyway. I assume you want me to do it in a way that doesn't make her suspicious we're trying to turn her loyalties back to us?"

"It won't be easy, I know, but it could really help us."

"I'll try," Fari promised.

It wasn't long after that the walls of a large estate loomed ahead of them, around a bend in the tree-lined road. The iron gates stood open, welcoming, a perfectly circular paved drive beyond—also cleared of snow.

A quick scan of the surrounds showed no guards posted at the gates themselves. There were no tracks in the mud to show that anyone had travelled in or out recently either. Lira urged Alfie into a trot past the others, taking a moment to adjust to his big stride before riding first through the gates. They all fell neatly into pairs behind her, having practised it over the previous days of riding.

Appearances would be everything with these people.

Once through, they covered half the distance to the house at a swift trot before Lira brought Alfie back to a walk. She wanted a chance to survey the grounds as they approached, and for anyone inside watching to get a proper look at them, too.

"No obvious guards," Tarion murmured. He rode immediately behind her, Fari at his left. "Odd."

"Not for a Shiven lord," Yanzi said. "This one is so confident in his power and wealth he has no need for a visible guard presence. They'll be there, though. Just a handful, probably, but well trained and good at staying concealed."

"Lord Yanzi is correct," Shiasta said. "Last time we met with Lord Anler in Dirinan, there were at least seven discreetly placed guards surrounding the location for the duration of the meeting."

Yanzi grinned—as he did every single time Shiasta used a title when addressing him—and Lira tried not to roll her eyes.

She looked over her shoulder at Shiasta, trying to keep her voice both casual and gentle. "Do you recognise this place at all?"

He seemed confused by the question. "Should I?"

"Not necessarily. I'm just curious."

"No, Lady Astor, I don't." But then he hesitated, taking a sweeping look around. "But ... it feels oddly familiar. Almost the same feeling as I have when you are near."

Fari and Tarion shot Lira curious looks, but she ignored them. Having firsthand experience of how Ahrin reacted when asked about her past and training as a Hunter, Lira was reluctant to press Shiasta unless she really had to. The sense of protectiveness she felt had only increased as she spent more time with him and his Hunters.

When they reached the end of the drive, Lira brought Alfie to a halt with a light touch, and he instantly obeyed. His dark coat was striking against the white surrounds, and the others were careful to rein in behind her, making sure Lira was marked as the leader for anyone observing them.

She swung out of the saddle with relief, pausing at the base of wide stone steps that led up to the front door. She took a quick inventory of her appearance. She was dressed more richly than she ever had been before. Fine woollen tunic and breeches tucked into kidskin leather boots. A jewelled dagger in her belt, matching leather gloves on her hands. A long, perfectly tailored coat that swung around her knees ... coloured deep violet, the same shade as her magic. As Shakar's magic. The amethyst-encrusted buttons of her tunic contrasted perfectly—a final touch of Fari's.

And, hanging in a new holster down her back, Cario Duneskal's mage staff, the one she'd stolen from Egalion. It was almost too long to look sensible on her slight frame, but she needed something to outwardly mark her as a mage, and she had been reluctant to give it up in favour of making herself a new one.

"Let's do this," she said without looking over her shoulder, and started up the steps.

Shiasta's three Hunters remained where they were, while the others trailed after her, staying a step behind. They made for an equally well-dressed, but motley, group. Yanzi, in what amounted to his idea of appropriate crime boss attire: tailored silks complete with a rakish hat and a bright orange feather hanging from his earlobe. She swore he must be freezing, though he insisted he was fine. Fari wore a fine Zandian cotton wrap under her cloak, like Yanzi in complete defiance of the cold, while Athira wore the split skirts and jacket of the noble-born heiress she'd once been, in matching shades of blue.

Tarion wore the simple breeches and jacket of a Taliath. With *Darksong* hanging at his hip, for the first time since Lira had known him, he looked like he fit within himself. Even some of his shyness had faded, and he no longer stared constantly at the ground when talking. Not only that, but the Darkmage's blade gave him an air of danger. Although maybe that had to do with the violent mage ability that lurked under his skin.

"I thought Underground was the champion of the poor?" Fari had asked when Lira told them to make sure they looked wealthy and impressive.

"They are. But if we want to fully resurrect Underground, we'll need those who supported the Darkmage—the ones who have all the money and resources. Both they and my grandfather leveraged the grievances of the poor for their own purposes, and I'll bet all the jewelled buttons on my new tunic that none of them gave two coppers about poverty in Shivasa. If we want them to take us seriously as the new and improved Shadowcouncil, we can't waltz in there looking like we're ruffians straight from the streets of a slum."

Fari snorted. "That's what I like so much about your rebel cause, Lira. It's so ideologically pure."

"It's not my cause."

Fari had looked at her sharply. "No?"

Lira hadn't replied, and Yanzi had made a joking comment about Lira ever looking like anything but a street rat, and their attention had been diverted. She'd breathed a sigh of relief and cursed herself for the misstep.

Now, Lira's gaze roamed what she could see of the estate as she reached the door and rang the bell, seeking any confirmation that this was the right place to be. There was a chance that Lucinda's contact was just a lackey, an unimportant middleman who'd be unable to tell them anything about Shakar's network. But Lira had gambled on the fact Lucinda wouldn't deign to deal with anyone *too* unimportant ... her need for iron-fisted control would have meant direct engagement with at least one significant member of the network. She had to hope Lord Anler was it.

The imposing nature of his estate seemed to indicate he was.

It was hard to see much of what lay beyond the manor house, but the place was clearly massive. Plenty of room for what she guessed had gone on here. Shiasta's stiffened shoulders and darkened eyes reassured her somewhat too—though she didn't think he was conscious of his reaction.

"You're hoping for more here than just a contact in your grandfather's network, aren't you?" Tarion asked now, his voice low. Clearly he'd paid attention to Yanzi's warning of hidden guards earlier.

"If I'm right about who Anler is, you'll see soon enough."

"And if you're not?"

Yanzi grinned. "Then we'll probably be leaving in a hurry."

"That's why you're here." Lira gave him a look. "Unless you've lost that silver tongue of yours since we last ran the streets together?"

He leaned closer, winking. "On the contrary. These days I can charm a lobster into a boiling pot."

"Delightful," Fari muttered, eyes rolling skyward.

"Lady Astor?" Shiasta asked quietly, one eyebrow raised. "Shall I?"

She nodded. "Yes, Shiasta. As we discussed."

He turned, took the steps two at a time, and then disappeared around the corner of the house. His three Hunters ran after him, silent and focused. Her gaze lingered on them until they disappeared from sight; she tried not to worry.

"Are we going to stand here all day?" Athira snapped.

Lira settled a look on Athira, letting the woman know she would do things at *her* pace, not Athira's, then turned back to the doors in front of her. She took a deep breath, ensured her grandfather's aloof expression was clearly in place, and then she knocked.

Time to take the first step in becoming the Darkmage in more than just name.

# CHAPTER 12

A moment later, approaching footsteps sounded, and then both doors swung open in a single sweeping movement. A well-dressed servant stood there with a politely enquiring expression, hands laced behind his back. He did not give any indication of surprise to see a random collection of well-dressed strangers show up at his lord's doorstep unannounced.

"My name is Lira Astor," she said coolly. "I'd like to see Lord Anler."

The man's gaze narrowed slightly. "Is he expecting you?"

"I doubt it very much."

"In that case, I—"

Lira cut him off. "You go and tell him my name. I'm confident he'll see me. We'll wait here."

He hesitated, but her name must have rung a chord, because he gave a sharp nod, then closed the doors in her face.

"Shiven hospitality, so warm and welcoming," Yanzi remarked.

"If he doesn't come back and let us inside in a timely fashion," Fari said primly, "I'm afraid I'm going to have to insist on Lira being treated with the respect Shakar's heir deserves. Those pretty doors might not survive my irritation."

Lira tossed her a quick look. How much did Fari truly want to follow Shakar's heir? Her motivations for joining Lira had been plausible, more, they'd sounded sincere. But still—

"You going to break them down yourself?" Tarion murmured.

Fari smirked. "That's what we have you for, Mage-Taliath."

"That won't be necessary. The lackey will be back quickly," Athira said.

She was right. They weren't waiting long before the footsteps returned and the doors swung open. This time, the man gave Lira a quick bow. "Please come in, Lady Astor."

"You'll have our horses stabled, rubbed down and fed, and quickly?" she asked as she stepped inside. Her voice echoed through the cavernous entrance foyer, edged with arrogance. Mindful of Fari's words about acting the part, she'd been practicing the tone, and it now came easily to her. "We've been on the road a long time and I want to ensure they're well cared for."

He bowed his head. "Very good, Lady Astor. I'll see to it at once."

Once he'd closed the doors behind them, the steward led them across the foyer and through an open door to their right. "Please make yourselves comfortable. Lord Anler will be with you shortly."

Those words spoken, he turned and disappeared farther into the house, presumably to organise to have their horses seen to.

The room was warm, a fire crackling in the hearth, long windows looking out over the front drive. Both Lira and Yanzi automatically scanned the space for potential threats and valuables while Fari went to sit on the couch nearest the fire. Tarion looked around with curiosity, one hand resting on the hilt of *Darksong*. Athira hovered just inside the door.

The steward was as good as his word. Within a few minutes, two grooms appeared through the window, approaching their horses.

"I hope they're not stealing those. They'll be expensive to replace," Yanzi said.

"A Shiven lord will not steal our horses." Athira snorted. "He'll have upwards of ten horses far superior in cost and breeding to ours in those stables of his."

Yanzi shrugged but didn't take his eyes off the grooms.

A brief silence fell, filled by the crackle and pop of the fire.

Lira spun at the sound of crisp, tapping bootsteps on stone approaching the room. A man appeared in the doorway a moment later, gaze sweeping them all before landing on Lira and narrowing slightly. "It really is you. I did briefly wonder if poor Herin was finally going senile when he told me who was claiming to be at the door."

She gave him an assessing glance. He was a tall, broad-shouldered Shiven man. Despite his clearly advancing age, he looked like he could take them all on in a duel and give a good accounting of himself. "Lord Anler, I presume?"

"I am." His dark Shiven eyes looked her up and down, slowly, assessing her in return. It was a considered, thoughtful study. She stood silently and bore it. Once he was done, he smiled slightly. "Well, there's no need for me to confirm your identity. You look just like your grandfather."

"So I'm told," she said coolly.

Anler's gaze shifted back to her companions then, but his gaze gave nothing away. "Please, won't you all sit down and make yourselves comfortable? Herin will bring tea and sandwiches as soon as the kitchen has prepared them."

He hadn't mentioned Shiasta and the Hunters or asked where they'd gone. So either his guards hadn't seen them as part of her retinue, or he wasn't willing to let on that he had concealed watchers. She'd bet everything on the latter.

Another shiver of worry went through her, but she dismissed it quickly. Shiasta and his warriors could and would take care of themselves.

At a look from Lira, Athira and Yanzi sat down on the couch near Fari. Tarion remained standing, stationed near the window where he could both see the front drive and the door to the room. Lira also stayed on her feet. She wasn't dealing with this man from a position of vulnerability.

Anler didn't seem bothered when she didn't sit. "What brings you here, Lira Astor?"

"It's rather simple. I'm here for your allegiance, Lord Anler, and your assistance."

"Allegiance? I rather wonder whether I should send a man to the Kharan barracks to fetch a unit of soldiers to arrest you."

She smiled thinly. "We both know you're not going to do that, so I suggest you stop wasting both our time with foolish posturing. I'm here to ask for the same allegiance you gave to my grandfather. The allegiance that you held to after his death." She let that land. "For example, in how you continued recruiting and training Hunters. Or magekillers, as I believe he called them." She paused again, lifted an eyebrow. "The same ones you have discreetly guarding your estate."

She clocked the quick shift of his gaze. The realisation in them, expertly hidden. Silence fell for a few beats as Anler walked to a side table, opened a decanter of spirits, and poured himself a glass. "And what is it that makes you think I did anything of the sort?"

"I am Shakar Astor's heir. Wouldn't you be more surprised if I *didn't* know about what you got up to?" She was bluffing, adjusting to leaning into her grandfather's legacy rather than trying to run from it. "I have proof, in case you were wondering, and killing everyone inside this room wouldn't prevent the information from getting out to the people you *really* don't want to hear it." She cocked her head. "Not that you *could* kill the people in this room."

His expression didn't change, and he gave a little shrug. "Even if there had been such a program, it would have ended long ago."

"Do you really think Leader Astohar would care about when things ended? Not to mention, just because a particular activity ended, your old allegiances didn't cease. You could be up to all sorts of things in furtherance of your goals. At least, that's how I imagine Leader Astohar and the Mage Council would see it."

Anler sipped from his glass, gaze hooded. "Say you're right. Am I supposed to consider the fact you're here talking to me rather than reporting me to Astohar as some kind of proof that I can trust you?"

"I don't see why you wouldn't. You were loyal to my grandfather. You believed in the same things he did. I am his heir."

"And who are these people?" A look of disdain flickered over his face as he gestured to her companions. Yanzi and Fari bristled. Tarion remained watchful. Athira smirked when Anler's gaze landed on her.

"My Shadowcouncil."

The click of the front doors opening echoed through the silence that followed. At the faint sound of booted feet lightly crossing the entrance foyer, her shoulders relaxed slightly in relief. Shiasta's tall form filled the room's entrance. He immediately sought Lira's gaze and gave her a quick nod.

"You might have met Shiasta already, during his Hunter training," Lira said conversationally. "He's also a member of my Shadowcouncil. Shiasta has been out having a chat with your estate guards." Lira enjoyed the quickly hidden look of shock on Anler's face. "If you try to call on any of those guards to protect you—or harm us—now?" She paused. "They would turn on you at a single word from Shiasta or myself. Isn't that right?"

Interestingly, Anler didn't seem afraid, even though he was effectively alone and unprotected in a room full of warrior mages and a heavily armed Hunter. Instead, his mouth thinned as he looked back at Lira and met her gaze. "Where did you find Shiasta?"

"Good, so we're not going to continue the useless merry-go-round of you denying everything."

He gave her a considering glance. "I admit to surprise at your knowledge. Last I heard, you were a council mage, Lira Astor."

"I was an apprentice," she spat. "I never took the Trials. But you know that too."

"You vanished from Temari Hall. Where did you go?"

"Keeping an eye on me, were you?"

He shrugged, gaze holding hers. "Consider it a favour to a long-dead friend. I'm an old man. Any revolutionary fire I might have felt died long ago."

"I don't believe that for a second." She paused a moment. "I *am* curious how much involvement you, and the others like you, had with Underground and the previous Shadowcouncil?"

"They were a rabble who had never had the ability to achieve your grandfather's goals despite their grandiose visions and big promises," Anler said, voice rich with contempt.

Lira almost smiled. It was as she'd thought. Lucinda had cut them loose when they no longer served her purposes. She risked a glance at Athira, but the woman's impassive expression told her nothing. "I think you'll find they had no intention of fulfilling my grandfather's vision. You were a means to an end, Lord Anler."

Recognition flashed on the man's face—ah, so he'd come to realise that Lucinda had ulterior motives too.

"Which is why you're so suspicious of me now," she continued after a beat. "I understand that. However, the Mage Council now believes Underground destroyed, their cause dead and gone, never to return." She didn't mention that Alyx Egalion knew full well that Lira intended to rebuild the cause. "This is our opportunity."

Anler sipped at his drink. She was quickly learning that this was a tell … a stalling tactic to give himself time to think. "And how are you going to convince me you're any more capable than Underground was? I concede to the prettiness of your companions, but dressing up in fine clothes and calling yourselves a Shadowcouncil isn't going to achieve what your grandfather sought."

Lira pointed to her companions one after the other. "My Shadowcouncil includes two mage councillor heirs, the only heir to one of the most powerful and influential pureblood Zandian mage families, and a crime lord who controls Dirinan's harbour. I can reach *everyone* with our message, our vision, not just mages. I have powerful magic. I have his name. I have the requisite ruthlessness." There was more she could offer him, too, but not while the others were in the room. "And as I have just demonstrated, I have the allegiance of your Hunter army."

After a long pause, Anler lowered the glass, placed it on the table. "All of that is a start, nothing more."

"Yet I think with our resources joined, we have more than just a start. We have a real chance to bring the Mage Council to its knees and install mage rule across this continent."

He held her gaze for a long moment, one finger idly trailing around the rim of his glass. She waited him out. Eventually, he straightened. "You and your Shadowcouncil are welcome to stay for the night. I'll have Herin set up rooms for you. But you and I will speak further alone. If we are to discuss an alliance, it won't be with your protectors hovering."

Lira smiled. Triumph fizzed in her veins. She had him on the hook.

# CHAPTER 13

L ira stood at an arched window, the fingertips of her right hand pressed lightly against the icy pane of glass. In the garden outside, Anler's grandchildren played with their nurse, resisting their mother's entreaties to come in for dinner now that the light was fading. Their shrieks rang with delight as they chased each other on the snow-covered grass. Even the frustration in their mother's voice was edged with affection.

The scene sat uncomfortably with her. That had never been her life.

It hadn't been Ahrin's either. Lira wondered sometimes whether that was why they'd always been so drawn to each other. So instinctively in tune. Neither of them understood what was "normal" to many others.

For the briefest of moments, she allowed herself to give into the stone-cold terror that simmered constantly under her mask of confidence and poise. What she was attempting—what she *needed*—to do was difficult. In the rare moments she was brutally honest with herself she acknowledged it was more likely than not to fail. But the thought of anything happening to Ahrin, of her Darkhand being at Lucinda's mercy for any length of time...

Oddly enough, though, the thought made her feel as different from her grandfather as it was possible to be. In her bravado, she'd once told Ahrin that she'd burn down the world if anyone touched Ahrin. And part of Lira *would* want that.

But Fari had been right ... after those days in the caverns under Rotherburn, thinking Ahrin was dead and lost to her forever, Lira had barely been able to put one foot in front of the other, let alone start a war. Maybe part of that had been magic overuse and injury, but Lira had overcome that before. She overcame everything. It was who she was.

Except losing Ahrin. Lira now knew that she could never overcome that.

That realisation had re-ordered everything she'd ever thought about herself. About Ahrin. It had occupied her ever since, sparked by Fari's questions. The realisation meant a conscious decision to step away from vengeance, from any need to belong, and pick the path that aligned with the pieces of *Lira's* true self; the one she was just beginning to learn about.

And the one most likely to result in Lucinda's defeat.

The door clicked open, signalling Anler's return, and Lira returned to the present, noting as she did that night had fallen and the children had long since gone inside.

Herin had escorted her to Anler's private study after their earlier conversation; this one not set out perfectly for guests, but more comfortable, messier. A place where the man clearly spent a lot of time. His desk was right near the window—she suspected he'd chosen this room because it allowed him to watch his family play outside while he worked.

Wanting to take control of this conversation from the start, Lira waved Anler to a chair by the fire and took the seat opposite. "Tell me about the Hunter program."

"You seem to know a great deal already," he said genially, taking the seat.

"I understand that you need to assess me, Lord Anler, but I also need to ensure that you can be useful to me." She knew far less than she'd pretended, so a little bluffing was going to be required. "For example—while I know you continued the training program after my grandfather's death, it seems to have ended abruptly at some point. About ten years later?" Lira had put this together from guesswork and the timing of Ahrin's arrival in Dirinan, and she relaxed when Anler nodded.

"Closer to twelve, but yes. The war decimated most of your grandfather's army and resource networks, but the core of his supporters remained and went into hiding. We never stopped working towards his aims. We just had to be far more discreet."

"What happened to make you stop the Hunter program?"

"We received word that Leader Astohar had learned it was ongoing, and intended to send his general, with an army at his back, to end it."

She frowned. "How did Astohar learn of it?"

"One of the nurses in the program developed a conscience and betrayed us." Anler's mouth curled in disgust. "We dealt with him, but it was too late. Our informant in his camp told us he intended to arrest anyone they found to be connected to the program and free the trainees."

"They didn't know who you were?"

"None of those administering the program knew our identities. We knew how to be careful." He gave her a scornful look. "Still, the betrayal was a blow. We terminated the program and shut down the facilities before Astohar could move. When his soldiers arrived, they found nothing. In the end, it wasn't all bad. The whole exercise served to reinforce to Astohar and Caverlock that Shakar's network was gone, which suited our purposes nicely."

"That's a positive spin to put on it," she said coolly. "In reality, you failed to adequately silo your activities and were therefore forced to shut down the entire operation rather than a single facility."

His jaw tensed, but he didn't dispute her.

"The ones who'd already completed their training, what did you do with them?"

"The magekillers were trained and conditioned in units. Once each unit had completed the program, we stationed them across the country at loyal lords' estates. There they prepared for what comes next." He paused, then at her look said, "At the time, there were thirteen trained units—all had been too young to have completed their training when

Shakar died. We moved them the instant the war ended and completed their training in secret."

"And where are they now?"

"Apart from those who remained here at my estate, we gave them to Lucinda and Underground." He shifted in his chair. "We don't know what became of them after that—we tried searching for them after Underground disintegrated, but we couldn't afford to draw attention to ourselves."

Rotted carcasses! This had been one of Lira's key goals in coming here, that Anler would know where the Hunters were after Lucinda had abandoned them. If he didn't know, then she had no idea where to even *begin* looking. Ignoring the dread sliding through her chest, she continued. "When your program was betrayed, what did you do with the children that hadn't completed the training yet?"

His relaxed expression didn't change. "We terminated them."

Horror rippled through her so strongly she barely saved herself from hesitating and betraying it to him. "To be clear, you killed them?"

"Yes. We had no ready hiding place to move them to, and no time to set one up. We considered it too much of a risk to hide them in our homes. Killing them was the most efficient way to address the threat to ourselves." He hesitated.

"What?" she snapped.

"We miscalculated how they would respond. Some escaped."

Anger, always waiting there, just beneath the surface, began boiling up. Ahrin had run away because they were going to *murder* her. She'd been only eight years old, and no doubt there'd been children much younger who hadn't made it out. All because these men had been afraid of being caught. How many *had* died? "How many escaped?"

He shifted, wariness flashing over his face at the sharp edge of her voice. He thought she was angry they'd gotten away. "It's unclear. Not many … less than twenty, but over ten, probably."

Lira took a breath, struggling to keep her fury in check. She needed to switch the topic or else she'd betray the true source of her anger to

Anler. Even then her voice came out chilly, almost threatening. "You said you gave all thirteen units to Lucinda—your entire remaining army after you killed the trainees, I take it. How many Hunters was that exactly?"

"Three hundred and twenty-five." A mix of deep regret and frustration filled Anler's expression. "It was a gross error in judgement, and I have no excuse for it. I can say only that Lucinda was highly convincing in her adherence to our cause and I believed that by allying with her we had a real shot at succeeding."

"With that many highly trained warriors immune to magic, why hadn't you already attempted to re-start Shakar's cause yourselves?"

"We needed more than warriors, especially given the growing number of fully trained Taliath." Anler reached up to rub at his forehead. "Immediately after the war, because the council had been exterminating them for decades, there were only ten or so Taliath. Within a decade, there were double that number and more being found each year. Our magekillers are elite—one of them is worth five Shiven soldiers—but they are on equal footing with a Taliath."

Excuses. Lira hid her contempt. Her grandfather's network might have some wealth, lingering ideological support, and an elite unit of warriors that could combat mages, but none of that brought them even close to toppling the strength of the Mage Council. A strength that only grew with every single year that passed.

They'd sat back and done nothing because there *was* nothing they could do ... yet they patted themselves on the back about keeping Shakar's cause alive. Pretended it *was* still alive. No wonder Lucinda had found them such an easy target for manipulation. "Tell me how you ended up working with Lucinda and her people."

Anler rose from his chair, crossed to his desk, and pulled out a drawer. Lira tensed, but he was only reaching for a cigar. "They came to us not long before your mother died, and the villagers sent you to the orphanage in Dirinan. We rejected their offer of a full alliance—it was too dangerous to reveal much about ourselves with people we didn't know or trust—but they knew about the training program." He lit the cigar, took a long drag. "They were smart, *energised*, and they had information we needed. In return for that, we agreed to a loose partnership."

"What exactly did they want from you?" Lira tracked the man as he returned to his chair, settled in, crossed his legs.

"The magekillers. Our knowledge of Shivasa and access to our extensive network of informants." A cloud of smoke wafted her way as he let out a breath. She wondered if he was trying to annoy her, or test her to see how easily she could be riled. She gave him no discernible reaction.

"And what did you get?"

"An actual plan for achieving our vision. Additional resources to carry it out. The chance that Shakar's death wasn't in vain. They'd almost entirely taken Aranan before they were routed!" he huffed a breath, closed his eyes and gave a little shake of his head.

"That was all?"

He hesitated, then said, "We also saw the advantages of them being the face of our resurgent cause. A useful front in the event it all went wrong ... nothing would lead directly back to us."

"But they wanted more than just the Hunters. You told them about me, too, didn't you?"

"That was a matter of great debate between us." Anler let out a sigh. "Many argued that we should help Underground as much as we could ... that maybe if they grew in strength, we could fully join forces. It was that hope that led to the decision to tell Lucinda about you. But you vanished from the orphanage before they could get to you."

Lira rose from the chair to stand by the fire, unable to sit still any longer. Her blasted name. She'd always been currency to someone, either something to fear or something to use. She'd never been just her, Lira.

Well, she could use that too.

Once she'd gotten a hold of herself, she turned, leaned against the cool stone of the hearth, and crossed her arms. "Tell me about the wrist tattoos."

"We acquired the Hunter trainees as babies. The training began from the moment they could walk, and as you know, it wasn't just physical training." Lira nodded as if she *did* know. "The nurses taught them to read and write and think strategically, to problem solve. We tested them at three years old, then again at five. Those with aptitude—only a handful achieved the scores required—were selected to be trained not only as strategists, but leaders. We intended these would be the commanders of our future army. The tattoos marked them."

"I applaud the preparations you've made." She returned to the chair, used the movement to hide the sudden ache of thinking of Ahrin being marked in such a way. "I need more specifics about the training your Hunters received. The better I understand their capability, the more effectively I can use them."

He frowned. "I haven't agreed to let you use anything, Lira Astor, even if the Hunters *were* still under our control."

She relaxed back in her chair, not wanting to press too hard. "Fair enough, but this is a mutual decision, Lord Anler. Like I said, I need to understand how you can be of use to me. If we did have the army, what could they do?"

"Very well." He paused a moment, presumably to collect his thoughts. "The trainees were separated completely from their parents. Their carers were under strict instructions to provide no softness, no affection, no comfort. The children were taught weapons from when they could walk, and given strength and stamina training, all of it tailored to their age. By seven they could take down a fully grown soldier—those that couldn't were removed from the program."

"And killed, one assumes?" She smiled thinly.

"We were very careful not to leave any evidence, Lady Astor." He nodded, pleased with himself. "Besides the physical training, they were put through trials designed to increase their resilience, mental strength, and ability to withstand physical and mental hardship. At three they were placed in a dark pit for three straight days, and again when they were four. Those that emerged insensible or damaged were terminated. Punishment for infractions of the rules resulted in whipping or other physically painful punishments, including starvation."

As the words rolled out of Anler's mouth, brisk, clear, without a hint of remorse, Lira came within literal seconds of clicking her fingers and setting him alight. She wanted to watch him scream, and she wanted him to die slowly, just like Greyson had. Everything in her burned for it.

But she didn't. This kill was Ahrin's, and Lira wouldn't take it from her.

"Was this program designed by yourself and your collaborators, or did my grandfather develop it?"

"It was his genius." A little smile flickered over Anler's face. "We merely refined it."

"I'm impressed, Lord Anler." She swallowed down the bile that wanted to rise at saying those words, at the knowledge *her* blood had been responsible for doing that to Ahrin, and Shiasta and her Hunters. Sweat beaded on her forehead. "Tell me about the mental conditioning."

He hesitated.

"Assume I know much more than you think I do," she snapped.

He lifted both hands in the air in concession. "From the time they could understand speech, the children were indoctrinated to believe the Darkmage was the one they owed complete loyalty to. The food they were given, the rest they were allowed, all of it was attributed to him. They were told stories of his victories, the power he held. He visited the training programs occasionally, to reinforce his command via his telepathic ability."

A chill rippled down her spine. "And after he died?"

"We modified the program slightly. We built loyalty to the tattooed trainees into the warriors through mental conditioning techniques developed by a telepath mage working with us. They were compelled to obey any command given to them and trained to follow without question any heir of the Darkmage."

She narrowed her eyes. "How does that work, exactly? Can any person approach one of these tattooed Hunters, tell them they're Shakar's second cousin twice removed, and they're compelled to obey?"

Anler chuckled. "Nothing so blunt, I assure you. No, the brainwashing was more nuanced. There are a set of specific phrases they need to hear, known only to the handful of trainers involved. Hearing the phrase would trigger the loyalty conditioning."

Lira fought not to lean forward in her seat. "And those words are?"

"We planned for you, Lira. In your case, the phrase is, '*My grandfather is Shakar.*'"

She stilled in her chair, the effort required not to show her reaction so intense that she literally couldn't say or do a thing. Those words. She'd spoken them to Ahrin the first time she'd met her in that snowy alley in Dirinan. It was a meeting forever etched in her memory, every single detail of it as clear to her now as if it had happened only a moment ago.

Lira had triggered Ahrin's conditioning the moment they met. And everything since...

Her chest was so tight she couldn't breathe, horror and grief competing for ascendancy. "And the other phrases?" she managed, hearing herself distantly through the roaring in her ears.

"Only two more. 'I am the heir to Shakar' and 'I am Shakar's heir.'"

"Too broad." She was hard pressed not to snap again. "Anyone could accidentally say those words."

"I beg to differ." He lifted an incredulous eyebrow. "Who would admit to having anything to do with Shakar in Shivasa bar someone who is loyal to our cause? We limited not only the knowledge of what the phrases were, but the fact they even existed, to a handful of highly trusted trainers. Some of my comrades would even object to me telling you now."

Somehow, she managed a haughty expression, kept her voice cool. She had to end this conversation now, before she lost her composure entirely. "Are you ready, Lord Anler, to finish what my grandfather couldn't?"

He smiled a cold smile, one that made her want to slap him. "Prove to me you *can* achieve his goal, and I will discuss an alliance with interested parties."

"I've shown you enough already," she countered. "I want your allegiance, and a promise to gather your lords, before I leave here."

"It has been a long day." He rose from his chair, walked over to stub out his cigar. "And dinner is shortly to be served. We can pick this up later. I'll send Herin to fetch you when it's ready."

She hesitated ... but pushing too hard now could ruin her efforts. Not to mention her emotions were roiling. "Very well."

Not waiting for a response, she strode from the room.

# CHAPTER 14

She barely made it to the guest room Herin had shown her to earlier. The space was dim, the curtains open to admit silvery moonlight. Lira closed the door behind her and sank down against the wall. She buried her face in her palms and tried to get her breathing under control, but it was a useless endeavour.

Anler's words reverberated through her thoughts over and over in an endless cycle. The brainwashing. The trigger words.

Lucinda had been terribly, horribly right.

What had Lira unthinkingly done that night in the alley? Bound Ahrin to her for life, subjugated that fierce, independent soul in a way she would have hated, would have fought bitterly against. She'd given up everything for Lira, and *none* of it had been her choice.

Lira swayed sideways, curling up in a ball on the floor, breaking into helpless, wrenching sobs, nails cutting into her palms from fists clenched so tightly they drew blood.

Alyx Egalion was right. She was no heir to the Darkmage.

She was a mess.

She barely noticed when the door clicked open, when someone sank down beside her, a hand touching her arm. All her usual instincts were drowned in grief.

"Lira?" It was Tarion's soft voice. "Lira, what happened, what's wrong?"

She shook her head, unable to stop sobbing. A moment passed, and then his arm came around her, tugging softly. She allowed herself to be lifted, brought gently to rest against his side.

"Whatever it is, I'm so sorry," he murmured in her ear. "You don't have to talk, but I'm here."

She nodded, curled further into him. Tears streaked her face. Her body shook with the force of her emotions, and she couldn't stop it.

"We're a pair, you and I." He rocked her a little. "I'm glad we have each other."

She was too. Gladder than she'd ever been of anything in her life. It compelled her to speak, stumbling between sobbing breaths. "I think I've done something awful."

"I'm here to listen if you want to tell me."

So she did, the words stumbling out of her between gasping breaths. Once she was done, Tarion sat in thoughtful silence, not horrified or angry or anything she'd thought he'd be. Her sobs had faded too, as if speaking aloud had drained away some of the intensity of what she felt.

"I understand why you're so upset," he said eventually. "But I know Ahrin Vensis. I don't think she's your puppet, willingly or unwillingly."

"She has to be. I spoke the words."

He smiled, gave her a little shake. "Come on, Lira. You know Ahrin better than anyone in this world. Better than Lucinda. Better than Anler and his trainers. Do you truly believe this of her?"

"I don't want to ... but she was *conditioned*, Tarion. There's no way around that." Even so, his words made her think. Ahrin was so independent, so fierce, so strong. It didn't seem possible that she would unthinkingly obey any order, even Lira's.

"When you see Ahrin next, you can talk about it, figure it out together. I don't think it's as clear as Anler has made it sound."

He was right, of course. Ahrin was going to escape Rotherburn, Lira had no doubt about that, had even included it in her planning. She might already be on her way to Lira, and when they met again, they could talk to her about it, get the real truth. And until then, the Darkhand wouldn't want it to ruin Lira's focus, her careful planning.

Hope unfurled, fragile, in her chest, making her want to cry all over again. "I won't hurt your mother, Tarion. I promise. I'll do what I must, but I won't hurt her, no matter what. Not her or Caria or your father."

"I already know that." He smiled and sat back. "Do you—"

A knock came at the door, cutting him off. Lira stayed sitting by the wall while Tarion went to answer it. Herin's voice floated through. "Lord Anler invites you all to join him for dinner, sir."

"Thank you. We'll be down shortly." Tarion closed the door without another word. "Fari and Yanzi will no doubt be thrilled at a bit of fine dining, but we can make excuses for you, if you like?"

"Thanks, Tarion, but Anler is still wavering on joining me, so I'm going to have to make an appearance." She scrubbed at her face. "Just give me a few moments and I'll join you downstairs."

He left without another word, closing the door softly behind him.

Lira picked herself up off the floor and walked over to the window. The glass was icy under her palms as she pressed both hands against it, allowing her forehead to rest there too. The cold was pleasant against her heated skin.

She took one breath in, held it, let it go. Then, slowly but surely, she tucked away the heartache and the fear. They had no place with what she had to do, and they wouldn't help Ahrin either. What came next was going to be difficult beyond measure, and there was no room for anything but cold, hard purpose. Resolve.

She would see this through. For Ahrin. And for herself. Once the council was dealt with, then she could turn her attention to Lucinda and destroying that woman from the inside out so she couldn't touch Ahrin, or anyone else Lira loved, ever again.

And if she had to use Ahrin to do it? Or Shiasta and his warriors? The traitorous question drifted up from the emotions she'd just locked away. Lira took a breath, pushed out everything but her goal, and curled her hands into fists.

Yes, she would. If it was necessary.

Then it would all be done. She would worry about what came next if she was still alive when it was all over.

The dinner was a polite and dignified affair. Anler's chef served an elaborate four-course meal, and while the lord wasn't overly warm, he kept conversation flowing easily. His wife seemed to serve no more purpose than to be an ornament at his side, which set Lira's teeth on edge, but she smiled and followed his lead in essentially ignoring her.

She hated every single second of it.

Maintaining the aloof arrogance of the Darkmage was difficult when she felt so ill at ease. Anler had arranged it all deliberately, she'd bet, knowing she'd grown up in poverty and would be completely unfamiliar with all the trappings of wealth he was throwing at her. He wanted her on the back foot, vulnerable.

It was a stark reminder that even though Anler had done very little to push forward her grandfather's cause in the years since his death, he was still a dangerous man to reckon with. Only her stubborn refusal to let him see her wilt gave her the strength to hold the façade.

Tarion, Fari, Athira, and Yanzi ate as if they engaged in this type of dining regularly, which of course they had, while Shiasta just seemed perpetually confused that he was joining them at the table. He, like Lira, was clearly uncertain as to which utensil went with which meal. The questioning looks they sneaked each other quelled her unease substantially. When Fari picked up their uncertainty and started proclaiming her views on which item of cutlery she preferred over the other, involving a detailed account of what they were used for, Lira wanted to hug her and never let go.

Not a fool, Anler registered what she was doing, but merely gave Lira an acknowledging nod.

First point to Lira and her Shadowcouncil.

As they finished a serve of perfectly seared duck slices and creamed potatoes—Lira had never eaten food this fine and her stomach was beginning to register discomfort with its richness—Anler waited for the servant to clear his plate, then languidly reached for his wine. "I've been thinking on your request, Lira, and I find myself unconvinced."

Lira stilled. The lord said nothing more, clearly waiting for her to fill the space, but she took a steadying breath, ignoring the looks shooting her way from her companions. "What exactly is it that you are unconvinced by, Lord Anler?"

"I'm not a fool, Lira Astor. You're a street rat from Dirinan and you grew up in a criminal gang. You and that crime boss at my table know how to run a con as effectively as anyone in the country. The Dirsk healer is a family outcast who failed her Trials, and the entire world knows that Egalion's son is a pale shadow of his mother. Your words are pretty, and you all look the part, but I won't be manipulated again into serving someone else's agenda."

All eyes were on Lira. If she crumbled now, in front of her new Shadowcouncil, she would lose any credibility she had with them.

With great effort, she kept her expression aloof, allowing a little smile to curl at her mouth. "It's your hesitation that's all for show, Lord Anler. Unlike Lucinda, I actually *am* the Darkmage's heir. His cause is mine. Yours too."

"So you say. Yet in reality you're merely one person with the right name and a handful of well-dressed followers. That means precisely nothing when it comes to defeating the Shiven Leader and taking down the Mage Council." Anler let the silence hang for a moment, placing his wine glass down as slowly as he'd picked it up. "If you want my allegiance, you need to prove that you can actually carry out what you're claiming."

"And how exactly would you like me to prove that?" As much as Lira's attention hadn't wavered from Anler during this exchange, she was acutely aware of her companions listening to this, studying her. She couldn't show weakness here.

"Deliver us our Hunter army."

Agreeing to conditions put her in a weaker position, but all her street instincts warned her Anler wasn't backing away from this. Damn

Lucinda for making him so suspicious. Lira didn't break eye contact, simply widened her smile a little more and kept her tone matter of fact. "Consider it done."

Anler blinked. Was he surprised by how quickly she'd capitulated? Or had he hoped his challenge would be enough to send her away so that he wouldn't be forced into doing anything?

"I'll gather *my* army." Lira rose slowly from her chair. "And bring them to you as proof of my capability. You'll receive a message within the coming weeks with a meeting time. In return for me completing your task you will be ready, as will *all* your allied lords. And not only them; I want the rogue mages too."

"I don't—"

She lifted a hand. "Don't dissemble. I know you probably aren't in contact with all the mages, that Lucinda did some recruiting she might not have told you about, but don't pretend you don't have your own. Those as loyal to my grandfather's vision as you are. I need to see all of you face to face, receive your sworn oaths of allegiance. Only then can I trust you. In return, at that meeting, I will prove to you I am the measure of this task."

He regarded her warily. "We don't move an inch until you prove your worth. And even then, you ask us to risk a lot by gathering in one place."

"Just as I risk a lot by coming here and revealing my intentions to you. We're done for tonight, Lord Anler." She stalked over to the door, pausing there to look back over her shoulder. "Oh, and one more insult out of your mouth directed at any member of my Shadowcouncil, and I let them loose. Trust me when I say you wouldn't enjoy that."

She swept out of the room, going straight back to her quarters, not wanting to risk questions from the others. Before she spoke to them, she had to figure out how she was going to find a lost army of Hunters.

# CHAPTER 15

After a night of restless dreams—and having come up with only one half-baked idea as to how she would meet Anler's demand—Lira rose and dressed early. Laun, one of the three Hunters that had accompanied them, stood guard across from her door. Tall and rangy like all of them, he had blonde curls and dark green eyes that held no emotion. Even so, she'd noticed him feeding a carrot to his horse before they'd left the inn at Kharan the previous morning. While his expression hadn't changed, the hand he'd lifted to briefly stroke the mare's nose had been full of affection.

"Lady Astor, good morning." He bowed his head in greeting.

"I'm just going out to the stables to get some fresh air and see Alfie before breakfast," she said. "You should take the chance to freshen up and eat yourself. It's going to be a long day on the road."

He frowned slightly. "I'd prefer to see you stayed safe." It was the closest he'd come to pushing back on her orders.

"Do you have reason to think I won't be on these grounds?" she asked sincerely.

"There are no active threats that we have identified, Lady Astor," he replied in crisp, clear tones. "The four Hunters Lord Anler has stationed here now consider your protection above his. The estate is secure. Therob and I did a full perimeter sweep overnight while Pestra stood guard here."

"In that case, I'll be fine, Laun. Do as I say. Tell Therob. Pestra, and Shiasta the same, please."

He bowed smoothly and strode away.

It was a frosty morning—the cusp of winter in Shivasa was synonymous with full winter—with pristine snow carpeting the ground and the air so still it felt as if it had been frozen in place. The doors of the barn next to the house were open, and a sharp whinny drifted out. Lira turned and trekked through the snow, following the prints already leading that way.

Surprise flickered through her at the sight of Anler inside, where he was grooming a tall bay stallion. The horse stood relaxed and content, eyelids drooping, one hind leg cocked.

"He's beautiful," she said politely.

"The prize of my stable." Anler smiled. "Your stallion is of fine quality too ... although not as strong-willed as I prefer in a mount. It's a shame the weather isn't suitable for a hunt, or you and your friends could have joined me on one before leaving."

Lira smiled as if she, too, were disappointed to miss out on such a thing, even though she'd rather have her fingernails ripped out than spend more time with this man. She felt equally reluctant to converse with him any more than necessary, particularly on a personal topic, but she had come here for answers, after all. So she stayed, leaning against an empty stall door, trying to look and sound casual. "Can I ask you something?"

"You may." He lifted the curry brush. "Is it all right if I keep working, though? He gets cranky if I stop halfway through."

She waved a hand in approval. "I assume you always knew Shakar had a daughter, a granddaughter?"

"Yes." Anler resumed slow, steady brushstrokes along the bay's side. "But your mother had no magic and was therefore useless to us. We hoped you would be different."

"My mother died when I was very young. I don't remember much of her." She paused, making sure that none of her eagerness bled into her voice. "Can you tell me what you know about her life?"

Anler's gaze turned distant, his movements slowing further. "I was still a relatively young man when Alyx Egalion killed your grandfather, not yet forty. My late father was one of his inner circle—Shakar visited here frequently during his time as lord-mage of Rionn. I knew your mother, though she was a good ten years younger than I."

"From what I've read of the Darkmage, he was broken-hearted over the death of his Taliath lover decades earlier." She stepped carefully, not wanting to offend Anler by pointing out that her grandfather's 'grand vision' had merely been a result of grief turned twisted. "How did he come to have a daughter?"

Anler shrugged. "I believe your grandmother was a lover he took in Alistriem; some minor nobleman's daughter besotted with the prestige of bedding a lord-mage. When she fell pregnant, it seems the idea of a child intrigued him, though he cared little for the mother. He revealed his identity to her, and she willingly joined the cause. A decision that saved her life, no doubt."

"So my mother fought for him?"

"She was no warrior." Anler finished and moved around to the bay's other side. "She lived well protected within his strongest base, and once the war ended, she stayed in the north of Shivasa until she went to Karonan. That's when we lost track of her. She went to significant efforts to remain hidden from us."

"Do you know who my father is?" she asked bluntly.

"No." He gave her a sidelong look. "We knew as soon as she returned to the north, of course, and that she'd fallen pregnant. As far as we understood, she told nobody of your father's identity."

"Were you the ones that killed her?"

He laughed, a cold sound. "I have no idea how she got herself killed. We were interested in your potential, and it suited our purposes for her to be alive, taking care of you."

Lira nodded, pushed off the door. "Thank you for your time."

"Breakfast will be served shortly. I'll be along soon." He gestured towards the other stalls. "My grooms have orders to have your horses saddled and ready for departure this morning."

"Thank you, Lord Anler. You've been a gracious host." She paused. "I hope you and your network will be prepared for my word. I don't like it when my expectations aren't met."

His eyes flashed, the strongest emotion she'd seen from him yet. "Neither do I. You could be our greatest opportunity yet, Lira Astor. I truly hope you can turn our vision into a reality. Deliver me our army, and we will speak seriously of alliance with you."

There was threat and hope both in his voice. She merely lifted an eyebrow, nodded.

And then she turned and walked away.


Lira almost collided with Athira coming out of the barn. "Checking up on me?" she asked dryly.

Athira didn't deny it. "You can understand why I'm suspicious."

"I can." Lira nodded back towards the barn. "I had some questions for him about my mother, my grandfather. I thought knowing more might help us succeed."

"Did he have the answers you were after?"

"Not the ones I really wanted."

Athira was silent a moment. "Are you sure Anler can help you achieve what you need?"

"I'd prefer it if he had a larger army and a network that reached more broadly than Shivasa, but I certainly won't be able to do Lucinda's bidding *without* him and his people." Lira shrugged, then slowed to a stop before the steps leading up into the house. Here was another opportunity to get some answers she needed. "While it's just the two of us, there's something else I need to know. What did Lucinda do with Tylender?"

"I don't—"

"Save it. Ahrin and I found the letter the Magor-lier wrote her on Shadowfall Island. I know they were allied—is that still the case after she left to go back to Rotherburn? Because if he is, that's going to make my job a lot easier."

"If you'd let me get more than two words out." Athira huffed. "I was going to say that I don't know the exact circumstances of what happened to Tylender as it wasn't my place to know. But I can tell you that the Magor-lier will be an ally."

Lira's eyebrows rose as Athira explained why that was the case. Rotted carcasses ... it explained a lot. And only deepened Lira's combined fear and awe of Lucinda's ruthless and strategic brain.

"You're right, that will be useful." She let out a breath, pushed a little harder. "Did Lucinda tell you that Tylender imprisoned me after she and Greyson set me up?"

"Yes. And she explained why it had been necessary." There wasn't a hint of emotion in Athira's face or voice.

"So you knew why I never came back for you?"

Athira stiffened slightly. "That doesn't matter anymore."

"When I left you on Shadowfall Island all those years ago, you sacrificed the opportunity to escape so that you could stay and spy for the council, to help me bring Underground down," Lira said carefully. "What changed?"

There was a beat of silence while Athira considered the question, gaze slightly narrowed. "What do you care?" she asked, eventually. "We're on the same side, at least for now. That's what matters, isn't it?"

"You know very well that I don't trust those whose motives I don't understand," Lira said smoothly. "The Athira I remember was a snooty, pureblood mage brat. Your grandfather is a mage councillor. What could have made you want to follow Lucinda, of all people?" Lira lifted a hand. "And don't tell me you feel some deep and undying desire to save the people of Rotherburn, because I won't believe that for a second."

The woman twitched. It was the faintest of movements, so small Lira wondered if she'd imagined it. "My reasons are my own, and they're none of your business," Athira said flatly.

With that, she turned and stalked up the stairs into the house, affront in every line of her body. Lira watched her go, thoughtful. That brief twitch had been strikingly familiar. She began to wonder if...

Tarion appeared at the doorway a moment later, breaking her from her thoughts. His hand rested on the hilt of *Darksong* as he came down the steps to join her, gaze scanning their surrounds. "Everything all right?"

"Don't tell me you're worried that Athira tried to kill me out here?" she joked.

"A smile. This is good." His shoulders relaxed. "And you've got your thinking face on. It was a useful chat, then?"

"Possibly." Lira looked up at him, shaking off her thoughts. She'd let her idea simmer away in the back of her mind for a while, look for further signs to confirm or refute it. It wasn't like Athira was leaving her side soon. "Come on, let's avail ourselves of Anler's rich larder. It's going to be a long day on the road."

"Are you planning on telling us what your next step is?" he asked as they climbed the steps. "Specifically, how you're going to meet Anler's demand. Was it a good idea to agree to that?"

She sighed. "Anler needs to be convinced that I'm the real deal before they'll give me their allegiance and go to war on my behalf. It makes sense after Lucinda betrayed them so thoroughly. I should have expected it, and was foolish not to," she admitted.

"He could be bluffing," Tarion pointed out. "He really has no other real hope of achieving what he wants without you."

"No, I get the sense these men are cowards at heart. They won't move unless the odds are overwhelmingly in their favour. That's going to make it much harder for us, but I'm confident they won't follow me unless I prove I can shift the odds their way." She nudged him in the ribs. "In addition to Shiasta's unit, there are another three hundred trained Hunters out there, according to Anler. That's some serious heft."

His eyes widened. "Do you have any idea where to start?"

She cocked her head. Gave a little shrug. "I have an idea that might send us in the right direction."

"And if you're wrong?"

"Then we come up with another way to find them."

"Bloody-minded persistence." He nudged her back. "That sounds like the Lira Astor I know and love."

# CHAPTER 16

"I'm sorry, you want to *what* now?" Fari asked, arms crossed.

They were gathered in Lira's small room at the inn in Kharan, having travelled directly back there after leaving Anler's estate earlier in the day. A wild wind whipped around the inn walls, and Lira was inordinately glad she was indoors and out of the weather.

"We need to find where the Hunters dispersed after Lucinda and Greyson sacrificed Underground," Lira said patiently.

"I understand that part. The part I'm not quite on board with is where we stroll into the Mage Council prison in Carhall, break out an Underground prisoner, and hope they know where the Hunters went."

"Fari is right," Tarion said. "Maybe if you hadn't killed Greyson..." He gave her a pointed look. "He was the only one we can be confident knew anything about Lucinda's plans. The risk of breaking another prisoner out is foolish given the unlikelihood they'll have the information we need."

Lira sighed inwardly. Tarion was right on both counts—Greyson could have been much more useful to them alive. Her desperate need for vengeance had led her to making a foolish mistake in killing him.

"Shiasta, are you sure you can't help?" Athira asked for the third time.

"He's said he doesn't know where they are," Lira snapped.

Yanzi weighed in then. "Is there anyone else who *would* know. Someone more accessible for us to kidnap and question?"

"What about Finn A'ndreas?" Fari asked. "He makes it his business to know everything, doesn't he?"

Tarion shook his head. "Don't forget the council had no idea the Hunters even existed until Shiasta broke Athira out of prison a few weeks ago."

Lira rubbed her forehead, trying not to betray her anxiety. She had to come up with *something* or her new Shadowcouncil were going to begin to lose faith in her. Dithering and inaction were the enemy. She needed Anler and his network *and* the Hunter army if she was going to successfully carry out her con, but she would also need ... Lira's gaze narrowed in thought. There was a place that might have useful information, even if it didn't lead to the Hunters.

If nothing else, it was something to *do*.

"You've got an idea, Lady Astor?" Shiasta seemed to notice the change in her expression.

"If we don't have a solid lead, we need to start somewhere we know Lucinda used regularly and considered safe," Lira said decisively. "DarkSkull Hall."

"You want to ride all the way to Tregaya on nothing but a guess?" Fari was already shaking her head.

"We can't sit around and do nothing. If I take too long to deliver Anler's Hunter army, we increase the period of time the council has to find and destroy us. DarkSkull is somewhere to start. I agree the chances of finding the Hunters there aren't high, but Underground might have left records behind that will help us—maybe they had other unknown bases."

Tarion looked at Fari. "I don't have a better idea."

Fari let out a breath and threw her hands up in the air. "Me either."

Yanzi shrugged. "If it suits you, Lira, I'll go back to Dirinan and work with Lorin to plan a bit of breaking and entering of the council offices there. If DarkSkull doesn't pan out, maybe we can find something there that will help—after all, if the council has worked out from Shiasta's attack that Hunters are back in the world, they'll be searching pretty hard for them. Our last resort could be waiting for the council to find them for us."

"Good idea," Lira said, relieved to have another avenue of hope. "Take one of the Hunters with you for protection, Pestra, and we'll keep Therob and Laun with us."

Yanzi rose from his chair and stretched. "If Lorin and I do find something, where can we get a message to you?"

"You'll have to wait until we return to Dirinan. If we find a lead at DarkSkull, we'll keep following it, but if it's a bust, we'll come straight back to reconvene."

"A lot of time could be wasted," Fari warned as she stood too.

"Do you have a better way of spending it?" Lira asked.

Silence greeted her words, and Fari managed a smile and a shrug. "This is why you're in charge."

A week later, driving snow whipped around them as they sat huddled on their horses, staring down into the valley holding the ruins of DarkSkull Hall. The old mage school looked lonely and abandoned in the stark winter landscape. They'd circled around to approach from the northern valley wall, not wanting to take the obvious road in or trek through the western valley wall where Underground had left a pit of bodies.

None of them wanted to go near that dark place again.

"Tarion almost died last time we were here," Fari said cheerfully.

Lira hid her wince. She knew how unlikely it was they would find the Hunters here, or anything useful, and that knowledge weighed on her with every day that had passed on their journey to DarkSkull.

She just didn't know what else to do. Her con was still in its infancy, yet she needed to be *ready* to strike the moment Ahrin freed herself and came to Lira—the final piece of the play. The plan felt increasingly impossible with every moment that passed that she hadn't actually achieved anything.

Tarion seemed to read her internal doubt. He shot her a little smile. "I promise not to almost die this time."

"Can we please move before I freeze into an icicle?" Athira demanded.

Lira urged Alfie back into a walk, allowing him to carefully pick his way through the trees down the rocky slope. They tethered the horses inside the treeline where they were out of sight and hiked across the snow-covered ground towards the remaining buildings of DarkSkull Hall. It looked just as abandoned up close as it had from a distance. A few birds circled above, but nothing else moved.

Disappointment lay heavy in Lira's stomach. If a large group of Hunters were here, they'd have walked into a void of magic by now. "They're not here, are they Shiasta?"

Shiasta glanced at Laun and Therob, who both shook their heads, then turned back to her. "I don't believe so, Lady Astor."

Lira didn't miss Athira's tightening expression, the weariness in Fari's. Only Tarion and the Hunters seemed undaunted. She did her best to force confident optimism into her voice. "Let's split up and search the grounds—we can cover more ground faster that way. Hopefully we finish the search during daylight hours, sleep here tonight, then leave tomorrow."

"And go where?" Athira asked pointedly.

"There will be something here that helps us figure out where to go next," Tarion said, matching Lira's confidence. "Lira, how about you and I take the main hall? Fari and Athira, you split up to search the dormitories—make sure you focus on the rooms that the Underground members were living in. Shiasta, you, Laun and Therob remain outside to watch our back."

They were good orders, so Lira let them lie. Nobody else complained either, and they split up to begin the search.

"I'll take the corridors where they were doing the experiments on us, you focus on the kitchen and storage area they were using?" Tarion asked as they climbed an exterior flight of stairs and pushed open the door at the top.

"Sounds good."

Innate caution had Lira entering the storage space via the narrow back stairs from what had once been the head cook's office. The sacks of supplies were still there, and a thin layer of dust covered the ground.

The trapdoor to the underground cells lay open, only darkness beckoning.

Lira lit a small flame and kept it hovering in the air by her shoulder. The moment she jumped down into the space, the scent of stale and rotting straw hit her nostrils, but nothing else loomed out of the dark. She increased the size of the flame until the entire corridor of cells was revealed.

All the cell doors stood open. Each cell was empty.

Lira walked all the way to the end, made sure it was solid earth and not a secret entrance somewhere else, then swore under her breath.

There was nothing here.

Her steps grew heavier as she climbed out, did a careful search of the storage area, then did the same in the kitchens. Nothing of value in there either.

She hoped Tarion, Athira, or Fari were having better luck.

They re-convened inside the main hall as the sun grew low on the horizon, already making the day seem dim. Lira couldn't help the snatches of memory that kept flooding her mind—*razak filling the place, Lorin on the ground with his injured leg, the others fighting around him...*

"There are remnants of the experiments, but no notes or records or anything like that," Tarion's voice flickered in and out of her attention.

"Same in the dormitories," Fari added.

*Lira and Garan, facing down a horde of razak while Tarion tried to get Fari and Lorin to safety...*

She snapped out of her thoughts as Athira's voiced sounded, angry and annoyed.

"So nobody found anything? No Hunters and no information that can help lead us to where they are? That's just fantastic. All this way for nothing." Athira shot her a filthy look. "You better not be carrying out some elaborate plan of stalling me, Lira Astor."

Lira blinked, a step slow in countering that attack, but Fari spoke into the pause.

"You're the one who's Lucinda's little puppet." The healer lifted an eyebrow in Athira's direction. "Are we supposed to believe Lucinda didn't tell *you* where she stashed her army?"

"Like I said, *repeatedly,* she didn't tell me," Athira said simply. "Because she didn't know."

"Wait, *what?*" Lira stared at Athira. "You didn't say that before."

Athira looked confused. "You asked me if Lucinda told me where they were. She did not."

Lira waved an impatient hand. "But you didn't say it was because Lucinda didn't know. What do you mean she doesn't know where they went?"

"Exactly that. If she'd known she would have told me. Her expectation that I help you in any way I can was made very clear."

Lira lifted a hand to rub at her eyes. Had she really been such a colossal idiot ...

"What are you thinking?" Tarion asked her.

"The night I fled Shadowfall Island, Shiasta was given an order to take his unit and assassinate Ahrin. She countermanded that order, instructing them to help her escape. But at the time, several other Hunter units were present on the island. If Lucinda truly doesn't know where they are ... maybe she didn't bother to give them any orders before she fled back to Rotherburn."

"That seems unusually careless for someone like Lucinda," Fari pointed out.

"Agreed, but if you think about it, what orders could she have given them? She was leaving with no immediate plans to return."

Tarion turned suddenly. "Shiasta, if you had been a member of one of the other units on Shadowfall that night, and Lucinda and her people departed without giving you any orders, what would you have done?"

"Stayed where I was," he said simply. "And waited for further orders."

Tarion shot a glance at Lira before turning back to Shiasta. "What about those who weren't on the island on that night?"

He didn't have to think about that either. "I would have completed whatever task I had been set, and then returned to the island to await further tasking."

Lira let out a long groan. Had all the Hunters been on Shadowfall Island, undetected, all this time? She'd been an utter fool not to press Athira or Shiasta harder before now. That mistake might have cost her precious time she wouldn't get back.

Fari's sigh echoed her groan. "I guess we're going to Shadowfall Island next?"

Before she could reply, Tarion froze, spinning around to stare through the main doors as if he could see something beyond them. Shiasta drew his sword and took a step closer to Lira.

"What is it?" Fari asked.

"Someone is here."

Lira followed as Tarion broke into a run down the hall towards the interior doors, weaving through the rubble. He quickly outpaced her, slipping through them, and then crossing the open foyer to where the outer doors stood only slightly ajar.

He peered through the gap and stiffened. Coming up behind him, she peered through too. It took her a moment to find what he'd seen, but when she did, she swore loudly.

Visible through gaps in the trees lining the southern valley wall was a group of riders making their way down the main road towards DarkSkull. Several blue-cloaked figures and a handful of Taliath.

"It's an ambush. Rotted bloody carcasses."

Tarion nodded. "We need to go, now."

He and Lira backed away from the door, then turned, only to come to a complete stop.

Garan Egalion stood between them and the interior doors.

He held his staff loosely in his hands, expression focused, blue mage cloak draped easily over his broad shoulders. "Hello Tar, Lira."

"Clever of the council, to look for me here," Lira said, heart sinking.

"Garan, let us go," Tarion said calmly. "We can be gone before your companions arrive. Lira and I don't want to fight them, or you."

"Really?" Garan's gaze swung to her.

"Truly," she said. "I don't want to hurt anyone if I can avoid it. I promise you."

His gaze slid over her shoulder, back to her. Then to his cousin. The hand wrapped around his staff clenched and unclenched.

Realisation crept over her. "Why did you come ahead of the rest of the ambush party, Garan?" she asked quietly. "You did it in case I *was* here. You wanted to be able to warn me."

Tarion shifted at her side but said nothing. He hadn't moved to draw *Darksong* either.

Garan's jaw tightened, but his hesitation was clear. "You're a traitor to the council, Lira, but you don't need to be. Come with me now. I'll make sure they treat you fairly."

"You can't make sure of that, and you know it," she said sadly. "And you know just as well that I won't leave Ahrin to die. You knew all of that and you still came here to warn me, didn't you?"

Garan's gaze shifted to Tarion then, his voice almost pleading. "Why are you with her, Tar? I don't understand."

It was on the tip of Lira's tongue to tell him everything, explain her con, make him understand why things weren't as they seemed. She wanted to so badly she could taste it—anything to take that look of betrayal out of her friend's eyes.

But she couldn't. Garan's mental shielding was appalling, and the council couldn't be trusted with the knowledge any more than Lucinda could.

"We need to go, Garan," Tarion said, quiet and calm. "Will you stand aside?"

Garan's gaze flicked over their shoulders again, then he took a deep breath. "I'll give you a head start only. I won't stop them coming after you."

"Thank you," Tarion breathed, stepping right up to his cousin and reaching out to squeeze his arm. "I'll see you soon."

Lira caught Garan's gaze, held it, and gave him a little nod. "Friends, Garan."

Then they both ran past him and back into the hall. When Lira glanced back, Garan was gone.

Laun and Therob were running through the hall from the opposite direction as Tarion and Lira returned. Lira's quick glance to Tarion said all it needed to—Athira was not to know about Garan's presence. He gave her a tiny nod.

"Mage Council attack party, sir," Therob reported to Shiasta. "Approaching from the south, both mages and Taliath."

"Probably reaching the valley floor about now," Tarion confirmed.

"Smart of Egalion to guess that we might go to one of Underground's known bases and come looking for us here," Athira remarked.

Fari shot her a glance. "Which means they'll probably go to Shadowfall Island next, if they haven't already."

Lira swore loudly and fluently.

"The council doesn't know about Lucinda using Shadowfall," Tarion said with a frown. "You said you never told them?"

"I didn't." Lira swore again. "But we have to assume Greyson said something when he was busy telling the council everything in order to frame me."

Which meant if the Hunters *were* there ... they had to get to them before the council did.

But first they had to escape this ambush of mages and Taliath.

"We should try and make it back to the horses before they spot us," Shiasta said. "My advice is that we avoid a fight if at all possible—their numbers are superior. The bulk of the buildings might hide us from view for a short time."

"Agree." Lira nodded. "Tarion, you teleport Athira and Fari straight to the horses. That way, at least the two of them get out if the rest of us are caught."

"I should take you first," he pointed out.

"I'm not leaving the Hunters, and you can't transport them because of their medals."

He clearly caught the thread of steel in her voice because he didn't argue any further, instead stepping towards and leading her far enough away from the Hunters that he could access his magic. They vanished from sight a second later.

Athira remained to wait for Tarion. The rest started running.

Lira and the others had only just reached the exit at the far end of the hall when Tarion reappeared and took hold of Athira. Lira did her best to keep up with the long strides of her Hunters as they burst out of the building and set off across the darkening valley floor at a sprint.

The footprints of their entry earlier were horribly visible in the carpet of white snow, even in the dimming light, and Lira kept throwing glances over her shoulder. At any moment the council searchers could round the buildings and spot them.

It happened just as Tarion flashed back into sight ahead of them and started running their way. Shouts ricocheted through the air, cries of triumph, and then the echoes of galloping hooves.

Lira glanced ahead of them ... it was too far. The council would be on them before they reached the treeline. Tarion saw the same thing she did. "I'll get the horses," he said, then vanished from sight.

The pounding of hooves grew closer and closer. Close enough that Lira could make out their faces—Garan wasn't among them. Laun dropped back behind Lira, even though he could run much faster, and Shiasta and Therob slowed their pace too, hovering protectively at each side of her. Ahead, the trees were a line of darkness.

Where were those damned horses?

A bow twanged in the stillness, and behind Lira, Laun gave a grunt. She turned as he stumbled, dropped to his knees. He was back on his feet a second later though—the arrow protruding from his shoulder, bright blood dripping to the snow.

A snarl tore from Lira, unbidden, and she scanned their pursuers. The three riders in the lead were Taliath, one armed with the bow. Another arrow ploughed into the snow beside Lira's foot as she slowed to help Laun. In a heartbeat, Shiasta and Therob had placed themselves between her and the oncoming Taliath.

"Get back!" she bellowed at them. "Keep running."

"Your protection is our priority. If we keep going, that archer will pick us off one by one now that he's in range," Shiasta said calmly. "We'll protect you until Lord Tarion brings the horses."

Lira's gaze fell on the blood running down Laun's arm, and her mouth curled. "Shiasta, do as I order!"

He wavered, then stilled. "We must keep you safe."

"I can't use all of my magic to defend us while you're so close to me!" But she had no further time to argue. The mages behind the Taliath were in range now, but far enough from the Hunter medallions. An ice spear launched at them, one after the other, so fast they were a blur.

Rotted carcasses. Nordan was with them—the combat master from Temari.

Lira summoned her magic, used flame to melt the first two spears, but it took too long, what she really needed was telekinesis too ... the third was arrowing in too fast and she didn't have time to pivot, to...

Laun stepped in front of her, taking the ice spear in the chest.

She stared, time slowing as he fell, already dead, his blood soaking into the white snow. Shiasta and Therob were already moving to fill the gap in front of her, swords raised as more arrows flew, more ice spears.

Lira screamed.

She summoned her magic, let it fill her, then with a shout wrapped her fire magic around the Taliath archer and set him alight.

The shock of seeing her magic work on a Taliath was enough to halt the rest as they reined in, uncertain about whether to keep coming. The man's screams echoed over the snow as he burned alive. Even so, her magic tugged at her, mixing with her anger and grief, wanting to be let loose. She wanted to burn them all, see them turn to ash—

"Lira!" Tarion's shout echoed over the snow.

She turned, snarling—he was almost there, leading Alfie and the Hunters' horses. The sight of Tarion checked her. Garan was with the force of mages. She couldn't kill them all—she'd ruin any chance of her con succeeding if she did. She took a handful of deep, gulping breaths, bringing her emotions under control.

Then, Lira stilled, focused her mind, and summoned every drop of magic she could gather. A roar escaped with her magic as she erected a great wall of white-edged flame between them and the mages.

"Laun?" she asked, gasping with effort.

"I'm sorry, Lady Astor." Shiasta rose from the Hunter's prone body.

"Lira, we have to go!" Tarion reined his mount in with a whirl of snow, tossing her Alfie's reins.

Lira stared at Laun for a moment longer, tears blurring her vision. She wiped them away and turned. Despite the chaos around them, Alfie stood quietly as she scrambled into the saddle, turned his head, and asked him to run.

She left the wall of flame roaring until they'd reached the valley summit.

# CHAPTER 17

The grey afternoon matched Lira's mood perfectly. A thick cloud of mist hung low over Shadowfall Island as they approached its southern coastline, shrouding the hills in the centre of the landmass and hiding from view anyone that might be watching their approach.

Almost three years had passed since Lira had left here, since Lucinda had abandoned Underground and returned home to Rotherburn. So long. Could they still be here? And if they were, had the council already beaten Lira here? They'd spotted no other ships on their approach to the island, but in this weather, that meant little.

Lira swallowed down another surge of guilt as she rhythmically lifted her oar in and out of the water, savouring the burn in her muscles. One of her Hunters had died because she'd made a bad decision—worse, she'd been reckless wandering into DarkSkull without considering the council might be there. Not to mention she'd had to kill a Taliath. Garan wouldn't forgive her that; he was no doubt already blaming himself for the man's death.

One mistake, and she'd made everything infinitely harder for herself.

If she didn't find what she sought here, she wasn't sure what to do next. There was no other obvious way to establish her legitimacy to Anler's people, short of staging a successful attack on the council—something more impressive than what Underground had managed, but she couldn't do that without his resources ... or the Hunter army.

Too much longer without progress and all the threads she was trying to keep hold of would slip through her fingers. Too much longer without progress and the Mage Council and all its formidable resources would catch up to her, risking more deaths of those she loved.

Part of her feared it was already too late.

Sending Fari back to Dirinan with Therob for protection, Lira, Tarion, Athira, and Shiasta had ridden directly south from DarkSkull in a race against time to reach Shadowfall before the council did. They'd gone direct to Port Rantarin, and after an afternoon spent walking and studying the docks, Lira had found what she needed.

Relief had thundered through her at recognising Ropin—another ship captain that worked with Yanzi's crew. Maybe her luck was changing. A legitimate merchant by day, Ropin also ran illegal goods when the profit was high enough. He'd agreed to take them south to Shadowfall Island for an exorbitant sum of gold coin.

She would have preferred to use Rilvitha's ship, knowing Ahrin trusted her. But Rilvitha would be making the third and final of her promised fortnightly runs past Rotherburn. If Ahrin had managed to escape … she would have a ride home. If not … Lira planned to make it worth the woman's time to keep making those runs. Ahrin would make one of them.

Ropin had lifted anchor in Port Rantarin ahead of the tide on Lira's request, and a day and a half's journey had brought them to Shadowfall Island, Ropin anchoring out at sea while the four of them went ashore in one of the ship's boats. The mist had closed in quickly around them; within a few minutes, they were rocking alone on the ocean's surface.

Shiasta handled the boat deftly despite the rough water, and Lira couldn't help her frequent glances at his wrist, where his tattoo was visible each time the cuff of his shirt rode up. Misery rose up to choke her each time. She couldn't get the sight of Laun diving in front of that ice spear out of her mind.

"You can't change what happened," Tarion said from where he sat beside her, rowing with the other oar, catching the direction of her glance. "What you're doing now is what's important."

"What I'm doing now is still using them, Tarion. Laun died for no good reason."

He was quiet a moment. It hadn't sat easily with him, the events at DarkSkull, particularly her killing the Taliath so brutally. He was still with her though, and she hoped beyond hope he would stick with her until she could reveal everything to him. "Even so. The way you treat Shiasta, how you speak to him, it's different to how Anler or Lucinda would. Or even Ahrin. You treat him as your equal, as a person who is just as valuable as you or me."

"That's because he is."

Athira scoffed from where she sat at the opposite end of the boat, the only one not working. "I never thought I'd hear you speak with such sentimentality, Spider."

Lira gave her a cool look. "It's not sentimental to respect the things that belong to you." She looked back at Tarion, lowering her voice to ensure Athira couldn't hear them this time. "You haven't changed in your sleep since we left DarkSkull."

Travelling with only Shiasta meant they'd been able to access their magic again, a relief for both Lira and Athira—though it meant a constant checking and focus on their telepathic shields—but clearly a double-edged blade for Tarion.

He'd slept close to Lira each night since—so that she could help if he changed, but also to prevent Athira seeing it—yet it hadn't happened once. Not wanting to add to the anxiety he felt about it, she hadn't raised it with him, but she hadn't missed the slight lightening of his shoulders every morning he'd woken after sleeping through the night.

He nodded. "Ever since Rotherburn, I've been practicing deliberately bringing about the change. The first time, I almost lost control again, but I remembered what you said about focusing on the thing that brings you hope, and I clawed it back. It's gotten incrementally easier ever since."

"And because you *are* using it, and learning control, it no longer needs to force its way out while you're unconscious," she said approvingly.

"I hate how it makes me feel, Lira. But you're right. I can't change it. So I'll learn to live with it."

"Good," she said.

He gave her a searching glance. "You're worried about something."

She dipped an oar in, felt the burn of her arm muscles. "If the Hunters *are* here ... all those medallions so close together. It wouldn't take Egalion and Dawn long to find them. That's how your mother found the Hunter base during the war, you know? She used her telepathy to track the void of magic a large group of them creates."

He frowned. "We'll have to do something about the medallions, then. Tricky, because it's their greatest advantage over mages, but it makes them easier to find. Not to mention it means our mages can't fight effectively alongside them."

Athira huffed an annoyed breath behind them. "Let's actually *find* our army first. Then we can figure out what to do about the medallions."


It wasn't much longer before they scraped ashore on the sandy beach. Tarion had teleported ahead to wait for them and clear the area of any potential danger. He cut a graceful picture on the sand as the mist cleared around him, *Darksong* drawn and held ready, head up and alert.

Lira, Athira, and Shiasta jumped into the shallows to drag the boat farther above the waterline. The mist was damp, cold, and the air was still, expectant. Lira let her shoulders relax, closed her eyes, sank into the night and the air. Nothing tripped her instincts. Her eyes blinked open.

Maybe the council weren't here yet.

Lira turned to Shiasta. "What do you think?"

His gaze took on a distant look. "I think they're here."

"If they are, they'll see us coming, right?"

"Yes. They'll have a watch set up to identify anyone approaching this area of the island."

"All right. You'd better lead the way then, in case they've got guards lying in wait, or decide to send an ambush party."

He set off with a long, swinging stride, an eagerness in his bearing that she was sure was unconscious. She couldn't imagine what it must be like … to have been ripped away from any affection or care from infancy, to be brainwashed to lead a particular life, yet to still experience feelings they wouldn't have a name for because nobody had ever taught them what they were.

She promised herself she would fix it. Somehow.

As soon as this was done.


They headed inland along a narrow track. The mist was so thick they could barely see more than a few steps into the trees on either side. Last time Lira had come this way, the day had been sunlit and breezy. Those thoughts inevitably led her to think of Ahrin, her Darkhand, the one who'd brought her to this island the only other time she'd been here.

She tried to breathe through the resulting ache in her chest, telling herself that Ahrin would be okay. Rationally, she knew that was true. But it didn't stop the worry and fear. It didn't negate the simple fact that Lira missed her like a constant, gnawing longing. She refused to even contemplate what would happen if Ahrin was unable to escape.

"Keep doing what you're doing and she'll be fine." Athira spoke suddenly, as if reading Lira's thoughts. "You already know Lucinda wouldn't kill a hostage if her leverage is working."

"And my father?" Tarion asked her, a note of challenge in his voice.

Athira shrugged. "Lucinda was clear on what would happen to him if your mother didn't carry out her wishes. I doubt he's still alive."

"You knew him, you *grew up* knowing him, and yet you can talk so casually of his death," Tarion said softly. There was no hiding the pain in his voice.

"Like Lira, I care very little for the mage councillors or their spouses," Athira said. "They left the both of us to rot, remember?"

"She's got a point," Lira said, playing her part, even though she hurt for Tarion, understood the fear he felt for his father. It was the same fear she felt for Ahrin.

At that thought, she blinked, startling herself. There had been a time when Lira had pretended not to feel that kind of empathy. Had ignored it, buried it, *hated* it. She'd treated it as a weakness. Now she freely admitted feeling it.

"*Lira, you are not him.*" Fari's words echoed through her memory, stark and clear.

The uncharacteristically dangerous note in Tarion's voice drew her sharply from her thoughts. "Lucinda knows that once Lira succeeds, if my father is dead, I'm going to come for her, right?" Something of the monster inside him burned in his gaze.

Athira huffed a laugh. "Lucinda is no fool. *You* are, though, if you think you can take her down."

"We'll see."

Lira shared a brief look with Tarion when Athira turned aside. They'd see, indeed. Lucinda still didn't know that her experiment of injecting Taron with nerik blood had worked ... that he had an ability to turn into a violent, deadly killer. The woman's paralysis magic would still work on him, but on Lira *and* Tarion at the same time? Lira wondered.

Silence fell then, and they walked on, the terrain growing ever steeper.

Then, abruptly, Lira felt a sharp dissonance wash over her. At her side, Tarion swayed, letting out a groan, and even Athira stumbled.

"Lady Astor, are you okay?" Shiasta asked.

She waved him off, trying to steady her breathing and fight off the instinctive panic of losing touch with her magic. After a moment, she summoned her violet-edged white flame. It appeared instantly, wreathing her hands and forearms. When she tried to access her telekinesis, however, it was gone.

Relief tumbled through her chest, so strong she swayed with the force of it, letting out a long breath that felt like it had been pent up for days. "Your fellow Hunters are here, Shiasta."

He straightened. "You have lost access to your magic?"

"All bar my new abilities, yes. Athira, Tarion?"

"I can't teleport," Tarion said after a moment's concentration. "You're right, Lira. A strong telepath knowing a general vicinity of where to look wouldn't have too much trouble finding the Hunters in a group. It hides *us*, but not them."

"Come on, let's keep going." Urgency flickered through Lira now. "If the council isn't here already, they will be soon."

They emerged from the forest onto a grassy clifftop above the ocean. Looming on the hillside to their left was the old Taliath training academy. To their right were the cliffs leading down to the jetty Lucinda and her Shadowcouncil had used to come and go from the island. A brisk breeze had sprung up, clearing the mist from the open plateau, revealing a grey, gloomy afternoon.

"Wow," Tarion murmured quietly, eyes drinking it all in. His left hand had fallen to the hilt of *Darksong*.

"If they're here, they'll have seen us, Lady Astor," Shiasta said. "I recommend we wait here in the open, weapons sheathed, where they can get a good look at us. Once they ascertain we're not an immediate threat, they'll come out to investigate our purpose."

It didn't take long. Within minutes, two tall figures emerged from the forested hillside and loped towards them. Lira almost started—she would never have known they were there, so close. Close enough to have taken them all out with an arrow if they'd been carrying bows.

Shiasta straightened his shoulders at the sight of them, and the moment they got close enough to recognise him, the Hunters' wary demeanour faded. They stopped and saluted sharply.

Lira and Tarion shared a look. More relief shivered through her.

"Antun, Renia." There was no trace of emotion in Shiasta's voice, merely the briskness of a commander seeking a report from his troops. "Are you well?"

"We are." The female warrior, Renia, spoke. "It is good to see you."

"How many are here?" Shiasta asked.

"All twelve units apart from yours, commander." A faint pause from Antun, then something unnameable cracked in his voice before it steadied. "The night your unit left … Lucinda and her mages did too. Within a month all other units had returned. We have not had any word since, so we've remained here, careful to keep ourselves hidden."

"What about supplies?" Shiasta asked.

"The Shadowcouncil kept a significant number of stores here, sir. We fished and foraged under cover of darkness to bolster our food stocks."

"You did well," Shiasta assured them, then gestured to Lira. "Lady Astor has come for us."

Relief loosened the shoulders of both warriors in a way that made Lira's heart flip. She smiled at them. "I'm sorry it took so long, but I'm here now. I won't leave you again."

Both bowed fluidly, Antun speaking, "We are yours to command."

"Our Darkhand lives too," Shiasta reassured them.

Lira nodded. "I'd like to speak with all of you. I can explain why I'm here and what I have planned."

Renia looked confused. "Explain?"

"Yes," she said briskly. "You are my soldiers. I want you to know what you're fighting for."

Renia and Antun shared a glance that was full of puzzlement. "Very well, Lady Astor, we do as you wish." Renia stepped aside. "Allow me to escort you in? Antun will go ahead and gather all of us together. It won't take long."

"Please be as fast as you can. We might not have long before my enemies come looking for us here."

As they walked, Lira turned to Shiasta, wanting to confirm what Anler had told her. "A warrior with a tattoo like yours commands each unit?"

"Yes," Shiasta said.

"Can I ask..." She hesitated, reading his features as best she could to make sure she wasn't causing pain. "You all accepted Ahrin as your overall commander, even though you and twelve others have the same tattoo as her. Why is that?"

"Commander Vensis possessed something we do not," he said simply.

"What is that?"

He froze, shoulders turning rigid. "I cannot—"

"It's all right, Shiasta." She touched his arm. "I'll figure it out on my own."

Lira slowed her pace a little to come alongside Tarion. "Any thoughts as to what it could be that made them accept Ahrin?"

"A deadly glare?" Tarion suggested with a little smile.

She elbowed him in the ribs. "You're hilarious."

He sobered. "Actually, given what Shiasta just said, I do have an idea."

"What is it?"

"Ahrin escaped, Lira. That's what she has that the rest do not. At eight years old, she had the strength to break through her conditioning and free herself."

Lira stared at him. Then tears pricked at her eyes.

She was going to fix this. She'd never been more determined about anything.

Three hundred elite warriors made for a packed training academy, though they'd been careful to leave no external signs of their presence. The exterior was exactly how Lira remembered it—weathered, falling down in places, an air of abandonment hanging over it.

Once inside, evidence of so many residents was more obvious, but—trained soldiers as they were—everything was neat and clean.

Renia escorted Lira, Tarion, and Athira to what had once been a large indoor training hall.

Lira sucked in a breath. They stood in perfectly neat rows of twelve warriors apiece, each unit commander standing two steps to the left of their unit's row. All three hundred moved into perfectly synchronised attention at Lira's appearance. The hall was utterly silent, rows and rows of unblinking gazes trained directly on Lira. Their stillness was uncanny. A shiver ran through her.

This deadly force of killers was hers to command.

It was an empowering thought. The familiar thrill rose through her chest, hot and seductive.

With this army, she could do whatever she wanted.

For the first time, she began to believe that she might be able to pull this off. She let the thrill race through her, giving her strength and confidence, taking away all the doubts that had been festering.

Athira immediately moved off to the side, while Tarion remained at her left shoulder, and Shiasta at her right. She wasn't thrilled with how short she looked in comparison to both men but was glad of their steadying presence nonetheless.

"You've all done an excellent job of remaining hidden," she said, projecting strength into her voice so that it carried through the large space. "Thank you for waiting for me, and I apologise for taking so long. I've come here because I need my army. Just like my grandfather planned, I'm going to bring down the Mage Council and restore his vision for the world, only *I* am going to succeed where he failed."

She paused, but there was no response from the warriors standing before her, only unwavering focus.

"They built you to help me achieve that goal, and now it is time for you to stand with me," she said, hating every word, knowing they had no choice *but* to follow her. "I'm here to take you away from Shadowfall Island for good."

Again, almost simultaneously, every warrior effected a crisp salute.

Lira Astor had her army.

# CHAPTER 18

As relieved as Lira was to have found her Hunters, to have taken the first concrete step forward, she didn't fail to notice Tarion's increasing agitation throughout the afternoon and evening.

She'd ordered Shiasta to organise the Hunters to systematically gather and pack any records or papers Lucinda and her mages left behind. If they could get that done by the end of the day, it allowed for them all to get a few hours' sleep before filing down to the jetty in the pre-dawn to begin ferrying out to Ropin's ship. If all went well, they'd be on board and Ropin could lift anchor with the dawn tide.

This plan didn't seem to calm Tarion though.

"What is it? You've been antsy for hours," she asked as they sat alone with Athira at a table in the mess area. The remains of their meal sat before them. The sound of cutlery and chairs scraping filled the cavern, but there was very little conversation. She remembered how odd she'd found these Hunters her first time on Shadowfall Island. Now their lack of chatter and laughter just made her heart ache.

"Not sure." His foot tapped repeatedly against the ground. "I'm uneasy."

"About what, exactly?" she inquired.

"Don't know."

She narrowed her gaze at him, her own instincts stirring to life. "Isn't that a Taliath thing, being able to sense approaching danger?"

"I'm not a Taliath."

She gave him a look. "We're not going to have this argument again, are we? Do I need to point out that back at DarkSkull you knew the council searchers had arrived before the Hunters even saw them?"

He didn't reply, but his foot kept jiggling. Up and down. Up and down. It was starting to make *her* antsy.

"Okay, you need to stop that," Athira snapped.

"Shiasta?" Lira called out.

The warrior was by her side an instant later. "Lady Astor?"

"Send more warriors out. I want enough lookouts that we'll see if anything approaches *any* part of the island's coastline." They'd been doing it throughout the afternoon already, with no sign of anything approaching the south of the island, but Lira suddenly wanted to be extra certain.

"I can't guarantee we'll have visibility of anything approaching in the dark, not until it's really close; night fell a half hour ago, and there's thick cloud cover in the sky."

"Understood. Do it anyway."

He saluted and slipped away. Within minutes several Hunters were rising and leaving the room, purpose written in their expressions. It must feel good, finally having something to do after years of waiting. Almost three years ... and now she was going to risk their lives before they'd even had a chance to know what it meant to live one.

It was necessary. And Lira could do what was necessary in a way Alyx Egalion couldn't. She didn't have that same compassion. Another little piece of knowledge about herself that she tucked away.

Athira cast Tarion a sidelong look. "Maybe you're so antsy because you can't access your magic. That's enough to make anyone uneasy. I've been itching all afternoon."

"It's not that," Lira said, gaze lingering on Tarion's jumping leg before returning to his face. His gaze was distant, like he'd not even heard Athira's words.

Athira glanced between them, then nodded slowly. "Far be it from me to go against your instincts, Lira Astor. But maybe it's just what we're expecting—that the council is on its way."

Shiasta returned a few moments later, a little frown on his face. Alea, one of the other unit commanders, followed behind. "Lady Astor. The orders you gave us ... is something wrong?" he asked.

Lira glanced at Tarion again, then made a quick decision. "Maybe, have the Hunters begin preparing for departure. Leave whatever records they haven't managed to pack up yet."

He saluted, then turned to Alea. "Pass the order to the other unit commanders. Tell each Hunter to prepare a pack of supplies enough to last three days. Light enough we can cover ground quickly if necessary." Once Alea nodded acknowledgement, Shiasta turned back to Lira. "I'll assist with that, unless you have other orders for me?"

"No, that's all for now, Shiasta."

He left, and Tarion fell silent at Lira's side, his leg still jiggling. Suddenly not hungry, she rose from the table and headed into the tunnels, making for the one she'd taken with Ahrin that night many years ago to spy on Lucinda from the clifftops.

A howling wind whistled off the ocean, sending her short hair whipping around her face and filling her senses with the salty scent of the ocean. To her right stretched the narrow ledge leading towards the cliff path. Darkness enclosed her like a welcome blanket. Her uneasiness eased. It didn't take long before Tarion joined her.

"Tarion, you're uneasy for a reason." She turned abruptly. "I've changed my mind. We're leaving, tonight. Can you signal Ropin?"

Tarion opened his mouth to respond, but boots rasping on rock sounded, heralding Athira's arrival. She cut them a suspicious glance before saying, "Leaving tonight is all well and good, but there are three hundred Hunters here. Where are you going to stash them after we leave? You haven't let us in on that part of the plan."

Because she hadn't made it properly yet. She'd simply been desperate to find them before the council did. She shoved hair out of her eyes as another gust of wind whipped around them and looked hopefully at Tarion. "Thoughts?"

"We'll have Ropin put them ashore in individual units at separate locations and instruct them to store their medallions at a safe location—preferably ones we've mapped out beforehand—before continuing to a rendezvous location. That way, if they're found, we don't lose all of them in one hit."

"Once they dump their medallions a telepath will be able to read their thoughts. They're not trained to shield," Athira pointed out.

"It is far easier for a telepath to locate a large void of magic blocking their access to peoples' thoughts," Tarion countered, "than search the thoughts of hundreds of thousands of unfamiliar minds to find a stray thought that identifies someone as a Hunter."

"He's right." Lira began pacing. "They'll be fine as long as they're not captured, and they're too good to be captured. We'll sail south, then east around the tip of Rionn, and start dropping them along the east coast up into Tregaya. By the time we sail back to Dirinan, they should be across the border into Shivasa. We just need somewhere to send them that they won't be too obvious."

"What about Shakar's old Hunter base?" Athira suggested. "Nobody uses it anymore."

A little thrill went through Lira at the idea. It was perfect in its symbolism. "Are you sure it's not being used?"

"Like DarkSkull Hall, the council preferred to just forget it ever existed after the war. Not to mention, it's in such an isolated location that it's not useful for anything. As long as we're careful and don't venture out too far, nobody will know they're there."

"It will be in some disrepair by now, but it shouldn't take too much to make it liveable," Tarion agreed. "Yanzi and the crew can funnel supplies up there discreetly so that we don't have to go near any of the villages in the region and risk tipping them off as to our presence."

"Done." Lira let out a breath. Her shoulders were tightening, her well-honed street instincts ringing more shrilly. "We'll figure out locations for hiding the medallions once we're back on the ship. We need to go."

Athira crossed her arms. "Even *if* the council is coming, I think we can take them. Every single one of these Hunters is wearing a medallion."

"I don't want to face them before we're ready, and I certainly don't want them getting a good idea of our strength," Lira said. "Even if they know about the existence of the Hunters, they don't know how many there are, *or* that I've found them all. We have to maintain every advantage we have. It's the only way we'll win."

"Lira's right." Tarion chimed in. "Once they know Lira has an army of Hunters, they'll be much better prepared to face us."

They'd barely got halfway back to the mess cavern when Shiasta came striding towards them, Renia a step behind him. "Lady Astor, Renia just reported back. Three large ships are approaching the island from the north."

Lira swore. "Tarion, go signal Ropin now. Shiasta, we're exiting via the cliff jetty tonight. Soon as it can be done."

"That's going to take time to—"

"Then we'd best get started," she cut him off. "Renia, you're going to take me out to where you saw the ships. Athira, you're with me. Tarion, you help Shiasta oversee the retreat. Any questions?"

"What are you planning to do?" Tarion lifted an eyebrow.

She shrugged. "If those ships are carrying a Mage Council attack party, I'll make sure to win you enough time to get everyone clear of the island."

Understanding dawned in Tarion's eyes. "Your water ability."

She saw the hesitation flit over his face, the concern, knew exactly what he was thinking. Possibly three ships full of mages and Taliath who might not all know how to swim. Wooden ships that could light up like kindling if Lira chose to make it so.

"I'll do what is necessary, Tarion. It is imperative we get the Hunters off the island. We can't do what I need to without them."

He clearly didn't like it. But he turned to Shiasta and said, "Are they still gathered in the mess?"

"Yes, sir."

"Let's go. I'll signal Ropin from the jetty, you start ferrying the Hunters down."

Dismissing Tarion, Lira turned to Renia. "How quickly can you get us out there?"

# CHAPTER 19

The mist from earlier in the day had cleared away by the time they emerged from the old Taliath academy. The night was cloudy, though, the air cold and damp. Lira and Athira moved at a swift jog, single file through the forest, following their Hunter guide.

It took them just over an hour to reach where Renia had spotted the ships, but Lira savoured the burning in her muscles, the quick rasp of her breathing. The physical exertion pushed away the constant simmer of anxiety she felt about the precarity of her plans. Not to mention that once they were a good distance from the Hunters, *all* of her magic returned, filling her with strength and confidence.

Eventually, they reached the summit of a tall, grassy hill looking down over the beach of the north-eastern coast of Shadowfall Island. A break in the cloud cover allowed faint moonlight to shine over the dark ocean and silvery sand laid out before them. Lira leaned on her knees, trying to catch her breath, her sweat-soaked skin cooling quickly as the breeze whipped around her.

"Where are they?" Athira asked impatiently.

Renia pointed, but it took several moments before Athira and Lira could make out the shadowy forms of three ships rocking at anchor—it was hard to tell accurately in the dim light, but it looked like they were roughly a mile out. Lira glanced at the Hunter. "Were they anchored when you left?"

"No, they were still on approach." Renia paused, studying the vessels. "Lady Astor, now that I can see them better, I believe they are Rionnan naval ships."

A shiver ran through her. "Are you sure?"

"We've been trained to identify such things." Renia nodded. "If their intention is to make landfall, they'll need to come ashore via the ship boats. We've monitored the trading ships that deliver supplies to the fishing villages along the coast—they usually anchor about the same distance out and send boats in. The water becomes too shallow closer to shore."

Lira thought about that for a moment. There didn't appear to be any sign of movement from the ships that she could see, but it was hard to tell how long they'd been anchored. A heavy cloudbank was moving in from the northwest, which would reduce visibility even further. "Renia, if they are intent on making landfall tonight, how long do you think it will take them to lower the boats and row in?"

"Not long, Lady Astor. Maybe an hour or a little more if the tide or wind is against them. Rionnan naval ships have troop-landing capabilities—they're constructed to carry multiple fast-moving ship boats on board."

Rotted carcasses. Smuggling ships like Ropin's were the opposite—space usually reserved for ship boats was instead taken up by discreet hiding places in the event the authorities searched them. Ropin only had two.

Lira stared until her vision went spotty. "There's no sign of lantern light on the decks, so if they're coming now, they're loading up in the dark. How long do you both think it will take to get all the Hunters out to Ropin's ship?"

"Three hours unless bad weather sets in. That cloud front isn't heavy enough to be a storm, but reduced visibility and stronger winds will make things harder." Renia hesitated, then, at Lira's encouraging nod, continued. "If we assume the navy is anchoring to the north of the island to avoid notice of any watchers at the Taliath base, then their intention is a surprise attack. In which case, they'll be coming quietly across the island, over terrain unfamiliar to them. That will slow them down. A good commander would plan a pre-dawn strike, hoping to catch us at our lowest level of alertness."

"They'll be on us before all the Hunters are out," Athira said.

"Lady Astor, look." Renia straightened suddenly.

Lira stared where the Hunter pointed, marvelling at her sharp vision. Something was moving along the side of the easternmost ship.

Athira hissed. "They're lowering the boats."

"We're going to slow them down, try to win as much time as we can for the Hunters to board Ropin's ship." Lira looked at Renia. "Go back, let Tarion and Shiasta know your assessment, that we're going to delay them as long as we can, but they need to hurry."

The Hunter hesitated. "What about you? I do not like to leave you unprotected, Lady Astor."

"Once I've done what I can, we'll be right behind you." Lira hardened her voice into a command. "Go, Renia."

Renia bowed her head and left, turning and vanishing into the darkness.

"You know the way back?" Athira asked idly.

Lira shrugged. "Pretty sure."

"Count me reassured."

Lira looked out at the three ships sitting out on the darkened sea, imagined those decks live with mage warriors and Taliath loading onto ship's boats. A flick of her fingers and she could set all three ships alight. But she couldn't kill them all—she didn't *want* to.

She needed the council to remain strong if her ultimate plans were to succeed.

If she wanted to change the world.

That meant her only option was to deflect and run. "I'm going to need your help with this one."

Athira lifted an eyebrow. "My help to do what, burn them?"

"My range with flame doesn't extend that far," Lira lied, then held out her left arm. "But I have another idea."

The young woman glanced out at the ocean, then back at Lira, seeming to wrestle with something. After a moment, she must have resolved whatever it was, because she reached out and closed her fingers around the bare skin of Lira's wrist.

The shock was immediate.

Lira's sense of the ocean around the island increased tenfold, the sheer volume of water flooding her senses in an overwhelming cascade until she was utterly lost in it.

Rotted carcasses ...

"Not so much. I can't...," she gritted out, her shoulders tensing as she fought to regain her focus and control over her magic. The intensity lessened slightly. When she had control again, chest heaving, she swore aloud and turned to Athira with wide eyes. "What did Lucinda do to you?"

"Made me better. Are you going to stop those ships or what?"

Lira grinned. Control regained, she *dived* into the water. With Athira's amplifying ability, she felt invincible, as if her magical strength was limitless. It seemed like nothing at all to extend her control of the water as far as the three ships anchored a mile away. From there, she spread it even farther, searching, sensing, until ... there! She'd found the first of the ship's boats on the water.

"A little more, please," she requested.

Athira was more careful this time, feeding Lira a slow increase rather than an abrupt burst. With it, Lira increased her focus. Then, she gathered and shaped the water around the first boat, rocking it, increasing the unsteadiness of the water's surface until she felt the boat tip over.

Sweat beaded Lira's forehead. Her breathing came faster, shorter, but she immediately spread her water sense out again until she'd located the next boat.

Magic thrilled through her blood, hot and heady and intoxicating. She lived for this.

Three boats capsized and still Lira didn't feel anywhere near the end of her strength, even though her head ached from the focus required to identify and concentrate on the water around each boat at such a distance.

By now they must know a mage was working against them, but there was little they could do at such a distance to counteract her without their own water mage.

"Mental shield!" Athira rapped out suddenly. "I can feel a telepath trying to get in."

How? But Lira didn't waste time with the question. Instantly, she re-routed her focus to her mental shields, making sure they were airtight. Once confident of that, she opened her eyes, scanning the skies. It was darker now, the ominous mass of the cloud bank drifting from the north having shifted across the moon. "Can you keep a close watch above? If the telepath is Egalion … we're right out in the open and neither of us is escaping a mage of the higher order if she pins us down here."

Athira shot her a startled look. "What makes you think it's her?"

"Nothing. Just … I want to be careful."

"All right. Will do."

"You doing okay strength wise?" Lira checked. "None of this will serve any purpose if you end up stricken with magic overuse and can't make it back to the other side of the island."

"I'm fine. Worry about yourself."

Lira accepted that and dived back into the sheer glee of wielding her water magic. Her senses rode with the waves, exploring, searching for more boats. A short time later, after overturning another five boats and enjoying every single moment of such a glorious use of power, Athira yanked on her arm and called her name sharply.

Lira opened her eyes, chest heaving, sweat running freely down her back. "What is it?"

"I think I saw something move into the sky above the middle ship—there was a brief break in the clouds and the light improved for a moment. It might be nothing, but you said—"

"Rotted carcasses. Run for the trees, now!"

Athira let go of her wrist and Lira swayed on her feet, the sudden exhaustion of so much magic use swamping her. She gritted her teeth and forced her body into a run. If Egalion caught them out here in the open ... well, Lira didn't have anywhere to flee here like she had in Dirinan.

She sprinted down the slope after Athira and dived into the safety of the trees. Once well inside, they pressed against a trunk under a thick canopy of leaves and stared up at what they could see of the sky. Despite her weariness, Lira reinforced her mental shield over and over.

"Maybe I imagined it?" Athira murmured.

"Maybe, but it's safer to assume she's with the force," Lira said. "They're after me, and Egalion wouldn't have trusted an assault force to grab me up without her leading it, not after what happened at DarkSkull."

Lira scanned the skies again. Nothing was visible, but the clouds were drifting ever closer to the island. "I think we got enough boats to stop them making landfall."

"If Egalion is with them, it would be safer to burn the ships. She can ferry her mages ashore if we leave now."

"I told you, they're out of my range." Lira shook her head. "Your amplification helped my strength just now, but not my range." She lied again, smooth and easy, a skill long since mastered.

Athira's gaze narrowed. "Are you sure you're not just looking for excuses not to kill mages and Taliath?"

"I've never needed excuses not to kill," Lira said coldly, sticking to the truth. "Evidenced by me burning that Taliath alive at DarkSkull."

"Fine." Athira stepped away from the tree. "You up to running?"

Lira didn't bother to reply. She merely set off at a run through the trees, following the path Renia had brought them along earlier.

Urgency and fear thrummed through her. If Egalion was here, a clean escape was going to be nigh-on impossible.

She'd promised Tarion she wouldn't hurt his mother, and she probably couldn't, even if she wanted to. But what would Tarion do if faced with her—would he remain by Lira's side?

The thought of losing him, his steady presence and support, was a gut blow.

*One step at a time.* Ahrin's oft-repeated words echoed through Lira's mind, the memory of her voice, the look on her face when she'd say them, having an instantly calming effect.

For now—she needed to get back to her Hunters. Her protective instincts over them surged.

Whatever else happened, she would make sure they were safe.

# CHAPTER 20

They arrived back at the old training academy to find Tarion down on the jetty, just off to the side of a long line of warriors snaking down the cliffside path and waiting to depart. One of Ropin's ship boats rowed towards them, ready to pick up another group, though the sea was growing rough, and it looked like they were making slow progress.

"We've got seven units out, five more to go." He spoke as soon as Lira appeared, her legs burning from the long climb down the steps set into the cliff. "You?"

"We prevented them making landfall on the north shore by taking out their ship boats, but we're far from clear. I think your mother is with them—and, if that's the case, she could be watching our exodus from above as we speak."

Tarion's eyes immediately went to the sky, concern and sadness both flicking over his face. "I don't think there's anything we can do about that, apart from keep moving as quickly as possible. If she attacks while one of the boats is out on the ocean—"

"Their medallions will protect them from her magic if she attacks from above. Not to mention if she gets too close, her magic will be cut off too, same as ours is right now."

Despite her words, he caught the underlying current of concern in them. "But if she *is* here, she'll attempt to use her telepathy to figure out who all these people are. If she hasn't already, she's quickly going to learn they're all impervious to magic."

"And she'll know she's found your Hunters," Athira said.

"True." Lira considered that. "But she'll also realise that she can't outright attack the ship. So her best course of action would be to fly back to the navy and bring them around to intercept Ropin before we can get clear." She glanced at Tarion. "I'll warn Ropin. Can you teleport Athira and me out to him?"

He shook his head. "Too many Hunters nearby."

Lira swore. "Right, of course. I'll take the next boat out there." She shifted from foot to foot, then glanced at Tarion. "Pull that hood on your cloak up, slouch your shoulders a bit, and keep *Darksong* hidden. The last thing we need is your mother recognising you and deciding to swoop down and 'rescue' you from my evil clutches."

Tarion frowned suddenly. "Athira, *how* did you even know a telepath was with the ships?"

"I can feel it in my head when a telepath reaches for my thoughts."

It was dark, visibility limited, but Lira thought she saw a stiffening of the woman's shoulders. She tried pushing a little to see what would happen. "What does it feel like?"

She paused. "Like ... claws raking over my brain."

"I imagine you must have tested that with the telepath the Seven has back in Rotherburn," Tarion said casually.

"Yes, I—" She stopped abruptly, eyes turning distant.

Lira lifted a hand, cutting off Tarion as his mouth opened to ask another question. "That's interesting, Athira. Let us know if you feel it again."

A soft call from one of the Hunters as Ropin's boat bumped against the jetty ended any further conversation. Lira was the first to clamber aboard, Athira and as many Hunters as could safely fit joining them.

Within minutes they were setting off. Lira watched Athira the whole time, considering. Maybe Lucinda hadn't won Athira's loyalty after all. Maybe something very different had happened.

Something to test later, when they were free of Egalion and her damned persistent search for them.

Ropin stood in the middle of his foredeck as Lira and Athira climbed up ahead of the Hunters that had travelled on their boat. He was oddly clean-cut for a captain that ran a ship engaged in activities that weren't always legal. His brown hair was cut short and neat, jaw clean-shaven, and he wore well-tailored clothing that made him look more like a wealthy merchant's son than a smuggler. Even his hands were without callouses. He was a far cry from Rilvitha's intimidating presence, but from what she'd seen on the journey here, he ran an efficient and tight-knit crew.

The man's eyebrows lifted slightly at Lira's appearance, but that was the only surprise he showed. "Have you finally come to explain our sudden departure?"

"There are three Rionnan navy vessels anchored off the north coast carrying a Mage Council strike force," Lira told him, quickly running through what she and Tarion had surmised.

Ropin's jaw tensed, gaze shooting to the sky. "You mean we're waiting here like sitting ducks while three naval vessels are likely sailing in this direction right now? Why hasn't Egalion attacked me if she knows you're here?"

"You've got enough Hunters on board that your ship is impervious to magic, which means she can't attack you with anything but her mage staff."

Ropin was quick. "So she'll monitor us while her navy moves to intercept?"

"Most likely, yes. How long do you think it will take them to get here from the north side of the island?"

Ropin cocked his head, considering. She liked how calm he was, despite her news. "The wind isn't strong, but it's against them. Rionn makes their boats light and agile. Maybe an hour, two at most."

"That might be just enough time," Lira said. "Have your crew ready to depart the moment the last Hunter group is on board."

Ropin crossed his arms. "My ship is fast, but not agile enough to outmanoeuvre three navy ships with mages aboard if they get too close. I can outrun them on open ocean, but not escape a cordon."

Lira glanced at Athira. "There are warrior mages with weather ability who could manipulate wind to make those naval vessels even faster. Even so, once our anchor is up, I can make us faster than any other ship in the world with my water ability."

Ropin's gaze narrowed. "How is it you can you use *your* magic?"

Lira grinned. "My flame and water abilities can break through the Hunter medallions and Taliath immunity."

"You forget I'm no member of your cause, Lira." Ropin's arms stayed firmly crossed. "I'm not risking my ship and crew for you."

"We'll make it worth your while ... and we'll cover the costs of any damage taken, not that there will be any." Lira paused. "You know Yanzi is good for it."

After a long beat, Ropin uncrossed his arms. "We'll wait for a little longer, but I'm raising anchor the second the Rionnan navy appears, whether or not all your people are on board."

It was the best she was going to get, short of forcibly taking over the ship, and that was the last thing she could afford to do. Hunters were skilled warriors but had no idea how to crew a ship. "Fair enough."

As time ticked by, the two boats ferrying Hunters moving faster thanks to Lira's magic—though she was careful not to expend too much—she anxiously scanned the skies for Egalion's presence. It was a useless endeavour. Either the woman wasn't up there, or she remained hidden behind the cloud cover.

Tarion scrambled aboard with one of the Hunter groups, gaze searching until he spotted Lira. "Just one more boatload waiting on the jetty," he reported. "As soon as they row out, we're good to go."

Relief shimmered through her, and she relayed the agreement she'd come to with Ropin. "We probably don't have much more time."

"Even if we get clear of the Rionnan navy, my mother will follow us. She can fly for days if needed," he pointed out. "And she can communicate with anyone ashore, as well as any pursuing ships, as long as there is another telepath within range."

"Right, so we need to figure out how to lose her, or how to get me and all these Hunters off this ship before it docks and we're met with a Mage Council boarding party." She looked at him expectantly.

"Range...," he murmured to himself, brow furrowed. Then, suddenly, he brightened. "She can't fly forever, and she can't fly so far that it would be impossible to make it back to land."

Lira nodded, following his train of thought. "We sail south, as far south as we need to go until she's forced to give up and turn back. Then we head northeast, using my magic to make us faster, up towards the eastern Rionnan coast like we said."

"Because she'll expect us to return to Shivasa," he agreed. "And by the time she reaches land, rests long enough for her magical energy to return, and gets back to where she last saw us, we'll be long gone."

"Meanwhile, we start dropping off small groups of Hunters along the eastern Rionnan and Tregayan coastline with instructions for them to make their way to Shivasa, like we'd already planned. We'll round Zandia in the north, then disembark last at Tarnor in Tregaya." Lira glanced towards the wheelhouse. "It's going to be a longer trip than Ropin signed up for. No doubt it's going to cost a lot to recompense him for missed trades."

He lifted an eyebrow. "Isn't that what we have your wealthy criminal network for?"

A single shout echoed through the night. It was Ropin's watchman up in the crow's nest, sounding the alarm.

"Astor, we're raising anchor!" Ropin called out a second later, unflappable. "I'm not lingering any longer. If I do, we'll be caught."

"Last boat's nearly here!" Tarion shouted, after striding quickly over to the railing.

The captain ignored him, snapping out a quick series of orders. Movement erupted across deck, the crew well-practised in responding to potential attack. The anchor creaked as it rolled up from the ocean floor and the boat rocked, sails going up rapidly. Ropin was already at the wheel, ready to begin tacking the moment the anchor was clear and the sails unfurled.

Lira ran to the railing to join Tarion, grabbing his arm and murmuring in his ear. "Distract Athira while we get clear. I can't have her asking me to burn the navy ships or wonder why I'm not when we'll probably be plenty close enough."

He didn't quibble. Instead, he peeled away, moving gracefully over the roiling deck and calling for Athira to help him settle the Hunters below.

Using more energy than she'd like, Lira's magic surged around the final boat, carrying it the final distance until it rocked alongside the hull. The Hunters immediately began scrambling up the side. Shiasta joined Lira at the railing, and they leaned down to help each one swing up and over, making room for the next, and so on. They ushered each arrival away from the railing, sending them belowdecks to join the others with instructions to brace themselves for some rough sailing.

There were still four Hunters to go when the anchor clanged onto the deck and Ropin spun the wheel. The ship turned into the wind, the two Hunters already on the rope ladder swinging wildly along the hull. Their elite agility allowed them to hang on, however, and it wasn't long before they were clambering onto the deck.

The final two had to leap the increasing distance from the boat as the ship faced south and began moving, sails filling. Lira's heart stayed in her throat until they, too, were safely aboard, a brief burst of magic sinking into the water around the boat to keep it close enough for them to make the jump.

Once all the Hunters were belowdecks, Lira went to join Ropin in the wheelhouse, staying back and out of his way. Immediately, she could see what had caused the warning from the crew watchman. The three

Rionnan ships were approaching from the west, angling to cut off Ropin before he could get clear and out into open ocean.

"It would be best if I conserve my magical energy as much as possible," Lira said. "Do you need it to get clear?"

Ropin shook his head. "Not yet."

A palpable silence fell over the wheelhouse. Around them, part of the crew worked calmly and efficiently while those that weren't needed stayed out of the way. All eyes were on the steadily approaching navy.

Lira's eyes narrowed as she studied the closing gap. She was no expert, but it looked to her like Ropin might just squeeze by them.

"Flaming arrows!" the watchman called down.

Ropin swore and spun the wheel to port, sending the ship on more of an easterly heading, trying to maintain distance between them and their pursuers. The crew that wasn't already working leaped into movement, moving pre-prepared buckets of water onto strategic points along the deck.

Lira's fists curled and uncurled at her sides. If the navy caught them … she would be forced to use fire. It was critical that she escape Egalion and her strike force—there were still too many things for her to do before she could reveal her true intent—but if she destroyed such a force? There was no coming back from killing so many mages and Taliath. "Can the Hunters help?"

"No." Ropin shot her a sideways glance. "Can you put out fire as well as make it?"

"Never tried, but I'll see what I can do if we get hit and you can't control the flames."

Soon, even Lira could see the pinpoints of orange light on the decks across the water, and they made a lovely sight as the arrows fired into the night sky. She watched their trajectory, arching higher and higher into the darkness, before reaching the zenith and arrowing back towards the earth.

They were going to fall short.

Relief shivered through her as they plunged into the ocean mere metres away from starboard, flames dousing in the cold water.

"The telekinetics will try next," she warned Ropin. "They can make the arrows go farther, and I judge they're still far enough away to be clear of the Hunter bubble."

He gave her a quick glance. "Maybe that's the answer. We turn towards them, get in close enough for the Hunter bubble to shut down those mages, but don't let them get close enough to board."

A smile flickered on Lira's face. "I like the way you think, Captain."

He called a quick series of orders, spun the wheel back west. They ploughed into a trough, seawater crashing over the prow. The gap between the ships grew closer and closer. Another wave of arrows flew at them. Many landed, causing spot fires to break out along the deck. The crew broke cover to toss buckets of water to drown the flames.

"Brace for one more wave!" Ropin called out, firm and clear.

Arrows hissed, thumped into the deck, bringing more flame.

Lira could almost make out the faces of the crew on the approaching ships now, but Ropin was tacking north, passing them and breaking free before they could hit.

In moments, he had a straight shot south into the open ocean.

Lira focused, sank into the ocean surrounding their ship, gathered as much of it as she could, and brought it up in a careful wave over the deck railing. It sloshed along the deck, dousing most of the spotfires. Ropin's crew took care of the rest.

Thudding bootsteps announced Tarion and Athira's arrival, crowding into the wheelhouse with them. She didn't risk a grateful look at Tarion, instead addressing them both crisply. "Tarion, stay in here. Your mother will be up there. Athira, you too. I don't want her to see either of you."

Lira left the wheelhouse, quick strides taking her to the stern, where she could watch the navy ships tacking south in pursuit. But already the gap was widening.

They were going to get clear.

Her gaze immediately lifted skyward. Dawn was rising, and the sky was lighter, glimmering with the beginnings of sunlight.

Egalion must have seen the same thing Lira did—that they were going to get away—because she appeared in the sky, dropping quickly towards them. When she landed on the deck, mere metres from Lira, she was unarmed.

"Where did you get a Hunter army?" the woman demanded, frustration narrowing her eyes.

"Wouldn't you like to know." Lira smiled, then lifted an eyebrow. "Have you come to concede?"

Egalion huffed a breath. "On the contrary. I've come for you."

"No you haven't. We both know you can't use your magic right now, whereas I could burn you alive if I chose to. Plus, this crew is handy with a weapon, even if you could take me in a hand-to-hand fight."

Egalion took a half step forward, right hand curling at her side. Lira recognised the gesture, that of a mage reaching for their magic. She frowned. It was almost like Egalion was holding back, though, rather than...

"You know I'll just keep following you," Egalion's voice rapped out, breaking Lira's train of thought. She was utterly relaxed now, stance steady and sure, hands uncurled and resting at her sides. "And we'll be waiting wherever you and your army make port."

"You can't follow us forever. There are limits to even your powerful abilities, Egalion." Lira pushed harder. "And don't think I've forgotten that little secret you're carrying, the one you're so terrified of everyone finding out about. If Lucinda can learn it, you better believe I can too. Perhaps you should leave me alone before I decide to put more effort into figuring it out."

Egalion huffed an amused breath. "You're far too occupied running and hiding from me to have time for ferreting out secrets."

"Am I?" Lira lifted her eyebrows again.

Egalion didn't say anything for a moment, then she looked around. "Where is my son?"

"Tarion is safe and well, and he is with me voluntarily."

Sadness and fear and grief—all intermingled in deep pain—crossed Egalion's face so quickly that Lira was left wondering if she'd imagined it. "I don't believe he would choose your side."

Lira cared nothing for Egalion, but she did for Tarion, and she knew Tarion was probably listening to this exchange. "I understand you think nothing of me, but I give you my word that Tarion is well, and the choice to be here was his alone. I will do my best to keep him safe. You will not lose your son like you have probably already lost your husband. Tarion loves you very much, and if at any point he chooses to return to you, I will not stop him."

Egalion flinched. "There doesn't need to be a war between us." Her face twisted. "We can work together against Lucinda."

*Not yet, we can't,* Lira thought, but kept her face expressionless. "I'm not willing to gamble with Ahrin's life. So unless you're willing to do as Lucinda has ordered us, then nothing has changed."

"I will never do what she wants." The words were clear and unhesitating.

Lira gave her a bleak smile. "Then what next? You have to know we're going to keep sailing until you can't fly anymore, so you've lost me for now."

"I'll find you again. You know I will."

"Not before I get what I want."

"Then you'd better move quickly." Egalion seemed resigned now. "I have a lot of strength at my disposal, not to mention the most powerful telepath in the world. It won't be long before I hunt you down wherever you go."

Lira inclined her head. "Until then, Egalion."

Without another word, Egalion lifted off the deck, soaring into the sky and heading towards the Rionnan ships. As her tiny form landed and disappeared from sight, Tarion appeared at Lira's shoulder.

"Thank you," he said softly.

"If you want to go to her, I won't stop you," she said. "I'm a bit surprised you're still here, to be honest."

"You asked me to distract Athira so you didn't have to burn those ships."

She looked at him in confusion.

"You've got a bigger plan brewing, Lira Astor, and I want to stick around to see what it is."

"Always too smart for your own good, Tarion Caverlock."

He grinned, then sobered. "By the time we return to Dirinan, Yanzi and Fari should have heard from Lord Anler." There was a questioning edge to his words. "Say you *do* win all the lords to your side, what comes next?"

She glanced at him, then looked out over endless ocean. "I do have a plan for that, Tarion, I promise you." What she didn't say was that her plan was contingent on other moving parts. Specifically, her Darkhand. Once she had the lords and her Hunter army ... she needed a war general to lead them. Ahrin would be the final piece that put all of this together.

"But you can't tell me."

"We'll soon be without the protection of the Hunter medallions." She let out a breath. "But your mother was right. Our time is running out. They'll find us again, sooner rather than later."

"And if that happens before you're ready?"

"Best case, your mother figures out how to destroy Lucinda, and I spend the rest of my life back in that prison cell. Worst case, Lucinda wins it all." Her jaw tightened, her knuckles on the railing turning white. "I refuse to allow either of those things to happen. I can't go back there, Tarion. I won't."

# CHAPTER 21

It was a long, tedious journey around the southern tip of Rionn and up the east coast. They began offloading units of Hunters ashore under the cover of night, always along isolated sections of shoreline. Lira instructed each group to split up and travel separately, so that their medallions wouldn't form a void to give them away, and to go to either Carhall or Karonan before heading on to the abandoned Hunter base in the north of Shivasa.

Alea, leader of the first unit to disembark, would divert through Dirinan to carry an update and orders to Yanzi at the headquarters of the Revel Kings.

Those travelling through Karonan would leave their medallions in the warehouse storage room where *Darksong* had been hidden all these years. Those going through Carhall would similarly leave their medallions in a safe location picked out by Athira, who knew the city well. In such large cities, frequented by Taliath, it was unlikely they'd come to notice.

Each of the twelve unit leaders had other instructions too. Working together, Tarion and Lira had talked them through leaving strategic signs of their passing ... a handful of comments spoken a little too loudly in an inn, a brief meetup to create a magical bubble that a searching telepath might find. Nothing that would be enough to get them caught ... but enough to give the impression the Hunters were heading for a spot in north-eastern Tregaya.

Lira tried not to worry about each group as they rowed away from the ship. Told herself they were capable and well trained. But having so much time to stare out at the ocean and think made that close to impossible. Instead, she tried to focus her thoughts in productive directions ... like trying to figure out what Alyx Egalion's secret might be, or who the spy in her inner circle was.

She still hadn't made her mind up on the latter, even though deep down ... Lira heaved a breath. She didn't *want* to make up her mind. Somehow, she was going to need to summon the strength to surface what she already knew. But not today.

As for the former, she went over and over in her mind that last conversation with Lucinda in Rotherburn. The panic on Egalion's face as Lucinda taunted her with whatever she knew. The oddity Lira's instincts had noticed only days earlier as they faced each other on the stern of Ropin's ship.

One afternoon, while Athira napped in the sunlight on the deck near the prow, Lira took the opportunity for a private conversation with Tarion. He might have information she needed to put the pieces together.

Leaning casually with her back to the rail, face tilted up to the faint warmth of the winter sun, she waited until he appeared from belowdecks and gestured him over. Athira was stretched out on her back several metres away, directly in her eyeline. Lira would notice the moment she even twitched.

"I'm pretty confident she's asleep," Lira murmured as Tarion joined her. "If she wakes up, I'll change to casual chat. Make sure you follow along."

"Understood." He rested his hip against the railing so he could see her and Athira both, but his posture stayed as relaxed as hers. To any observer, it would look like they were simply soaking up the sun and enjoying a comfortable silence.

"We need to talk about Cario Duneskal."

His eyebrows flew upward in surprise, and he let out a genuine chuckle. "I did not expect a secret conversation to be about Mama's long-dead best friend. Are you sure you don't mean Rawlin?"

Lira suppressed a shudder at the mere mention of that name. A supercilious coward, Cario Duneskal's surviving brother, Rawlin, was the Mage Council representative in Karonan. He had been nothing but a thorn in Lira's side since they'd met.

"No, I mean Cario. There's one thing I didn't tell you and the others about the conversation your mother and I had with Lucinda before leaving Rotherburn." She risked a glance at him. "Not because I was trying to hide things from you."

He waved a hand to dismiss her concern, voice rich with curiosity. "Whatever it was had to do with Cario?"

"Yes. And your mother." Lira glanced at Athira—still asleep, her breathing slow and even—then relayed what she'd held back. The taunt Lucinda had made that had clearly terrified Egalion.

Tarion's expression turned to worry. "Mama has a secret that Lucinda knows about?"

"Yes. Lucinda threatening to reveal it genuinely terrified your mother—the woman who faced down and killed the Darkmage. Whatever it is, it's big. I need to know what it is, Tarion. It's something I can use if she catches up to me before we're ready."

He was silent a moment, one hand idly lifting to push back tendrils of hair that the sea breeze had blown over his face. It had grown long in the past weeks and months. Once again, Lira was testing their friendship, asking for his support in something that would be difficult for him. "What does Mama's secret have to do with Cario?" he asked eventually.

"Lucinda said, and I quote, '*Do you know the story of Cario Duneskal's death, Lira?*'" She paused, shaking her head. "The look on your mother's face when Lucinda said those words, Tarion. It was sheer panic."

He frowned. "Everyone knows that story, though."

"Will you talk me through what you know?" When he hesitated, she continued. "I know what I'm asking of you—if you don't want to help, I accept that."

Tarion let out a breath. "All the monarchs were gathered in Alistriem to make a plan to deal with Shakar and his encroaching Shiven army. Leader Astohar and his Shiven rebels were there too. Shakar attacked the meeting—he sent Hunters to surround the room and cut off all magic to those inside so that he could assassinate Mama and the leaders. The Bluecoats closed down the room as soon as Mama and Aunt Dawn sensed the Hunters approaching, seeking to keep them out and protect those inside.

"But that's what the Darkmage had planned for. He'd smuggled a Hunter assassin into the room, stationed up in the gallery with a bow. He took a shot at Mama, and Cario jumped in front of the arrow when his telepathy didn't work. He died quickly."

Lira frowned. Tarion's account was no different from the one she'd read. "What happened after he was shot?"

"The Bluecoats and Taliath eventually fought through and killed the Hunters surrounding the room. Magic was restored within a few minutes, but it was too late for Uncle Finn's healing magic to help Cario."

*A few minutes.* Lira stuck on that ... "Wait. Why didn't the assassin take another shot? If your mother was a target, why didn't the Hunter take another shot at her after Cario was down? Nobody had access to magic, right? Don't tell me he only took one arrow in there with him."

Tarion's gaze turned distant. "Da told me that after Cario was shot, Mama lost her mind with grief. She brought half the room down on top of the assassin. Crushed him under a couple of marble pillars. He didn't have time to get off another shot."

Lira stared at him. "She did *what?*"

Tarion shrugged. "Her best friend had just been killed right in front of her, *saving* her. And you've seen how powerful she is."

"But you just said it was a few minutes before the Bluecoats and Taliath killed enough of the Hunters outside the room to restore magic. How did she bring down half the room before that happened without using magic?"

"I..." Tarion's eyes went wide.

"How has nobody ever noticed that discrepancy?"

"The timing in the official accounts must have been wrong. Maybe magic was restored faster than people thought, maybe—"

"If magic was restored fast enough that Egalion could prevent that Hunter loosing a second arrow—something he could have done in literal *seconds*, Tarion—then Finn A'ndreas would have had time to help Cario. At least keep him alive long enough to do proper healing work."

"She..." Tarion let out a long breath. He turned away from her, starting out over the ocean. Lira gave him a moment to think it through, keeping her gaze on the still-sleeping Athira. She hadn't moved the whole time they'd been talking, her face turned away from them, blond hair lifting in the slight breeze.

Eventually, Tarion turned back to her. "That's why Lucinda took Mama. Somehow, she knew. Mama's magic can breach Taliath and Hunter immunity, which means she can probably use her magic on razak and nerik too."

Lira whistled softly. "If the world knew that not only was there a mage of the higher order alive who was herself immune to magic but could also breach the immunity of a Taliath or anyone wearing a medallion..." She trailed off, shaking her head. "Rotted hells, Tarion, no *wonder* your mother was utterly panicked at Lucinda telling everyone about it."

"It would all crack open again. The council, Taliath, the monarchs." An echo of the same panic was on Tarion's face that Lira had seen in his mother's. "The fear, the distrust, it would all return."

Lira let out an admiring breath. "Your mother's self-control is impressive. So many times she could have used that ability back in those tunnels under Rotherburn, but she didn't, all for fear of what would happen if her secret got out."

His voice dropped to an undertone. "Lira, we can't breathe a word of this to anyone. It's too dangerous."

"What we do with the knowledge is less concerning than what Lucinda will do with it."

"How did she even find out?"

Lira gave him a look. "I just found out by asking you a few questions. Your mother got lucky that what she did was covered by the chaos of an attack where people were terrified and not paying attention to what was happening. But the secret is there to be found by anyone who looks for it."

He caught her gaze. "What are *you* going to do with it?"

Sudden anger bubbled up in her, hot and fiery. "Now that your mother knows that my flame magic can breach immunity, the minute she catches me, she's going to lock me away again for the rest of my life. She's going to treat me as even more of a danger to the world. Even though she has the *exact* same ability."

"She doesn't know you, Lira." His gaze was downcast, words mumbled, a hint of the old Tarion bubbling back to the surface.

"She never *tried* to know me. She made up her mind about me before I had any chance to prove different." If she only knew what Lira's true intentions were—not war, but unification, a better way forward for all of them. The frustration was overwhelming, and she briefly wondered if she shouldn't change her mind, take the simpler path, just do what her grandfather had wanted.

Tarion suddenly broke into a smile, a chuckle escaping him as he pointed out at the ocean where a cormorant diving after a fish had been knocked off course by an unexpected swell.

Not glancing in Athira's direction—where she assumed the girl was waking up—Lira rolled her eyes and huffed. "How is that amusing?"

"Come on, Lira, it's the simple things. It's not like there's much else to do just sitting around on deck all afternoon."

"I'm fine with enjoying the sunlight in peaceful contemplation, thank you."

Tarion snorted. "You? Peaceful contemplation? Ha."

Athira wandered over, rubbing sleep from her eyes. "What about a sparring session? I've been doing far too much napping."

Lira straightened with alacrity. "That sounds great. Should we get Shiasta out here too?"

Tarion went to fetch him, and Lira and Athira moved out into the open space of the deck to stretch and warm up. As they sparred, part of Lira enjoyed the quickening of her breath, the sweat slicking her skin, the challenge of trying to outlast her opponent.

The rest of her wondered. Egalion's secret was enormous. And useful ... very useful indeed.

Lira might just have found the thing that could ensure the success of her con. Always, *always*, Lira's primary focus had to be on making the world believe she was carrying out Lucinda's orders. Timing was crucial, and if Egalion found her before she was ready, then Lira could wield her secret as a shield, a way to keep her at bay. Until all the pieces were on the board, and with a single tip of her finger, Lira could set them all into motion.

Just like dominoes falling.

Dominoes that would re-shape power across this continent and bring Lucinda to her knees before she even saw it coming.

They eventually made port at one of the smaller cities along the northern Tregayan coast, where Ropin had lucrative financial arrangements with a handful of key port officials. None would report their presence.

From there, they'd contemplated travelling overland to Dirinan, but to do that swiftly meant running the gauntlet of road checkpoints no doubt staffed with mages and telepaths. Instead, they'd bought passage on a ship known to Ropin.

"He's quick and discreet," the captain promised. "And he stays out of the way of the authorities. I've asked around, and he's one of only three ships heading to Dirinan direct from here. I wouldn't recommend the other two."

"Thanks, Ropin." She took the captain's details from him with a grateful smile.

"You know, it's going to take weeks for us to overhaul my ship, change our markings and flag, alter its appearance, and source new forged paperwork," he told Lira. Calm as always, it was nonetheless clear that he was unhappy. "And that's going to take coin. Lots of it."

"When you're done, bring your bill to Dirinan. Yanzi will pay it, with interest on top," Lira promised.

"He'd better. Or the Mage Council are suddenly going to find themselves in possession of a lot of information about you," Ropin said amicably. "The coin they'll pay for it will easily cover my costs."

Lira smiled and shook his hand in farewell. "Consider me adequately warned. Safe travels, Ropin."

Another week-long ship journey, and they finally reached port in Dirinan. Warned by a message sent ahead from their last port, Yanzi, Fari, and Lorin were waiting for them.

"Alea came through just over a week ago," Lorin said as they gathered in the Revel King's gambling hall. "He reported no issues on the way and had successfully stored his medallion in Karonan. Based on your instructions, we sent supplies north to the old Hunter base. They should arrive shortly."

"Thank you." Lira glanced at Shiasta. "I'd like to get up to the base soon as we can, make sure they've all arrived safely."

"Not all of them will be there yet," he said, looking unworried.

"We've heard from Anler too," Yanzi said. "Just last week. The message was admirably vague—he certainly knows how to conduct a secret alliance. He invites you to 'visit him at your convenience, and he will have things in place.' He also added that no further discussions will be entered into, or preparations made, until such time as you have completed your 'work.'"

Lira nodded wearily. "Send a message tonight and tell him we'll be there in two weeks. Then prepare our horses and supplies. I want to ride out the day after tomorrow. Fari, Tarion, Athira, you're with me. Shiasta, I want you to go north to the Hunter base, make sure our Hunters are safe and that everything there is running smoothly. Then meet us in Kharan before we go to Anler's."

Yanzi frowned. "You're going somewhere else first?"

"Yes." She lifted a hand before any of them could ask the questions already forming in their expressions. "No more Hunter medallions means we're open targets for telepaths. We all know mental shielding isn't foolproof. All I'm going to say is that we need more than just Anler and his network and the Hunter army."

"How wonderfully cryptic," Fari said mournfully. "Can you at least tell me how warmly I need to pack?"

"*Very* warmly." Lira grinned at her, then sobered. "Which reminds me. Here's where you make yourself useful, Councillor Dirsk. Before we leave Dirinan, you'll make sure we're all fitted and dressed for a dramatic show. Anler has already proved resistant, and we can assume his fellow lords will be similarly so. I want to give them no reason to refuse to ally with me—and that includes our appearance."

"Oh, I can make them so impressed with the visual they'll be scrambling to pay attention to the details," Fari promised. "But I want free rein. No 'but that high collar chokes me, Fari,' or 'velvet makes me itch, Fari.'"

Lira sighed. "Fine."

"And we're going to do something with your hair, too."

Yanzi brightened. "Finally, no more rats' nest!"

"I would like to come with you," Lorin said. "Shouldn't you have most of your Shadowcouncil at your side when you make your pitch to Anler's people?"

"Given my natural aversion to locations requiring *very warm* clothes, I'm happy to stay here and run things," Yanzi said.

She shook her head, trying to hide her irritation at being questioned. "Sorry, Yanzi, you'll travel north to meet us at Anler's too—I just don't need you for what I'm doing first. Lorin, I have reasons for needing you here."

Lorin at least had the grace to wait until they were alone, everyone else having filed out to either get some sleep or attend to crew business, before questioning her further. "Why do I need to be here?"

"You know why," she said, the irritation bleeding into her voice. "If Yanzi catches even a hint that Ahrin is a prisoner, we'll lose his support in a second. If that happens, I need you to step in and take control of the crew. I can't leave Athira behind to do it, or she'll become suspicious, and as critical as Fari is, she's no warrior. I'm deploying my Shadowcouncil according to their strengths, Lorin. We can't do anything without the resources the Revel Kings give us."

"I do appreciate your trust in me." He made a rueful face. "I just didn't quite expect running a criminal gang would be my part in taking over the world."

"I couldn't do any of this without you," she said, meaning it, then hesitated. Fari, Lorin, Yanzi. The names still swirled around and around in her mind. "Are you sure that this is what you want, though? I know better than anyone how badly you've always wanted to be a mage warrior."

He touched his arm, memory making his eyes go briefly distant. "I still have nightmares about the terror of breaking this arm so badly when I was a boy ... of the interminable wait for a healer, hoping desperately they'd arrive in time to prevent permanent damage so I could still go to Temari Hall." His gaze cleared and he smiled at her. "You saved me from that fate a second time, risking your life to save my leg at DarkSkull, convincing me that I could still be a warrior, despite the limp. If I have to choose between you and the council, I choose you, Lira. I always will."

The pain in his eyes, of his boyhood injury ... that was real, Lira felt it deep in her bones. And something in her twisted.

She smiled at him. "I hope you know I don't take that for granted."

"You know I won't fail you." He gave her a little smile. "I take it from your warm clothes comment that you're heading farther into northern Shivasa? That's a pleasant travel location for the middle of winter."

She sighed. "You're right, but unfortunately it's necessary."

"Good luck, Lira. I'll be here for anything you need." He smiled, then left, following after Yanzi.

Rather than joining the others in getting some rest, Lira slipped out of the gambling hall, taking a long walk through the streets of Revel King territory. She breathed deeply of the familiar briny air, always edged with the rotting hint of sewerage and damp. It wasn't just that she wanted some time alone to clear her thoughts.

She was hoping to receive a message that she'd been waiting for. That she *needed*. But despite over an hour of walking, through dark alleys and narrow, winding streets—she even passed by their old loft, hands deep in pockets to ward off the cold as she looked up at the dark, cracked windows—nobody but a foolish pickpocket approached her. Worry and anxiety churned in the pit of her stomach as she returned to the gambling hall.

Ahrin hadn't broken free yet.

It was taking longer than she'd expected, but all wasn't lost yet. Trying to dismiss the worry nagging at her, Lira finally went in search of a bed and some sleep. She'd rise early in the morning. Maybe a message from Ahrin would arrive by then. If not, well, there were things that still needed to be accomplished before she needed her Darkhand to step in.

It was time to pay a little visit back home.

# CHAPTER 22

Wind whipped from the east, turning snow into icy sleet. Their horses plodded along the empty and pitted road, as miserable as their riders. After setting off from Dirinan just over a week ago, they'd left the nearest large town two days earlier and were now truly in the depths of isolated northern Shivasa. The southern border of Tregaya was barely three days ride away.

"Remind me again why we're wasting time doing this?" Athira brought her mare up alongside Lira and Alfie. "You're the one who keeps saying the council is going to catch us sooner rather than later."

"Thanks to the distractions our Hunters left while travelling through Tregaya, I'm hoping the council will concentrate the search there for the moment. And this will only take us a few days out of our way."

"What *is* this, exactly? You're supposed to keep me informed."

Lira fixed her with a steely look. "You know why it's important I keep information locked down. And I've told you—I need to make sure that by the time we meet Anler's full network, we're in as strong a position as possible. We can't afford to spend *more* time convincing them to join us. You will see soon enough what I mean, I promise you. I'm not hiding anything."

Athira huffed her breath and kicked her horse forward. Alfie—ironically the last in their group of horses' pecking order—immediately sidestepped to give the mare right of way. Lira glowered at the back of his head. As much as she liked the sweet horse, he really needed to grow a backbone.

By the time she'd shifted to regain her balance, the village they were heading for had become visible in the distance through a gap in the stark white landscape. She stilled in the saddle, staring ahead, spirits growing heavy. Alfie turned his head to look at her, as if sensing her distress. She gave him an idle pat.

As much as she needed to do this, she suddenly wished she'd gone with Shiasta to their new base. It wasn't too far to the west—maybe she should just turn around now. Lira sighed. No, this was necessary. At least Fari and Tarion were with her. That was something.

As if summoned by her thoughts, Fari rode up on Lira's right. "You okay?" she asked.

Lira looked away from the distant village to offer a small smile. "I'm always okay."

There was a moment of silence, then, "Lira, if you don't want to do this anymore, then—"

"We're taking down the Mage Council," Lira snapped, her fire sparking, "so quit trying to find ways to change my mind."

Riding ahead with Tarion, Athira glanced back, lifting an eyebrow at Lira's raised voice. She didn't say anything though, merely smiling a little when Lira glared at her. Therob—the Hunter bodyguard Shiasta had assigned them—rode even further ahead, his gaze constantly studying their surroundings.

"That's not what I was doing," Fari said mildly, keeping her voice low. "I was just recognising that soon we'll be going to meet with Anler and his people and, given Anler is one of the most awful people I've ever met, it would be absolutely fine if you were having second thoughts about working with him."

Lira glanced at her, let out a steaming breath. "All right. Sorry for snapping."

Fari smiled. "I can't imagine the pressure you must be under, going at the entire Mage Council when even your grandfather failed, not to mention figuring out how you're going to beat Councillor Egalion, *and* worrying about what Lucinda might be doing to Ahrin at the same time. I can handle a little short temper."

Lira hid her relief that, at least as far as Fari was concerned, there was no doubt she was still following Lucinda's tasking. "You're just as much a traitor to the council as I am now. You'll be going up against Egalion and her people too."

"Sure. But I'm not in charge. I'm following you."

Lira huffed a breath of amusement. "And you're not worried that I'll fail miserably, and you'll spend the rest of your life in jail, or worse?"

"Oh, I'm absolutely worried about that. But my choice is made. I can't go back now. I wouldn't even if I could." Fari flashed another smile her way. "Plus, I figure you like me enough by now that even if we all do end up in prison, your Darkhand will break me out too when she comes for you with her pack of elite killers."

Lira chuckled as she studied the healer, still trying to figure out how sincere she was. She'd set her pieces on the board carefully, arrayed them according to instinct and judgement, but she still didn't have enough to be certain of the spy. The traitor who'd pretended friendship from the beginning. If she was wrong about any of it...

A low whistle from Tarion had them both glancing sharply to where he pointed. Trees lined the southern side of the road, but they were planted sparsely, providing enough of a view through to the ruins of where a cabin had once stood. There wasn't much left, just the foundations and a handful of lonely, charred beams rising out of the ground. Weeds and grass—mostly covered in snow—grew all over it.

Fari shot a quick look between Lira and Tarion, then said in realisation. "This was the village you were born in, isn't it?"

Ignoring her, Lira reined Alfie in and dismounted without conscious thought. Her fine boots sank ankle-deep into icy snow as she walked through the trees, coming to a halt only a handful of steps from where the front door had once been.

A soft footfall beside her heralded Tarion's arrival, but he said nothing. Athira and Fari remained mounted on the road; Athira watching the area, Fari watching Lira. Therob was out of sight.

"They burned it down after they sent me away," Lira said, not directing the words at anyone or anything in particular. She bit her lip.

This village had once been loyal to Shakar, part of his fight against the Mage Council. But sometime after the war that loyalty had changed, faded to wariness, doubt. When her mother had come back here looking for safety, they'd taken her in because they'd felt they had to, but they'd been terrified of what it would mean for them.

And it seemed as soon as both mother and daughter were gone, the village had destroyed all remnants of them. So much fear—of what? What a five-year-old girl might become? Why was she surprised?

"How did your mother end up out here?" Tarion asked softly.

She turned, glanced towards the distant village. "That's what I plan on asking them."

"You were five when she died?" He knew this already, but his voice was soft, casual. He was looking to focus her on the little details, keep her from being lost in memory. It was something she'd done for him before, an easy shorthand of support between them. It calmed her.

Lira nodded. "She didn't come home one night. They came the next day to take me to the orphanage in Dirinan. They must have told the matron there who I was, because she reported it straight to your mother. Your parents came to see me a month later, then left me there, telling me to come to Temari when my magic broke out."

"I wish my parents had taken you with them." He gave her a little smile. "We might have grown up together."

She looked away. What would she have become if she'd grown up with a brother like Tarion, a cousin like Garan? She might have learned how to trust. She'd never have met Ahrin, in that life. Never have said those fateful words to her. Lira didn't know what she felt about that, only that it was an unbearable sensation, so she buried it away. "I think that would have been nice."

"I would have been a lot less lonely," he admitted. "You've always understood me in a way nobody else does apart from Sesha."

Lira leaned into him. "What would your princess think of you joining me to take down the Mage Council?"

"I haven't spoken to her in a long time, but ... I believe she would support me doing what I felt was right. She would trust that I had made the right choice, even if she didn't understand it."

The pain in his voice touched hers, making her speak when otherwise she never would have. "I miss Ahrin so much. I feel the ache with every breath I take."

"Every single breath," he agreed softly.

A comfortable silence fell between them. Eventually Lira's thoughts returned to what they were about to do. She hesitated. "It's not going to be pretty, Tarion. I'll limit the damage as much as I can ... but to do this successfully, it will need to be quick and brutal. If you want to wait here until it's done, I'll understand."

He considered that a moment, gaze still on the burned-out remains of what had once been her home. "I'm coming. I trust you."

She huffed a breath. "Even though I haven't told you what my plan to take down the council actually is yet?"

"If only I had a Taliath's immunity to telepathic magic," he said ruefully. "Then you could tell me. But yes, even though I don't know what your plans are, I have faith in you."

"That's a wonderful gift. Considering who you are, and what I'm trying to do. To have faith in me despite it..." Lira let out a sigh. "I'm not sure what to do with that."

He smiled. "Who says you have to do anything? Come on, let's get this over with."

Fari was still staring at the burned remains through the trees as Lira and Tarion walked back. "That's where you lived?" she asked Lira.

"It was."

She scowled. "Want me to give the whole village a case of the boils? The painful type, with lots of pus?"

Lira smiled. "If they don't cooperate, you're free to give them a case of whatever you'd like."

Athira let out an irritated sigh. "It's freezing out here. Can we please move on rather than spend any longer feeling maudlin over a burned cottage?"

Fari gave her a sideways look. "Each time I think I've plumbed the depths of how unlikeable you are, Athira Walden, you go and better it."

"I'm crushed, really." Athira rolled her eyes.

Therob interrupted the bickering with a quietly spoken, "Do you expect danger here, Lady Astor? If so, I would prefer that you remain close to me at all times."

"There will be fear, Therob, a lot of fear," Lira murmured. "But nothing in this village is a danger to me."

Lira Astor wasn't a five-year-old child they could discard like yesterday's trash anymore.

Now she was what they'd always feared she would be.

# CHAPTER 23

Given the awful weather, Lira was unsurprised to find the main street of the village empty. Its muddy surface was spotted with frozen-over puddles, and snow had been half-heartedly swept to the curbs. The place looked no different to her fuzzy memories of it.

It certainly didn't seem to have grown in size since she'd left—a handful of streets branched off from the main thoroughfare, along which was a smithy, an enclosed market, and the inn. A square—green and bright with flowers in summer but stark and snow-covered now—for a larger Seventhday market cut the main road in two. Most of the village's residents came from the hundreds of acres of farmland surrounding this small huddle of buildings. It took a certain kind of rugged hardiness to survive amidst such isolation and ruthless weather. It was a quality that had served Shakar well.

"Where do we go first?" Tarion asked.

"Where everyone will be in this weather." Lira pressed her right calf into Alfie's side, guiding him off the road and over to the inn. There, she dismounted and loosely tied his reins to a free spot on the hitching rail. His big head swung around, giving her a gentle nudge in the chest. She smiled and stroked his nose while the others dismounted too.

Eventually she stepped away and looked at them all. "You remember what to do?"

Fari let out a theatrical sigh. "My difficulties were with book learning, not memory. Look intimidating, don't speak unless you direct us to. Ignore whatever you say and don't let any reactions show on our faces, even if you start burning people to cinders." She jerked a thumb sideways. "Athira and Therob are going to be great at that. I'm less sure about Tarion."

"I'm just hoping that you're soon going to make it clear what in magical hells we're doing in this backwards falling-down collection of buildings claiming to be a village," Athira remarked sourly. "Trust me, it's not going to be hard to look thoroughly unimpressed."

"Good." Lira's gaze lingered on Tarion a moment, until he gave her a little nod. He'd be fine. "Let's do this."

She paused only a moment at the entrance, taking a breath, focusing on being what she needed to be. The heir to the Darkmage.

It took only a second for that skin to slide over her, and then she pushed the door open, took three steps inside, and halted, allowing her eyes to adjust to the dim, smoky light.

The air was thick with the scent of ale, cigar smoke, and old food. Her boots squelched against a sticky floor and the windows were hazy with grime. At a quick scan she counted roughly fifteen patrons scattered around the dim space, mostly men, a handful of women. No children. No weapons in sight.

Tarion and Fari stopped beside her, one at each shoulder, a half step back, marking her as the leader. Therob and Athira halted just inside the door, blocking it. It took a few seconds for everyone in the room to notice there were new arrivals, to look at them and take in their appearance. Realise they were visitors from a long way away.

And a single heartbeat to recognise her.

Lira was a grown woman now, nothing like the child she'd been. Yet they knew. Most of them froze. Some glanced around as if looking for an escape route. One picked up his ale and chugged it down in several swallows.

"Good," she said, pitching her voice to carry through the room. "You know who I am, so I don't have to bother introducing myself."

One man, bearded and old, braver than the rest, rose to his feet. "We told you never to come back here."

Her gaze narrowed in on him and she studied him a moment. His hair was much greyer and thinner, shoulders stooped with age, but... "You're the one who came to my door to tell me my mother was dead."

"Yes."

"What's your name?"

He hesitated a moment before reluctantly spitting out, "Rojan."

She nodded, careful to keep her face expressionless, and took a few steps farther into the room, holding his gaze. "You were right to be afraid of me." She let that settle, savoured the fear in his eyes. "I'm here with questions. I'd like honest answers, or I'll burn this village to the ground just like you did to my mother's home. Is that clear?"

To her left, a younger man rose from his chair and scrambled for the open door into the kitchens. He made it a third of the way before Lira's telekinetic magic slammed the door shut, then picked him up and sent him flying across the room to hit the wall hard. He slumped to the ground, out cold.

Then she lifted her left hand, summoned more magic to wreathe her entire arm in violet-edged flame. "Would anyone else like to question my sincerity?"

Silence crept through the space. It was thick with a fear that spread like wildfire through the room until even the faintest shift or movement was audible.

"Good." She flicked her hand, dragged one of the tables away from its terrified occupants to the open space in the centre of the room, savouring the loud screeching it made against the wooden floor. Once it was in place, she sent two chairs flying through the air to stand either side of it. Then she pointed at Rojan, still standing. "You. Sit."

His gaze flicked around, clearly considering his options, before he realised he had none and gave in. Slow, wary, strides carried him to the table where he perched gingerly on one of the chairs. Lira walked over to sit opposite him.

Therob took up a position at the front door. Fari and Athira moved to stand at the exit to the kitchens, while Tarion hovered behind Lira's chair, cloak pushed back to display where his hand rested on the hilt of *Darksong*.

Rojan paled even further when he saw it, sweat beading on his brow. Lira almost smiled. So, he recognised her grandfather's Taliath sword. Those in this village really had been among the Darkmage's closest supporters.

She kept her gaze on him, a small part of her monitoring the rest of the room. She didn't beat around the bush. "Who are you, Rojan?"

"My boys and I run the smithy," he said, jaw set with defiance.

"Good. Now, who was my father?"

His jaw tightened further. "I don't know."

"Explain why you don't know."

He swallowed, glanced around the room, got help from nobody—none of the cowards would even meet his gaze—and looked back at her. "Your mother came here after the war, and we took her in. She left after a few years to go to Karonan, and when she came back, she was pregnant. She never talked about who your father was."

"Why did she come here, to this particular village, after the war?"

Sweat beaded the man's forehead. "I don't know."

"You're lying." Her voice was granite.

"This entire region was your grandfather's stronghold." He bit the words out. "She had nowhere else to go and she knew we'd have no choice but to take her in."

So far that fit with what she already understood, but still, she wanted to make sure. "Why did you take her in if you were so scared of her?"

"She had no magic ... and..." He licked his lips. "The war had only just ended. We were still afraid. Most villages in the north had actively supported Shakar, but some of us only ever did so because he terrified us into submission. She used our fear against us."

Her gaze narrowed. This was new. "My mother was part of his army?"

"She was his administrator in this region—she made sure all the villages contributed soldiers to his army, provided food and other resources, and paid taxes. She knew how involved we'd been, and she threatened to report us to Leader Astohar if we didn't let her stay here."

Lira blinked, but otherwise didn't let on her surprise. Her mother had been more involved with Shakar than Lira had realised—or that Anler had let on. And she'd clearly possessed his ruthless streak. "What was her name?"

He let out a breath, looking suddenly defeated. "Niria."

A name. Her mother had a name. *Niria.* She liked the sound of it on her tongue. Lira leaned forward over the table. "Where was she during the war?"

"I don't know, I swear it. She never talked about the war afterwards. But I assume she lived at his stronghold, the Hunter base northwest of here." Any defiance he'd felt was dissipating rapidly. "And before you ask, she left here to go to Karonan because she wanted a better life. She looked down on us, on our farming and our poverty. She thought she was too good for us."

"If that's true, why did she come back?"

"She never said. But she was afraid, that was obvious to everyone. She was afraid of what having a child meant. I think she came here to hide, to hide *you.*"

Lira's gaze narrowed. "How long was she gone?"

"Almost two years."

Lira paused a moment before asking her next question, making sure she was ready to hear the answer, that she wouldn't betray anything but calm in front of these people. "How did she die?"

Rojan shifted his gaze away again, but this time it settled on another older man across the room.

"My patience is thinning rapidly, Rojan."

More sweat beaded on his forehead at her tone—it began sliding in multiple droplets down to his jaw. She savoured that fear. Was glad of it. A small taste of the fear she'd felt as a discarded five-year-old girl. "Teren found her in the woods near your hut when he went out early to hunt that morning. It looked like she'd died from exposure."

"It *looked* like?" she snapped.

"There were no signs she'd been attacked, no wounds, nothing untoward. And..." He hesitated.

"What?"

"She probably hadn't eaten for several days. She'd come begging at the market two days earlier, pleading with us for scraps. She told us she'd only had barely enough to keep you fed but that she had nothing left."

Her mouth tightened, rage rising like a flame in her chest. "And did you give her any food?"

His voice came out as small as a squeak. "No."

"Was that the last time you saw her?"

"No." Rojan's shoulders sagged, breath starting to come in quick pants, like a cornered animal. "The night before Teren found her ... we have a town meeting every Fifthday evening. She came along. She wanted to borrow money. She said she planned to leave, never come back, but she needed coin for the journey, for food."

Lira's voice was ice-cold, barely containing her anger. "Did she say why?"

He swallowed. "She said she'd discovered you were a mage, and that changed things. She said even though your father hadn't wanted a child, his family might want you. She was planning to take you to them in Carhall."

Silence caught. Held. Then—

"*Carhall?*" Lira asked, stunned enough that the surprise echoed through her voice.

Behind her, Tarion shifted, but he held to his promise and didn't say anything. Although Lira was entirely focused on Rojan, her peripheral vision told her everyone in the room had gone still where they sat, drinks untouched.

"She said your father's family was from there, even though he was in Karonan at the time she met him." He lifted a hand to ward off the questions forming on her face. "She didn't even want to tell us that much, but she was desperate. I know nothing else. She didn't give us their name, *or* his name. She just wanted money for the journey."

"And did you give it to her?"

He hesitated. Lira clicked her fingers and a bright flame flared into life, dancing across her fingertips. Rojan mumbled, "No. We refused."

A longer, heavy silence filled the room as Lira struggled to keep a hold on the fury and grief storming inside her before it erupted into violence. She needed information, not dead people. And killing them now wouldn't bring her mother back.

Before Lira got a handle on herself enough to ask her next question, Fari abruptly stepped away from the kitchen door, strolling over to the table, as if sensing Lira's need for a moment to gather herself. "Let me get this straight," she said. "Lira's mother died, and instead of taking her child to Carhall where you knew she had family, you dumped her at an orphanage in Dirinan and told the whole world who she was?"

Rojan swallowed again, gaze darting between Lira and the visibly angry Zandian. "I—"

"No need to stammer uselessly, we all know what the answer is," Fari cut him off. "You're a rotted piece of slimy fish carcass, you *do* know that right? All of you." Her gaze took in the room. "If Lira truly was what you were all so terrified of, what do you think comes next?"

The fear in the room deepened.

Lira let it settle, holding Rojan's gaze for a long moment. "If I leave here, and I learn that you knew something you didn't tell me, I'll be back. And I'll do to your village what you did to my home. Do we have an understanding?"

He nodded. "Yes. There's nothing else."

She leaned forward, voice cold as ice. "I'm not a helpless five-year-old anymore, so don't imagine you can take your petty revenge on me by announcing my presence to all and sundry."

Terror had sweat dripping down his face and his hands trembling on the tabletop. She savoured it like a fine wine. "Now, before I go, I need two more things from you."

"Whatever you want. Just don't hurt us. Please." He was practically whimpering now.

"First—did you tell the council any of this when they came asking questions about me after you dropped me at the orphanage?"

"No." The relief on his face at telling her something she *wanted* to hear was comical. "We pretended to know nothing. It was safer that way."

"Good. Now, you're going to tell me which Shiven villages remain loyal to my grandfather, and which are turncoat cowards like you." She leaned back, looked around the room. "Someone better get some parchment and ink. Quickly."

The silence held for a quivering moment, like a drawn bowstring, before Fari snapped, "Now!"

Immediately, a chair scraped backwards and an older woman, about Rojan's age, went over to the bar. She dug around behind it for a moment, then came up with a ragged piece of parchment, which she carried over to Rojan. She looked at Lira the whole time, fear and defiance in that gaze. Lira didn't look away until she did.

"There's ink and quill in the back office," another man said quietly.

Lira glanced over her shoulder at Tarion. He nodded and vanished from sight. Within a few moments he reappeared, holding the ink pot and quill, which he placed in front of Rojan.

Lira looked at him. "Start writing."

He scrawled out a few lines without protest, then seemed to hesitate. He looked at her—instinct told her he was weighing the odds of not giving up everything he knew—but at the expression on her face he sighed and looked around the room. "Tarrna? Teren? I'm going to need your help to finish this—I don't know as much as you do."

An elderly man, with hunched back and a shock of wispy white hair, rose from a chair at the bar and came over. He gave Lira a glance that was both considering and full of contempt, then took the seat next to Rojan's. He crossed out one of the names Rojan had written, then scrawled out several more. When he was done, he waved over the woman that had fetched the parchment. She reluctantly got up and took his chair before scrawling out a few more names.

When she was done, the parchment was covered with writing, and she shoved it over the table to Lira. "You're going to die a failure just like he did."

Someone at the back of the room gasped at her defiance, and Rojan tensed, knuckles whitening.

Lira merely smiled, folding the parchment and tucking it inside her jacket. "If I were you, I'd start paying attention to news coming out of Carhall. And when you hear that the Mage Council has been taken down, my Shadowcouncil sitting in its place, you should start preparing for my next visit. Because, like my grandfather, I reward loyalty."

She let that sit for a moment, pushing back her chair and standing up, her gaze sweeping the room. "As for traitors …. well, what I do with those will soon become quite clear. Until next time."

And Lira Astor turned and strode out the door without another word.

Her Shadowcouncil swept out after her.

# CHAPTER 24

"Well, we got out of there without you burning anyone alive," Fari said cheerfully as they filed down the steps into the street. "I count that a win."

Lira paused, glancing back, the rage inside her still threatening to boil over. The way those cowards had turned their back on her mother ... she'd died because they'd refused to lift a finger to help. All she'd needed was some food and coin.

"Lira." Tarion stopped dead, ignoring both of them. The sleet had cleared off, and now a light snowfall drifted around them. "I think I know who your father is."

Lira snorted, distracted from her lingering anger by the outrageousness of his statement, and lifted an eyebrow at him. "Oh really?"

He didn't smile. He was completely serious, hazel eyes wide. "You said that Lucinda told you that your father's identity could help you get the power you wanted?"

She shrugged. "Lucinda was just waving carrots in front of me to get me to do what she wanted."

"No, no, think about it." His words were tripping over themselves, trying to keep up with the speed of his thoughts. "That staff you carry ... Lira, who was considered the most skilled telekinetic mage alive before Shakar killed him? Who is the mage they keep comparing *your* skill to? The one whose brother sits on the Mage Council, whose family is based in Carhall, but who lives in *Karonan*?"

Before Lira could even think about what to say to that, Fari let out a shriek, eyes going wide as saucers. "Oh magical hells, Tarion, are you saying you think Rawlin Duneskal is Lira's father? That Lira is Cario Duneskal's *niece*?"

He nodded firmly. "That's exactly what I'm saying."

Fari stared at him for a long moment, then dissolved into outright laughter. "Oh that's perfect. It's so perfect. Just look at her face ... the superciliousness all over it. That's not Astor arrogance, it's Duneskal arrogance. How did we not see this before?"

Lira looked between them, frowning. "You're not serious."

"Rojan just said your mother was going to take you to Carhall because your father's family would be willing to take you in," Tarion said eagerly. "She had to have been talking about the Duneskals; a pureblood mage family like them would have *absolutely* wanted you once they learned you had mage ability."

Lira rolled her eyes. "Tarion, there are a hundred pureblood mage families in Carhall."

"Sure, but none who have a mage councillor family member based in Karonan," Fari chimed in, sobering. "Your mother would have known who Rawlin was, how powerful his family was, even if he didn't know *her* identity. When your mother found out you had magic, she would have known they would take you in."

Silence settled over the street. None of the villagers had followed them out—they were probably watching fearfully at the windows for them to ride away before emerging. Part of Lira noticed Athira standing a short distance off, her face white, jaw set, but the rest of her attention was stuck on Tarion's words.

He jumped in again, "Lira, you're not just the heir to the Darkmage. Lucinda was right. You're the direct heir to the Duneskal seat on the Mage Council. Rawlin doesn't have any other children. Cario died childless. And their only sister married a Walden, so their children are heirs to the Walden seat..." Tarion's eyes went wider, and he spun around to stare at Athira. "Magical hells, Athira is your cousin!"

Athira didn't react. Didn't move. Lira merely blinked at Tarion. This was too much to take in—the revelations about her mother's death already enough. But the fact that she might be a Duneskal, that she might have living blood family out there that had no connection to the Darkmage ... it was too much. "What you're saying is just speculation. I don't think—"

"It's not. It's true," Tarion said quietly. "I know it in my bones. Mama talked about Cario a lot when I was growing up. You're so much like him, Lira. Not just your telekinesis ability, but... he always acted like he didn't care about things, even when he did, deeply. She said he could be cold, practical, able to focus on what was necessary irrespective of the emotion of it. That's you."

"I agree." Fari stepped forward, squeezed her arm. "Welcome to the fraternity of pure magebloods, Lira."

"Athira, what do you make of all this?" Lira looked at her.

She was silent a moment, then the pale shock on her face cracked, faded, and her expression returned to normal. "I think it doesn't matter a jot who your father is at this point. You can't prove it, and even if you could, it won't give you a seat on the council now, while Rawlin lives."

"Lucky you, having such a warm and supportive cousin, Lira," Fari remarked.

Therob's cleared throat broke the ensuing silence. "Lady Astor? I'd prefer not to linger here in view of those in the inn much longer, unless you deem it necessary? They were all deathly afraid, but fear can turn to anger quite quickly."

"You're right." Lira shook herself. "Let's go. Time to return to Anler and see if he's done what I asked. Athira has a point. I've learned what I needed to here, and the identity of my father isn't it."

Still, as they mounted their horses and rode from the village, the idea of being a Duneskal circled through Lira's head on repeat. Rawlin Duneskal. She couldn't stand the man, found him rude and supercilious and intolerant. But Cario had been the opposite of that ... he'd given his life for his best friend. Were there other living Duneskals like him? Was Athira's mother more like Rawlin or Cario? Did she have other cousins?

She might be the heir to the Duneskal seat on the council.

Lira focused on that, pushing the other questions out of her mind, dismissing them as irrelevant. This part though ... this she might be able to use.

Lucinda had been right indeed.

From Lira's home village, they turned southwest, heading straight for Kharan. It was a silent journey—if nothing else, all were tired of travelling through such awful weather. Athira remained uncommunicative and even Fari's ebullient nature dimmed. Lira pushed the pace hard, wanting to reach their next destination, hating having too much time to think, to dwell.

Her mother had wanted to take her to Carhall. It was hard to imagine what that life might have been like ... although even if Tarion was right, she doubted growing up amidst the Duneskal family would have been as warm as the life she'd found for herself with Ahrin and their crew in Dirinan. And her name would have been even more of a factor living amidst the centre of the Mage Council world. Still ... she wondered.

"You grew up in Carhall, right?" Lira asked Athira idly one afternoon as they rode through a heavy snowfall, shoulders hunched against the driving snow in their faces.

Athira flicked her an unreadable look. "I did."

"What was it like?"

"I don't know. It was a normal childhood for a mage pureblood, I guess. I had nannies while my parents were off doing more important things. My councillor grandfather regularly lectured me on the importance of upholding the honour and strength of the Walden name. I had whatever I wanted in terms of clothes and toys and horses. A private tutor. All the things you sneer at."

"Were you happy?"

Athira snorted. "Really? What do you care about that, Lira Astor?"

"I'm just wondering if maybe you weren't ... if that's why Lucinda was able to manipulate you into joining her."

"Lucinda didn't manipulate me into anything." Athira cast her another sidelong glance. "You've become a lot more introspective since I knew you last. It doesn't suit you."

Not liking the tone of suspicion in Athira's voice, Lira changed the subject. "Have you communicated with Lucinda recently?"

"We're in touch."

"That's annoyingly vague. I'm making quite an effort here to do what she wants, to make sure you have access to everything I'm doing so there's no room for doubt. A little information in return isn't too much to ask, surely?"

"I've made Lucinda aware of your efforts. You don't need to worry on that score," Athira said. "But don't think I'm fooled, either. You're only compliant so long as we hold Vensis. I know you burn for the Seven's destruction."

"Does that bother you?"

Athira merely gave her a cool smile.

It was confounding. Athira had believed enough in the Mage Council that she'd voluntarily remained a prisoner of Underground, willingly stayed behind when she could have escaped to undergo more experiments. Yet in the space of two years, she'd become a loyal follower. So loyal that Lucinda of all people trusted her to be free of the woman's control.

Two years was a long time, but even so ... Lira couldn't quite pin down Athira's motivations. And that bothered her. You couldn't defeat your enemy unless you understood what drove them.

For now, Lira was doing what Lucinda wanted, and it suited her purposes for Athira to be spying on everything she did. But in the long term ... Athira was a problem that needed to be dealt with.

She let out a long breath. Juggling so many balls in the air was becoming exhausting, not least because she was the only one who knew the full entirety of the plan. She couldn't share the burden with anyone, sense check it, not until...

She dismissed that thought. Best to focus on one thing at a time. Hopefully she'd done enough now to win Anler to her side and bring all of Shakar's network into the open. Now she'd just have to see if it worked.


Shiasta waiting for them at the agreed-upon inn at Kharan was a welcome sight.

"All Hunters arrived at the base without issue, Lady Astor." He looked pleased to see her. "Are the other members of the Shadowcouncil with you?"

"All but Yanzi are waiting outside. He'll join us in a few days," she said. "How did things go in the north?"

"The Hunters are settling in well," he said. "The size of the old base is suitable for our needs, and the necessary repairs provide a way for our warriors to stay busy." Shiasta hesitated, but only for a moment. He seemed to be growing increasingly comfortable with giving his opinion unasked. "Lady Astor, I am uncomfortable with your decision to remove our medallions, although I understand the tactical reason for doing so. You should be aware that if a telepath searches the area around the base, they will likely find us."

"There is no reason for a telepath to be diving into specific minds in such an isolated area of Shivasa," Lira said. "I understand that it's a calculated risk, but you'd be far more likely to be found by a telepath scanning for a large magical void. And they *will* be searching for that."

He bowed his head. "I understand."

"The twelve other unit leaders have their orders?" she confirmed.

"They've already moved, Lady Astor."

She straightened. "Good. Then let's go. I'd like to ride straight out to Lord Anler's estate."

He followed without a word.

Anler emerged from his imposing house as they rode up the long drive. His expression was impossible to read, but Lira's instincts were quiet, and Shiasta didn't look in any way alarmed, so she judged they were safe.

The rest of her Shadowcouncil hung back while she rode forward to greet him.

"Lord Anler." Lira greeted him from horseback, preferring to remain taller. "It's good to see you again."

He bowed his head. "Am I to take your arrival to mean that you've fulfilled your end of the bargain?"

"I have. I hope you have held to *your* end of the deal and are prepared to gather your entire network?"

A cool smile spread over his face. "I have been in frequent communication with them since we last spoke, Lady Astor. My fellow lords are prepared to move and await only my word. Our mages have been gathering in the region since I first sent out the call."

"What numbers are we talking?"

He didn't hesitate. "Including myself, there are thirteen lords that represent the core of your grandfather's network. Between us, we own a significant portion of northern Shivasa. We control the country's internal trade networks almost entirely, though the level of our control has been obfuscated in various ways. There are nineteen mages loyal to our cause."

"Very good. How long will it take to bring them all together?"

"A week, no more." He smiled. "But first I require proof that you have achieved what I have requested."

"You'll get your proof when your network shows up, Lord Anler."

"That is not what we—"

She lifted a sharp hand to cut him off, voice cold and hard, fuelled with the intense dislike she felt for this man and her lingering grief over Laun. "I lost a valued warrior doing as you demanded, and I have no further appetite to accede your whims. I have your army and I expect you to take my word for it. If you want your cause alive, your army behind it, you will now meet *my* expectations. You should be in no doubt that I am very prepared to walk away from you if you test me further."

He gave her a long, considering glance. She held that gaze, cool and aloof, confidence oozing from her entire bearing as Fari had taught her. If she was to become the Darkmage, then she had to force him to her will. Her grandfather would have shown no further lenience.

Anler eventually bowed his head. "They'll all come here, if it suits you? And of course you're welcome to stay here while you await their arrival."

"That's fine. Thank you, Lord Anler."

Lira finally dismounted, stifling a groan as aching legs hit the ground. Grooms swarmed to take their horses, and Lira followed the others up into the house.

Some of the tension in her shoulders loosened. She'd forced Anler to fold. Egalion and the council hadn't caught up with her yet, and she was about to take another key step in her plan.

Now she just had to convince a group of proud Shiven lords and rogue mages that she could succeed where her grandfather had failed.

# CHAPTER 25

A nler's lords began arriving within days. All were cool and distant—clearly as unconvinced that Lira could take down the Mage Council as Anler had initially been. The mages were no different. Curiously, none were familiar to Lira. The mages Lucinda had introduced to her at Shadowfall Island when pretending to bring her into the movement must have been Lucinda's creatures. Rotherburnian mages.

Tarion had demanded a list of their abilities, and provided Anler had been honest, they were dealing with a handful of telekinetics, two healers, a single concussive mage—the rest would have been referred to as lesser mages by the council, having an assortment of abilities that would be of little help in a mage battle. It made Lira wonder how much of that fed into their desire to join Shakar's cause. Lira herself had always been bitter about her lack of power.

Watching them all arrive ... her plan unfolding before her ... Lira had known it would be an uphill battle to convince them, but the reality of it made her edgy, unsure of herself. She wasn't an imposing leader, or a particularly influential orator. Convincing these Shiven lords and mages to not only swear allegiance to her, but to also put their lives and wealth at risk to follow her in a war against the imposing might of the Mage Council ... she had to admit that it might be outside her capabilities.

But this was why she'd established her Shadowcouncil. She didn't have to do this alone. They could help her.

Once she had their allegiance, if all went well, she wouldn't have to hold it for long. Just enough to use it as the leverage she needed to build a force truly powerful enough to bring down Lucinda and her Seven.

While waiting for Anler's network to arrive, she spent a lot of time in the private study he had provided her for use, closeted with her Shadowcouncil. They deliberately stayed out of sight over the days of the lords' arrivals. Part of the show she was going to put on was in the aesthetics, using their anticipation of seeing the heir to the Darkmage and her Shadowcouncil in person to enhance her status and mystique.

Yanzi arrived four days after Lira. He filled them in on the activities of the Revel Kings as they gathered late that afternoon. A fire crackled in the grate, and a teapot steamed on the table between them. Snow drifted outside the window. It was as peaceful as Lira had felt in months.

"In short," he finished. "No problems other than the usual. No overt Mage Council interest in us, or the docks. The search for Lira has moved on from Dirinan and is currently focused in Tregaya, thanks to your Hunters."

Tarion leaned forward. "What about supplies for the Hunter base?" he asked. "The last thing we can afford is a hungry army."

Yanzi nodded. "We're working through a trader operating in the northern towns—but he only moves the supplies so far. He doesn't know the location of the base or who's there. I *am* getting some questions from the crew as to why we're acquiring and shipping so much food without any profit, however."

Fari frowned. "Manageable questions?"

"Your man Lorin is doing a pretty good job keeping the boys and girls under the thumb," Yanzi admitted grudgingly. "While I've been ensuring the crew is still running the usual cons and jobs. It will be fine for now. As long as we're still turning a profit overall, the grumbling will be nothing more than a minor issue."

"Once we have these wealthy lords on board, I expect them to dip into their coffers to support our army, so the Revel Kings won't have to do it too much longer," Lira said. If her plan succeeded, none of that would become necessary, but always, *always*, Lira spoke as if Lucinda's spy were in the room with her.

"That assumes we *do* get the lords on board. You've been pretty vague about how you're intending to do that, Lira," Athira remarked.

Lira sighed, sank back in her chair. "That's because I'm not entirely sure how I'm going do it."

For a moment they all looked stunned that she'd admitted such a thing. Well, all of them except Shiasta. It tugged at her heart that he merely looked ready to carry out what she asked, irrespective of its chances of success.

"Maybe if you told us what your plan was beyond 'get the lords to swear loyalty and then take over the Mage Council' we could help you with what to say to them," Athira said.

"Do that and she risks the council learning what those plans are," Fari countered. "Which you already know. Do you truly distrust Lira's intentions at this point, or are you just being irritating?"

Athira gave her a cool look. "I absolutely distrust Lira's intentions. I need to be completely satisfied that she is carrying out Lucinda's orders to the letter, which *you* already know. Who is the one being irritating?"

"What else exactly do you *think* I'm planning to do by gathering the Hunter army and my grandfather's network? The Revel Kings are risking arrest by running supplies out of Dirinan to a secret army. I just killed a Taliath at DarkSkull, attacked Rionnan naval ships back at Shadowfall, and I'm doing my darndest to keep us all hidden." Lira lifted an eyebrow, her casual demeanour belying how much she *didn't* want Athira asking that question. A good con was always about misdirection. If Athira called it...

But she merely scowled and acceded. "Fine."

Lira nodded, relieved. "I understand why you distrust me, but surprise is the only advantage I have. If the council learns what my plan is, we *will* lose. Then how is Lucinda going to save her people from being destroyed either by monsters or a very angry Mage Council wanting revenge for the murder of Dashan Caverlock?"

"I said fine. Let's move on." Athira didn't seem any more bothered by that prospect than she did by the idea of Lira betraying them. Lira didn't know what to make of it.

"I understand your tactical reasoning, Lira, but I have questions too," Yanzi said languidly. "Where is Vensis, and what is her role in this con, exactly? I continue to question what interest she has in any of this, and I'm growing increasingly uneasy at the length of her absence."

A knock at the door thankfully interrupted before Lira had to come up with a response to that. "Come in," Lira called out.

Anler appeared, bowing his head in a faint show of respect. "Lady Astor. The last of those I invited has arrived."

Lira's heart thudded. The time had come. "Thank you, Lord Anler. My Shadowcouncil and I will address them tomorrow morning." A little bit of waiting, building anticipation, would only help the theatrics.

He lifted an eyebrow. "Along with your army, I hope?"

"I assure you, after tomorrow morning, there will be no more room for doubts."

He smiled. "I very much look forward to it."

As he closed the door, Lira looked to the motley group surrounding her, ignoring Yanzi's question and hoping he'd let it go in the distraction of Anler's news. "Are you all prepared to be at your intimidating best tomorrow morning?"

Shiasta sat up straighter. Athira gave her an ironic salute. Yanzi grinned.

"Thanks to me, you've got the visuals down," Fari said. "But apart from your appearance being suitably terrifying, you'll need to sound like a charismatic villain looking to bring down the world order. Do you know what you're going to say?"

"Not besides the obvious—talk up my grandfather's vision, make a big deal of the fact I'm his heir, point to the Hunter army ... but that's all words, and I'm not sure if it will be enough. I don't have the presence

Shakar clearly did." She sighed. "But at least I have a whole night to dwell anxiously on it."

"Actually." Tarion spoke into the ensuing silence. "I have an idea of what to say that might help."

"Good." Fari rubbed her hands together. "Now get up out of that chair, Lira, and start talking. We're going to practice until you've got the best speech in the world running smoothly off your tongue."

Yanzi leaned forward in his chair, dark eyes twinkling. "This is going to be fun."

Lira dropped her face into her hands and let out a miserable sigh.

It was going to be a painful afternoon.

Early the next morning, Tarion found Lira in the barn, where she stood outside Alfie's stall, keeping him quiet company while he happily munched away on his morning's grain.

Clad in a velvet midnight blue jacket over black tunic and breeches—all tailored perfectly to his tall frame. Silver buttons adorned the jacket and the buckle of the belt that held *Darksong*. He looked tall and darkly handsome, leaner than his Taliath father, but just as graceful, and with more of an edge. It wasn't just the whispering blade at his hip—today some of the monster gleamed at the back of his hazel eyes.

For her. He was uncaging it for her, because he knew she needed them to make an impression of strength.

"Thank you," she said simply.

He looked her up and down, giving her a crooked smile. "Well, Fari certainly got rid of the rats' nest."

"Don't you start," she warned.

Her boringly brown hair was slicked back behind her ears, curling slightly at the ends, highlighting her sharp features—those of Shakar Astor, her grandfather. Muttering something about vertical lines making her look taller, Fari had dressed her in a long violet jacket that fell just above her ankles, over knee-length kidskin boots that had a discreet heel. Jewels glittered on the buttons, hem, cuffs, and collar of the coat. It fit so snugly it was incredibly uncomfortable, its high collar threatening to cut off her air supply, but Lira had to admit it *did* make her look taller, the collar accentuating the severity of her face.

"Shall we?" He offered his arm.

She smiled a little, remembering that night on the steps of Temari Hall, where she'd offered *her* arm to escort him down to the party so he wouldn't feel the pressure of so many eyes on him alone.

The Lira back then would have resisted such support returned in kind, would have dismissed it as a weakness, something that could only hurt her if she allowed it.

This Lira took his arm without hesitation and felt the stronger for it. "Let's do this."

Fari, Yanzi, Shiasta, and Athira waited for them in the foyer. Fari had done an amazing job with all of them. She and Yanzi looked like Zandian royalty in brightly coloured silks, both their eyes darkened with kohl that made them look as dangerous as they did elegant. Athira wore velvet tunic and split skirts in shades of green, her blonde hair in a perfect braid coiled at the back of her head. And Shiasta was dressed much like Tarion, his dark clothes stark against his pale Shiven skin, the weapons he carried today jewelled and expensive. Her heart clenched at how powerful and capable he looked.

Anler's steward stood there, too, speaking as soon as she appeared. "They're waiting for you, Lady Astor."

She sent a single questioning glance at Shiasta. He nodded. Her shoulders relaxed.

"Thank you, Herin, we're ready."

The steward led them through the house to the formal dining room where Anler had gathered all the lords and mages. Herin paused with his hand on the door handle. "My lord has dismissed all staff from this area of the house. You will not be overheard. I will remain out here to ensure it."

"Thank you, Herin. Please announce us."

He bowed, then opened up the doors and stepped inside, voice ringing out. "My lords, Lady Lira Astor and her Shadowcouncil."

Lira swept in, shoulders straight, head up, Shakar Astor's aloof arrogance firmly set in her expression. She came to a halt at the head of the table, Fari and Tarion standing at either shoulder, with Shiasta, Yanzi, and Athira along the wall behind them.

Her quick glance noted the arched windows lining the wall to her left, letting in the wintry morning sun, the long table, and the thirteen cool, unblinking gazes of the men sitting around it. Their dress and posture instantly marked them as Anler and his lords. The mages stood gathered along the wall at the other end of the table, far more rumpled in appearance. All gazes were fixed on her. She wondered how long they'd give her to make her case before dismissing her as not worth their attention.

Hesitating wasn't going to help.

*You can do this Lira.*

"I am Lira Astor, granddaughter of Shakar Astor, the Darkmage." She spoke clearly, using the cool, arrogant tone she'd been told was so like her grandfather's. "I am the most skilled telekinetic mage alive. I also have fire ability and the ability to manipulate water. Both those abilities can penetrate Taliath and Hunter invulnerability to magic."

To give the effect to her words, she raised both hands in the air, allowing her magic to wreathe her hands and forearms in violet-edged white flame. Its fiery crackling broke through the silence of the room. At the same time, she drew the water out of the jug sitting in the centre of the table, twirled it around in the air, then placed it neatly back inside without losing a drop.

She extinguished the flames, lowered her arms, and let her display of magic settle for a moment. None of the lords were particularly expressive, but she didn't miss traces of surprise in some, interest in others. A handful were unmoved. The mages looked fascinated—they'd all unconsciously taken a step forward during her display so they could see better.

She smiled inwardly. She had them already. Now, the lords.

"Unlike my grandfather, I have diverse allies. Powerful ones. And *that* is why I'm going to succeed where he failed twice." She smiled coolly, then inclined her head in Tarion's direction. "Lords, mages, meet my Shadowcouncil."

Tarion took one graceful step forward and drew *Darksong*. It whispered its melody through the room, dark and beautiful, instantly capturing the lords' attention. "I am Lord Tarion Caverlock of Rionn. I am both mage warrior and Taliath, and I carry Shakar's Taliath sword. I am heir to a council seat and to the general of Leader Astohar's armies."

He held the blade out for a moment longer, correctly reading the lords' and mages' fascination with it, before spinning and sheathing it in a single, devastatingly quick move, and stepping back to his place at Lira's side.

"Fari Dirsk." The healer stepped forward next, a marvellous combination of stunning and haughty in her Zandian silks. "Single heir to the most powerful pureblood mage family in Zandia. I bring the weight of my family's strength and influence behind Lira Astor."

"Athira Walden." She was short and sharp. "Single heir to both a Mage Council seat and one of the most powerful and influential Tregayan pureblood families."

Yanzi swaggered forward last, the feathers in his ears swinging. His hand caressed the dagger sheathed at his waist. When he spoke, everything about him exuded dangerous criminal, including the edge he gave his voice. Silver-tongued indeed. "Yanzi Ardesk. I run the most powerful criminal gang in Shivasa. I already own the docks in Dirinan, and within a year I'll have the whole city paying tithe to me."

Again, Lira let those introductions sit for a beat or two.

"These are powerful men and women, my lords, fellow mages, and they bow to *me*," Lira said. "You can see I already have the foundations of a new council, one that can reach well beyond Shivasa. That's more than what my grandfather had."

"You won't take the Mage Council without force of arms." One of the lords spoke up. Lord Roan, the same age as Anler, just as tall and spare. She'd memorised Anler's list of names and descriptions—it hadn't been easy given how similar they all were to each other. How had her grandfather ever thought this narrow group of interests could ever succeed at taking over anything? "Your words are pretty, but you don't have the magical strength to counter theirs."

"Agreed, Lord Roan." She settled a long look on him, then glanced over her shoulder. "I introduce you to the fifth member of my Shadowcouncil here today. Shiasta?"

He moved gracefully to the door, opening it and calling out a soft order. One by one, all twelve Hunter unit leaders walked through the door to line the walls surrounding the dining table. As instructed, they all had the left sleeves of their shirts rolled up, and now lifted their arms in the air to show the black tattoos etched on the inside of their wrists.

Surprise and fear both rippled through the lords. They understood what those tattoos meant. They understood what Lira's presence here *with* them meant. They no longer had control of the killers they'd brainwashed and trained.

"I couldn't bring all three hundred and twenty-five Hunters here for obvious reasons," Lira said. "But I hope this convinces you that I have full control of the entirety of your Hunter army."

"How did you find them?" Anler asked sharply, a light on his face that she thought might be dawning hope. "And where are you keeping them?"

"At a safe location, which is all anyone needs to know."

"Good," he said firmly. "I will admit you have surprised me, Lady Astor, and I'm sure my fellow lords too. You are closer than we could ever have imagined to achieving our shared vision."

"Closer, yes," one man spoke up. Lord Prosin. The man Anler had told her would be most resistant of them all. "But three hundred-odd

Hunters and some influential mages and criminals doesn't win us a war against the Mage Council."

"My grandfather waged open war with the council twice and failed both times," Lira said. "I don't plan to repeat his mistakes. You're right, we won't win a war. Instead, we will cut the head off the snake before they even see us coming. We will do things differently, my lords, and this time we will win."

One of the mages stepped forward then, a tall and gangly young man. "How exactly do you plan to do that?"

"What is your name?" she asked him.

"Terrens. I speak for this group." He waved a hand. "I have concussive ability."

Ah, the strongest among them. She took a breath, dispelling the anxiety that wanted to rise. She was coming to the crux of it now ... had she done enough already to win them? She was about to find out.

"I will not tell you. Not yet. The council has powerful telepaths at their disposal, and I don't know any of you well enough to trust you with the details." She paused. "I can tell you that I do have a plan. One that takes advantage of our strengths. One that I am confident will succeed."

Prosin's mouth curled. "You ask us to have faith, to risk our lives and homes, on someone we don't know."

"That's exactly what I'm asking." She held his gaze. "You followed my grandfather on faith and trust, and you will have to do the same with me."

"Lady Astor isn't asking us to trust her on words alone," another lord spoke out. "She has made demonstrable steps already."

A brief silence fell, then Anler spoke. "Once the Mage Council is gone, then what?"

For him, her strongest ally so far, to still question her ... they still wavered.

Lira had expected that, though. As with any good show, she hadn't yet revealed her best hand. She tugged a creased parchment from her jacket, unfolded it, and laid it out on the table. "Lords, I understand that you control a large portion of Shivasa's wealth. *I* control the beginnings of an elite army. The only thing missing is the people supporting us. What you see before you is a list of those villages still loyal to our vision. Once we topple the council, it is these people who will allow us to *hold* our power, making Shivasa an unassailable base of support."

She paused, watching them glance at each other, saw the dawning hope in Anler's face begin to be reflected on others.

"Assuming we give you our faith and trust, that we swear allegiance as you've asked," Terrens said, holding her gaze. "Talk us through what it looks like once you cut the head off the snake."

She didn't hesitate. "I replace the Mage Council with my Shadowcouncil. We will control the mages, and then, one by one, we will subdue the kingdoms under our rule. First will be Shivasa—I estimate we can take it within weeks given our combined control of Dirinan harbour and the Shiven trade networks."

At her words, anticipation rose through the room in a series of shifting seats and rustling clothes, heady, almost palpable. Intense hunger replaced doubt and suspicion in their eyes.

She held those looks, then played her trump card, what Tarion had suggested the previous day. "And once Shivasa is ours ... well, our very next step will be to take what has *always* rightfully been yours. Rionn. Alistriem will burn, my lords. Port Rantarin will belong to you again."

Her words were followed by energetic nods. Anler shared a look with Prosin, then looked at her, holding her gaze without hesitation. "A sound plan, Lady Astor, and one I think we can all get behind."

Lira smiled, cold and triumphant.

She had them.

# CHAPTER 26

L ira stood on the battlements, shoulders hunched against the bitter cold, breathing in the still morning air. The old Hunter base was surrounded by a carpet of stark white after a heavy snowfall the night before and the trees of the surrounding forest were equally laden with it. Every now and then there was a distant thud as a clump of snow fell from a tree branch to the ground, but otherwise everything was eerily quiet.

Almost like the world was holding its breath.

There was no reason for her to be out here. Hunters manned the walls and patrolled the forest surrounding the base. It was too cold to be comfortable. But she hadn't been able to stay indoors any longer, had needed to feel the endless sky above and the fresh bite of winter air.

Lira's gaze settled on the single set of tracks in the otherwise unbroken carpet of snow, hoofprints that marked Shiasta's departure earlier that morning. Her Hunter had been away from the base tracking more Hunters ... those who'd still been undertaking their training when Leader Astohar had learned about the program, and who'd escaped Anler's purge.

But the news he'd brought with him had anxiety eating at her bones.

The Mage Council's search for them was shifting away from Tregaya and back to Shivasa. They'd figured out the false trail Lira's Hunters had left for them. Soon, Egalion, A'ndreas, and any other telepath at the council's disposal would be honing their efforts on Lira's location.

She stared harder out at the snow, the forest, wondering if Taliath and mage warriors were creeping through it towards them right now.

It was foolish thinking. Her Hunter scouts would have picked up the approach of any attacking force. But she couldn't help worrying.

If they were found, they'd have to run, but there was nowhere like this to flee *to*. They'd have to break up into smaller groups, which would make coordination of her forces much more difficult. Without a secure base, they'd be on the run from council mages constantly, always looking over their shoulders.

She had Egalion's secret to wield ... but given even Lucinda hadn't been able to wield it as a successful threat against her, Lira worried that it might not be enough to make her back off entirely. And if Egalion found them, it would all be over.

The success of winning the loyalty of the Shiven lords was a double-edged blade. She needed them, but she'd awakened their bloodlust, their hunger for power. After so long waiting, the realisation that victory might be in their grasp had galvanised them. She'd promised them she had a plan, but now they wanted to see it enacted.

Anler kept pressing her to announce themselves to the world. To make the new Shadowcouncil public knowledge, to begin instilling fear in those loyal to Astohar and joy in those loyal to her and her grandfather. But if she did that, it would only widen their exposure, increase the threat of being discovered.

To succeed where her grandfather had failed, she'd insisted, they needed to surprise the council, take them unawares. It was a point she kept re-iterating, and for now it was working. But Anler's patience would run out eventually ... their confidence in her turning to doubt.

Lira had to move, and soon. She had gathered all the pieces she needed, balanced in a fragile house of cards. But to carry out what came next, she needed the skills of her Darkhand, a general to lead her army in a strike that would land the blow that changed everything. Lira didn't have the mind to pull that off. She wasn't even sure that Tarion did, but she might have to turn to him soon.

Because there had still been no message from Ahrin.

Surely she'd managed to break free of Lucinda by now? Or had Lucinda proved too much of an adversary even for Ahrin Vensis? Lira's stomach churned at the thought, grief and fear making it momentarily hard to breathe.

Her musings were disrupted by Tarion's appearance, his long strides carrying him quickly towards her. "Any reason you're voluntarily freezing yourself out here?" he asked, huddled inside a thick cloak.

"I needed to think."

"Ah. I find thinking clearly much easier when I'm warm and comfortable, but that's just me."

She managed a small smile, but it faded quickly. "How long do you think we have?"

"Gathered all together like this? Weeks, at most." Tarion didn't sugar-coat the truth. "Aunt Dawn and Mama working together will find us here now that they're re-focusing on Shivasa. It's just a matter of when they turn their search on the north of the country."

"We need to move before then, break up into smaller groups to make it harder to find us." She let out a breath. "But go where?"

He gave her a searching look. "Whatever your plan is, you didn't bargain for needing to stay ahead of the council much longer."

"No," was all she said, then she turned to him. "What brings you out here in the freezing cold anyway? Nothing is wrong, I hope."

A concerned look came over his face. "Not exactly, but ... a message came for you."

Lira's heart thudded, stopped, then resumed with a too-quick beat. "Who delivered it?" she asked carefully, taking the folded and sealed parchment from him.

He frowned. "I assume it was one of your Dirinan folk, a message from Yanzi or Lorin. A non-descript man on an equally non-descript horse passed it to a Hunter on the front gates not long after Shiasta left this morning."

"Did the messenger *say* he was sent by Yanzi?"

"No, he said he'd been sent by Jessin." One of the Hunters in Dirinan with the Revel Kings. "So I assumed Yanzi or Lorin is the ultimate source. One of our scouts trailed the messenger for a while to be extra careful, but he didn't do anything out of the ordinary, just headed back in the general direction of Dirinan."

Lira turned from him, fingers trembling, and ripped open the note, her gaze devouring the brief contents. Once she was done, she stared unseeing out at the snow, holding herself rigid in an attempt not to betray what she was feeling. The relief made her momentarily light-headed.

"Should we be worried?" Tarion asked when her silence drew out. "If that messenger knows where we are, and he's not from Yanzi or Lorin, then ... is something wrong?"

She spun, shoving the note into the pocket of her jacket and meeting his gaze. "No, we're fine. I've been waiting on this message. I have to go. You're in charge until I get back."

Surprise flashed over his face. "Wait, *where* are you going? What's in the note?"

"I can't answer either of those questions, not yet," she said. "I'll be back inside a fortnight. Tell the rest of the Shadowcouncil to begin preparations for moving out of here, and send a message to Anler that he and the network should prepare themselves too."

His eyes widened in realisation. "The note is a signal. That's what you've been waiting for before making your next move."

"It is. At least, I hope so." Either that, or someone was setting a finely laid trap.

"Not that I doubt you in any way, but all we've got right now is a few hundred fighters and a group of old—albeit wealthy—Shiven lords. And you think now we're ready?"

"If this is what I hope, I'll soon be able to tell you the whole plan. Can I ask you to trust me until then?"

He smiled. "You can."

She returned his smile and pushed past him. "See you in a fortnight, Tarion."

"What if the council find us while you're gone?" he called after her.

"If they're a small enough force, take them out. If not, retreat to Dirinan. I'll find you there."

"And what about Athira?"

"Figure out something to tell her that doesn't make her suspicious—tell her I needed a break or something."

"Lira!" Exasperation tinged his voice. "Take one of the Hunters with you, at least."

"I can't. Besides, nobody would expect the most wanted traitor in the continent to be travelling alone. I'll be safer this way."

That was only part of the reason. What she was doing needed to remain secret from every single person in her small army. One leak and it would all be over.

Hope burned in her chest even as she fought to douse it with rational thought.

She might finally be able to make her move.

# CHAPTER 27

Lira rode hard and fast, pushing Alfie at a gallop until the big horse's strength flagged, then chafing at the slower pace until she eventually had to stop to let him graze and drink. Then more galloping. She tried to rest when Alfie did but struggled to do so. Hope and anxiety twisted her stomach into knots and set her shoulder muscles rigid with tension. Her thoughts wouldn't quiet enough to sleep.

Dirinan was a welcome sight on the horizon when Lira approached it as dusk fell on her fifth full day of riding. None of the other travellers on the main road in had looked at her with anything more than passing interest. Clad as she was—she'd switched the violet jacket for one in grey, but otherwise wore her expensive wardrobe—she looked like a wealthy young woman; not too rich to be overly important, but enough to have her own fine horse.

Once through the gates, she found a decent, non-descript inn where she paid for a room and a stall for Alfie. Once alone in her room, she changed into the clothing she'd carried in her saddlebags: weathered breeches and shirt and a winter jacket patched at the elbows. Boots worn thin at the toes. Feeling instantly more like herself, she slipped out the window and into the night.

Part of her was tempted to head to the harbour district gambling hall, check in with Yanzi and Lorin and make sure all was well with the crew. But it was better they not know she was even in the city. Not yet, anyway.

Everything she'd done so far—since that morning at the ship's railing coming back from Rotherburn—had been about carefully managing the information flow, speaking *always* as if Lucinda's spy was watching. No matter who it was, there had been nothing in her actions so far to make them think she was doing anything but carrying out Lucinda's orders. But tonight, everything was going to change.

Her feet padded the familiar streets of her childhood as she slowly weaved her way into the lawless harbour district. She took care to keep her head down and out of sight as much as possible, not wanting any of the gangs to recognise her or mark her as an interloper in their territory.

As she grew closer to her destination, her pace slowed, her focus on making sure she wasn't being followed ... and that she wasn't walking into a trap.

Nothing seemed out of place, and her instincts were quiet, not warning of any danger unusual to being in this area of the city after dark. Hope began to beat a steady tempo in her chest...

Once she reached the street across from her destination, she pulled the now-crumpled parchment from her pocket and re-read the instructions. It was a nervous habit—she'd already memorised them—but despite her increasing confidence that the note was genuine, she knew she could potentially be walking into a trap.

The house was quiet, sandwiched as it was between multiple other identical houses in the street. They were only two blocks back from the northern side of the harbour: a rundown district in desperate need of repair, and home to dockworkers, sailors on long shore leave, and criminals. The Revel Kings had owned this patch when Lira had lived here last.

After a final hesitation, Lira tore the note into tiny pieces and scattered them on the ground before using her boot to grind them into the foul-smelling puddle at her feet. Then she crossed the road in quick strides, both hands curling slightly in her pockets as her magic stirred in readiness.

She made quick work of the locked front door—a simple mechanism that conceded quickly to her telekinetic magic—then ducked inside and closed it behind her. She found herself in a narrow foyer, lit only by the moonlight coming from a room off to the right. That room was empty, no furniture, nothing. Dust and other detritus littered the floor. A set of narrow wooden steps rose immediately in front of her, leading up into a dark second level.

After casting a longer glance at the front room to make sure she hadn't missed any indications of an ambush, Lira started up the stairs. They creaked loudly, announcing her presence to anyone inside, so she gave up on the pretence of stealth and allowed her violet mage light to glow around her hands in warning. Eagerness beat at her, threatening to override her caution.

At the top of the stairs, a landing led away to the right, a door standing open at the end of the hall. To her left a closed and locked door was only two steps away. Lira went right, strides quickening, her heartbeat growing louder as it beat faster in her chest.

If this were a trap, she would bring down the entire building on anyone trying to ambush her like this. And then she'd burn them alive.

She took one step inside the room at the end of the corridor, eyes scanning the interior, sliding past the two uncurtained windows, the dusty floorboards, the equally empty walls, to...

"You took your time. I expected you hours ago."

All the breath left Lira's lungs in a rush, and for a moment she couldn't move or speak, so profound was her relief at the sight of Ahrin Vensis standing in the corner of the room, arms crossed, staring at her with a little smile.

"You're here." She swallowed, had to lean over and brace herself on her knees for a moment when her legs threatened to buckle in relief, then she was straightening and flinging herself across the room.

Ahrin met her halfway, and they collided furiously, stumbling, almost falling over with the force of their embrace. Lira closed her eyes and buried her face in Ahrin's neck and decided she was never going to let go ever again.

"I'm here," Ahrin eventually murmured, holding on just as fiercely. "And it wasn't easy, I tell you."

"I knew you would get out." Lira whispered against her skin. "I was so scared for you, but I knew."

Ahrin eventually pulled back a little, one hand lifting to push Lira's hair behind her ear, the other still curling around her hip. "I admit to experiencing mild concern about you as well. You're all right?"

"Better now." She nodded, trying and failing not to get lost in the delight of seeing Ahrin's face, breathing in her vanilla scent. "You?"

Ahrin's eyes were dark, and there were shadows under them, but she nodded. "I am."

Lira leaned in, pressed her mouth to Ahrin's, eyes sliding closed in bliss. And then she remembered ... what Lucinda had claimed, what Anler had confirmed. And even though Tarion had made some good points, even though she'd *agreed* with them, now that Ahrin was here it didn't feel so simple. She pulled away, guilt writhing inside her.

"Something wrong?" Ahrin frowned, trying to pull her back in.

Lira stepped away instead, putting some space between them. "How did you get away?" Even though she'd believed it possible, had faith in Ahrin's skill and smarts, she couldn't envision *how* it could have happened. Lira doubted she could have done it.

"That's a very long story, and one that can wait for another time because we have too many other things to discuss." Her voice turned businesslike. "What's your play? I assume you have one."

Lira went over to the window, staring down to the street below, then took a breath and began explaining. It was the first time she'd spoken her ultimate plans out loud, and as she said the words, she winced at how flimsy it all sounded. How unlike her. How foolish. But at the same time, it was such a relief to be able to say it after months of having it locked inside her mind. Once she finished, she turned to Ahrin. "You see why I needed to wait for you."

Her Darkhand was silent, gaze inward as she thought through what Lira had told her, not betraying any particular shock or surprise ... or contempt. Lira hoped that was a good sign. Eventually Ahrin moved, coming to join her by the window. "It's not bad. You've kept the details sufficiently locked down, provided you made the right call on your allies, and I can certainly do what you need of me." A flicker of a smile. "I taught you well."

"But?"

"It's rather a large betrayal." Ahrin didn't sound bothered by this, just curious.

"Isn't that the reason I was born?" Lira said bitterly. "To betray everyone and everything."

Ahrin scoffed at that, ignoring her petulance.

Lira cleared her throat, pushed her maudlin thoughts away. "You know I'll do anything to see Lucinda burn, but that has blinded me in the past. This way seemed different ... something she wouldn't see coming."

Another flicker of a smile. "I agree. I applaud the ruthlessness of it too, even if I don't like how close it brings you to the council."

"I need them to defeat Lucinda. I can't do it alone."

"You *have* learned," Ahrin said approvingly. "But you're still taking a risk, a gamble that the council will—"

"I know." Lira dismissed that with a wave. "But now that you're free, Lucinda is a bigger problem. We'll have to move quickly to convince her we're still doing what she wants. If she doesn't believe she has any leverage over me, she'll act to try and regain it unless she thinks I'm still following her orders."

A little smile played at Ahrin's mouth. "She won't be as certain as you think that she's lost her leverage."

Lira grinned, delight seeping through her. "What did you do?"

"When I escaped, I made sure there was a pursuit, and I made sure that my pursuers saw the boat I escaped in crash into the rocks and disintegrate. Lucinda will suspect I survived, of course. But what she *won't* know is that I timed my escape for one of Rilvitha's fortnightly stops." Ahrin paused. "Thank you for that, by the way. I had to hope you'd pay her to keep coming."

"I knew you'd get out, it was just a matter of time," Lira said simply.

"Well, I was off that island under the cover of darkness and before Lucinda could get any patrols out to look for me. No search party will be able to find me, and she won't be able to figure out how I got off the island, so she'll likely assume I either died in the crash or got eaten by monsters up on the surface."

Lira let out a breath. "And in her mind, even if you did somehow make it back, she's always been convinced you'd betray me, so she won't know for certain that we've reunited."

"Exactly." Ahrin paused, her wicked smile widening.

"There's something else." Lira narrowed her eyes, fighting back another smile. "You only grin like that when you've done something particularly impressive and you think I'm going to be awed."

Ahrin winked. "I brought you a present."

# CHAPTER 28

"**C**ome with me." Ahrin took Lira's hand, tugging her down the dark hallway to the room at the top of the stairs with the locked door. Orange flamelight spilled out when she unlocked and opened it, and once Lira was inside, she saw why—there were no windows in this room for the light to betray their presence to anyone outside.

But that was her second thought. The first was stunned recognition at the sight of Dashan Caverlock sitting in a chair by the fire. His ankles and wrists were locked in manacles, but apart from some cuts and bruises on his hands and face, he looked alive and well.

Like Ahrin, though, he was pale, eyes shadowed, and he had a restless energy about him. At the sight of Lira, anger clouded his face.

"You got him out with you?" Lira turned to Ahrin, both impressed *and* awed.

Ahrin shrugged. "I needed someone skilled enough with a boat to get us out of the ravine city, then make it look legitimate when we crashed, without killing both of us. We got back to that abandoned fishing village, held out there for a night, and Rilvitha appeared right on schedule just before dawn the next morning."

"At which point your Darkhand ordered the crew to take me prisoner," Dashan snarled. "After I saved her life."

"He was quite useful, I admit. Boat handling is not among my many skillsets." Ahrin turned to Lira. "He fits quite nicely with your plans, no?"

"As long as we keep him hidden until they're in play," Lira said thoughtfully. "I don't want Lucinda's spies reporting him appearing here alive and well, or she'll know you're alive too."

Dashan shook his manacles furiously, interrupting their conversation. "I don't particularly care what you want, Astor. *I* would really like to go and find my wife and children. You can't hold me forever."

Lira met his gaze. "I'd rather have your cooperation, but I think you know by now I'm not averse to killing you if you try anything stupid."

Fury rippled across his handsome features. "If you think for a second that I'm willing to sit here and cooperate with Shakar's granddaughter when I don't even *know* if my family is safe—"

Lira cut him off. "I am willing to answer all your questions. *After* you agree to calm the hell down."

He paused, mid-tirade, eyes narrowing. Lira recognised the signs of battling a temper that wanted to burst free and waited him out. Eventually he gritted, "Even if I did agree to be nice and docile ... when can I see my family? Your Darkhand refused to tell me anything."

Lira summoned magic, readying it. Between her and Ahrin, she was confident they could contain the world's greatest Taliath even if he did manage to break out of his shackles, but she didn't underestimate how difficult it would be, and they wouldn't be able to do it unscathed. "Lucinda made a deal with your wife and me. We take control of the Mage Council, make it a tool of hers to use as she wishes, and she keeps you and Ahrin alive. I agreed to the deal, your wife did not."

Panic, despair, all of it flitted over his face. "Is Alyx okay?"

"As far as I know," Lira said. "But I *am* going to take over the Mage Council, Caverlock. And you need to be out of the way until it happens. I give my word here and now that I will not hurt your wife, your son, or your daughter, unless in self-defence."

He wasn't stupid. "You're going to use me as a bargaining chip."

"Something like that."

"Why bother? I'm free, Ahrin is free." His dark Shiven gaze turned to Ahrin. "And she wouldn't be here without me. Lucinda holds no leverage over you or Alyx anymore. You don't need to do what she wants."

"I didn't agree to what Lucinda wanted to save Ahrin. I knew she could save herself." Lira stepped closer to him. "I agreed because it's what *I* wanted."

He frowned, studying her. "I never bought into the fear that you were just like your grandfather. It's just not logical. I'm one to know—I spent years terrified I'd turn out just like my father. And I still don't believe it, Lira Astor."

"That's where we're different, Caverlock," she said softly. "Now, do I have your word that you will remain here and not try to escape? If you agree, we can make things more comfortable for you."

His gaze shifted between Lira and Ahrin, his expression shifting from anger to realisation; as powerful a warrior as he was, he couldn't take them both together.

"You give your word that Alyx, Caria, and Tarion will not be touched. That you won't hurt them no matter what ... that even if your life comes under threat from them, you find another way to defend yourself." He held her gaze, eyes hard. "You swear that, and I will give you my word to remain here."

"I swear it." She nodded. She'd already made the same oath to Tarion, willingly, so it was an easy bargaining chip to give away. Ahrin gave her a quick sideways glance but said nothing.

"Alyx will crush you," he said quietly, not like he was threatening her, but warning her. "You know that, don't you?"

"She's already tried once." Lira smiled bitterly. "But I'm not so easy to kill, and if I get what I want, it won't be necessary for either of us to die."

That was when he saw the staff hanging down her back, and he went white. "You didn't—"

"No, she bloodied me up pretty good," Lira admitted. "But I will hold to my oath next time we meet."

"I wish I could trust you." There was no anger in his voice now, just pain.

"Tarion is with me." The words spilled out before Lira could stop them, and even Ahrin shot her an astonished glance. Lira had already told her that Lorin, Fari, and Tarion had chosen to join her, so she assumed Ahrin's surprise must have been about her willingness to tell Caverlock.

Dashan's gaze turned thoughtful. "He knows what you plan to do, and he chose your side?"

"He did."

Another brief silence, then, "In that case, if I'm to sit around waiting until you complete your no doubt criminal machinations, I'd like some creature comforts please." The man's demeanour had completely changed. From anger and despair to cheerful bonhomie. "Some ale, to start with. Lots of it. Fresh bread and a wheel of cheese ... a bowl of olives. And a comfortable bed. These manacles can come off too, at your earliest convenience."

She huffed an amused breath. "I'll do what I can, but those shackles are staying. I'm not a complete idiot."

At that, Ahrin, who'd been silent this whole exchange, opened the door and slipped out.

"She's something, your girl," Dashan settled back in his chair. "I don't know how she escaped—I spent hours trying to figure out a way out of my cell and failed miserably. But there she is one day, unlocking the door to my cell as if in the middle of a country stroll."

Lira shrugged. "Your girl is something too. I assume you know about her big secret? The one about being able to breach Taliath immunity."

He stilled. "How do—"

"Lucinda knows. That's the bigger problem, don't you think?" Lira paused. "Has Egalion told anyone else?"

"Just me. My Taliath invulnerability means nobody can read it in my thoughts." He leaned towards her, urgency in his gaze. "Lira, you can't tell anyone. You know what the consequences would be."

"It would crack open the Mage Council, again. And that would happen because, despite your wife and her friends' best efforts, the mage order remains an intolerant and narrow-viewed entity at heart. It needs to change, Caverlock."

His urgency faded to consideration. "What are you planning, Astor?"

Lira didn't reply. She left the room, locked the door behind her, then trailed Ahrin back down the hall and into another room with a closed door. This one had no lamps either, but moonlight shone through its single window. An old bed covered in blankets sat in the corner, but the room was otherwise empty. A musty smell hung in the air.

Ahrin was pacing back and forth. When Lira entered, she lifted her head. "What if I don't agree with how your plan plays out?"

Lira spoke carefully. "Would you do what I need anyway?"

Ahrin stiffened slightly, gaze turning to stare out the window, voice cool and distant. "I'm not your tool, Lira."

"That's not why I asked." Lira hesitated, stomach plunging in fear. She didn't want to have this conversation, was terrified of where it would lead ... but she'd done enough to Ahrin. She couldn't let it go any longer, not now that she knew. "I know that you bow to nobody, that you've already stood by me more than you probably ever wanted to—"

"That's not—"

"Was that by choice, Ahrin?" Lira forced the words out. "Or was it because you were brainwashed as a child into being loyal to me?"

Ahrin was biting her lip so hard, Lira unconsciously reached up to touch it with her thumb, an awkward attempt to soothe her. "Tell me the truth. Please."

The Darkhand yanked her head away from Lira's touch. "Why are you asking me this now?"

"I found my grandfather's network, the ones who created you. I learned the phrase." She choked on the words. "It was the first thing I ever said to you, and I had no idea."

"What phrase?" Ahrin asked carefully, midnight eyes glittering. Quiet menace oozed from her, something that quelled anyone Ahrin directed it at. All but Lira.

"I spoke to one of the lords who ran the Hunter development program. He told me the trigger phrase that you were conditioned to respond to. The one that, when spoken aloud to you, forced your loyalty and obedience."

Ahrin had gone so rigid it was like she'd turned into a stone statue, her eyes black as night. In a movement so abrupt Lira didn't see it happen, she broke away to stride across the room. "And, what, now you think I've been under your control since the night we met?"

"No! At least, I hope not. But I have to ask." Her voice sounded desperate.

"How could you..." Ahrin paused, ran a hand through her hair, uncharacteristically agitated. "How you could *ever* believe that? That all these years I was just a dog following your whistle?"

"Ahrin, I don't—"

"Is there anybody in your entire life that you *don't* doubt, Lira? Do you truly think everything between us was a lie, something you forced me into?"

"I am terrified that it was," she cried out, tears welling in her eyes. "The thought that I might have caused you pain all this time, that I might have been the cause of you almost dying against your will, it's unbearable."

Ahrin simply stared at her, cold fury on her face.

"I used the phrase, Ahrin," she said helplessly into the silence. "On you, the person most precious to me in this entire stupid, rotted world. What else am I supposed to think?"

Ahrin's anger vanished at that, replaced with weariness. Tiredness. A sadness Lira had never seen before. "The brainwashing never worked fully on me." She eventually spoke the words, clipped and brusque. "I hid it from them as soon as I realised ... managed to keep it a secret by pretending obedience. It's how I was able to get out before they killed us. In fact, when we met in Dirinan and you told me your name, I almost killed you then and there for what had been done to me."

Lira stilled. "Why didn't you?"

"Because in that same moment I saw *you*. I saw your toughness, your determination, your will to survive. It was like a bright burning beacon inside you. I held back for reasons that have nothing to do with who your grandfather was, and everything to do with who *you* are, Lira. I saw someone I wanted with me always. I didn't understand why, or how, not after an entire life of knowing nothing but violence and hardship. But I still knew."

Lira was silent a moment, throat closing over, then, "The best thing that ever happened to me was meeting you that night."

"You mean that?" Ahrin's eyes had gone dark.

She didn't hesitate. "Yes."

"I won't ... *this* won't ever be normal. Not like what everyone else has. No house and yard and kids and reading books by the fire at night."

"I—"

"I'm not going to do everything you want, or be your tool, because I'm *not* brainwashed to follow you. I'm not going to tell you I love you more than once a year, or smile sappily at you, or stay my hand just because you ask it." The words came out of her in a rush, and she stepped closer, till there was no space between them. "But I want you so much. I always have. Only ever you."

"And I want you." Lira held her gaze. "I want everything you are, no changes, nothing different. Just you, Ahrin. I am happy as long as you are with me, in my world, no matter *how* that looks. So we'll figure it out."

Ahrin closed the remaining distance between them and kissed her, and Lira's eyes closed in sheer delight at the taste of her after so long apart. Ahrin's hands went straight for skin, and clothes came off quickly. The mattress was unexpectedly soft, Ahrin's skin even softer, her touch a live flame. "I choose you freely, Lira Astor. I always have."

Many hours later, sweat-slicked and languid, Lira lifted an eyebrow and looked at her Darkhand. "How did you survive the fall into the river? I only survived it because of my water ability."

"I *didn't* fall into the river." Ahrin smiled slightly. "I learned that trick of yours with telekinesis, using it on yourself. I'm not as skilled as you, but mid-fall I managed to throw myself against the cliff face where I could grab onto an outcropping in the rock. The impact knocked me senseless and dislocated a shoulder. It was a long time before I could manage to start climbing upwards, and by then you were all long gone."

"Why didn't you come after us?"

"That would have been a foolish move. I had no way of knowing where you'd gone, and I was alone in the dark without supplies or the ability to penetrate razak immunity with my magic. I judged it smarter to head back up to the city. I thought I could use the time until you returned learning more about Lucinda and the Seven, figure out a weakness we could use to attack her." Anger rippled over her face then. "I didn't expect to be captured the moment I got back. Not anticipating that was my error, and a stupid one."

Lira let that settle for a moment, then turned to her, serious. "I'm pretty sure Lucinda has something else in play."

Ahrin listened as Lira explained about what Tarion had seen being carried onto their ship by Athira, then taken ashore into Dirinan. Once Lira was done, Ahrin nodded. "It makes sense. Lucinda always has a backup plan. She knows full well you'll be looking for any way of getting out of her hold on you and wants something in place for if you fail."

"It's a problem."

"It's a *big* problem." Ahrin agreed, stretching. "Even if your highly risky plan succeeds, even if you lock it down well enough that she doesn't catch wind of it ... even if you *win*, Lira ... she has something else in train that you know nothing about."

Lira let out a sigh. "Will you willingly and voluntarily be my Darkhand until I see this thing through, or will you leave tonight and return to your crew? Whichever you choose, I accept it, though I hope you know if you leave, I'll be tracking you down as soon as it's all over."

Ahrin rolled towards Lira and pressed a kiss to her mouth. "I will stand at your side, Lira Astor, until this thing is done. I like the idea of being the Darkhand of the Shadowcouncil again. Like I always told you—leading them is *our* place."

Lira closed her eyes, relief making her body feel lighter than air. "Good."

"But I will not take orders from you."

"Agreed."

"And when this is done, we will decide, *together*, what comes next."

"Also agreed." Lira opened her eyes again. "And since you've already said yours for the entire year, let me repeat here and now, that I love you too, Ahrin Vensis."

Ahrin considered that for a moment. "Now that I'm not trapped in a cage, hearing that gives me a pleasant kind of warmth. And delight. It's really rather odd. Say it again."

"Nope."

"Go on."

"If you're only saying it once a year, then I'm only saying it once a year. You can wait another twelve months to feel your odd feelings like a normal person."

Ahrin laughed, deep and melodic, Lira's favourite sound in the entire world.

"I thought you were dead after you went off that precipice," Lira said a few moments later, staring up at the ceiling.

"This isn't turning sappy is it?"

"No." Lira turned to look at her. "It just made me realise some things, that's all."

"What things?"

"Maybe one day I'll tell you." She snuggled closer, closed her eyes. "Wake me at dawn? We have to get back to the base. Now that you're back, I can finally move. And not a moment too soon. The council is closing in on us rapidly."

She chuckled again. "It's already almost dawn, Lira."

But she was already falling asleep, content and warm. Happy.

# CHAPTER 29

"**Y**ou sure you're ready?" Ahrin asked as Lira prepared to leave the safehouse. It was well after dawn.

Lira scoffed. "You think I've forgotten how to run a con? I'm insulted. I *was* managing just fine until you bothered to show up."

Ahrin flashed her a quick smile. "You haven't run a con without me before, Lira Astor."

"Well, I learned from the best."

"Just remember. Enough truth to make it believable. You can let things slip that Lucinda will already know, or be expecting you to learn, to help maintain the trust you need."

Lira fixed her with a look. It was exactly what she *had* been doing.

Ahrin lifted her hands in the air. "Fine. You go deliver the news that you're ready to make your move. If your spy is here, then that is something they'll want to report to Lucinda right away." Lira had given Ahrin her list of possible spies the night before; Fari, Lorin, Yanzi. It had made her stomach sink when Ahrin had firmly agreed with her theory that one of them had likely been a spy from the beginning. "I'll watch them and see if anyone makes a move. Then I'll come after you."

Lira hesitated. She needed more surety about who the spy was before moving ahead, but the risk of Ahrin being spotted by anyone in the crew, let alone the spy, would have even worse consequences. But after a moment she shook her head—Ahrin didn't get spotted when she didn't want to, and she knew these streets even better than Lira. "Good, and Caverlock?"

"Before I leave, I'll make sure Jessin is sorted here to babysit him. I don't trust him, despite him giving his word, but she'll make sure he stays secure."

When the Darkhand had arrived in Dirinan, she'd immediately co-opted one of the Hunters working with Yanzi's crew. Jessin, conditioned to obey only Ahrin and Lira, was the ideal go-between who could be implicitly trusted to keep Ahrin's presence a secret from everyone.

Lira leaned up to kiss her. "Ride safe. I'll see on you the road."

Lira took a circuitous route from Ahrin's safehouse just to be careful. She walked through the streets of the harbour district, making for the Revel Kings' gambling hall. Runners took off the moment they spotted Lira approaching the hall, so Yanzi was already walking out the front door and down the steps to greet her as she arrived. When he reached her, he swept into an overdone bow. "Lady Astor, how lovely to see you."

"You're ridiculous," she told him flatly, her mouth quirking at his theatrics at the same time as she felt a sharp pang. She didn't want it to be Yanzi, not the smooth-talking criminal who'd looked out for her, always, when they were crew. "Let's talk inside."

Lorin appeared the moment they walked into the main hall, a welcoming smile on his face. "Lira! It's so good to see you."

"And you, Lorin." She returned his greeting with a matching smile. Not Lorin either. Not the earnest young Shiven mage who'd stuck by her no matter what. Abruptly she felt tired and worn. Would her life ever be anything but a series of betrayals?

It would. She would make it different.

None of them said anything further, not until they were in the boss's office, the door closed firmly behind them. Sun shone through the window and cigar smoke scented the air. Yanzi immediately went to the chair behind the desk and dropped into it with a sigh of contentment.

Lira sniffed, but there was no trace of the sweet scent of cloudweed. Good.

"Is the plan finally in motion?" Lorin asked eagerly. "I feel like we've been sitting around here doing nothing for too long. Who knows what Lucinda has done to Ahrin by now."

"Hang on, what now?" Yanzi sat up straight and almost overturned his chair in the process. "How would Lucinda be doing anything to Ahrin?"

Lira caught her breath. Yanzi's response seemed entirely sincere, as if he truly was unaware of Ahrin's capture, which would rule him out as the spy. But he'd always been so good at acting...

Lorin meanwhile ... Lira shot him a furious glance. He paled, jaw tensing, but didn't compound his mistake by speaking any further. She turned her attention to Yanzi. "Ahrin and I have been running a play against Lucinda as part of my attempt to take the council down," she said. "You know that already."

"Yes, but what did he mean about something being 'done' to Vensis?" Yanzi asked the question mildly, but there was a dangerous glint in his eyes. Spy or not, it was all too easy to forget that the silver-tongued Zandian was as much dangerous criminal as anyone else here in Dirinan.

Lira avoided shooting another glare in Lorin's direction, despite how badly she was tempted. Best not to make it too obvious bow badly the mage had messed up. She scrambled for the best way to explain the situation, trying to keep her voice casual, unconcerned. "Ahrin is currently being held hostage by Lucinda in order to force me to carry out her wishes."

The Zandian's eyes widened. "Vensis let someone capture her? No way."

"Exactly!" Lira said, relieved by the opening he'd inadvertently given her. "Ahrin's capture was arranged in the interests of the con. But the situation is firmly under our control, trust me." She glanced at Lorin, tried to make her change of subject smooth, "And yes, I'm here to start putting our plans into motion."

Yanzi leaned forward then, rubbing at his eyes, clearly not swayed by her casual words. "Hold up. This con you and Vensis are running involves letting Ahrin be captured by Lucinda ... so that Lucinda will force you to do what you want to do anyway?"

"That about sums it up."

His face turned hard. "How exactly is that a con? You know what seems suddenly more likely to me? That Lucinda captured Vensis *in reality* and you're dancing to her tune to save her life. Vensis knows nothing about what you're doing does she?"

"How many more times do we have to do this dance, Yanzi?" Lira made her voice hard, cold. "Ahrin knows exactly what I'm doing. You keep baulking and she's going to hear of it. Am I clear?"

"I'm a dead man if you're lying to me, Lira." All the criminal was gone from his face and voice now, leaving the young man who'd once been part of a family she'd made for herself.

It wasn't Yanzi. He was genuinely terrified for his life and crew, she could feel it in his every tone and gesture, every word. He'd had no idea that Ahrin was being held by Lucinda.

Yanzi wasn't the spy.

Lorin had inadvertently done her a favour by letting slip about Ahrin's capture. But if *he* was the spy, surely he wouldn't have made such a mistake, one that risked losing Yanzi's support for Lira's venture?

It was all so murky. Lira took a breath, refocused on this moment, this meeting, before they started to wonder why she was hesitating.

"I won't let anyone touch you," she promised Yanzi, just as softly. "Ahrin *is* a part of this."

Lorin's voice broke the tense silence, then. "I assume once you've taken the council, your attention will turn to Lucinda herself?"

"Oh, she'll burn," Lira said. "Eventually. First things first, though." She turned back to Yanzi. "I'm headed back to the Hunter base. You stay in charge here until I return."

Yanzi looked puzzled. "What brought you here in the first place?"

She smiled, cold and vicious, laying the bait for Ahrin to pounce. "I came to let you know in person that I'm ready to move."

Lorin straightened, fierce glee flashing over his face.

Yanzi's smile beamed out, although it was a little more tentative than it had once been. "We stand ready to enact your world domination plans. You just make sure you do it right, Lira. You fail, and we're going to be in a world of trouble."

She nodded, turning serious. "Part of the reason I wanted to come and tell you in person—I recommend you start implementing contingency plans in case things don't go our way. Your crew knows how to protect itself, but it's time to start making those preparations."

"Understood," he said grimly. "We'll be ready to go to ground if the worst happens."

"Thanks, Yanzi." She gave him an encouraging smile. "And of course, the worse *won't* happen, so what you really need to prepare for is helping me and the Shiven lords take over Shivasa. You'll hear from me soon."

He gave her a salute, and Lira shifted her attention to Lorin. "Walk me out?"

Lorin fell into step with her as they left the office. Lira waited until they were halfway through the hall and two crewmembers passing through were out of hearing distance, before stopping and rounding on him. "That back there was a damned stupid mistake," she hissed under her breath. "Yanzi and the resources he controls are critical to what we need to do. You know that."

Regret flashed over his face. "I'm sorry, I didn't think."

"He has to believe we have Ahrin's authority, or we're done." Lira held his gaze. "Is that clear?"

His jaw hardened. "Very. I'm truly sorry, Lira. I'll fix this."

"You'd better," she snapped, and continued walking.

He followed, keeping his voice low. "Am I coming back with you?"

"No, I have a more important job for you." She smiled. "I'm going back to prepare the Hunters to move. Wait four days, then go to Lord Anler. Instruct him that he and all his lords and his mages need to be in Carhall by the appointed date. I want them there for when we claim victory."

Lorin's eyes gleamed. "I can do that."

"This is crucial, Lorin, which is why I'm trusting you with it." She held his gaze. "If I don't convince them I've subdued the council, I won't be able to leverage them for what I need to take Shivasa next. And I won't have them hiding in the shadows while I do the dirty work and then turning on me if everything goes wrong."

"I will make sure they're all in Carhall, every single one," he promised solemnly. "You can count on me."

"I will take the council as a sign of good faith and to prove my capabilities." She gave him a fierce look. "But you make it clear to the mages and lords both that my expectation is they'll be joining my army and fighting alongside me when we take Shivasa."

"Consider it done."

Sunlight spilled over them as they walked out into the street. "Once you've done that, I need you back here in Dirinan." She lowered her voice. "I trust Yanzi only so far, and for taking Shivasa I'm going to need to lean heavily on his crew in ways he may not like. Can I trust you to cover my back here?"

"I'd like to be there when you take the council, Lira."

His shoulders had slumped, so she reached out to touch his arm. "I want you there too, but you're one of my most trusted allies, Lorin. I need you here, or I might not succeed. Can you do that for me?"

"Always," he said simply. "You know that."

"The moment I've taken the council and made sure things are under control, I'll return here. Wait for my arrival. You'll be at my side for what comes next, I promise you that."

He smiled. "That's all I ask. Good luck, Lira."

Lira glanced back at him once as she walked away, making for the public stables where she'd left Alfie the day before. She couldn't help remembering that night at DarkSkull, Lorin screaming in pain as his leg was crushed, the reckless decision she'd made to sacrifice her escape to go and help him.

It still sat uncomfortably with her, that choice, but she no longer saw it as a weakness. A vulnerability ... yes. And vulnerabilities could be dangerous, especially in her world. But without them the world was a much colder place.

That was something she'd realised too.

# CHAPTER 30

A hrin caught up to Lira on the road five days later. Even though she knew the Mage Council searchers could be closing in on the Hunter base at any moment, Lira had deliberately lagged, wanting her Darkhand's report before arriving back at the Hunter base. Whatever news she brought, Lira wanted time to process it and decide next steps before speaking to her allies again.

"Well?" Lira asked as Ahrin rode up alongside Alfie, her mare giving Alfie a quick warning nip that he should keep his distance.

"Nothing. Neither Yanzi or Lorin made any unusual moves after you left the gambling hall, and two mornings ago Lorin left the city, heading for Anler's estate as you ordered."

"Could you have missed anything?"

"No."

Lira swore. "Rotted carcasses. If it's neither of them, then..."

Fari. Sorrow and despair washed over her—not Fari.

"I wouldn't be so certain. Whoever your spy is, Lira, they're good. So good that they've existed in your inner circle for years without tripping your instincts, *or* mine," Ahrin pointed out, then hesitated. "To have done that, they've had to *live* their cover for a long time, completely *be* the person they're pretending to. Part of them is your friend, Lira, and not a small part."

Lira gaped at her. "Are you trying to defend whoever it is?"

"Don't be ridiculous. I'm making sure that when the time comes to deal with them, you don't baulk because of sentimentality."

"I won't." she said, jaw tightening. "But before I can do that, I need to be certain as to who it is."

"Well, we can run the same play on Fari once we're back at the base."

Lira nodded, not wanting to say how sick that made her feel. "I think I've managed to rule Yanzi out at least." She explained what Lorin had accidentally done.

Ahrin took that in with a thoughtful hum but said nothing further. Presumably she wasn't convinced it was enough to rule Yanzi out either.

The Darkhand stayed cloaked and hooded as they rode, not unusual given the icy weather, keeping her features hidden from whoever they passed. Within a couple of days, however, they moved into the more isolated region of northern Shivasa and saw few others travelling the backroads in either direction.

"I went back to my village," Lira told her one afternoon as they rode at a walk, giving the horses a rest from a morning of galloping. Alfie trundled along happily, making sure to keep his distance from Ahrin's feisty mare, who liked to snap if he got too close or moved ahead of her.

Ahrin glanced over at her. "How did that go?"

"They gave me the information I needed. They told me what they could about my mother, too, how she died." Lira related the details. "Tarion thinks he's figured out who my father is."

"Oh?"

"Rawlin Duneskal."

Ahrin's grin flashed over her face, bright and beautiful. "That doesn't surprise me in the slightest. Tarion Caverlock has a brain, doesn't he?"

Lira glowered at her. "Thank you."

"I always knew you were pureblood mage, Lira. You were the one who refused to see it," Ahrin said, then, "Well, that will help with what you're planning."

A moment's silence passed before Lira spoke again, "I almost killed Anler. Barely stopped myself, actually, and only because I wanted you to have the right."

"My, you're chatty this afternoon."

Lira looked over until Ahrin met her gaze. "Once this is done, I'm going to figure out how to break the conditioning. I want them to have choices, Ahrin, like you."

The Darkhand thought about that for a moment. "It won't be easy for them. I hope you understand that. It's been difficult enough for me, and I had the ability to fight myself free of the conditioning. Life for them is simpler in many ways. They don't need to think about what to do or why. Giving them choices won't give them the ability to understand how to *make* choices."

"Do you think it's the wrong thing to do, then?"

An even longer silence passed then Ahrin steered her horse closer, reached out to take Lira's hand, tangle their fingers. "No. I don't."

Lira hesitated. "I wasn't sure if you would want me to take away their conditioning, their loyalty to you."

"I am one of them, Lira." It was all she said, urging her mare back away as her ears went back and Alfie snorted nervously.

"I won't abandon them either," Lira promised. "I hear what you're saying, and I'll do what I can to help them adjust, to learn."

Ahrin flashed her that wicked smile. "After you free them, I *am* going to recruit them, though, to come work for me."

"As long as it's their choice. They can choose whatever life they like."

Ahrin gave her a considering look. "Like you want to."

Lira looked up, startled. "What do you mean?"

"That's what all this is about, isn't it? You've finally figured out you're not Shakar Astor, and you're not a council mage either. You're trying to work out what being *you* means."

"I ..." Lira thought through those words, testing them. "Maybe."

Ahrin abruptly changed the subject. "What are you going to do about this counter-plan of Lucinda's?"

Lira sighed. "I honestly don't know. Do you have any advice?"

"Only the obvious. You need to know what it is, and you need to know before you move on her. Otherwise, you'll be caught blind, just like we were in Rotherburn, and that didn't turn out so well for us."

"Yes, but how? We don't know where the package was carried, or what was in it. We have no way of finding out."

"You do know what the goal is, though. She wants to rule this continent. It's a convenient way of saving her people, or at least giving them a safe home, but what she really wants is the power."

Lira gave her an irritated look but played along. "So whatever it is, the plan achieves that goal. And it assumes I've either failed at taking over the council and am dead or imprisoned *or* I've betrayed her in some way and am no longer doing as she asks."

"Yes."

"But my current plan is very carefully structured so that she thinks *neither* of those things. If it succeeds, we'll take her before she realises anything has gone wrong. Surely that will stop her from instigating her backup plan."

Ahrin gave her a look that suggested trusting in that would be the height of foolishness. She was right.

"I hear you, but the best I can do is take her by surprise, and ensure that before I do that, all her pieces here in Shivasa are taken off the board. That at least limits what she can do," Lira said.

"To make sure, she has to die, Lira, and she has to die the moment you have her. None of this compassionate prisoner-keeping."

"Oh, we both agree on that, don't worry," Lira said coldly.

They waited to approach the Hunter base until after nightfall, and once it was dark enough, they left the horses and Ahrin weaved them through the cordon of Hunters out patrolling as if she knew the pattern by heart.

Which she probably did.

They aimed for the southern wall, where the location of the moon meant the area along the base of the stone was cast in shadow. The two of them climbed quickly, pausing at the top until the patrolling boots of Hunters passed by. Then, they had only a handful of seconds to scramble to the top, cross the battlement, and drop down the other side, so they went one at a time.

"You need to fix that gap in the patrol quick," Ahrin muttered as they crouched amidst the snow piled up against the inside of the wall.

Lira nodded, then rose and led Ahrin towards one of the back entrances. It wasn't going to be possible to sneak past the Hunters guarding all doors into the base, but she was glad to see it was Therob standing still and silent outside the barred door she'd aimed for, leading into what would be empty kitchens at this time of night.

"Lady Astor. Commander Vensis." His eyes widened when she and Ahrin appeared out of the darkness. "You're back."

Lira held a finger to her lips, murmuring, "Nobody is to know we're here. That's a direct order, do you understand?"

He bowed without hesitation. "Yes, Lady Astor."

"Let us in please, and quietly. How long are you on watch?"

"Till dawn," he replied as he unlocked the door and cracked it open, ensuring it made no noise.

"Good. I'll be coming back this way before then. Keep an eye out for me."

He saluted, then closed the door behind them, plunging them into darkness. Lira made her way through the kitchens, Ahrin close behind, and up the servants' staircase to the floor where she and the rest of the Shadowcouncil had their rooms.

It was the work of seconds to pop the interior latch on Tarion's door and slip inside. He woke almost instantly, hand reaching for *Darksong*, before he saw it was Lira. Once again, she placed a finger at her mouth, warning him to stay quiet.

He nodded, then murmured, "Everything okay?"

"Very okay. Can you teleport and fetch Fari? Make sure you don't wake Athira—that is *critical*, Tarion. She can't know we're meeting."

He nodded and vanished from sight. As he did so, Ahrin entered, pushing off her cloak and going over to the windows, checking to make sure the curtains were fully drawn and there were no gaps. At one point she glanced over her shoulder, murmuring, "He's a good second for you."

Lira read the implication clearly—Tarion was a good replacement for the time when Ahrin would no longer be at her side. "I won't need one, if this all goes as planned."

By the time Fari and Tarion reappeared in the middle of the room, Fari looking slightly nauseous from the trip, the Darkhand was pacing the floor by the unlit fireplace.

"This is all very cloak and dagger." Fari yawned. "Though I'm glad to see you, Lira ... is that *Ahrin Vensis* pacing a hole in the floor, or am I still dreaming?"

Lira couldn't help a smile. "Shush. Nobody can know either of us is here."

"Ahrin, my da, what happened to him?" Tarion's voice was low, but urgent.

Ahrin glanced at Lira, who gave a little nod. "He's fine, little Caverlock. Alive and somewhere safe."

Tarion's gaze narrowed. "What does that mean?"

"He's safe and well, I promise you," Lira reassured him. "If you could please be patient and hear me out before peppering us with questions, I'll explain everything."

Tarion shivered. "It's freezing in here. I'm guessing lighting a fire is out?"

Ahrin fixed him with a look. "You want Athira or one of the Hunters noticing a light under your door at this hour and wondering what's going on?"

He grinned at her. "In that case, come on over here."

Tarion clambered back into his bed and lifted the thick quilt he'd been sleeping under in invitation. Fari immediately crossed the room and scrambled onto the mattress beside him, crossing her legs and dragging the quilt around her shoulders.

Lira shrugged and followed suit, settling in on Tarion's other side, Ahrin following reluctantly while muttering, "This has just gone from cloak and dagger to ridiculous. What are we, having a cosy midnight friend chat?"

"You don't have friends, Dearest, remember?" Lira nudged her under the admittedly warm doona. "Friends make you feel odd feelings."

Ahrin pinned her with a scowl.

Tarion ignored the banter, his gaze meeting Lira's. "Tell us everything."

And she did. Well ... she told them most of it. Even now, she couldn't afford a telepath on either side reading their thoughts and learning too fast what was going to happen. "You've probably already gathered by now, and I've said as much to Anler and his lords, but I don't plan on waiting until we're powerful enough to face the council on open ground and defeat them in battle. It didn't work for my grandfather and it's not going to work for me. We're going to take them by surprise instead."

"A targeted attack." Fari glanced at Ahrin. "That's why you've been waiting ... you needed our Darkhand."

"Precisely. Ahrin commands the loyalty of the Hunters, and she was literally trained for this. We've spoken, and she's already come up with a plan of attack."

"That's ... you *planned* for Ahrin being able to escape Lucinda and get herself back here?" Fari hissed. "That's either a foolish gamble or a big leap of faith. I'm not sure which."

"Nobody can hold me for any length of time," Ahrin said simply.

A beat of surprised silence then Tarion's eyes went wide. "You're ready *now*, aren't you?"

Lira couldn't help it; she grinned. "Damn right I am."

"What is this plan exactly?" Fari enquired.

Ahrin glanced at her. "Essentially, we're going to skip the pleasantries and go straight for the throat."

Silence filled the space again, and Fari and Tarion shared a quick look.

Fari frowned. "I'm sorry, but I have to ask the obvious question. Why are you still doing this if Ahrin is free and Tarion's father is safe? Lucinda has no leverage over you anymore."

"She doesn't know that." Lira explained the precautions Ahrin had taken in escaping.

"Even so. You don't have to do what she wants anymore, Lira," Tarion said quietly.

Lira took a breath, wondering if this was the moment that everything fell apart. She could do what came next without Fari and Tarion, probably, but it would be much easier with them. And deep down, she couldn't help but want them with her. Want them to choose to stand with her. "I'm aware that neither of you have a good reason to do this, to put your lives and futures at risk. But that was true when you decided to help me back on that ship, and you knew then it wasn't just about Ahrin. Nothing has really changed. I ask you to stay with me."

Ahrin had stiffened slightly at Lira's side, and neither Tarion nor Fari missed it, though they clearly misread the reason for it.

"Is that why she's here?" Fari asked quietly. "To execute us if we say no?"

It was Ahrin who responded. "I have no orders to kill or hurt you, and no desire to do so either."

"Why not?" Fari looked startled.

"I..." Ahrin didn't look sure, but then said, "You are Lira's friends. You have stood by her when I couldn't. You have protected her and lent her your strength, and you have clearly been worthy of the trust I told her not to place in you. I will not hurt you."

Lira reached out, took Ahrin's hand where it rested beside hers, tangled their fingers together.

"Unless of course you try and hurt her," Ahrin added, cooler this time. "Then I'll gut you like a fish."

Fari giggled, then clapped a hand over her mouth to stop the noise.

"Lira..." Tarion let out a long breath. He looked conflicted.

"I meant what I said about leaving now, so the both of you need to be sure." Lira looked at them. "When we're in that Mage Council chamber, you need to be completely with me. You can't break in the middle of it, or we'll lose."

Tarion and Fari shared a long glance. Eventually Fari turned back, looking troubled. "You won't kill unless necessary?"

"That promise is easy to make. I will only use violence when I need it to win the day. It's part of the reason I'm doing it this way rather than building up arms for an open war."

Fari let out a long sigh. "Lira ... when I told you back on that ship I would join you, I meant it. But I no longer understand what we're seeking to achieve now Ahrin and General Caverlock are free. Is bringing your grandfather's vision to life really what you think is the best thing to do? *I* don't want to see people like Anler and his lords ruling Shivasa, even if us forming a new Mage Council might ensure better outcomes for mages."

Lira took a breath, took strength from Ahrin's hand still tangled in hers. "If *any* telepath happens to find your minds between now and when we attack, I need the only thing they see in there to be my intent to bring down the council."

"*Any* telepath...," Tarion said slowly, realisation dawning in his eyes. So clever, her best friend in the world. "I see."

"I don't." Fari snorted.

"What Lira is saying is that it is imperative that Lucinda, or anyone working for her, including a telepath, believes that Lira is still carrying out her wishes," Tarion said carefully.

"But why do you need..." Fari trailed off, eyes widening. "Because in reality you might *not* be—" She cut herself off. "Better for me not to think about why, because you don't want a telepath to see anything else in my head apart from the fact we're on our way to take down the council."

"Exactly." Lira shifted closer, holding her gaze. "Lucinda has to burn, Fari. You and I both know that—she's a threat to everyone here. And you've also seen how dangerous, how effective, how clever she is. To defeat her, I need full control over every bit of fighting strength the council has." It was close to the full truth, and Fari read the sincerity in her face.

"My head officially hurts," she said mournfully. "But all right. I can get behind that. I just hope by doing what is necessary to defeat Lucinda, we're not making things worse in our world."

"Before you make a decision, here's the plan," Lira said. "We leave the day after tomorrow. Fari, Tarion, Athira, and myself will ride separately with Shiasta. The Hunters will move in units—some via Karonan to pick up their medallions—and we will all rendezvous in Carhall."

Tarion's eyes widened further. "You're going to attack the council building."

"We're going to take it over," Ahrin corrected. "And we're going to hold the Mage Council hostage until they submit to our wishes."

Fari cleared her throat into the silence that followed. "That's it? That's your big plan?"

"That's most of it." Lira shrugged.

"What about Anler and his lords?"

"They're moving too. I've told them they need to be in Carhall, ready for when we take over ... they won't be part of the attack, but they'll be there afterwards to help us claim victory, to see us win, and to help guide the new leadership."

Tarion started talking, "You won't be able to hold the council building for more than a day, maybe two at most. Then the Tregayan militia will be on us—not to mention all the mage warriors and Taliath in Carhall—if we don't contain them straight away."

"We don't need to hold the building for more than a day," Ahrin said. "We only need to hold it for a few hours."

"How do you plan on achieving council submission in just a few hours?" Fari asked.

"Through fear," Lira said quietly. "I can't tell you the exact details of how, just to be safe, but I do have a way of getting it done, and it is going to be brutal. Especially if they resist."

She let that sit for a moment, making sure they heard and processed it, before saying, "This is the part where you can walk away if that's what you want. No questions asked, no offence taken."

"What about my da?" Tarion asked.

"Once it's done, I'll ensure he's reunited with your mother, I promise you, Tarion," Lira said. "Nobody in your family will be hurt if I can help it."

His gaze shifted to Ahrin. "You really got him out?"

She shrugged. "I needed his help to navigate the rapids and make the boat crash look real. He left Rotherburn with me on Rilvitha's ship."

Tarion still didn't seem sure. "You could have killed him once he was no longer any use to you."

Ahrin gave him a sharp look. "Like Lira, I don't kill for the fun of it. Only when it serves my purposes. He is your father, and as I've already said, I am not unaware of your importance to Lira."

Tarion lifted his hand, offered it to her. "Thank you for getting him out. I love my father more than I can say. I am glad to have you standing with us, Ahrin Vensis."

Ahrin inspected his hand like it was a particularly disgusting piece of rotting offal. But after a moment she reached out and took it, giving it a single sharp shake before letting go.

"Are you sure?" Lira's gaze snagged on Tarion. By deciding to stand with her, he was agreeing to take down the Mage Council, something both his parents had fought for, and making that choice knowing his father was safe. As much as she'd hoped for it, she didn't understand how he *could* make that choice.

He inclined his head. "I have faith in you, Lira."

Fari rubbed her forehead. "My head still aches, but if you're asking me to trust you, then I do. I hope I don't come to regret it."

Presumably having had enough of the heart-to-hearts, Ahrin abruptly moved, sliding off the bed. "I'm going to stay hidden in this room until you move for Carhall. Lira is going to sneak back out but ride through the gates first thing tomorrow as if just arriving back from Dirinan. Any questions?"

"What do we do with Athira?" Fari inquired.

Lira cleared her throat. "When I arrive tomorrow morning, we'll go through this whole song and dance again. A secret meeting, just you and me and Tarion, but Athira and Shiasta will be present this time. I'll lay out the whole plan again, leaving out Ahrin's involvement. You and Tarion will do your best to look surprised and ask me all your questions again." Lira shrugged. "We'll then make sure Athira has the opportunity between here and Carhall to get a message off to Lucinda to let her know I'm doing exactly what she wants me to do."

"And Yanzi and Lorin?"

"I gave them their instructions before leaving Dirinan. They're ready too." Lira left it at that. Each person involved in the con now knew what they needed to, whether wittingly or not. It wasn't easy, keeping so many differing strands alive in her brain, but having Ahrin with her now made it so much easier.

Fari stood too. "This is really happening, huh?"

"It's really happening," Lira said soberly.

"I'm scared," she admitted. "I trust you, Lira, but I really don't like how uncertain all this is."

"Do you have a plan in place for if we fail?" Tarion asked, gazing shifting between Lira and Ahrin.

"You mean if we fail and are still alive and not in prison?" Lira lifted an eyebrow. "Ahrin and I flee, we take the Hunters, and we keep running. Tarion, you go back to your parents, who will protect you. Fari, you will be welcome with us if you choose."

"We won't fail," Ahrin said before either of them could reply. "I'm the one leading this attack. I don't do failure."

"Well, that's an excellent point." Fari cracked a smile. "Okay, I'm off to get some sleep before all the play acting required tomorrow."

"I'll walk you out." Before leaving, Lira met Ahrin's gaze. The Darkhand gave her a little nod.

Fari would be watched like a hawk. If she tried to get a message to Lucinda to tell her that Ahrin was alive and with Lira, they would know. And Lira would have confirmation of her spy. And now that Fari knew Ahrin was alive, she would be dealt with before any message could be sent—they simply couldn't risk it.

As they stepped into the hall, Fari glanced towards the closed door of Athira's room. "What are we going to do about her?"

"Once we win?" Lira asked. "I have some thoughts, but there are a few complications." Not least of which was that Athira probably knew at least some of the details of whatever backup plan Lucinda had in place.

"We can't hurt her, not after everything she went through." Tears glistened briefly in Fari's eyes. "We got to go home, Lira. She never did."

"I know." Lira reached out to touch her arm. "We'll make sure she's okay."

"That doesn't sound very Lira-Astor-like."

Lira smiled at her. "Why, because it doesn't sound like Shakar Astor?"

Fari matched her smile. "Touché. All right, you'd best get out of here before someone sees you. Try not to freeze to death and I'll see you in the morning."

Lira's thoughts were full as Therob ushered her back out the kitchen exit and she climbed the walls and slipped through the gaps in the Hunter patrol. Once she made it back to Alfie, he butted her with his nose, pleased to see her again.

She was about to go at the Mage Council. And in the process pull off the biggest con of her life.

Out here, in the dark and the snow, the thrill of danger rose up through her, potent enough to warm her through despite the cold. A smile tugged at her mouth, spread across her face as she let it free.

Lucinda thought she was bringing down the council.

The council thought she was bringing the Darkmage's vision to the world.

Neither would see what was coming next.

She couldn't wait.

# CHAPTER 31

L ira strode down the middle of Centre Square, violet coat swirling around her knees, back straight, shoulders square.

Tarion Caverlock walked at her left shoulder, Fari Dirsk at her right. Athira Walden two paces behind. They all wore clothing as rich as hers, but simple, comfortable for fighting in if needed.

Tarion, moving with the grace of a Taliath warrior, wore *Darksong* at his hip. His face was calm, his shoulders straight, no trace of the discomfort that had once always been present in his bearing. Fari's mage staff hung down her back, Zandian arrogance in every inch of her expression, while Athira looked as if walking into the Mage Council chamber was just an ordinary task on an ordinary day for her. Which it probably had been once upon a time.

Lira fought the urge to search the square for Ahrin, who would be there, waiting and watching, ready to make her move. It was enough to know her Darkhand was there.

They'd received plenty of glances as they left their inn near Centre Square—they'd arrived in the city the day before in vastly plainer attire to ensure they attracted no notice—and walked into the bustling square. People clearly wondered who these four young people were who walked with such confidence, such obvious mage power, yet weren't wearing the tell-tale blue cloaks of council mages. Lira ignored them all, her gaze focused unerringly on what lay ahead.

The domed roof of the council chamber loomed ahead, towering over the other buildings of the square. It soared several stories high, and it, the pillars, and window edgings were all engraved in silver and blue marble that gleamed as brightly as the surface of the square.

And then, on her right, the council mage prison where Lira had spent over two years of her life. She glanced up at the windows, quickly narrowing in on which one had been her cell.

Things were so different now. And, as much as she'd spent endless hours in that cell planning for an eventuality like this, the reality was nothing like *any* of the plans she'd made in that tiny room.

Her gaze shifted to Athira, and she gave the woman a small nod. Athira peeled off without a word, heading towards the prison. As she did so, others loitering along the edges of the square, dressed far more plainly, fell in behind her. Therob's unit of Hunters.

The mage warrior guards stationed at the main doors to the council building shifted their attention to Lira and her companions the moment they broke free of the crowds thronging the square and started up the steps. They were halfway up before Lira and her party were close enough to be recognised.

Lira didn't give them the opportunity to react.

She summoned the magic she'd been gathering with every stride across the square, wrapped both guards in her telekinesis ability, and sent them soaring high above the crowds before dropping them halfway across the square. They landed in a tangle of limbs and cloaks, winded and bruised, but alive.

Shouts of alarm broke out at once.

The crowd in the square began scrambling away in all directions. The two warrior mages staggered to their feet, adding to the yelling as they raised the alarm, running back towards the steps. Militia soldiers guarding the Centre Square gates ran towards them.

Ignoring the hubbub breaking out behind them, Lira and her companions reached the top of the steps and walked through the open double doors into the council building.

The shouting behind them grew louder, more alarmed, more and more voices adding to the cacophony. Lira waved a hand, and the front doors slammed closed behind them, cutting off the sound. Then she used a quick, more focused, burst of magic to turn the locks. It wouldn't hold the mages long, but she didn't need it to. She just needed to delay them.

She spared a quick thought to hoping that all the other pieces of Ahrin's plan were moving as expected—now that they'd begun, there was no way of knowing until it was too late if something failed—then focused her thoughts entirely on what came next.

Now inside, Tarion took the lead without comment, leading them across the entry foyer and taking a right turn down a wide, wood-panelled corridor. As he did, a loud pounding on the main doors started up.

A set of arched double doors stood closed at the end, and two more blue-cloaked mage warriors stood guard before it. They'd clearly heard the ruckus because their staffs were drawn and they looked wary, ready to deploy magic. The mage to the left challenged them the moment they came into sight.

"I don't know what you think you're doing, but council is in session. You stop right there, or—"

Lira gave Tarion a small nod. He blurred out of existence, reappeared behind the mage speaking, and placed a knife at his throat. It happened within a heartbeat. The mage's words died, eyes widening in fear. The mage opposite him dithered, half lifting her staff then halting, clearly not knowing what to do. Her face was white with shock.

Lira came to a stop a few paces in front of them.

The second guard spoke, swallowing. "You're Lira Astor."

"I am. Fari?"

Fari walked over to the mage and touched her shoulder. A moment later her eyes slid closed and she crumpled to the floor. She did the same to the guard Tarion was holding, and he stepped away, sheathing the knife before lowering the man's body to lie beside his companion's.

Lira glanced back. The loud banging on the front doors was rapidly increasing in volume and intensity. She was surprised nobody inside had heard it yet and come to see what the fuss was about.

As Tarion stood from settling the second guard gently on the floor, a loud crash reverberated down the hall—the front doors smashing open. The sound of shouts and running feet spilled into the quiet hallway. Seconds later, mage warriors and armed militia soldiers appeared around the corner.

Lira turned to the doors in front of her and threw her telekinesis against them. They flew inwards, crashing into the walls either side.

It was all about the theatrics. To take power she had to show power.

Tarion and Fari fell into position behind Lira as she stalked through, and as soon as they were all inside, she sent the doors slamming closed again. One part of her focused on using a thread of magic to hold them closed, but the majority of her attention was on the room before her.

Stunned silence pervaded the space.

A round table sat in the middle of the domed chamber; the eight overly ornate chairs set around it filled with mage councillors wearing blue cloaks. No other furniture or adornment filled the cavernous space. The galleries overlooking it from above were equally empty. Good.

The shocked silence quickly shattered as the mages and soldiers outside reached the doors and proceeded to do their best to break through. One of the mages out there had telekinesis—Lira felt their magic push against hers, trying to force open the doors. She fed more magic into her efforts, holding the other mage off. Whoever it was couldn't match her skill or power with telekinesis. For now, anyway. But it was a constant drain on her energy.

Lira kept her breathing even, thoughts focused. She could do this.

Alyx Egalion was the first councillor to rise to her feet, expression furious, magical energy crackling around her. She looked like she was about to pulverise Lira then and there, one hand already lifted, concussive green magic flaring in her palm, until her gaze landed on Tarion. She went white. "Tarion?"

"Mama." He inclined his head.

"Councillor Egalion." Lira drew the woman's attention away from Tarion. "It's good to see you again." She channelled her grandfather's arrogance. "Before any of you decide to attack me, consider how close I am to Masters Duneskal and Walden and how quickly I can turn them into a human bonfire. Your precious Magor-lier isn't too far away for me to light up either."

At the mention of his title, Tarrick Tylender leaned back in his chair, a little smile on his face. "How long do you think you have before the guards outside break through and overwhelm you? Your magic skill might be superior to that of a single mage, but not a group of them, not as many as we have in proximity to this building. Not to mention the Taliath no doubt already on their way."

"Oh, but I can light up a Taliath just as well as anyone else." Lira smiled. "But you already know that."

"You're evading the point," Egalion said. "You can't defeat those in this room, let alone those who will come at you through the balconies above if the door proves too much of an obstacle. So what exactly is it you think you're doing?"

Lira kept her gaze on Tarrick Tylender, responding to his original question. "You mean, how long do you think *we* have?"

He chuckled, but then cast a disgusted gaze at Fari. "Did you really have to bring a Dirsk with you?"

Lira shrugged. "She sits on my Shadowcouncil. I'd take a Dirsk over a Tylender any day. They're far more willing to do what is necessary."

"What is going on?" Jamer Walden, Athira's father, demanded, gaze shifting between Lira and the doors. "Girl, I don't know what you think—"

"I'm here to finish the job my grandfather started and take control of the Mage Council." Lira cut him off. "Didn't Councillor Egalion tell you about the deal I made with the ruling Seven of Rotherburn? You've certainly been hunting me these past months like you knew about it. Or maybe you were hunting me because you're just as scared of me as you were of the Darkmage. Either suits my purposes just fine."

Walden sneered. "You can't just walk in here and take over the council. You've got maybe minutes before those outside break in. You're insane, just like your grandfather."

Lira moved towards him, slowly, as if she had all the time in the world. When she got there, she braced her hands on the back of his chair and leaned down to murmur in his ear, just loud enough for the others to hear. "My grandfather wasn't insane, Councillor. And neither am I."

The door thudded, and Lira closed her eyes briefly, needing a new burst of strength and focus to hold back the mage outside. Damn, he or she was persistent. Tarion's gaze flicked to her, concerned, but she gave a faint shake of her head. She could hold. If the other parts of her plan were going smoothly, she wouldn't need magic much longer.

A knowing smile played at Egalion's mouth, and she cast a glance upwards. "You haven't got long, Lira. Get on with whatever it is you're here for and leave my son out of it."

Lira held her gaze. Remembered Egalion and her council locking Lira away for life without a trial or a chance to defend herself. And smiled. "Tarion is with me voluntarily, as I've already told you. He's not my prisoner, and I won't hurt him, no matter what he decides to do."

"Tarion?" Egalion asked, though she never moved her gaze from Lira.

"I'm with Lira, Mama. My free choice." He spoke without a trace of doubt.

A beat of silence, then, "What do you want, Lira?" Egalion's voice turned to granite.

"It's simple. I want that chair." She pointed at Tylender. "And control of the Mage Council, just like Lucinda ordered, so that Ahrin is returned to me. Those who agree to that get to live. The rest can leave and never return or be executed."

"There has to be a vote," Rawlin Duneskal drawled. His supercilious expression dared her to keep challenging them, "to install someone new on the council."

Lira stared at him, momentarily wavering. Tarion thought this man was her father. She couldn't wrap her head around that ... he couldn't be. She shook her head, forced all distractions away. Then she laughed coldly. "And what possesses you to think the heir to the Darkmage is here to abide by a *vote*?"

"You plan to kill us all?" Egalion asked, glancing up again with a little frown. The balconies above were still empty.

"Not by choice. But if I have to, *if* you refuse to give me the council, then yes. You know I can."

"Not before I kill you," Egalion said.

"Maybe not, but it's not just you and me in here, is it? Unlike my grandfather and I, you're not willing to let anyone die for you. Not anyone *else*, at least." Lira moved closer to Egalion, savouring her slight flinch at the reference to Cario. "I could light up three people before you got your magic anywhere near me. Who are you willing to sacrifice first, Councillor Egalion?"

Her green eyes turned flinty. "You underestimate me, Lira."

"Do I?" Lira held Egalion's gaze for a long moment, the woman's silence giving her the answer she needed, then abruptly she shifted her eyes to Tylender. "Do I have your nomination to sit on the council?"

The amused smile was still playing at his mouth, but he nodded. "You do."

The ripple of shock around the table was almost palpable.

"What are you doing, Tarrick?" Egalion rounded on him.

Lira smiled. He'd done exactly as she suspected he would.

Which made what came next much easier.

Lira glanced upwards. The balconies were still empty. The cacophony of fighting beyond the arched doors had quieted to a muffle, too, but nobody in the council had noticed that yet. Anticipation began to creep through her then, fierceness, the first hints of triumph. She'd just gotten the confirmation she needed from Tylender, which meant it would only be moments now before ... she took a deep breath in, waited, and then...

Almost simultaneously, the councillors started, one letting out a groan. Egalion took a step back, eyes clouding over in concentration. Lira herself took a moment to ride out the instinctive panic of losing access to her telekinesis magic. But then she relaxed.

Nobody inside this chamber could access their magic anymore. Nobody except Lira and Egalion. The main doors stayed closed even though Lira wasn't using magic on them anymore.

"I can't access my magic," Duneskal said uselessly, glancing around as if the answer to what was going on would suddenly appear out of thin air.

"What have you done?" Egalion asked Lira, hands clenching and unclenching.

Walden looked at Lira. "*You* did this?"

Lira ignored him, instead nodding at Tarion and Fari. Each began moving, circling the council table to the left and right, drawing the attention of the councillors. She turned her gaze to Egalion, giving her a knowing look. Were the circumstances dire enough for the woman to reveal she could still use her magic?

"Lira Astor can have a seat," Tylender said into the increasingly fearful silence. "She can have my spot as Magor-lier too. Who else votes with me?"

The silence deepened. It was thick with confusion and fear. But nobody voiced support for Tarrick's nomination. Lira almost felt sorry for them. *Almost.*

"What a shame," Lira drawled. "I had so hoped to avoid bloodshed. Unless of course you're all willing to vacate your seats and leave now? That option remains open to you."

"Tarrick, what is going on?" Egalion demanded.

"Why haven't the guards come?" Duneskal finally noticed how quiet it had gotten beyond the doors. His gaze flicked between Lira and the empty viewing balconies above, his calm demeanour beginning to fray.

Lira could have hugged him for the utter perfection of his timing.

Because the very moment he spoke, sending every councillor's gaze upward to the galleries, was the same moment Lira's Darkhand appeared at the central balcony overlooking the Magor-lier's chair.

With a single, graceful, move, Ahrin swung over the railing and dropped to the marble floor below. She was dressed all in black, long coat falling to her ankles, dark hair loose around her shoulders. Violet trimmed her cuffs, her only nod to Lira's position. She wore her predator's smile, and danger thrilled in the air around her.

"How are we progressing?" she asked Lira in a casual drawl.

Lira cocked her head, considering. "The Magor-lier has nominated me for the council. The others so far refuse to endorse it, although they're getting a little curious about where their mage guards and soldiers are, and why they haven't burst in here to save their privileged skins yet. They've also lost access to their magic." She sent a knowing glance Egalion's way. "Well, not *all* of them."

Egalion spun suddenly, gaze searching for her son. "Tarion, explain this to me. Please?"

"I'm here for Da," he said, calm and quiet, no trace of wavering. The faith he was showing in Lira ... it took her breath away. "I suggest you do what Lira wants. If you do, nobody will be hurt."

"Indeed." Lira said. "I'm prepared to be a little less bloodthirsty than my grandfather. Nobody will die unless they oppose me."

"How disappointing," Ahrin said. "My blades hunger for blood. Shall we try the vote again?"

The councillors looked at each other, but eventually all their gazes shifted to Alyx Egalion. They weren't going to do what Lira wanted, not while the most powerful mage in the world was there to protect them. But Egalion wouldn't move against her—not unless one of her councillors' lives were directly threatened and she had no choice. Lira was confident of it.

Lira was looking forward to this next part. When the silence drew out again, Egalion clearly trying to figure out what to do without conceding to Lira's demands or revealing her potentially catastrophic secret, Lira glanced at Ahrin, inclined her head slightly.

Ahrin slid her hands into her pockets and began circling the table like a wolf rounding up its prey. "We seem to be at a stalemate of sorts." Her voice was cool, edged, and her graceful stride held the gazes of the room.

"How is she here?" Egalion asked, voice shaking with anger. "And why are you doing this if Lucinda no longer has any hold over you?"

"That's easy. I'm doing it because I want to," Lira said.

"Your guards aren't coming, by the way," Ahrin said, drawing closer to the Magor-lier. "They've been contained. Every single soldier and mage warrior in this place. I have control of Town Hall and Centre Square. There's no help coming for you."

"You're bluffing," Duneskal scoffed.

"Am I?" Ahrin paused, lifting an eyebrow. "Where do *you* think the guards have gone? How do you think we're blocking your access to magic?"

"The Darkhand leads *my* army now," Lira said. "An army of elite Shiven Hunters immune to mage power. You're all old enough to remember my grandfather's Hunters, I'm sure?"

A collective gasp went through the room.

"I have mages too, of course." Lira gestured at Tarion and Fari. "My Shadowcouncil holds all the power here. I'd really rather you admit I've won and give me what I want. That's the simplest way out of this."

"You can't defeat Egalion," Walden said tiredly. "You know it. Your Darkhand knows it. Even if we ceded you the council now, we'd re-take it the moment we came back with a mage and Taliath army that would crush yours."

"I beg to differ," Lira said coolly.

By now Ahrin had reached the Magor-lier's chair. In a move too quick for anyone to see or stop, she'd drawn a knife and stepped up behind him, reaching around to slice the blade across his throat.

A quick, efficient kill.

# CHAPTER 32

B lood sprayed, the cut so deep that Tarrick Tylender instantly slumped back in his chair, eyes glassy, one hand reaching halfway to his throat before falling limp. He hadn't even had time to react to the death blow.

Egalion let out a stricken cry, hand pressing to her mouth, while everyone else leaped from their chairs in reactions ranging from shock, to horror, to grief like Egalion's. Tarion twitched, made as if to step forward, then looked at Lira. She held his gaze for what felt like an interminable moment, then he nodded and stayed where he was. Fari had paled slightly but otherwise her expression hadn't changed.

Thank everything they were holding with her.

Ahrin stepped back from the chair and slid the knife back inside her coat. Lira glanced at Tarion. "Go."

Egalion was already moving to Tylender's side, no doubt hoping her limited healing magic could somehow help him. Her face was bloodless, eyes glistening, but she wasn't caving, not even close. Lira was impressed with the woman's fortitude, despite herself.

But Tarion got there first. He'd moved up near Tylender's chair, and in a quick movement lifted the man's body and carried it towards a side exit. At his sharp knock, the door opened and he disappeared from sight. Egalion stared at the space where Tylender had been, now an empty chair surrounded by a pool of blood. Her eyes were glassy with grief.

Once the initial shock had faded, a terrified silence fell over chamber.

"Does that convince everyone that I'm serious?" Lira asked them.

"I'll kill you for this," Egalion said softly, turning to face Lira. No, she wasn't broken. She was aflame with the same fury Lira was all too familiar with. She would have to be careful here. One wrong step and Egalion would rip her to pieces before she could do what she needed. The *only* thing holding her back was her stubborn refusal to reveal her power. So far Lira's gamble was holding.

Lira spoke calmly but firmly, "Agree that the council is mine, and then you can do whatever you like. I won't hurt anyone else. You have my word."

Tarion came back through a door a few moments later, walking straight over to his mother. Tylender's blood spotted his jacket and tunic. He reached out, squeezed her arm. "Do what she says, Mama, please. Trust me."

Egalion looked at him for a long moment, then she gave a faint nod. "Fine. Take the chair you've always wanted, Lira. Let's see how long you can hold it."

The fight went out of the rest of the room then, fear replacing the wariness and stubbornness that had characterised the other councillors' main reactions until Tarrick's death.

Fear of *her*. At least this time the fear was there because of something *she'd* done. Not because of her grandfather's legacy. She looked at them all in turn. "Are there any remaining dissenting votes?"

One by one, they all shook their heads.

"Congratulations, Magor-lier." Ahrin dropped into Tarrick's abandoned chair, put her boots up on the bloodied surface of the table and gave her that wicked smile.

"Tarion, remove your mother. I can't afford to have her in here, she's too much of a liability," Lira said. She kept her voice clipped, cold, but inside everything was drawn tight in anxiety. Everything relied on him being able to convince her to leave this room. If he couldn't, she'd have to make another display of strength to make it happen, and she wasn't sure she'd defeat Egalion again in a battle of wills. The woman was formidable despite her grief.

But she shouldn't have doubted Tarion. He leaned down to murmur something in his mother's ear, then gestured towards one of the side exits. Egalion settled a long, lingering look on Lira, then turned and followed Tarion out without a word.

"Don't worry, I don't intend to harm her," Lira said in response to the horrified gazes of the councillors watching their most powerful protector walk out the door without protest. "She'll be confined, of course, but as long as she remains manageable, she'll be fine."

"Forgive us if we don't believe a word you say," Duneskal snapped.

"That's fair." She shrugged, barely hiding her sneer. She detested each and every one of these arrogant, powerful, fools who thought they were superior to her because of their mage blood and status. Duneskal was the worst of them. She didn't care if he was technically her father. It meant nothing beyond what use his name could have for her.

"What now?" Walden asked. "You can't hold Town Hall hostage forever."

"I can hold it for as long as I need to," she said crisply. "You will all wait here, and not move. I'll be back. Fari, if one of them so much as twitches, lock them up tight."

"Will do," the healer said cheerfully.

"And I wouldn't try to overwhelm her," Lira added. "One call from Fari and my Hunters will fill this room. They won't be as nice as her."

"I thought you were going to let us go if we acceded to your wishes," Walden said.

"I will. But first I need to be sure of your loyalty." She lifted her eyebrow when nobody moved. "I'll be back soon, and we can discuss the new Mage Council."

Ahrin rounded the table to join Lira and the two of them headed for the main doors, opening them to find Shiasta waiting outside, two warriors with him, all three unharmed.

He bowed to them both. "We have control, Darkhand, Darkmage."

"Any deaths?" Lira asked.

"Only one, accidental. None of ours. The mages are locked up separately from the soldiers, as you asked, within the boundaries of the magical void created by our medallions. Town Hall is fully under our control, but I expect those outside will notice something is wrong sooner rather than later. When they do, we'll have to fight to hold the walls. That will mean more casualties."

"We need an hour, maybe two," Lira told him. "Can you keep everything under control until then?"

"I can, Darkmage."

"Good. Well done, Shiasta. Can you send one of your Hunters to Athira? Let her know things are progressing well here, and as soon as I'm comfortable that I have full control, I'll come to her. Then send three of your Hunters in there to help Fari in the event any of the councillors get restive. We won't be long."

He saluted, waved the Hunters with him into the room, then closed the doors behind them.

As soon as they were alone, Lira asked Ahrin the question that had been burning in her mind since leaving the Hunter base. "Fari?"

"A Hunter monitored every single movement she made since you left the base. She made no attempts to get a message to anyone."

Not Fari then. Lira closed her eyes. Was it relief she felt? Or more doubt?

"I re-iterate my point about how good this spy is."

"I've known this whole time, Ahrin, deep down, who it is," Lira said slowly. "But there is one more thing I can do to confirm it before I move on them."

"Until then, I wouldn't—"

"I know. No trusting anyone just yet," Lira agreed, then changed the subject as they turned a corner and headed up a side staircase. "No unexpected trouble?"

Ahrin sniffed. "I don't have unexpected trouble."

Lira chuckled. "Not even with the package?"

"I am offended that you're even asking."

"I am glad you're on my side, Ahrin Vensis."

"Why? Because I'm the only one in the world who could defeat you?"

"You and Egalion," Lira conceded.

"Hmm. I think you could take Egalion." Ahrin's gaze held hers briefly. "But not me."

Lira almost smiled, but by then they'd reached a door being guarded by Tarion. His pale Shiven skin was even whiter than usual, hazel eyes dark. "She's inside."

"Thank you, Tarion," she said. And she meant it. "You'll be ready for my signal?"

He gave her a little nod. "Be careful. I won't step in when she tries to kill you, not against my mother—I've never seen her this angry before."

"It will be fine." She touched his arm. "I promise. Just be ready when I call for you."

"You..." He hesitated, then his expression cleared. "I don't know what you're doing. But I've got your back."

"I'll never forget it," she said quietly. "And I hope to earn the faith you've placed in me."

"Excuse me while I vomit," Ahrin snapped. "Could we get on with things, please?"

"Of course, Darkhand." Lira grinned. "Let's do this."

The controlled concussion burst came flying at Lira's chest the instant she opened the door. Cursing, she barely ducked aside in time to avoid it, forced to scramble desperately away. The bright green ball of energy flew through the opening and hit the wall opposite the door, exploding in a deafening boom and gouging a massive chunk out of the marble.

"Stop!" Lira bellowed. "One minute, that's all I want, and then you can try and kill me. All right?"

Egalion hesitated, another green concussive burst already summoned and hovering in her palm.

"One minute is all I'm asking!" Lira cursed the note of desperation in her voice but couldn't help it. If Egalion killed her now, it would all be over. "Besides, Tarion's outside. Do you want to accidentally hurt him in your temper?"

"You have one minute. Make it good," Egalion snarled, lowering her arm.

At those words, Ahrin slipped into the room before Lira, closing the door behind them both. It was a large sitting room, sunlit from arched windows behind where Egalion stood. To her right was a closed door leading into another room.

"First, is anyone nearby? Anyone close enough to hear our conversation? Telepaths included," Lira asked.

"I've already ensured we're clear," Ahrin said in irritation.

"I want her to check with her telepathic magic," Lira said, gesturing at Egalion.

"There's nobody outside but my son," Egalion said tightly, barely controlling herself. "Your minute is rapidly running out."

Lira turned, rapped twice on the door. "I meant what I said earlier, Egalion. I'm not here to murder everyone or make a bloodthirsty grab for power."

"You could have fooled me." Tears sheened in her eyes then, a soul-deep sadness. "You just spilled Tarrick's blood all over the council chamber floor."

"Not exactly."

On cue, Tarion came through the door, cradling the dead body of Tarrick Tylender. Only, while the corpse wore the same clothes Tarrick had been wearing, had the same gaping cut throat, the face wasn't his. The body was roughly the same height and weight, but he was clearly Shiven.

"That's..." Egalion stared at it, confusion written all over her face. "That's Warrior Tersha. He's been missing for years."

"Three years, to be exact," Lira said. "That man was a spy, a mage with shapeshifting ability. He inveigled himself into a position as the Magor-lier's aide, so he could learn everything about the man and his day-to-day activities. Once he was ready, Underground killed your friend and Tersha stepped into his place. Lucinda has had the Magor-lier under their control for three years, Councillor Egalion."

Egalion took a deep, shuddering breath, and then she tore her eyes away from the body to look at Lira. "Tarrick died three years ago?"

"What happened to the real Tylender is the only part I'm not certain about, but I can't see how he could still be alive. I'm sorry." Lira paused, some of that old anger rising up and filling her voice, even though she tried to stop it. "I did try and tell Dawn, when she and Tersha locked me up in prison almost three years ago, but she didn't believe me."

Those green eyes whipped to hers. "You're *sorry?*"

"Don't get me wrong, I'm not drowning in sympathy for you, Egalion, but I know he was one of your oldest friends."

Egalion bit her lip, spending a few breaths piecing herself back together. It was another impressive show of strength and fortitude. "What is it you want, Lira?"

Lira looked at Tarion. He gave his mother a comforting shoulder squeeze, then left the room, returning to his post outside the door. Ahrin took up position before it, a silent but reassuring presence.

Lira met Egalion's gaze. "I have gathered all the remnants of my grandfather's army. All of his Hunters, every one of the Shiven lords who supported him, and all their money. The rogue mages who believe in his cause. Every Shiven village that continues to support Shakar's cause to this day. Every single living supporter of the Darkmage is now banded together under my leadership."

"Well done," Egalion said in resignation. "You've achieved what your grandfather failed to do. Temporarily, at least. It's what you've wanted all this time, isn't it?"

"The only thing I ever wanted was for people to see *me*. Not him. At first, I thought I could do that by helping you bring Underground down, do something that would win your respect. I figured I'd keep achieving great things until I got a spot on the council, make them all forget him."

She narrowed her eyes. "But that was never going to happen, was it? I learned that the day you locked me away."

"You wanted power," Egalion said bitterly.

"I did. I *still* want power. I want more magic." Lira shrugged. "I don't apologise for it. Why should I?"

"Well, you have power now. But you won't be able to hold it."

"I don't intend to." Lira crossed her arms over her chest. "I have every single remaining piece of Shakar's army under my control, all of them loyal to me. I know all their secrets." And even though she hadn't looked at her, even though the Darkhand hadn't moved an inch or changed her expression, she could feel Ahrin's disapproval intensely as she said, "And I'm here to hand it all over to you, Egalion, so you and your council can destroy Shakar and his vision forever."

# CHAPTER 33

A full beat of silence filled the room.

Egalion stared at her. "*What?*"

Lira smirked. "You heard me."

Comprehension slowly slid over Egalion's features. "If that's true, why not just walk into the council chamber before and say that. Why all the theatrics?"

"I still don't know the full breadth of Lucinda's capabilities, but I do know she's had an inside look into everything I do for years. Since the moment I agreed to do what Lucinda wanted, every single person around me had to believe I was fulfilling my side of the bargain. That way, no matter who her spy is, they saw only what I wanted them to see. Nobody but Ahrin knows what I'm doing in this room."

Egalion hesitated, glance flicking from Lira to Ahrin and back again. "You killed a Taliath recently, not to mention risked the lives of multiple mages by overturning boats back at Shadowfall Island. How do I know you're telling the truth?"

"Necessary actions. But not once did I gratuitously hurt any council mages or Taliath, Egalion, which you know full well. I could have burned those ships and everyone aboard, and your Taliath died because he killed one of mine." She bit her lip, grief for Laun still there. Then took a breath, steadying herself. "Also, I brought you a peace offering. A gesture of my sincerity."

Ahrin strode over to the room's other door without needing to be asked, opening it and gesturing beyond. "Get in here."

Seconds later, Dashan Caverlock strode in. His gaze went straight to Egalion, and before Lira could blink, they were in in each other's arms.

A few moments later, Ahrin sighed in irritation. "I think I might vomit again." She turned to Lira. "Are you really sure about—"

"Yes."

Her mouth was taut with disapproval. "You could have everything. *We* could have everything, like we always planned."

"I know."

"You could succeed where Shakar failed."

"I know."

"Then why not take it?"

She thought back to standing on the prow of that ship returning from Rotherburn ... the crazy plan Lira had devised, when she'd taken away her need for vengeance on either Lucinda or the council, when she'd thought about doing something that her friends would respect, something the old Lira would *never* have considered.

A united Mage Council, one with a better makeup of mages—change that would be effected as the price of delivering Shakar's entire network, even though Egalion didn't know it yet—one that didn't face any internal threat because Shakar's lingering support would be utterly destroyed.

*That* Mage Council had a real chance to defeat Lucinda.

But how to explain that to her Darkhand, who wouldn't understand why Lira couldn't still rule the council. How to explain that *that* kind of power, the kind Ahrin coveted, wasn't what Lira wanted. She'd never wanted it.

She was saved from answering by Dashan and Egalion finally disentangling themselves from each other. The Taliath's furious gaze raked the room. "What the magical hells is going on?"

"It's a long story. I'll give your wife time to explain." Lira turned for the door, opened it, and waved Tarion over from where he stood watch a little farther down the hall. "Tarion, you might want to get in here."

Frowning a little, he walked towards her, freezing on the threshold. Joy lit up his face at the sight of Dashan. "Da!"

Relief cascaded over Dashan's face. "Tarion! You're all right. Caria?"

"In Alistriem with Dawn and Ladan and Garan. They were all fine last time I saw them," Egalion assured him, still gripping tightly to his hand.

Dashan nodded, wrapping an arm around her and closing his eyes as he pressed his face into her hair. "Good. That's good."

Lira cleared her throat. "Egalion, we'll be out here when you're done. Don't be too long about it."

She slipped out without another word, Ahrin following behind, and she closed the door to give them their privacy. The hall around them was utterly deserted, but wanting to make sure, she walked down to the end and peered around the corner. Also empty.

Ahrin leaned against the wall near the room's door, legs crossed at the ankles, the massive gash from Egalion's magic immediately to her right. Rubble carpeted the floor. "I could be Lucinda's spy, you know," she remarked as Lira joined her. "Yet you haven't put me on your little list."

"I know," she said, leaning one shoulder against the wall so she could face Ahrin.

"You're not even going to ask me if I am?" Ahrin looked troubled.

"Even if you were, you're a good enough liar that I'd believe your denials."

She looked away, then back. "Why be foolish enough to trust me completely?"

"I don't," Lira said simply. "But I *want* to believe that no matter what happens, you are mine, and I am yours, and that is the most important thing in the world for both of us. I know that might end in disaster for me, for everything I've built, because I *don't* trust you completely, Ahrin. I want to, but I don't know how. I never have."

"You *do* realise how foolish that is, what a weakness it is?" Ahrin murmured. "It goes against everything I've ever taught you."

"I do. I know I'm risking disaster." She smiled sadly. "But it's what I choose."

Ahrin straightened off the wall. "Will it undermine your credibility as the terrifying heir to the Darkmage if I kiss you right now?"

"Seeing nobody is around at this moment, I don't see how."

"Good."

Before she knew it, Lira found herself pressed against the hallway wall, Ahrin's mouth on hers, their bodies pressed so tightly together there was no space between them. After the events of the morning, the anxiety, the strength needed for the façade she'd had to put on, Lira wrapped her arms around Ahrin's neck and let her kiss send all the emotion melting out of her body.

After a long, glorious moment, Ahrin pulled back a little, unable to meet Lira's eyes as she whispered, "I think you should have taken all that power for your own, Lira."

"I know you do." Lira nodded, sliding her hand into Ahrin's hair and cradling her head as Ahrin closed her eyes and pressed her face into Lira's neck.

The moment only lasted a handful of seconds before Ahrin stiffened and pulled away, grumbling in annoyance. "We're just as bad as those two in there."

"Perish the thought."

"Can we get on with things now, please?"

Lira pushed away from the wall and grinned. "As you wish, my dearest Darkhand. Why don't you go and make sure the councillors remain sufficiently quelled and we're not about to face an invading army of Tregayan militia? If Egalion isn't out in a few minutes I'm going to go break up their little reunion. Time is running short."

"While I don't take orders for you, that sounds a far sight better than hanging out in this corridor, so I shall do as you ask. I'll be back soon." Ahrin left without a backward glance.

Lira watched her go, a helpless smile on her face until she'd vanished from sight.

Then the door in front of her opened. "Come in," Egalion said. "We've got some planning to do and not a lot of time."

# CHAPTER 34

"You've got a mind like a Taliath," Dashan said admiringly as Lira joined them.

Lira snorted. "Good, your wife explained what I'm doing here."

Egalion barked a laugh. "I'm far from convinced you mean anything you say, Astor, especially when you've got the Darkhand of the Shadowcouncil at your side."

"Mama, Lira is to be trusted. Believe me if you won't believe her," Tarion weighed in, giving Lira a little smile from where he stood by the window. Joy lit up his eyes—joy that his faith in her had been rewarded. She couldn't help how warm that made her feel. For a moment, the chasm in her chest was gone entirely.

"Here's my question," Caverlock chimed in, thankfully getting right to it. "Do we continue the charade that Lira has taken over the council until Rotherburn and the Seven are dealt with, or do we move immediately on Shakar's network?"

Lira replied before Egalion could say anything. "First you need to wrap up Shakar's network—we have to assume Lucinda has her own people embedded within that group. While it's happening, I need to simultaneously remove her remaining spies. A single, precise operation. Once that's done, we'll have a short window—during which she'll be completely blind. *That's* when we act against the Seven."

"You're really going to hand your grandfather's network over to us?" Egalion still doubted. "Just like that."

"Subject to two conditions." Lira hoped that seeing Caverlock safe and sound had sufficiently softened Egalion. After all, Lira had come here with a purpose, and it wasn't just to hand over Shakar and his people. No, that was only the leverage for what she truly wanted.

The councillor's face tightened. "Of course there are conditions."

"How do we know you're telling the truth?" Dashan asked reasonably. "That you aren't doing what you claim Lucinda did—sacrificing unimportant pieces of your grandfather's network to make it *look* like they're gone?"

Lira had expected this question. "All of the lords and mages involved are here in Carhall. They're in a safe location waiting to sweep in and help take control once I subdue the council. Additionally, a unit of my Hunters is currently raiding those lords' estates in Shivasa, collecting all the records they can find. Not only will you have the entirety of the remaining network, but I'll also give you all the information you'll ever need on them. And, I can give you a list of every village in the north of Shivasa still loyal to the vision."

Caverlock and Egalion shared a glance heavy with silent communication.

"I can verify everything Lira says," Tarion said. "I've been with her these past months. I watched her convince the lords and mages to swear allegiance to her. She has everything you need to take them down, quickly and easily, in a single strike."

Egalion turned back to Lira. "What are your conditions?"

"First, the Hunters are mine. They weren't bred for violence; they were brainwashed for loyalty and unquestioning obedience. I want your guarantee that you'll give them access to your healers and telepaths ... I want their mental conditioning undone, and I want them free to pursue as normal a life as they can."

"Agreed," Egalion said without hesitation. "Provided their medallions are handed over and our healers and telepaths confirm that they are no threat to the general population."

Lira knew the healers and telepaths would find no concerns, and it was better the medallions be controlled by a council she trusted than out in the world where people like Lucinda could find them. "Your counter is acceptable."

Surprise flashed momentarily over Egalion's face. "And your second condition?"

Lira took a breath. Here it was. "You need a new Magor-lier."

"You are not *ever* going—"

"I don't want the spot," Lira cut over her. "But before anyone votes on who gets to be Magor-lier next, you're going to give Garan and Fari positions on the council."

The combined looks of puzzlement made Lira smirk inwardly; Tarion hadn't known this aspect of her plan either, but after a moment to process, he nodded eagerly.

Lira continued, "Before you come at me with how Garan and Fari are too young and immature and can't be trusted and all that nonsense, don't. Yes, they're young. And yes, Fari didn't even pass the Trials, and Garan can be too confident and a little judgemental at times. But he thinks things through carefully, he's willing to consider other viewpoints, and, even more impressively, he's willing to admit when he's wrong and change his thinking. Fari is smarter than anyone gives her credit for, and she's tough. Most importantly, both of them have good ideas on how to improve the council—changes you'll need to make if you want it to survive and prevent issues like this in the future."

Egalion let out a breath. "Council seats are decided upon by a vote among all councillors. If I unilaterally nominate Garan and Fari, it will be seen as nepotism, the very thing I've been fighting against my whole life. It will shift the balance of power in the council to me, and I don't want that."

"Then convince the councillors to vote both of them in." Lira shrugged. "Yes, Garan and Fari will have to fight the perceptions that they're puppets propped up by you, but I have no doubts they can overcome that challenge."

"What do you get out of all this?" Dashan asked. "A council seat of your own?"

"I no longer have any desire to sit on one of those chairs for the rest of my life," Lira said. "In the short term, however, to ensure I continue to have a voice and that my conditions are adhered to, I will take my father's seat. I want him permanently removed from the council."

Dashan looked puzzled. Egalion did not. Tarion smirked.

"How long have you known?" Lira asked.

"For certain? When that staff went to you during our fight in Dirinan." Egalion smiled sadly. "But there were times I saw you using your magic and … it took my breath away. It was like watching him. That same joy, the same skill."

Caverlock frowned. "Are you talking about Cario? She can't be his daughter, she…" Realisation crossed his face, and then he laughed. "Oh, please tell me I can be there when you tell Rawlin Duneskal he fathered the heir to the Darkmage?"

Egalion let out a long sigh, gaze on Lira. "You say you're going to hand over the remains of Shakar's network. But what about the protests, the strikes, the unrest?"

"I can give you his network, but I can't take away the underlying grievances that fuel it," Lira pointed out. "That's on you and the council to fix, and *that's* why I'm making these demands. You know that Duneskal is half the problem, yes? You sent him to represent you in the most troubled country on the continent. You should be glad I'm taking his seat."

Dashan's hand shot up. "I volunteer to tell him that too."

"Dash, please," Egalion snapped. "This is not a joke."

He leaned closer to his wife, capturing her gaze. "Are you going to agree to Lira's conditions?"

Egalion let out a long breath, then turned back to Lira. "Say I do agree. What happens next?"

"We continue the façade that I'm in control until we've wrapped up Shakar's network and taken out Lucinda's spies. Then we fetch Garan, re-constitute the new Mage Council, and act fast to take Lucinda down before she figures out we're coming."

"You keep saying spies. Who are you talking about?" Dashan frowned.

"Like I said, we should assume at least one of the individuals in Shakar's network is loyal to Lucinda, which is why I want them imprisoned quickly and completely. But there is someone else ... that will be for me to deal with. Once that happens, we'll be clear."

Tarion looked between Lira and his parents, thoughtful. "Estimating how long it will take Lucinda to figure out she's lost her coverage, I think we'll have maybe a month at most."

Egalion looked at Lira. "Do *you* have a plan for Rotherburn?"

"I want Lucinda to burn," she said firmly. "Outside that, no. I've been a little busy orchestrating this little coup. I figured that if I managed to pull it off, we'd be able to work together to come up with a plan. That's the only thing powerful enough to defeat Lucinda—a Mage Council that is unified and not undermined by rebellion."

Dashan began pacing, plans spilling out of him. "We'll need to keep the council members confined to the building while we maintain the show. Lira, we'll make sure Ahrin and your Hunters are visible around Centre Square. I'll talk to King Mastaran as soon as possible, tell him what's going on; him and a trusted militia commander—Rodan. They can help us project the façade that you've taken over. We can run a few half-hearted attacks on the walls, have your Hunters push them back, that sort of thing." Dashan's gaze flicked to Lira. "I can guarantee you neither King Mastaran nor Rodan are compromised."

Lira nodded "I take your word on that. And it's a good approach—you'll run it by Ahrin, make sure she agrees and doesn't have any further suggestions."

Dashan's eyes twinkled in amusement. "I dare her to pick any holes in my flawless planning."

"Will King Mastaran be willing to announce publicly that the Mage Council has been taken over by Lira and her allies?" Egalion asked her husband. "We need word to spread so that Lucinda's spies hear it."

"No, we don't." Dashan grinned. "Lira brought Athira with her, for exactly this purpose, I'm presuming? All we need do is maintain the façade long enough to convince her so that she writes a report to Lucinda."

"And the moment that message is sent, we move on Shakar's network and the spies," Tarion said. "If all goes well, we only need to keep up the pretence here until Lord Anler and his allies ride into Centre Square. A day at most."

Lira thought for a moment. "At which point we can release the councillors. Egalion, your job will be to convince the councillors of the changes that are coming, particularly the additions of Garan and Fari."

"Works for me," Dashan said cheerfully, jumping in before the protest written all over his wife's face could be verbalised.

"Wait, there's another problem." Egalion cast an irritated look at her husband. "You and the Darkhand escaped Lucinda's control—she no longer has leverage over you. She's going to question why you're still carrying out her plans, Lira. At the very least she'll question the authenticity of what you're doing."

"Something Ahrin already handled." Lira explained the circumstances of her and Dashan's escape. "Lucinda won't know what happened to Ahrin or your husband. Nobody in my inner circle, bar Tarion, Fari, and the Hunters conditioned to obey, are aware that Ahrin is with me. Athira won't see either of them, and I'll be making some showy, high-handed demands about Ahrin's safety now that I've purportedly done what I was told to do."

Egalion glanced at her husband. "Then you can't be seen either. Not by anyone outside this room."

"I can get to Mastaran without anyone seeing me," Dashan said confidently. "And if it makes you both feel better, I'll hide out at the palace until you send word it's okay to emerge."

The door opened then, Ahrin stepping in, casting a quick, practised glance around the room. "The councillors are petulant and grumbling but sufficiently quelled," she told Lira.

"Good. We've just been talking through the plan." She gave Ahrin a quick outline.

The Darkhand considered it for a long moment, eyes narrowed, but eventually nodded. "It works." She flicked Lira a glance. "I'll be joining you in Dirinan."

"Dirinan?" Egalion frowned.

"To ensure Lucinda's spies are fully dealt with, I'll need to leave Carhall," Lira said. "While I'm gone, Tarion will take point on handing over Anler and Shakar's lords and mages to you. Anler knows Tarion is my second and he trusts me. Tarion also has the lists of villages you'll need."

Tarion nodded. "I can do that."

"You'll need to be careful," she warned him. "The lords are toothless, but Terrens has concussive power, and don't overlook the telekinetics."

"I can handle it," he said confidently. "And I'll make sure there are Taliath amidst those rounding them up."

"To confirm," Caverlock said, "with King Mastaran's help, we continue the charade that Lira has taken control of the council until Athira has sent her message to Lucinda and she rides out of the city to accompany Lira to Dirinan. Once they're gone, Tarion will deliver Anler and his network to us here in Centre Square. We arrest them and hold them here in the prison. Astohar will need to decide what he wants done with them, but that can happen later."

Egalion nodded. "After that's done, we release the councillors and travel to meet you in Alistriem once you're done in Dirinan."

"Couldn't we just send for Garan to meet us here?" Tarion asked.

Ahrin shook her head before Lira could. "I'd prefer any planning regarding Rotherburn happen in Alistriem. It was a place Lucinda never infiltrated—she didn't see it as important enough. I am confident Lira has the spy situation under control, but I'd like to be careful anyway."

Lira hesitated. "Those in this room are the only ones who now know the full extent of what's going on. I'd prefer to wait until we're in Alistriem before anyone else learns of it, including Fari. As far as those who travel with us will know, we're going to Dirinan to begin the next step of taking over Shivasa now that the council is under my control."

Egalion fixed her with a look. "You want me to convince a group of aggrieved councillors to travel to Alistriem with absolutely no explanation of why they were attacked and held captive in the council chamber for nearly two days?"

Lira shrugged. "I have faith in you, Egalion. Once you're on the road and clear of Carhall, it will be fine to let them in on what's going on. You'll need to if you're going to soften them up about Fari and Garan."

"This is why I'm not Magor-lier," Egalion grumbled to her husband, who gave her an amused grin.

Lira let out a breath. "Everyone ready to play their parts? I need to get to Athira before she starts wondering what's taking me so long. Once I leave here, everything is pretence. She'll be permanently at my side."

"I'll slip out now for the palace." Dashan rose too. "Good luck everyone."

Egalion smiled a little as she looked at her son. "Would you do me the honour of imprisoning me so that I can practice my affronted fury in time for Athira to see me?"

He matched her smile. "There's nothing I'd love more."

Ahrin lingered to leave with Lira, her voice only a murmur as she asked. "Why nominate Fari for the council if you still think she might—"

"It's like you always taught me," Lira cut her off. "Keep the con as realistic as possible."

"If you turn out to be wrong in this, Egalion and the council will have a fit. You might lose the credibility with her that you need."

"This whole charade has been a gamble that I made the right call on this one thing, Ahrin." Lira sighed.

"How confident are you?"

Lira leaned into her briefly. "It breaks my heart, but I'm sure."

"Instinct is not enough, not for something this important."

Lira hesitated, nodded, then turned back to Egalion. "Can you reach Finn A'ndreas from here?"

"Just, if he's awake. Why?"

"Will you ask him to do some research for me?" Lira explained what she needed. "I can't tell you why, but it's important."

"I'll do it." Egalion seemed curious, but didn't protest. "Good luck, Lira."

"I will be at your side when you do what needs to be done," Ahrin said once they were outside the room. "Are you going to tell them about Lucinda's other plan?"

"Not yet. Not until we're in Alistriem—by then I'll more confident about sharing the information." Lira stopped, caught her hand. "I won't see you until Dirinan. Be safe, my Darkhand."

Ahrin leaned down, kissed her briefly. "You too."

They diverged in the hall, Lira not looking back as she made her way towards the exit. After six months, she was about to voluntarily walk into the prison that she'd sworn she'd never return to if she ever got out. So much had changed in that six months. So many things were different.

Lira Astor had finally cast off the weight of her grandfather's shadow. Now she had the opportunity to properly figure out who *Lira* was. A prospect both exhilarating and terrifying.

First, though, Lucinda and the Seven.

# CHAPTER 35

It was surreal, walking down the same corridor she'd stared out at for two long years, this time not as a prisoner trapped within its walls. Lira wasn't alone this time either—Shiasta and one of his warriors followed a few paces behind, a reassuring presence.

Not only that, but barely an hour had passed in which Lira had gained complete control of the Mage Council and Centre Square of Carhall and then ... handed it all over to Alyx Egalion.

That crazy, foolish plan worked out over hours at the prow of Lucinda's ship—it had somehow come to fruition. It was more than surreal. After a moment, she shook those thoughts away. She could dwell later—the con wasn't over yet.

She found Athira inside the cell Lira had once been kept in, standing with her hands clasped loosely behind her. The woman wore a distant expression. At the sound of Lira's entrance, though, she turned and her expression cleared. "Shiasta told me it worked?"

"It did." Lira smiled, putting on a look of triumph. "Tarrick Tylender is dead and the Mage Council is mine. Centre Square too. My Hunters have done a flawless job."

Athira's eyebrows rose. "So you killed the shapeshifter? I admit to some surprise."

"You really had so little faith that I could defeat Egalion and the council?"

Athira's mouth quirked. "I was confident you couldn't."

"I do like it when I'm right and you're wrong, Athira Walden. I apologise for taking so long to come and get you—I wanted to make sure the councillors were properly subdued before leaving the council chamber. Right now, Fari is keeping an eye on them. How did things go here?"

Athira gave her a look. "Therob and the Hunters did their jobs. The Underground prisoners have all been freed and were directed to the safehouse where Anler and the others are waiting for them."

"I'm glad to hear it. And the mage prisoners?"

"Awaiting your judgement. I suspect there are more than a few who will be willing to join our cause." Athira hesitated, eyes narrowing slightly. "I didn't fail to notice that you separated me from your part of this mission."

"For good reason. I needed someone competent to make sure our allies were freed." Lira allowed her voice to turn wintry cold. "Lucinda has Ahrin. I have no intention of doing anything that would cause Lucinda to harm her in any way. I have done as she asked, and I'm here to prove it to you."

Athira hesitated only a moment longer before stepping out of the cell. Lira gestured for the woman to join her as she began walking back down the hall. Shiasta fell in behind them, a quietly protective presence.

"How did you best Egalion?" Athira asked.

"As expected, she was unwilling to sacrifice anyone to kill me, and so she stood down." Lira gave a more detailed account of how it had gone down, leaving out only Ahrin's involvement. "We're going to see the councillors now, so you can be convinced I'm telling the truth."

"We'll see," Athira murmured.

Lira stopped at the door, one palm holding it closed as she turned and stared straight into Athira's eyes. "And then you're going to write to Lucinda, or her contacts, or whoever it is you're supposed to ... because I've held up my end and I want Ahrin freed. Is that clear?"

"Your job isn't just to take over the council. It's to use the council to quell the kingdoms."

Lira didn't look away. "I've demonstrated my good faith. I want a similar gesture of good faith, or I might get to thinking Lucinda never intends to hold up her end of the bargain."

"Like I said, we'll see," Athira murmured.

"You will, and then I'm going to expect that my demands are met. *Quickly.*" Lira hauled open the door. "Let's go."

When Lira approached the doors to the council chamber, the two Hunters on guard opened them without hesitation. She paused to speak to them before going through. "No troubles?"

"None, Lady Astor. They've been talking a lot, but there haven't been any attempts to escape."

"Thank you." Lira turned back to Shiasta. "Can you go and make sure Centre Square is still under our control and the captured mages and Taliath you're holding in the building aren't causing any problems? If you judge it safe enough, it might be a good time to start moving them into the prison."

"Lady Astor." Shiasta bowed and strode away.

Anxiety lurked in the pit of Lira's stomach as she opened the doors. Athira was about to see everything she expected to, but if one of the councillors mentioned the Darkhand ... it had either been risk that or brief them all on what was happening before letting Athira see them. She'd decided the risk of the councillors being unable to act well enough to sell what was going on much higher than one of them mentioning the Darkhand. Even so, it was a gamble.

Fari waited just inside the doors of the council chamber. She gave Lira a little nod of greeting, then turned to Athira. "Everything went smoothly on your end, I take it?"

"Without a hitch." Athira glanced around, turning to the council mages. They were still sitting around the table. Food and drink had been provided, and most had taken off their cloaks and removed mage staffs to get comfortable. They stared sullenly at the new entrants.

It didn't take long for the councillors to realise who'd entered the room with Lira, though.

"Athira! We thought you were dead." Walden's voice rang out, his tone an amusing mix of injured and disbelieving as he looked at his granddaughter. There was no trace of grief, or relief or joy at seeing her alive despite the circumstances, just astonishment. "Why have you betrayed us like this?"

Athira shrugged, appearing similarly unmoved by seeing her grandfather for the first time in years. "You left me to rot as a prisoner of Underground. Don't blame me for deciding to take what they offered me."

The doors opened, admitted Tarion, and swung closed. He stood silently, hand on *Darksong*'s hilt, looking broody, as if he weren't entirely pleased with what had gone down. Athira didn't even glance his way though.

"Which was what, exactly?" Walden sounded puzzled. "You would have had all the power you wanted here—my seat on the council after my death and a genuine shot at being Magor-lier one day."

Athira twitched. It was the barest of movements, but Lira caught it. It wasn't a hint of emotion, not guilt or regret. No, it had been more like ... Lira's gaze narrowed. It was the second time she'd seen it now, proving the first hadn't been her imagination.

And it was familiar. She'd seen it often. In Ahrin. In Shiasta. Whenever Lira had pressed them to talk about topics that pressed up against their mental conditioning.

Realisation snapped through her, clear and resolute. It told Lira what had happened to Athira, explained her loyalty to Lucinda. Her mind raced. She had to figure out how to use that. She glanced briefly at Tarion, then back at Athira as she replied to her grandfather.

"Your kind of power is not what I want," she said flatly.

He looked flummoxed by this, mouth opening and then closing.

Duneskal glanced at Walden, then at Athira, a calculating look on his face. "What kind of power *do* you want? Come back to us now, help us destroy Astor, and it's yours."

"It's not anything you can give me." Athira turned away from him deliberately, holding Lira's gaze. "Where's Egalion?" she asked sharply.

Lira scoffed, "I couldn't afford to leave her loose with this lot to help plan a mutiny. She's in a room surrounded by Hunters that cut off her magic. Don't worry, we're going to go and see her next."

Athira pointed at the councillors. "And what are you going to do with them?"

"They've—reluctantly—agreed to make me Magor-lier. I'll leave them here to stew a little longer until any remaining defiance bleeds out of them, and then we'll open the doors and tell the world who's in charge now." Lira shrugged, pointed to the pool of blood on the floor by Tylender's chair. "That's all that remains of their previous Magor-lier. They know if they display any hint of defiance ... well, they've seen how good my Hunters are at executions."

Athira's gaze narrowed and she seemed deep in thought. She'd clearly been deeply doubtful about Lira's ability to carry this off. Lira found herself irritated and offended by the thought. Still, she let Athira have all the time she needed to be convinced.

Eventually she let out a breath. "I want to see Egalion, now."

Lira nodded. "Absolutely. Let's go."

"Lira?" Tarion's voice held a note of irritation, matched by the thin line of his mouth. "A moment, please?"

She halted and waited for him to approach. He gave Athira a hard look when she didn't move away. "This is personal."

She huffed, reading his tone and expression. "Fine, cry about your mother. I'll wait outside, Lira. Don't make me wait long."

As soon as she was gone, Tarion stepped closer, lowering his voice. "Sorry, I didn't want to risk making her suspicious, but I saw that look on your face just now. You need something?"

"You're brilliant," she murmured with genuine feeling. "After Athira and I have visited your mother, can you speak to her? I need someone to meet me in Dirinan, and your mother's telepathy is the fastest way to deliver that message."

He looked curious when she spoke the name, but didn't say anything further, only stepping away and smiling. "Consider it done."

"Fari, you're okay?" Lira called across the room.

"Never better," the healer reassured her. "Getting a little bored watching this lot, though."

"We'll get you out of here soon," she promised.

Egalion was cool, arrogant, and believably angry when Lira and Athira entered the room in which she was being held. She whirled as soon as the door opened, eyes flashing, "Of course *she's* with you," Egalion snapped. "What is it the both of you think you're going to achieve, exactly?"

"You know the answer to that. We're going to achieve what Lucinda wants so that I can get Ahrin back," Lira said reasonably. "Athira is going to tell Lucinda that *I'm* doing as ordered."

"I didn't appreciate being locked away in a cell back in Dirinan," Athira said. "Be assured I've already informed Lucinda that you *did not* uphold your end of the bargain. I think we both know what that would have meant for your husband. You have my condolences."

Fear that looked completely genuine filled Egalion's face. Lira's shoulders relaxed a little—she hadn't been sure of the woman's ability to play a role convincingly. But she was flawless. Impressive. Another small bit of admiration filled her. Damn, she *really* didn't want to like Alyx Egalion.

"If Lucinda has touched him—" Egalion snarled.

"You'll do what?" Athira scoffed.

"I'll burn her and everything she loves to the ground."

"No you won't." Lira laughed. "That's not how you operate. It's how *I* operate. It's why you're in this room and I'm now in control of the most powerful organisation in this land."

Egalion shook her head, arms crossed, defiance in every line of her body. "You know you can't hold that power. I give you a few days at most before you're overwhelmed and killed."

"Yes, but that's what you said about me being able to gain control in the first place, and look where we are now." Lira shrugged.

"She has a point," Athira drawled.

Lira looked at Athira. "Are we done here, or do you have more questions for her?"

Athira shrugged. "I'm done. What are you going to do with her?"

Lira's smile was slow and full of triumph. "I'm going to put her in the same cell I spent two years rotting in. She won't speak to another soul but her guards for the rest of her life."

"Good." Athira nodded and turned for the door. "It was nice knowing you, Egalion."

Lira didn't bother to wait for the mage councillor's reply before closing the door in her face.

"What's next?" Athira asked as they walked away.

"What's next is you're going to tell Lucinda that I've succeeded," Lira said flatly. "What do you need to make that happen? Parchment, a messenger? Do you need to be left alone so I don't ferret out the secret details of your contact?"

Athira gave her a cool look. "Nothing so convoluted as all that. I'll require a parchment and ink, and one of your Hunters to take the message to a contact."

"First, come with me to meet with the rest of the Shadowcouncil. As you said before, Lucinda wants more from me." Lira held her gaze. "I will demonstrate how I intend to achieve it, and then you will arrange to have a gesture of good faith made before I do anything more."

Athira snorted. "You really think she's going to give up her leverage over you?"

"If she wants the kingdoms she will." Lira stopped walking, stepped even closer. "And if you don't convince her of that, you're going to find yourself in a very precarious position, Athira. Because your *only* use to me is as a conduit to Lucinda."

Athira's eyebrows lifted, unmoved. "And what, then you'll kill me? Your own cousin?"

"You know what I did to Tersha. What I did to Greyson. I won't hold back when it comes to you." Lira let that sink in. "You might nominally be my cousin, but that doesn't mean anything to me. I just took the Mage Council. I'm not someone to be messed with. Lucinda needs to know that."

Athira held her gaze a long moment then let out a breath, finally looking convinced that Lira was genuine. "I'll do my best with Lucinda. You have my word."

"Good. Then let's go meet with our Shadowcouncil so you can write a nice and detailed message to her."

Athira smiled as she fell into step with Lira. "Not a *Shadow*council anymore, are we? Now we're the real thing."

Their gazes met and held, sharing triumph, and Lira felt it deep in her chest. *There* was Athira Walden, the real woman, her cousin. The woman who'd once risked her life to hold a door open for Lira. Lucinda hadn't succeeded in burying her completely.

In that moment of shared feeling, Lira realised she didn't want to see Athira hurt any more than she did Fari, Garan, or Tarion.

She let out an internal sigh. Rotted carcasses, the list of people she cared about was only getting longer.

# CHAPTER 36

"I need to go to Dirinan," Lira told her assembled inner circle a short time later. "I leave first thing tomorrow. Tarion, you'll—"

"Why are you going *there* in such a hurry?" Athira interrupted sharply.

"You were there when I told Anler and his lords and mages my plans—Shivasa is the next step after taking the council. If I'm going to do what Lucinda wants next, then I need resources. Ahrin's crew in Dirinan is the largest crime gang in the country. I need what they can give me." Lira paused, meeting Athira's look. "Not to mention, if we take control of Dirinan before moving on to Karonan and the rest of Shivasa, that gives Lucinda and her people a safe harbour to arrive in, no?"

"What about Lord Anler and the other lords, and your mages?"

"Tarion will manage their role in our next steps." Lira gestured in his direction. "Some will remain here to help keep an eye on Carhall with the backing of the Hunters, while the rest will go back to their estates and begin exerting the control we need over Shiven trade. Our mages will underpin the new council. The lords will take day-to-day control of running Shivasa."

Athira nodded, satisfied with that.

The thrill of playing a con shivered through Lira delightfully, and she had to work hard to hide it from her face. "As we did today with the council, we will offer Leader Astohar a choice. Submit to the Mage Council's overall authority or find his country taken out from under him."

"We won't be able to hold Carhall for long," Fari pointed out, frowning.

"We won't need to. The new Mage Council will carry on as normal until we've taken Shivasa—we'll make apologetic noises to King Mastaran and assure him today's events were the result of an internal mage issue that has now been resolved. Once we have Shivasa, we'll withdraw the seat of the council to Karonan until we've subdued the rest of the kingdoms."

"Tregaya and Zandia won't submit without war, and there's a good chance they'll send their forces to help Rionn," Athira said thoughtfully. "But if we can take Rionn before they move, you'll hold the entire south along with most mages and Taliath. From there it will only be a matter of time."

"Agreed." Lira turned her attention to Tarion. "While I'm gone, you'll work with Lord Anler and his people to begin planning the details of how we take Rionn quickly. Shiasta, you'll stay to support Tarion in case there's any trouble, although I'm confident the councillors are sufficiently subdued. Fari and Athira, you're with me." Lira faced the others. "Any questions?"

"What about my parents?" Tarion's voice was laced with an undercurrent of concern.

"What of them?" She lifted an eyebrow. "Your father is being held by Lucinda—this will hopefully free him along with Ahrin, *if* she hasn't killed him already. That's why you're with me, no? And your mother will be held in a nice prison cell with sufficient creature comforts. I will hold to my agreement not to harm her in return for you allying with me."

"What about my sister?" he persisted.

"She will have the choice to join me, like you have." She kept her voice crisp and firm. "And if she doesn't, she won't come to any harm as long as she doesn't act against me."

"Fine." He subsided, looking the perfect mix of accepting and unhappy. He wasn't bad at playing a con either.

Lira ran her gaze around the room, her expression triumphant, confident. "You've all done well—I couldn't have pulled this off without you. *We* are the power in this land now."

She didn't quite get the response she wanted. Both Tarion and Fari nodded half-heartedly, neither looking convinced about their future plans. Athira just looked bored, like she just wanted to stop talking and get on with it. And Shiasta just looked happy to have orders.

"You should all get some rest. It's been a long day and I want to be on the road early tomorrow. Rooms have been set up for us." Lira rose and stretched, making a show of yawning. "I, for one, am exhausted."

Fari fell into step with her as the left the meeting. "Are you sure about what comes next?"

"What do you mean?"

"Is taking over the world really what you want?" Fari's dark eyes looked troubled, as if she didn't quite understand.

"That's what I've said from the beginning. This wasn't just about getting Ahrin back. Once we control everything, we can *destroy* Lucinda, Fari."

"And then what?"

"And then we can run things the way that we want to." It was Lira's turn to give her a questioning look. "If you want out..."

Fari yawned. "I'm tired and still uncertain of where we're heading."

"Stick with me until Dirinan, and then we'll talk properly, I promise." Lira held her gaze. "Deal?"

Fari managed a smile. "Deal, Astor."

Lira made a point of sharing a room with Fari and Athira to forestall Athira becoming suspicious. But as soon as Athira was asleep, Lira slipped out, asking Therob to show her to Shiasta. He quietly led her through the dim halls to where Shiasta stood alert outside the closed double doors to the council chamber.

Lira paused before going to him. "Therob, go back and keep an eye on my room. If Athira wakes, come and tell me instantly. The story is that I got hungry and went to the kitchens for something to eat, okay?"

"Yes, Lady Astor." He bowed his head and returned the way they'd come.

"Lady Astor," Shiasta murmured in greeting. "We did as you asked, and he's ready for you."

"Good. Take me to him, please."

Shiasta led her to a room not far from the council chamber. The light was dim, only a single torch flickering in its bracket on the wall. Two Hunters stood guard outside the entrance, and one silently opened the door to let her in.

She waved off Shiasta when he wanted to come in with her. "I'll be fine."

"We'll be here if you need anything," he said, waiting until she walked inside and then closing the door behind her.

It was a small office. Rawlin Duneskal sat on a chair in front of a desk piled high with papers. A tray of food and water sat on the table near him, and a fire crackled in the hearth. Curtains had been drawn over the narrow window behind the desk.

Duneskal looked up at her entrance, eyebrows raised. "Have you separated me out because you want to kill me yourself?" The arrogant ease of his tone suggested he didn't truly think this was the case.

"I have no intention of killing you," Lira said anyway. "You'll be put back with your fellow councillors shortly, but you and I need to have a chat first."

He leaned back in his chair. "I have no interest in conversing with a deranged mage who has delusions of being another Darkmage. He would have crushed you like a bug."

"Maybe." She shrugged, remaining standing. "But he's long dead."

Duneskal said nothing, merely crossed his arms over his chest and gave her a challenging look.

Lira leaned back against the door, making sure that every part of her looked and sounded casual. "Not long after you were first posted to Karonan, you had an affair with a woman named Niria. She got pregnant, and you told her you weren't interested in being a parent." She paused. "Do you remember that?"

His eyes narrowed, incredulity seeming to overpower his determination not to talk to her. "You wanted to chat with me about an affair I had over twenty years ago?"

Something inside her clenched tightly at his admission, the chasm opening wide and yawning, but she took a single breath, thought of Tarion and Ahrin, and relaxed. "I do."

"What of it?" He shrugged. "I haven't seen Niria since she left Karonan. I didn't want the entanglement of a child, or a wife, and she took that badly."

"And you never bothered to look for her, find out what happened to her and the child, ensure they were well?"

"No. She chose to leave, and I accepted that." Disbelief filled his voice. "What has this got to do with anything?"

"Niria was my mother."

Duneskal scoffed, then stilled. He stared at her, the blood draining from his face. His arms uncrossed and fell to his sides. "No."

"*Yes*, in fact," Lira said. "She left Karonan when you abandoned her and returned home. She had me, and then she died from hunger and exposure several years later. At which point your five-year-old daughter was tossed out of her home and dumped at an orphanage in Dirinan like an unwanted sack of potatoes."

He stared. "How ... how long have you known this?"

"I wasn't sure, until right now." She cocked her head. "The council is going to love learning you fathered the heir to the Darkmage before abandoning her. Imagine if you'd wanted me? Imagine the life I might have had if I hadn't grown up on the streets. I might have turned out to be the perfect little mage warrior you all hoped for."

He scoffed, voice full of scorn. "You made your own choices, Lira. I have no fault in any of it."

"You really believe that, don't you?" It was her turn to be incredulous. "I wonder what the Duneskal clan will think, knowing that you abandoned a pure mageblood heir that could have added to their strength and prestige. All because, what, it was too annoying to have a child in your life?"

He said nothing, but he'd turned even paler, his jaw working.

"Well, they're all going to find out now." She pushed off the door and took a step closer. "I'm leaving tomorrow, but when I return, I will be taking your council seat—*my* council seat. You're going to retire and ... well, you can do whatever you like as long as it doesn't involve getting in my way."

That familiar superciliousness flashed over his face. "You won't hold the council longer than another day." His voice was rich with scorn. "And then you'll be back in jail where you belong. I will dispute this conversation ever happened. Nobody will believe you're a Duneskal."

"We'll see." She shrugged. "Remember what I said. I want you gone when I return."

She didn't wait for a response, opening the door and closing it firmly behind her, hand lingering on the handle as she took a deep breath to steady herself.

Her father was Rawlin Duneskal. The knowledge left her feeling raw, exposed.

Shiasta waited patiently for her. "Lady Astor, is all well?"

She made herself smile at him. "Keep him in there until I'm gone tomorrow. Then he can re-join the councillors."

"Yes, Lady Astor." The Hunter hesitated, looking a little confused. "I wished to ensure your safety, and so I listened to your conversation. I apologise if that was not what you wanted."

"It's all right, Shiasta. I appreciate that you were trying to keep me safe."

Shiasta flicked a glance beyond the door, still looking confused but forging ahead anyway. "I do not like that man. It makes me feel ... upset, that he ... he does not deserve a child such as you, Lady Astor."

Lira stared at him, eyes welling with unbidden tears. "I think it's me that doesn't deserve you, Shiasta. Walk with me, will you?"

"Did you need something?" he asked, voice returning to its even tone.

She kept her voice low. "Once you and Tarion have delivered Lord Anler and his associates to the council, you and all the Hunters are to remain here in Carhall."

He frowned. "We are not to join you in Alistriem?"

"No. Your part in all this is done." She stopped before they could reach her room. "Your lives are going to be your own now. You're going to stay here, and mage healers and telepaths are going to work with you. They're going to help lift your childhood conditioning."

The frown deepened. "I don't think I understand."

"I know you don't." She stepped closer, placing a hand on his arm. "This is going to be my final order to you, Shiasta. Once Anler and his friends are in custody, you and your Hunters—every single one of them—will remain here with the healers and the telepaths. You will let them help you. And when the day comes, and you are able, you will choose to do whatever you want to do."

"I..." He looked at her. "What about the Darkhand?"

"She's already free, Shiasta." Lira searched his face. "I think deep down you already know that, all of you. It's why you chose to make her your leader."

He was silent for such a long time she worried that she'd said something wrong. But eventually he nodded, his gaze on her hand where it rested on his arm. "I still don't think I understand, not completely, but there's a part of me ... we will do as you order." His gaze shifted to meet hers, his shoulders straightening, "And then we will come to you."

She smiled through her tears. Somehow, thinking of her Hunters as free, of how she'd helped make that happen ... it made her feel free too. "But that's the beauty of freedom, Shiasta. You won't have to."

# CHAPTER 37

L ira sent a message ahead to Dirinan before riding out of Carhall. Athira had queried why the Hunters weren't accompanying them, and Lira had pointed out what would have been the absolute truth if she were truly doing as she pretended. "Tarion will need the army to hold position in Carhall until King Mastaran and his Tregayan militia are convinced that the new council is here to stay. There are enough Hunters in Dirinan to support the Revel Kings."

In reality, word would never spread beyond Carhall of what had happened, and now that they were gone, things would quickly revert to normal as Egalion imprisoned Anler and his friends and re-took control. Lira would have to act the moment she reached Dirinan—if she waited too long, she risked Athira becoming suspicious as to why news hadn't spread of the takeover.

Her stomach churned with growing anxiety the whole way, even though she had to maintain an air of confident triumph. It was finally the time to deal with the person who had been a traitor from the beginning.

The thought of Ahrin—who'd ridden ahead, ready to play her part in what came next—calmed her ... but even thinking of her Darkhand wasn't without a flicker of anxiety. Ahrin had stuck by her this far, but there were limits to what she'd be willing to do.

Part of Lira hoped that when Egalion did as Lira asked, she'd find something that would prevent this trip from being necessary. Maybe there never had been a spy, maybe she wouldn't have to ... but no. That was a foolish hope. She'd gone over and over it in her head. Lucinda had known things it was impossible to know unless she'd been told by one of only a handful of people.

And then, two nights after they left Carhall, Alyx Egalion slipped into her thoughts. Lira had been travelling with lowered mental shields for this eventuality. *"Lira? Anler and his lords are all in custody, the mages too. No casualties on either side, just a lot of angry Shiven men."*

*"I'm glad to hear it. The Hunters searching their estates should be with you in a matter of days, bringing whatever they found. I trust you'll look after them as we discussed?"*

*"I'll make sure of it personally before we leave for Alistriem,"* Egalion promised. *"Also, I've been in contact with Finn and I have the information you were after."*

Lira took a breath; dread and anticipation both squeezed her chest. *"Lay it on me, Egalion."*

*"Finn spent several hours searching through his records but was unable to find the information you sought. I asked him to double check, which he did, and still found nothing. He's insistent that if the event had occurred, it would be in there."* Egalion paused. *"Nobody loves record-keeping more than Finn. If he says it didn't happen, then he's right."*

Lira bit her lip, then let out a long breath in an attempt to ease the tightening of grief in her chest. One last betrayal. Proof that trusting anyone completely was a mistake, no matter how much you cared about them.

*"This news upsets you,"* Egalion noted, not unkindly.

*"More than it should,"* she said softly. *"It merely confirms what I already knew. Thank you for the help."*

Her foolish hopes erased, Lira focused her mind and re-set her mental shields.

"Lira?" Fari called over from her horse. "Everything okay?"

Catching her voice, Athira turned back from where she rode slightly ahead, eyebrows lifted.

Lira's gaze settled on Fari for a moment, considering, then she summoned a smile and addressed both women. "I was just thinking about the different crews in Dirinan, and which would be the weakest to go after first. Once the Revel Kings have control over all the gangs, taking over the city proper will be easy."

Fari didn't seem convinced by Lira's lie, but presumably aware of Athira listening, she merely shrugged. "Let us know if you want to run anything by us."

Lira said nothing, her thoughts no longer in what had already happened, but on what came next.

She wasn't going to flinch from it.

The weather was dull and grey, thick cloud hanging over the city as they entered it. The lack of any breeze made the usual stench in the harbour district even stronger than usual. Lira's mouth quirked as she caught Fari surreptitiously lifting the hem of her Zandian wrap to cover her nose. The smile died quickly though.

They made no attempt to slip into gang territory unnoticed, and the moment she and her retinue crossed the boundary into Revel Kings territory, runners darted ahead with the news of her arrival.

Nobody tried to challenge them. As violent and brutal as the street gangs of Dirinan were, none were so foolish as to challenge three mages riding openly through their streets in broad daylight. At least, not without planning a good ambush first.

A hushed silence hovered over the area, as if even the most hardened criminals knew something was about to go down and preferred to stay out of sight until it was over. She could feel the weight of multiple watchful gazes keeping an eye on proceedings. Even the normally steady Alfie was a little skittish under her, his head up high and ears pricked back.

Once they'd dismounted out the front of the gambling hall, Lira shifted her gaze to accommodate Fari and Athira. "Focus and strengthen your mental shields. I can't be sure there aren't telepaths lurking in Dirinan searching for me."

As they stepped through the door Lira checked and re-checked her own mental shield. A couple of steps inside, she hesitated, then cursed herself for it. She could not afford a single shred of weakness.

Clearly noticing the hesitation, Fari opened her mouth, as if to ask what was going on, but her gaze shifted to Athira, and she simply continued scanning the hall with her gaze.

A moment later, Yanzi's voice shouted Lira's name, and the man himself appeared at the end of the hall, waving them over. "We're ready for you."

"Yanzi!" Fari reached him first, giving him an enthusiastic hug, which he returned just as enthusiastically.

"We're meeting about how to take over the country in a gambling den?" Athira asked as she and Lira joined him.

"Actually, we're having a meeting in a room *near* the gambling den," Lira said with a little smile.

"Pleasure to see you again, Athira." Yanzi smiled, easy and warm.

Athira merely gave him a cool look.

He smirked. "Such a friendly lot you keep around you, Astor."

Lira shrugged. "I do need to maintain a certain image. You're looking at the new Magor-lier of the Mage Council."

The smirk faded to a troubled look. "I guess we're in a whole new world now."

"A better one, Yanzi. Provided we can keep the momentum going."

A tattooed woman with multiple knives strapped around her body stood outside a non-descript door in the hallway Yanzi led them down. A Hunter stood there too—Alea, the unit commander of the Hunters left in Dirinan to support Yanzi and Lorin. The woman opened the door at a gesture from Yanzi, then stepped away. "Anything else you need, boss?"

"Could you go and fetch our first guest, Ordra? Once you have, please stay with our second guest and make sure she doesn't go anywhere. Lady Astor will let us know when we need to see her."

Yanzi's instructions had Lira's shoulders relaxing slightly. He'd gotten her message and was carrying it out as asked, despite his clear reservations about what was going on.

Now Lira just needed to be able to carry it out. Her palms were sweating, and she surreptitiously wiped them on her breeches. Dread squeezed her chest tight, and she hoped her drumming heart wasn't audible to anyone else.

The woman nodded and strode off. Athira, Yanzi, and Fari went into the room, all three looking uncertain. Alea remained outside after a glance from Lira.

It wasn't a large space but had been set up as if for a meeting. A narrow rectangle of glass set high in the wall let in a watery grey light that illuminated a table holding food and drink. There were no other exits from the room.

Lorin waited for them inside, rising from one of the chairs with a smile. "Lira, Fari! You have no idea how excited we were to get your message, to know things went as planned in Carhall. Not that I ever doubted you."

"Lorin." Fari beamed, going over to punch him affectionately in the shoulder in greeting. He slung an arm around her shoulders to give her a quick hug before letting go.

"Good to see you too, Athira." Lorin gave her a nod.

"Lorin Hester." Athira greeted him with equal coolness.

Before anyone could say anything further, the door opened again. Alea appeared, waving in another individual.

Ahrin Vensis.

Lira made no sound of acknowledgement but felt herself relax. Having Ahrin here was going to make this so much easier. Not to mention she'd simply missed the woman since they'd parted in Carhall. Something she wasn't used to admitting to herself. It remained an uncomfortable experience.

Once Ahrin was inside, Alea closed the door. He would stand guard until all this was over to make sure nobody entered ... or left. Lira had made sure he had instructions too.

"Greetings all," the Darkhand said coolly.

"What is she—"

"How did she—"

Lorin and Athira spoke simultaneously, voices loud, drowning each other out.

Ahrin lifted an eyebrow, menace oozing from her. "Surprised to see me? Or disappointed? From the looks on your faces, I'd say it's both. Plus a healthy dose of fear. That's good."

"Lira, what is going on?" Athira demanded, rounding on her in fury. "You don't look surprised to see her. How long have you known she was free?"

Lira said nothing, merely nodded in Ahrin's direction.

The Darkhand moved in a blur, stepping around behind Athira, drawing her wrists back, and locking them in a pair of bracelets so quickly that Athira didn't even begin struggling until her wrists were already confined.

Lira looked at Yanzi. "You're sure they cut off magic access?"

He waved a hand. "Tried and tested." He glanced at Ahrin, something like relief and discomfort in his gaze. "The boss insisted on it when she finally swanned in here two days ago."

"Good." She couldn't afford Athira helping her ally in this room. They could be in genuine trouble if she did.

Athira snarled. "What is happening here? Explain yourself at once, Lira, or—"

"You'll what? Report us to Lucinda?" Ahrin hissed, voice low and dangerous. "You won't be making any more reports to her, Athira Walden, so count us *very* unconcerned on that score."

Sweat beaded Athira's brow, gaze darting from Lira to Ahrin. Not scared, or angry, or even thwarted, she looked ... uncomfortable. Extremely so. Deep down, Lira hoped she was right in what she'd guessed about Athira. But that was for worrying about later. Now that the woman was neutralised, she could finish what she'd come here to do.

Lorin spoke into the baffled silence. "Lira, what is going on?"

Lira shifted her gaze from Athira to Lorin. "If you'll indulge me for a moment, I'm happy to explain."

Fari dropped into a chair. "I have to admit to being completely lost. Although..." Her eyes narrowed. "If we're revealing Ahrin and imprisoning Athira, that means you don't think you need to make Lucinda believe you're doing what she wants anymore. And now I'm recalling a certain conversation at the Hunter base in Dirinan ... yes, please, do go on."

"Don't hold back on my account. I love a good story." Yanzi stretched, settled himself in another chair, and gave her an expectant look. She didn't miss the uncertainty in his gaze though. Even Ahrin's arrival hadn't settled his doubts about their plans.

Lira allowed herself the indulgence of a single glance at Ahrin; at soaking in the cool confidence in her expression, her stance, letting it bolster her own confidence, then faced the seated group.

She took a breath, and she started talking, weaving a story that had only ever been spoken aloud to Ahrin Vensis. "Here's the thing. Lucinda has *always* been one step ahead of me. She had spies in Temari Hall when I was there, of course, but it was more than that. At some point she learned that I was a traitor to Underground, that I was spying on them for the council. I had a lot of time to think about that in my prison cell, and I began to wonder how she'd found out."

A quick pause—scan of the room. They were listening intently. All bar Ahrin, who was watching *them*, not Lira, with the silent stillness of a predator ready to pounce if needed.

"The obvious answer was that the Magor-lier had told her. Tarrick Tylender had been replaced by her shapeshifting mage around the same time Lucinda found out about me being a spy," Lira said. "But after careful thought, I realised that it wasn't the *right* answer, for two reasons. First, the way Lucinda and Greyson set me up took time and planning, weeks of it at least ... which means Lucinda knew I was a spy before they replaced Tylender."

"That doesn't necessarily mean anything," Fari pointed out. "Both Tylender and Lord-Mage A'ndreas knew you were a spy—a telepath loyal to Lucinda could have read it in their thoughts."

"True. I dismissed the chances of any telepath being capable of breaching the thoughts of Dawn A'ndreas, the most skilled telepath in the world, but even *I'd* heard Egalion refer to Tylender's sloppy mental shielding," Lira said. "However, second, and most importantly, Lucinda didn't just know about me being a spy. The night I escaped Shadowfall she went after Ahrin too. She knew we were working together."

A silence fell while Lira let that sit, let them process her words and realise what she was saying.

Fari came to it first. "Tarrick Tylender didn't know about you and Ahrin."

"No. I kept our relationship hidden from the council. It was one of the things that undid me, the secrets I kept."

Lorin frowned, shooting the Darkhand a suspicious look. "How do you know Ahrin didn't betray you?"

"Simple. If she had, they wouldn't have gone after her too," Lira said. "So I figured there had to be another spy. And *then* I thought ... the Mage Council accused me of joining Temari Hall in order to spy for Underground. It wasn't true, of course, but that didn't mean someone else hadn't done that exact thing. Someone who would be in a position to spy on both me *and* Egalion. It's just the sort of complex and long-term plotting Lucinda loves."

Yanzi had begun leaning forward in his chair, eyes narrowed. Something flickered over Fari's face. The woman, far more intelligent than most had ever given her credit for, was starting to realise where this was going. Lorin simply looked confused, as if he wasn't sure why they were talking about this. Athira stared at the ground, convulsively tugging against her restraints.

"When the seven of us were kidnapped by my Darkhand here"—Lira glanced at Ahrin with a little smile. She scowled—"we wondered why us, of all the students at Temari? Ahrin answered that for me. Lucinda was trying to create mages whose magical abilities could break through razak and nerik immunity. Her healers thought they might have the most luck with test subjects who carried a bloodline with very rare combination of mages of the higher order who had absorbed Taliath immunity."

"Oh, that makes sense!" Fari said in excitement.

"It does. I am the granddaughter of such a mage. Garan and Tarion are grandsons, and in Tarion's case a son, of such a mage." She paused, looking at Fari. "And, after doing some digging during my time in prison, I learned that your grandfather on your mother's side was a Zandian prince who was one of the mages that went missing before the last war—killed by a Hunter."

"Yes, the Hunters were secretly taking out the most powerful mages on Shakar's orders. My grandfather was one of the last remaining mages of the higher order." Fari nodded. "But what about..." Her voice trailed off as she glanced over at Lorin.

"What about Lorin?" Lira asked. "That's a very good question. No mages of the higher order in your family?"

"No, none." He frowned. "We're not a mageblood family. I'm the only one born with magic that I know of."

"So why did Lucinda kidnap you along with us?"

"How should I know? She took Haler too, remember? And he wasn't even a mage."

"Yes, another good point. That's two apparent mistakes from a woman who doesn't make mistakes." Lira looked at them all, watching their reactions.

"She was very clear with me on who to take," Ahrin drawled. "The instructions left no room for doubt. She wanted all seven of you. Lorin and Haler weren't taken by mistake."

Lira's gaze settled on Lorin. "She took you for a reason, Lorin, and I started to think about what that reason could be if it wasn't your bloodline. An obvious answer presented itself, and when I started to place all your actions in the context of that answer, it just made too much sense. Tell me ... when you broke your arm as a child—the terrible break that threatened your future as a mage warrior—who was the healer that fixed it?"

He frowned. "I don't remember his name. I was a child."

"Fair enough. But here's the interesting thing. I had Master A'ndreas do some digging on my behalf this past week. He insists on Mage Council healers keeping accurate and thorough records. He is confident that no council healer has ever visited the area of Shivasa where you lived."

"Then the records are wrong." Genuine anger filled Lorin's face. "I broke my arm—it happened. Are you suggesting I'm lying?"

"This past *week*?" Fari jumped in. "How were you communicating with Master A'ndreas—"

Lira cut her off, gaze on Lorin. "I don't think you were lying about the break. What I *am* suggesting is that it was an Underground mage that fixed your arm and saved your future. I'm suggesting from that moment on you were loyal to Underground and the Shadowcouncil. I'm suggesting that you joined Temari Hall in order to spy for them, and I'm suggesting you were kidnapped along with us to win my trust and gain access to me. The death of Haler, your 'best friend' was a lovely touch to win our empathy. A poor farm boy from the rural regions of Shivasa—who better to draw my attention and get under my guard?" Lira's voice was laser-like, cold and cutting, filled with the long-buried fury of what she'd figured out.

The room fell deathly silent. Yanzi now looked bewildered, as things took a turn he hadn't seen coming. Ahrin was watchful. Fari's dark skin had turned bloodless. Lorin's expression hadn't changed from its usual haughty look.

"You have more than one mage ability, don't you Lorin? Lucinda *gave* you more." She pushed harder. "You can create illusions. I think back to that night in Temari tower ... when we were all staring out of Egalion's office at the 'deserted' city of Karonan. You were sweating, your shoulders tense. At the time I thought it was well-concealed fear, but it was *exertion*. You were creating the illusion. Despite your injury, you were the one who helped get us back inside Temari Hall without anyone seeing ... impressive. Tell me, was the crushed leg intentional? Or a mistake because I knocked Dasta out and he lost control of the razak? I'm betting it was the latter."

"You've lost your mind," he said, the volume of his voice growing louder with each word. "I can't believe you would accuse me of any of that. I've been the one person to stand by you no matter what."

She cocked her head. There was no dread or anxiety anymore, not now she was looking into the face of her greatest betrayer. Now it was just cold fury and ruthless purpose. "And that's what undid you in the end. I saved your leg, Lorin, but there is no good reason you would throw away your life, your career as the mage warrior you supposedly so desperately wanted to be, to break me out of prison. To then agree to overthrow the council you supposedly loved so much. I wanted to believe it, but it's just not plausible."

His mouth tightened. "What about the others? They helped you escape too."

"Garan and Tarion were desperate to find Egalion and Caverlock. For them, breaking me out of prison was foolish, stupid, but understandable. Garan walked away from helping me overthrow the council and Tarion stayed with me to save his father."

"And Fari?"

Lira's gaze swept to the healer, settled on her. That had been the hardest decision. Which was the spy—Fari or Lorin? "I admit I was never completely sure, but Fari had a genuine grievance with the council after they refused to let her pass the Trials for grossly unfair reasons. And she had the right heritage for the experiments Lucinda was doing."

Lorin looked genuinely stricken. "After all this time, you are truly willing to believe that I'm a traitor? That I was a traitor all this time."

"I don't just believe it, Lorin," she said it without hesitation. "I know it."

"Lorin, is she right?" Fari asked him in a shaky voice.

He glanced between them, thoughts clearly working furiously, but there was no give in Lira's expression, and he seemed to realise that claiming innocence wasn't going to work. It was too late. So he said, with his characteristic hauteur, "She is."

Silence, deep and thick and choking filled the room. As certain as she'd been, to *hear* those words ... Lira almost rocked back on her heels. Fari let out a gasp before covering her mouth with her hand.

Lorin looked at Lira. "I am still your ally, Lira, your friend. I want the same thing you do, to have mages rule this continent. Imagine what you could achieve if you worked *with* Lucinda."

"You're not my friend. You're a traitor," she spat at him. "And I don't want mages ruling this continent any more than I want Lucinda taking another breath."

Realisation crept over his face, and he stared around, as if he couldn't believe it, his gaze finally returning to hers. "A con. You ran a con on *me*? On all of us?"

"Damn right I did," she said quietly.

She ignored Fari's gasp, Yanzi's confused grunt, a sudden jerk of Athira's wrists against her bindings, and she watched the Shiven mage sink back into his chair, jaw set.

"What happens now, then?"

"What happens now is that you won't be leaving this room. I'm sorry, Lorin."

Lorin was already summoning his magic as he rose from his chair, hands shimmering with concussive magic.

But Ahrin had already moved.

With one hand, she tossed one of her knives towards Lira, while in the same movement she stepped up behind Lorin and wrapped an arm around his neck.

Lira caught the knife. She didn't hesitate. Before Lorin could let loose his magic, she stepped forward and buried the knife in his heart.

He sagged instantly in Ahrin's hold, eyes going glassy, and Lira pulled the knife out just as quickly. Ahrin let go and stepped away, allowing Lorin's body to slump to the floor.

Lira lowered her hand to her side, grip steady, but inside, the grief crashed through her chest like a tidal wave. Lorin Hester had never been her friend, but he'd stood by her when most hadn't. She'd loved him.

She took a deep, steadying breath. She accepted the grief as necessary, as necessary as killing him had been, then lifted her gaze from his body.

It was done.

# CHAPTER 38

The Darkhand looked at Lira. "He reacted fast. It would have been safer to light him up."

Lira merely shook her head. "Not Lorin. A quick death for him."

A heavy silence filled the room, finally broken by Yanzi, who looked a little shaken. "Well, that was quite the meeting."

Lira's gaze searched out Fari. "You okay?"

Her dark eyes were sheened with tears. "You thought it might be me?"

"I did."

"That's why you never told us all the details of your plan, even though you hinted..." Realisation spread over Fari's face.

"You stuck with me anyway," Lira said. "I will never forget it. And I will never doubt you again."

Fari held her gaze and gave her a slow nod.

"And now..." Lira hesitated, pulled up a chair before Fari, ignoring anyone else was even in the room, knowing Ahrin would be covering her back. "I'd like to reward your faith in me." She reached out and took the healer's hands. "I didn't really take over the council, Fari. It was all for show. Anler and all his people were arrested by Egalion and the council three days ago. There will be some changes to the council, but I am working *with* them. Now that Lorin is dead, Lucinda is blind to us and has no leverage to wield over Egalion or me. We can now move on the Seven as a united force."

Fari stared at her for a long moment. "So instead of taking on your grandfather's mantle, you've destroyed Shakar's network right down to its roots?"

"You were the one who said it. I'm not him. I don't want to be him."

Fari's mouth opened, closed.

"There's another thing." Lira couldn't help the grin spreading over her face. "You and Garan are going to be mage councillors. From here, we're riding to Alistriem to meet the rest of the Mage Council to have you formally invested. You both will have a vote on who the new Magor-lier will be and a say on what the council becomes in the future. What's your proud Dirsk clan going to think about that? You may not give them an heir, but you've just given them a seat on the Mage Council."

Fari swallowed, blinked, then she launched herself forward, wrapping both arms around Lira's neck. "I don't care what they think, but *I* think that I am so glad that I chose to stay with you, Lira Astor."

Lira hugged her back fiercely. "I'm glad too."

The sound of Yanzi clearing his throat loudly behind them had Lira letting go and standing up. "Hold up. Just to clarify, we're *not* taking over the world? It was all a ruse you and the boss cooked up together?"

"Is that okay with you?" she asked, inwardly bracing for his response.

Yanzi dropped back into his chair and let out a loud sigh of relief. "Thank everything for that. I really just want to be a crew boss in Dirinan, not emperor of the world."

"*I'll* be the crew boss," Ahrin said sharply. "But you've done well, Yanzi. Your place as my second is secure."

Lira let out a relieved breath. "Now that we're sorted, Yanzi can you ask Alea to bring in our other guest and have someone remove the body?"

He nodded and headed for the door. Seconds later, the tattooed woman was back, along with another crew member. They hefted Lorin's body and carried it out.

They'd barely gone when Alea waved in the lord-mage of Rionn, Dawn A'ndreas.

It was the first time Lira had seen the woman since she'd helped the false Tarrick Tylender lock her away for life. She hadn't been sure how she'd feel on seeing her again, but in the end, she felt only a slight ache that had once been fierce grief and anger. "Thank you for coming, Lord-Mage. I'm hoping Egalion filled you in on everything that's happened."

Dawn nodded. "Under the strictest instructions that I was to tell nobody, not even my husband and son, and that I travel here secretly. I'm aware that there's a lot to be said between us, but I assume you need me for something important?"

"I do." Lira waved a hand in Athira's direction. She was still tugging compulsively at her bonds but hadn't reacted to Lorin's death, or Lira's revelations after. Something in her had gone quiet, almost like a switch being flicked off. "I'd like you to help her, please."

Dawn frowned. "Is she ill? Wouldn't my brother be better to—"

"She's not ill." Lira stepped closer to her cousin, resting a hand tentatively on her shoulder. "And I don't think she's truly loyal to Lucinda either. I think they conditioned her, forced her loyalty, like the Hunters. I want you to help her break the mental conditioning, Lord-Mage."

Silence fell. Athira still didn't say anything, but her jaw tensed, and her shoulders turned rigid. It was almost identical to the way Ahrin had looked every time Lira had pressed her for information about her childhood.

Dawn nodded briskly, crossing the room. "I can help her."

"She won't be able to have contact with anyone until you're confident the conditioning is broken," Ahrin said sharply.

The lord-mage gave her a considering glance. "Understood. I'll take her back to Carhall with me—I understand that's where the Hunters are being treated?"

Athira shoulder's relaxed suddenly. "Yes, Carhall. That's where I want to be."

Dawn smiled in understanding. "Home is always best for healing."

Fari rose from her chair, turning businesslike. "Let's get to Alistriem then. I'm guessing we don't have a huge amount of time until Lucinda realises we've destroyed her spy network." The woman's gaze lingered on the blood on the floor, the grief in them belying her briskness.

Lira touched her arm, bringing Fari's gaze back to her. "I'm still no hero."

"Oh, I know." Fari cleared her throat, turned, and headed for the door. "You're something much better."

Exhausted, Lira sought solitude once Dawn took Athira in hand and the others went to catch up on some much-needed rest. She'd only just dropped onto the bed, though, shoulders heavy with weariness and an odd sort of flatness, when the door clicked open softly to reveal Ahrin. She scanned the room before settling her gaze on Lira. "It's rather dark in here."

Lira didn't reply. It *was* dark.

Ahrin crossed the room in a blink, reaching down to take her hand and haul her upwards. "Come with me."

They left the gambling hall, heading through the dark streets of the harbour district. Lira followed in silence, content to be led, calmed by the feel of Ahrin's hand in hers. A little smile flickered at her mouth when it became obvious where they were going.

The loft where they'd once lived with their crew.

It was empty now, the floor covered in dust, old belongings strewn around. The windows had the same cracks she remembered, the floor the same holes. Even the curtain that had once divided off Ahrin's personal space still hung from the ceiling. Lira stopped in the centre of the space, breathing it in, the memory of that warm contentment she'd once felt serving to soothe the edginess of her heavy mood.

"When I came back to Dirinan after leaving Underground and took down Transk, I ordered the crew who'd been living here to clear out." Ahrin's hands were in her pockets as she strolled over to the windows. "I'd come here sometimes, when I needed to think."

"We were happy here," Lira said with a sigh.

"I didn't know what happy was, then. I'm still not sure, not really." Ahrin turned, leaned against the wall. "But I like to come here and remember those days. It makes me feel … good. Warm. I thought maybe it might make you feel the same way. You've had quite a time recently."

Lira couldn't help it, she grinned. "Are you concerned about me?"

Ahrin scowled. "Yes. When you decide to care about people, they can hurt you. I know that Lorin's betrayal, killing him … you did what was necessary, but it hurt you."

"I'm all right, Ahrin." She lifted a hand to rub the back of her neck. "You're right, having to drive a knife into his heart, it hurt in a way I *never* want to hurt. But … I accept now that the risk of pain is part of letting myself care, and it's what I choose."

"You and I are different there," Ahrin murmured, then lifted her head. "I'm not coming with you when you leave Dirinan."

Lira let out a breath, nodded. "No, I didn't think you would."

"I've helped you get here, but now you've got the full might of the council and kingdoms behind you, and you don't need me." Ahrin shrugged. "Lucinda isn't my fight, and I have no interest in trekking all the way back to Rotherburn. I want to stay here. Start growing the crew again. It will be harder now without the Hunters; I'm sending Alea and his unit to Carhall with Athira and the lord-mage."

It wasn't what Lira wanted, but it *was* what Ahrin wanted, and that was what mattered most to her. So she squelched the aching sadness she felt at their imminent parting and kept her voice brisk. "All right."

Ahrin's quicksilver smile flashed out. "Really? Just like that."

"Just like that. You've done more than enough to help me, Ahrin." Lira smiled, and meant it. She would trust that they would find each other again. "I'll be riding out for Alistriem in the morning. Once everything is done, I'll come back here and tell you all about how it went."

"Assuming you manage to survive Lucinda," Ahrin muttered.

"So much doubt." Lira shook her head. "Well, just in case I never see you again, how about you come over her and kiss me like it might be the last time ever?"

Ahrin's wicked smile spread further over her face, and she pushed off the wall, stalking towards Lira in a way that had her stomach doing flips. "That I can do."

They gathered outside the gambling hall the following morning, Lira and Fari, Dawn A'ndreas and Athira, Alea and his Hunters. Yanzi and Ahrin saw them off.

"We'll keep a close eye on all ships leaving the harbour over the next few weeks," Ahrin promised. "Any we suspect of heading towards Rotherburn will be stopped."

"Appreciate that," Lira said.

Ahrin cocked her head. "You'll need to move fast. I can't stop all messages going west, and you can't be sure she doesn't still have spies—"

"I know."

"And even if you win, she's got something else planned. You're going to have to figure out what that is before—"

"I know."

Her eyes narrowed dangerously, but then she sighed. "Be safe, Lira."

"I'll do my best." She kissed Ahrin, then turned to Yanzi, throwing her arms around his neck. "I'll miss you both."

"Me too," he said gruffly. "Just make sure you come back here in one piece to visit us, all right? And don't leave it years this time."

"I'll do my best," she promised.

Lira swung into the saddle, lifting a hand in farewell, before urging Alfie into a quick trot. The others came streaming after her.

She didn't look back.

# CHAPTER 39

Two weeks later, Lira and her party met Egalion, Caverlock, and the rest of the Mage Council delegation on the main road that wound into Alistriem from the east. It was a bright, sunny morning, the air warm, the sky a cloudless blue.

Tarion was with his parents and the councillors, and as soon as he caught sight of Lira's group, he urged his horse into a gallop before reining in alongside Alfie. "You're well?"

"I am." She returned his smile, pleased to see him.

"And Lorin?" His gaze searched hers, concerned. "Aunt Dawn told Mama that everything was okay, that he had been the spy, but she didn't pass on all the details."

Her smile faded. "Lorin is dealt with. He won't be reporting to Lucinda anymore."

Tarion let out long breath, looking stricken. "I had hoped somehow you were wrong. He was my friend, and I..." He shook his head as if to dispel the sadness, then in a sudden movement leaned over to wrap his arms around her tightly. "Missed you, Lira. I'm glad you're okay."

She hugged him back. "Missed you too, mage-prince."

"No Ahrin?" Tarion asked.

Lira shook her head. "Her part is done."

"Do I get a hug too?" Fari enquired from behind them.

Tarion beamed at her, then urged his horse over to give the Zandian healer the same treatment.

Fari accepted the hug, then gave him a scowl. "Don't think I've quite forgiven you yet for thinking I might have been a spy. I know Lira wasn't sure whether it was me or Lorin, yet she never suspected you."

Tarion reached out to touch her arm. "When Lira told me what she suspected ... I didn't believe it was either of you. I'm so glad, Fari, you have no idea."

She blinked, seeming startled by his sincerity. "All right, I suppose you're forgiven."

Lira, still smiling, glanced away from them to meet Egalion's gaze. The woman was watching them. She looked puzzled, but also thoughtful. Lira lifted her hand in greeting. Egalion merely nodded in response, but Caverlock gave a hearty wave back.

They merged the two groups of riders, with Lira and Egalion up front, and continued towards Alistriem. The carriages carrying the councillors trundled along behind them.

The only time Lira had been to Alistriem previously, it had been after nightfall and she'd been exhausted and suffering from magic overuse. This time she had the opportunity to admire the soaring golden palace perched on the hillside above the city, its harbour gleaming deep blue in the sun.

Alistriem was beautiful. Lira no longer wondered why Egalion had tried to make Temari Hall more like her home. If she'd grown up here, she'd never want to leave. Egalion had made a lot of sacrifices, and not just during the war.

"Is Athira safe?" Lira asked, trying to breach the space between them. It wasn't like she wanted to be best friends with the woman, but the stiff silence was making her itch.

Egalion glanced at her. "Dawn arrived in Carhall with her two days ago. She'll stay there for now, to help with the Hunters too."

"Thank you."

There was a moment's silence, then Egalion cleared her throat. "When Dawn sends me updates on how they're doing, I'll let you know."

Lira buried a smile. "I would appreciate that." She gestured over her shoulder towards the councillors. "What do they know?"

"I told them before we left Carhall that things weren't as they appeared, and that they needed to maintain the façade of being overthrown, but from an abundance of caution I didn't say anything further until a couple of days ago." Egalion grimaced. "The full story didn't put them in any better mood, but they've come around to the necessity of it all."

Lira huffed a breath. "I can't believe I ever wanted to be a councillor and sit with that lot for the rest of my life."

"Be thankful you weren't born with the type of power that demands that kind of duty," Egalion said quietly.

Lira blinked in surprise. She'd never thought of it that way. That her lack of magical power, power like Egalion and her grandfather had, would be a kind of freedom.

But it was.

Before entering the city, Egalion turned them off the main road and onto a quieter one. The turnoff was guarded by two Bluecoats sitting their horses, straight-backed, hats perfectly in place. The paved road led up into the hillside above Alistriem, winding between sun-dappled trees. At one point they crossed a rushing river, hooves echoing on the wooden bridge, then the road turned a corner and the walls of the Egalion estate loomed on their right.

It was just as beautiful as the city it sat above.

That was Lira's first thought as they slowed their horses to a walk through the open gates and along a pebbled drive towards a graceful three-story mansion. Arched windows faced out over the front of the property. Stables sat to the left of the main house, a long terracotta-roofed building adjacent to an exercise yard for the horses. The remaining visible space of the main property was covered in beautifully landscaped gardens running all the way up to the boundary of what Lira assumed was the palace lands.

"You grew up here." Lira looked at Egalion, unable to hide the note of wistfulness in her voice. It couldn't have been more starkly different from the draughty shack she and her mother had shared.

Egalion smiled. "I was fortunate."

Lira nodded slowly, then glanced over her shoulder to what had grown into a rather substantial convoy. Counting the three carriages carrying councillors, and their mage and Taliath guards, there were upwards of thirty riders. "Are you sure there's enough room in there for all of us?"

Unexpectedly, the woman chuckled. "I've no doubt there'll be many complaints about room size or lack of view, but Ladan has space to put them all up. And the Bluecoat barracks behind the house for his private household guard will be comfortable for the councillors' guards." Egalion glanced at her. "You didn't bring any guards."

"The Hunters aren't mine anymore, and I am no longer the heir to the Darkmage." Lira shrugged. "I'm just me, Lira, and I don't warrant any kind of retinue."

"Nor do you need one," Egalion said, giving her a little smile. "You can look after yourself better than anyone I've ever met."

The arched double doors at the front of the house opened as Lira and Egalion approached, Tarion and Fari not far behind. The carriages had come to a halt, and the mage and Taliath guards stayed close as councillors clambered out and stretched. Caverlock stayed with them. Lira had already noted multiple instances where his charming, jocular manner quickly served to soothe tempers or spurts of irritation. The man was as impressive as his powerful wife.

Garan and Ladan Egalion emerged from the house, looking so alike it made Lira shake her head in amusement. Garan was the more expressive of the two though, and the look on his face at the sight of Lira Astor and Alyx Egalion riding together in apparent harmony down his driveway made Lira break out in a chuckle.

"Aunt Alyx. Lira," he said cautiously, coming to a halt at the top of the steps as Lira and Egalion reined their horses in below. "I'm going to skip the pleasantries and demand you tell me what's going on."

"What my son said," Ladan added firmly, one hand on the hilt of *Mageson.*

"It's pretty simple." Lira smiled at Garan. "We're here to make you and Fari mage councillors."

At her side, Egalion sighed.

"What?" he said, a blank expression on his face.

"She's not joking, cousin." Tarion called out jovially. "The whole council is here to swear you both in."

Ladan cleared his throat, giving his son a sympathetic look before addressing his sister. "Could you kindly explain what is going on?"

"It's quite a long story," Egalion told her brother soberly. "Which, if you invite us in, we'll share with you. Once we've told it, we can answer all your questions. We're under quite a time imperative, so the sooner we can talk, the better."

Ladan Egalion scowled, jaw set. "You want me to host a Mage Council meeting in my house. What's wrong with Carhall?"

"I'm afraid I must insist on it." His sister dismounted, waving for the others to approach as well. "But I bring you a gift in recompense."

Dashan Caverlock rode up to the steps then, dismounting and climbing them in three easy strides to wrap Ladan Egalion in a fierce hug. "It's good to see that ugly face of yours again, my friend."

"Dashan." Ladan's eyes closed momentarily, before he pushed Dashan away. "Once again you return from the dead. Alyx, you'd better have a damned good explanation for all this."

"She does!" Dashan said cheerfully. "Garan, good to see you too."

"And you, Uncle Dash." Garan looked completely dazed.

Egalion spoke then, issuing a series of orders. "Tarion, you'll join us. Dash, will you go over to the palace to brief Cayr and Jenna on what's going on? Cayr's less likely to lose his temper if you're the one carrying the news."

"With pleasure. I'll make sure to impress upon them the secrecy of it all too." Dashan grinned, then offered his hand to Garan. "I'm sorry I can't be there, but good luck, Garan. I'm so proud of you."

Garan took the offered hand and shook it, still dazed. Dashan gave him a slap on the back, nodded at Ladan, then strode back down the steps to remount his horse and ride off at a canter down the drive.

Egalion started up the steps then. Ladan seemed to realise this was actually happening and muttered something about letting his steward know to prepare for guests before striding after his sister into the house.

Grooms appeared from the stables, and the yard became a bustling chaos of neighing horses, clopping hooves, and councillors and guards milling about. The councillors eventually began heading up the steps, making noises about food and drink after a long ride, while one of the mage warriors started gathering all the guards to lead them around to the barracks.

Lira headed up the steps with Tarion and Fari. Garan still stood there, looking rather lost as he watched mage councillors file one by one into his house. He grabbed Lira's arm as she reached him, pulling her to the side. "What is going on?"

She met his gaze. "The council and I came to an agreement. The entirety of Shakar's network has been rounded up, gift wrapped, and handed over to them. In return, you and Fari get seats on the council. I'm on the council for the next little while too, though that will just be temporary."

He shook his head, pinched the bridge of his nose. "That ... I am my father's heir. I can't...."

"One hopes your father has many years to live yet, and in the meantime, you can do some genuine good for the mage world," Lira said. "And when the time comes, the choice will be yours which life you want."

"What about Uncle Tarrick?"

She gentled her voice. "The man who took his place and has been pretending to be him for the last three years is dead. There is no Magor-lier right now."

Garan reeled, shock filling his face. Tarion moved over to sling an arm around his cousin's shoulder. "I'm sorry for the awful news."

"It's true, what she says?" Garan searched his cousin's face, clearly hoping he would refute all of it.

"It is." Tarion hugged him tighter, then let go. "We don't know for certain yet what happened to Uncle Tarrick, but it's very unlikely he's still alive. A mage with shapeshifting ability has been impersonating him for some time."

Garan turned back to Lira. "You were right about him."

"I didn't want to be. I'm sorry it turned out this way," she said, meaning it.

Silence fell as Garan processed his, one hand distractedly lifting to run through his hair. He let out a long breath. "So you weren't ... you never intended to destroy the Mage Council and do what Lucinda wanted?"

"No." Lira paused. "Your aunt and I are going to explain everything in there, but suffice to say everyone had to believe that's what I was doing. It was the only way I could figure to keep Ahrin and Caverlock alive until Ahrin could get them out."

"Ahrin's alive too?"

Lira smiled. "She got herself and Caverlock safely out of Rotherburn while making Lucinda think they both died in the escape attempt."

Joy began to break through the dazed look in his eyes, that his uncle truly was returned alive. He blinked, shook his head. "But I refused to join you. Why would you make me a councillor?"

"You did what you believed was the right thing, as difficult as that was," she said. "You're a good man, Garan Egalion, and the council needs someone like you. Just promise me you'll keep listening, especially to those who've had a very different life to yours."

Tarion laughed and gave Garan a shake when he simply stared at her. "She's not kidding. You've got to lose that vacant look from your expression before you face the council."

Lira stepped away. "Come on. We don't have time to waste. We need to get you both installed so we can figure out what to do about Lucinda before *she* figures out what's going on."

Lira tried to quell the anxiety curling in the pit of her stomach as she went into the house. She'd gotten this far, but there was still so much more to go. Not to mention whatever else Lucinda had planned.

But she wasn't alone anymore. Lira almost laughed as she realised that she was about to go to war alongside the Mage Council.

She just hoped it would be enough.

# CHAPTER 40

They hosted the council meeting in Ladan Egalion's formal dining room, a location that had plenty of space for the six councillors, along with Lira, Garan, Tarion, and Fari. Rawlin Duneskal was a notable absence, but it was Tylender's empty seat that cast the largest shadow over the proceedings. For all the council's faults, Tylender had been universally loved and respected.

Once food and drink had been laid out on the table, Alyx Egalion didn't waste any time. Knowing what was coming, the five remaining councillors wore expressions ranging from resignation to almost-contempt. "As you now know, Lira made two conditions in handing over all remaining vestiges of Shakar's network. I propose that we get those formalities out of the way immediately. Then you can all rest after a long journey, and we can reconvene as a full council first thing tomorrow morning to agree on a plan of attack against the Seven and Rotherburn."

Walden let out a heavy sigh. "I propose that Lira Astor take Rawlin Duneskal's position on the council."

"Seconded," Egalion said without hesitation. "Are there any dissenting votes?"

Silence filled the room. It was a sullen silence, but nobody objected. Lira wondered whether it was because Egalion had truly convinced them, or whether they just wanted to get it over with so they could eat and go to their soft beds. She'd take it either way.

Keeping the spark of triumph off her face, Lira stepped forward, pulled out one of the empty chairs, and dropped into it. Before anyone else could speak, she said, "I nominate Garan Egalion and Fari Dirsk as new members of the Mage Council."

"Seconded." Again, Egalion didn't hesitate. "This council was re-constituted after the war to improve the lives of mages, to destroy the prejudices of the past. While we've made some strides towards that goal, we are far from achieving it. If we want to survive, we must adapt. And to do that we need councillors with different viewpoints, different ways of doing things. Are there any dissenting views?"

There was a lot of shifting in chairs, muttering, and scowls, but nobody said anything. Lira rolled her eyes. What a bunch of spineless old men.

"Garan, Fari, please join us." Egalion waved them to the two remaining empty chairs at the table. Once they'd seated themselves, Garan still looked a little dazed, Fari fiercely proud. Egalion continued, "We need a new Magor-lier. Traditionally, we would seek a unanimous vote from among the existing council members." Egalion took a deep breath, her gaze settling on Lira for a long moment. Lira couldn't force what came next ... she no longer had any leverage or power over the council. Her single vote wouldn't make the Magor-lier, and Egalion clearly held the most influence with the councillors, especially now they knew Lira was no threat to them.

"And that's what we should do this time," Walden barked. "Especially now, when we're facing the first serious threat since Shakar."

Egalion's gaze was still on Lira. A silence stretched out. Though all the other councillors had nodded at Walden's words, none of them spoke. They waited for Egalion's view. She eventually nodded and sat down.

"Right, I'm going to be very clear." Fari spoke up then. "There is nothing—not even hot pincers driven deep under my fingernails—that will *ever* convince me to vote for any of the pre-existing members of this council not named Alyx Egalion."

"I have the same view." Garan sat up straighter, his voice clear and penetrating. He and Fari shared a nod.

A little smile on her face, Lira drawled. "Same. I guess that makes things easier. Egalion, you're it."

Garan smiled at his aunt, and Fari gave her a nod.

"Take it, Egalion," Walden grumbled. "You're the most powerful mage alive and you've always wanted more change than the rest of us."

Egalion shook her head. "I've never wanted to be Magor-lier. I don't think a mage with my power *should* be Magor-lier. I am content with running Temari Hall. And I'm not the only option."

Walden barked out a laugh. "If you think any of us are voting for one of the children you just used your influence over us to add to the council, you're sorely mistaken."

They were close to a stalemate. Lira could see it clear as day—Egalion wouldn't agree to take the job and Lira concurred with her reasons for not taking it. But the old men would never agree to it being Fari or Garan either.

"I propose a compromise." Garan Egalion spoke into the thick silence. "We have an existential threat before us. Let's deal with that first. Once we come out the other side, we'll turn all our efforts to learning what happened to Tarrick Tylender—he deserves that much from us. If and when we confirm he is no longer alive, *then* we will discuss who becomes Magor-lier. Not before."

"I second that." Lira spoke immediately in support. It was the best solution before them.

Alyx Egalion ran her eyes around the table. "Are there any objections?"

There were none.

She sat down. "All right. Session dismissed. Let's aim to be back here first thing tomorrow morning to discuss Rotherburn."

A short time later, while the councillors were resting in their rooms, they held a much less formal meeting in Ladan Egalion's study. Now,

Lira's inner circle joined with Egalion's. It made for a crowded space, but a hopeful atmosphere pervaded the room.

Cayr Llancarvan, the king of Rionn, and his queen, Jenna, had appeared unexpectedly, Dashan Caverlock in tow. Throughout Egalion's explanation of everything for her brother and the king's benefit, Cayr had worn a bemused expression while Jenna kept darting thoughtful glances in Lira's direction. Garan's father was grumpy—having already made several pointed comments to his sister about who would inherit his estate and position now that Garan was a mage councillor.

Eventually all the relevant information had been related, and questions answered. Lira almost laughed when—once the servants delivering hot mugs of spiced cider to everyone had left the room—they all turned to her expectantly.

All the master strategists and experienced leaders sitting around the lord-Taliath's study, and they turned to the heir to the Darkmage to start them off. Then, when that thought properly settled, she almost burst into tears.

They *weren't* seeing the Darkmage when they looked at her.

They were seeing Lira Astor. And they wanted to know what she thought.

Tarion seemed to realise she was frozen. The most shy and awkward man she'd ever known promptly opened his mouth and addressed the room in quiet but confident tones, one hand resting on the hilt of *Darksong*. "The most important factor now is moving before Lucinda can put a response into play—because we know she has one." He explained briefly about the bulky package that had travelled on the ship from Rotherburn.

By then Lira had recaptured her equilibrium. "Lucinda will react the moment she realises she's blind. We have an advantage now, but only a small one, and it will vanish soon."

Egalion's gaze turned thoughtful. "We'll go in with a specialist strike team to—"

"No. I think we have to send everything we have," Fari said. "It's not worth underestimating Lucinda. If we're going at her, we'd better make damn sure we can take her. Half measures will fail."

"I don't think we need a whole army." Lira sided with Egalion. "We can't creep up on the Seven if there are hundreds of us, not to mention how many more ships and boats will be visible hovering off their coastline. The home ground is theirs, which means they'll have the advantage, even if we have superior numbers."

"Both points are well made," Garan said thoughtfully. "We keep it small, then, but we send our best. Our most powerful mages, most skilled Taliath."

"Don't forget we have a potential ally in Rotherburn," Fari pointed out. "Lira's anonymous telepath. What if we reached out to them when we arrived, asked for their help?"

"We don't know them well enough to trust them with this." Lira shook her head immediately. "And we can't risk them telling the Seven we're there—we have to assume Lucinda's control over them has only grown since we left."

"Once we take her out, though, we should make contacting the telepath a priority," Dashan said. "They'll be able to help us smooth things over."

Egalion nodded at her husband. "I'll ask Dawn for a recommendation, but I think Warrior Rani would be the best option. His telepathic range isn't very powerful, but like Dawn he can sense the emotion behind thoughts. It will help you discern your mysterious telepath's honesty."

"Good," Lira said. "Egalion, you'll have to stay here. You too, Garan." They simultaneously opened their mouths to protest, and Lira shook her head. "Egalion, you're the last line of defence for Shivasa and Tregaya. Lucinda has a failsafe, a counterstrike planned, and we have no idea what that is. If we don't take her out quickly enough to prevent her initiating that plan, leaving our most powerful mage alive behind to deal with it is the best way I can think of to counter her. And Garan, your aunt will need an ally on the council to help do what is needed."

Garan did not look happy about this. At all. But he didn't protest. "Fine. We'll make sure the continent is prepared in case the worst happens. We'll ride for Carhall tomorrow with the councillors. Perhaps, King Cayr, you or Lady Jenna would be willing to travel with us? Some joint conversations between you and King Mastaran would be useful. Actually, Uncle Dash, could we get Leader Astohar there too? If you succeed in taking out Lucinda, then we'll need a united front."

Ladan looked at his son with a frown. "For?"

"We need to decide, kingdoms and Mage Council together, how we can help Rotherburn rebuild," Garan said simply.

There was a beat of silence, but Fari continued, "Once you take out their leadership, things will be even more difficult for the people there in the short term. We should be ready to provide aid—even if it's just immediate supplies of food and weapons, and mage warriors and Taliath to help them hold off the razak and nerik while we work with them to come up with a long-term plan so that they don't have to abandon their home."

"You shame me, Garan, Fari," Cayr Llancarvan said quietly. "It is something I should already have thought of. I will travel with you to Carhall, and I will write to the Zandian emperor first thing tomorrow, requesting his presence there also."

Dashan nodded. "If I ask, Leader Astohar will come too."

Lira cleared her throat. Magic save her from bleeding hearts. "While I agree from a tactical standpoint that neutralising any future threat from Rotherburn is in our best interests, I'd prefer to focus first on actually making sure we take out Lucinda."

"She's right." Jenna spoke for the first time, cool and imperious. "Even with a specialised strike force, how are you going to get close to the ravine city without the Seven's forces seeing you coming?"

"That actually won't be too difficult." Tarion shot a little smile at Garan. "I have a way in."

"Each member of the strike team needs to be trusted implicitly by at least one of those here in this room," Garan said. "And even then, they shouldn't know where you're going until after they've set sail."

Ladan frowned in thought. "Following those parameters, I can think of, say, twenty Taliath off the top of my head. Jenna, what do you think?"

"No more than that," she said. "I'd rather not have all our trusted Taliath offshore at once."

Egalion looked at her brother, also clearly thinking. "Mage warriors who can be effective without being able to directly target their magic in case you encounter the monsters ... trusted implicitly ... and keeping some in reserve here for if things go wrong, we'll struggle to give you more than twenty or so."

"It's not as many as I'd like, but I agree that we should prioritise having trusted warriors." Caverlock nodded. "Alyx, can you and Dawn telepathically contact those we need in Carhall and Karonan? We'll need them to get messages to Ladan's Taliath too. If the rest of us leave Alistriem first thing tomorrow, we can rendezvous with everyone else in Tarnor." He named the Tregayan port just over the border with Shivasa. "Lira, I recommend avoiding Dirinan; it's a place Lucinda knows and may still have contacts in."

"Agreed." Lira shrugged.

"Good." Dashan rose to his feet and stretched. "Now I recommend we repair to the kitchens where there is hot food. I want our strategy hammered out tonight before we ride out for Tarnor."

"We'll need to get the council's approval tomorrow morning," Garan added. "Otherwise, there will be no mage warriors for your strike force."

"They'll follow Councillor Egalion's lead on this," Fari said. "Not to mention you, me, and Lira have votes now."

"They'll also be thrilled they don't actually have to *do* anything," Ladan muttered.

Everyone chuckled.

Lira went last out of the room, her head spinning a little. It was so odd, planning something on this scale without needing to hide in the shadows or watch over her shoulder. She wasn't sure she liked it … it felt so unexciting, despite the scale of what they faced.

Maybe it was just that she was chafing at the delay. All the obstacles in front of her now were gone. Nothing was stopping her from going at Lucinda.

The spark lit and burned through her, and her stride quickened despite herself. She wanted this planning done so they could stop *talking* and start acting.

It was time for Lucinda to burn.

# CHAPTER 41

L ira stared out from the prow of their ship. A cloudy night kept the coastline of Rotherburn mostly hidden beneath a curtain of darkness, but the gap in the cliffs where the ravine sat was a darker spot that just made it discernible.

Around her the ship was a hive of quiet activity. Ropin—freshly signed Mage Council immunity in hand—had anchored far enough offshore that any observer on the cliffs would be hard pressed to see them on such a dark night, even if they knew exactly where to look. All the deck lanterns had been extinguished. To reduce visibility even further, one of the mage warriors with them, Skot, had shrouded the ships in a natural-looking fog.

All the potential problems tossed over and over in Lira's thoughts. Once they all piled into three ship boats and approached the ravine, they risked being seen by any observers on the clifftops.

The Seven would be watching, she was almost sure of it. Even if Lucinda hadn't noticed that her spies had gone dark yet ... the woman had an uncanny knack for knowing when things weren't right.

And even if they did make it inside the ravine without being seen, they'd have to navigate along the unruly rapids for what Tarion estimated was several miles. His way in was perfect ... *if* they could find it in the dark. A tunnel opening in the ravine wall several miles east of the ravine city. He and Garan had come across it while searching the undercity for Ahrin after she'd fallen off that cliff.

Then it was navigating miles of undercity while avoiding nests of razak, before going deep into the heart of Rotherburn's remaining population with only a small strike force. There was no safe harbour for them inside the city, nowhere to escape to, no defensible location. If they didn't cut the head off the snake quickly and efficiently, they might never get out.

Tarion's voice drew her sharply from her musings. "How are you feeling?"

Lira glanced up, shifting to make room for him at the railing beside her. "My overwhelming desire to see Lucinda burn hasn't served me well in the past, and I'm trying to keep in mind that I've never come close to outwitting her."

"You haven't given up yet, either, Lira, and that means something. If the worst happens, and she's prepared for us, then we'll do our best. I certainly don't count us out easily."

She glanced over her shoulder. They weren't visible in the dark, but this ship was full of skilled mages and Taliath, not to mention Dashan Caverlock. Lucinda wasn't invincible. She tried to take heart from that. "Neither do I."

Silence fell then, but Lira studied him. There'd been something different about him since they'd left Alistriem, a heaviness. In some of the tactical discussions they'd had on the journey, he hadn't been anywhere near as energised as he usually was when talking strategy. "Did you see Sesha while we were in Alistriem? I noticed you disappeared there for a while."

His shoulders turned rigid for a moment, then he let out a soft breath. "I saw her. We officially ended things. She's..." He swallowed. "I think there might be a match in mind for her. Which I'm actually glad about, because the thing I want most of all is for her to be happy. If I know she's happy, then I can be okay."

Lira hesitated, then reached out to rest her hand over his on the railing. Despite his brave words, the grief oozed from him, and she wished she could ease it somehow. He leaned into her briefly, and they stood there in companionable silence.

Sometime later, a low whistle had them both turning to see Caverlock lifting a hand and gesturing them over.

It was time to go.

Fari slipped in beside Lira and Tarion as they gathered with the others around Caverlock.

"Everyone ready to go?" the general asked. They numbered forty-six warriors in total. All wore dark, non-descript clothing, though it was easy to tell mages from Taliath by who had a sword at their hip versus who had a staff hanging down their backs. Each warrior carried a small pack with rations enough to last a few days if they got lost or held up in the tunnels.

Caverlock and those on his boat would be the vanguard. He was the most skilled sailor among them, not to mention the strongest fighter. Tarion would travel with him to direct his father to the ravine opening. All would be trusting the Taliath's unnaturally sharp eyesight to spot it quickly enough that they could direct the boats over to it. The telepath, Rani, would also travel with that group to maintain contact between the three boats.

Lira, with her water ability, would travel on the third and rear boat in case anyone got separated. Cario Duneskal's staff hung from Lira's shoulders, its heavy weight long-since adjusted to, and she carried a knife at the small of her back.

When everyone gave a series of nods, Caverlock straightened. "Good. Let's start lowering those boats. Rani, make sure you can easily reach the minds of someone in each of the rear two boats before we set off."

"Yes, sir," he said.

"Not me." Lira gave the telepath a look. "My shields are too strong and instinctive."

"You can use me," Fari offered. "I'll be on Lira's boat. It will be a relief having a short break from shielding."

"My shielding is bad anyway." Toola, a female telekinetic riding in the second boat, offered Rani a smile.

Anticipation and fear both kindled in Lira's stomach as she clambered down into the rocking boat and took her seat on one of the benches, Fari pressed against her left side. Their plan was a solid one ... endorsed and refined by Dashan Caverlock, the finest strategist alive. But Lucinda was a fearsome adversary, and deep down, Lira knew that the woman would have some counter to this.

She just had to hope they'd be able to meet whatever the counter was and still come out the other side.

A stiff breeze had whipped up earlier, and now sizeable swells propelled the boats inexorably towards the cliffs. The Taliath manning their tiller kept his gaze unerringly on the lead boat as it angled towards the ravine. When it felt like they were lurching too far off the correct angle of approach, Lira used a touch of magic to help the rowers keep them under control. Ropin's ship quickly vanished from sight behind them, wreathed in fog.

"I'm so glad I don't get seasick," Fari muttered as the boat plunged down the side of a wave, sending their stomachs plummeting with it.

Despite her words, the woman seemed more subdued than usual. In an attempt to distract her, Lira asked, "How do you feel about going back into those tunnels?"

"About the same as I did last time. Either way, I'm glad it's with you." Fari leaned into her as the boat lurched to starboard. "What about you?"

The words came out without Lira really thinking about them, "I feel like I'm going back a completely different person."

"Not a different person," Fari said. "But someone who's stopped living in everyone else's skin and started learning what it's like to live in their own. If we survive this, what are you going to do next?"

"I still don't know." Lira shrugged. "But that doesn't scare me anymore."

"Well, whatever it is, it better involve a lot of visits to Carhall. If I don't get my regular snarky reminders about pureblood mage privilege and ignorance, I might start turning into one of those old fossils I share a council seat with."

Lira smiled. "Count on it."

She hesitated. "If we survive this, could you keep your council seat a few weeks before giving it up? There are some changes Garan and I would like to propose immediately—adjusting the Trials for one, and making Temari Hall more accessible for those from poor or badly educated backgrounds. It will help to have your vote."

"You'll have it," Lira promised.

The dark gap of the ravine loomed closer and closer, and the sea was rough, crashing against the cliffs, loud and roaring the closer they came. A tense silence fell over everyone as their boat angled after Caverlock towards the ravine.

Lira focused, kept her magic sunk into the water around them to keep the boat steady as they shot towards the gap. For a moment, it seemed as if they were going to crash straight into the rock looming up out of the water. Lira braced, moved her body with the boat's sudden turning to port...

And then they were through.

From there it only grew more difficult. The dangerous underwater rocks and choppy surface meant that directly following Caverlock's route was impossible—their rowers had to do the best they could to avoid hitting rocks or the ravine's sides. They plunged and veered through the rapids, spray soaking them within moments.

"Rani says they're about to reach the gap!" Fari called out suddenly. "Northern rockface, roughly fifty metres up."

"Keep a look out for the lead boat where they've anchored against the ravine wall," the Taliath on the tiller replied.

After some interminable period of Lira holding on for dear life and trying to see through the darkness and spray from the boat, one of the sharp-eyed Taliath caught sight of the other two boats bobbing on the water by the ravine wall.

As soon as they had line of sight, Lira sank her magic into the rough water, using sheer brute force this time to bring them smoothly up alongside the other boats. Once they were alongside, she worked to calm the current around all three boats, using her telekinesis at the same time to hold them all closely together so they didn't go rocketing off past the opening in the rock.

Everyone cast uneasy glances at the sky as she worked magic. They had to hope no nerik or razak were close enough to sense it and dive on them. It was a risk they had to take—trying this without Lira's magic would be impossible without a jetty to tie up to.

The river poured out into the ravine from the opening Tarion had identified, an imposing torrent of water. The young mage flashed in and out of sight as he teleported himself inside, then caught the rope his father tossed up to him, aided by one of the mages with telekinesis. A moment later, he'd secured it, then did the same for the other two boats. Once the boats were moored, the raiding party moved one by one up into the tunnel opening.

It took almost an hour, but everyone got inside without injury, and the night remained dark and cloudy, hiding them from any nerik flying above. A handful of the Taliath withdrew torches and flint from their packs. It took some work to get them lit in the damp surroundings, but soon flickering firelight illuminated the rocky tunnel walls.

Caverlock addressed the group once they were gathered. He was calm, relaxed. They huddled on a section of rock just above the flowing river, boots inches deep in puddles formed from the spray. "I estimate we're a handful of hours off dawn. As soon as it's light enough, a patrol could spot our boats out there, so we move fast and hard from here. Tarion will take point with Fari and Lira—they've been here before and are more familiar with the undercity. I'll bring up the rear with the Taliath to make sure nothing tries to creep up on us from behind. From here on out, nobody uses magic unless I say so. If you do, we'll find ourselves fighting through razak to get to the Seven and probably warning them of our approach in the process. Any questions?"

There were none. They'd been over this before, many times, on the journey. But Caverlock was a seasoned leader, knew the value of calming any nerves with repetition of details and his confident manner.

"Right." Caverlock's grin flashed out. "Then let's dive into the belly of the beast."

Lira felt an echo of the thrill on his face leap to life inside her.

# CHAPTER 42

T he strike team moved quietly down into the undercity, following a tunnel leading away from the riverbed that wound inexorably downward. They'd only travelled a short distance when Lira first sensed the razak. It was faint, like a tiny niggle in her thoughts, something she barely noticed. But as they moved deeper into the tunnels, heading down under the waterline, the faint nag became noticeable pinpricks in her brain. Like little sparks of heat zapping her.

She'd often wondered if she'd somehow imagined what she'd felt after killing the queen razak, but clearly she hadn't. When the queen razak's blood had spattered into her open wounds as Lira killed it, it must have caused some sort of ability to break out. Much faster than injections of regular razak blood had.

Tarion noticed when she started shaking her head to try and dislodge the odd sensations there. "You can sense them again?"

"I can sense *something*. I'm assuming it's the razak."

"Are they anywhere near us?" Fari asked.

"If I try and actively use it to pinpoint their location, we risk them sensing my use of magic," she said quietly.

Tarion said, "It's worth the risk. If the worst happens, you'll at least sense them coming and we'll have time to move."

Reluctantly, she concentrated, trying to focus and lean into the sensations rather than shy away from them. Almost immediately she had to fight being lost in the rush of using her magic. It took a moment to steady herself, then, taking deep, steady breaths, she focused on the sparks of heat in her head, jumping from pinprick to pinprick, mapping the spots that her magic could sense.

Eventually she opened her eyes. "Keeping in mind that this is a new ability and I have no sense of distance or perspective yet, I can't feel any particularly close to us. And none in the direction we're heading … I think."

"Good news. Let us know if that changes."

Fari's eyes scanned her face. "Your reserves okay?"

"This ability doesn't seem to need a lot of energy to use." She waved off the healer's concern. "I had to use a lot more back at the tunnel entrance manoeuvring those boats."

It felt like a long walk, but eventually the incline began to even out, and they came upon another rushing river—the one upon which Lira had washed ashore after diving after Ahrin. A chill trickled down her spine at the memory of those moments, thinking she'd lost Ahrin forever...

"This way," Fari murmured, turning west along the shoreline. "We're not far from the undercity proper."

Tarion gave Lira a look, as if sensing her unease, but she ignored it. Ahrin was alive and well. Lira just needed to deal with Lucinda and she could go home to her Darkhand.

Their pace slowed a little. Fari and Tarion had to rely on their memories—Lira's weren't any help; she'd been so out of it with magic overuse and grief. Tarion was confident, though, and led without hesitation. Every now and then he'd stop and consult with Fari, and they'd decide on the best way forward.

As they continued along, Lira kept part of her attention on the annoying pinpricks in her brain, slowing them if a razak seemed to be close to ensure they didn't run into it, and speeding them up when they were moving through an area free of the creatures.

If only she'd had this ability the first time Lucinda had sent them down here.

If only Lucinda and the Seven *knew* she'd had this ability. Lucinda would have lost her justification for making war on the Mage Council. A mage who could lead elite strike teams directly to the creatures ... it would take time, but it would maximize the likelihood they could find and eradicate them entirely. Lira kept that thought in the back of her mind—it might be something she could use if things went wrong.

Lira's ability meant they made much faster progress than Caverlock had estimated. Her inner sense thought it was probably only just past dawn when they reached the more familiar upper levels of the underground city.

Tarion had already picked out the best approach in, explaining to his father back on the ship, "The door they let us through when they sent us after the razak ... when we returned, they took us straight from there to the Seven's assembly hall. It was a direct route. I remember it."

Lira had agreed. "And we barely saw anyone on the way there. They were deliberately keeping us isolated from their citizens."

Now, as they approached that door, Tarion sent a signal down the line, and Caverlock came forward to join them. The four of them paused behind the thick steel door.

"Tarion, you're up," Lira said unnecessarily.

Dashan cast a worried glance at his son but, to his credit, didn't try and delay him. Tarion gave them both a reassuring smile, then vanished from sight. Behind them, the strike team settled into resting positions along the walls.

Lira stared at the door, as worried about Tarion as his father was. He had the most dangerous job of all: teleporting himself through the ravine city, based only on his memory of the route they'd travelled twice, to get himself to the Seven's hall and wait for them to gather inside it.

They'd considered going after Lucinda alone in the house where Lira and Egalion had met with her, but Caverlock disagreed. "If we take the Seven together, it prevents any of them slipping away and gathering mages and soldiers to fight back. We don't have the strength to stage a war on the streets of the city, especially on unfamiliar ground when we can't use magic because of the nerik flying above. This needs to be clean and surgical."

Lira paced the top of the stairs as she waited, while Fari took the opportunity to rest her legs, and Caverlock moved among the warriors, a smile or joking word for each and every one of them. She saw the effect it had on them, how it kept them focused but relaxed, despite the danger they were in.

Very few of these men and women had been in a real fight before, risked their lives, experienced danger. Caverlock knew that. She trusted that if things went awry, he had the ability to keep them together.

She was also glad to give him that responsibility. She didn't want it. Preferred to be answerable only to herself, her own survival, as much as possible.

The plan was for Tarion to return at midday if the Seven hadn't gathered beforehand, to let them know he was all right, then again at nightfall. But they were only waiting just over an hour when he flashed into sight. Weariness from magic use tugged at his expression, but his hazel eyes were alight. "They've just gathered in the hall. There are a few clerks and lots of papers, so I'm hoping they plan to be there for a while. I couldn't see anything different from the same configuration of guards they had when we were here last."

Dashan's glance shifted from the door to Lira. "Can we risk magic?" he asked her.

She nodded. "I can't sense any razak close enough to reach us before we're through the door, even if they sense me using it and come looking."

"Good." He moved aside for her, and she pressed her palm against the smooth metal, wrapping the door with her telekinetic magic and frowning in concentration.

Two locks and three bars on the other side. Exactly as she'd remembered.

She picked the locks first, and they gave two satisfying clicks, then she lifted the bars out of their brackets. In case there was anyone passing within sight of the door on the other side, she lowered each bar painfully slowly, then gently placed them on the ground, so they made no sound.

"Done," she murmured. "Door's open."

"Give them the signal," Caverlock said.

She lifted her hand, allowed enough of her magic to leak out to light up her hands and forearms in a violet glow. A signal to the mages and Taliath arrayed on the stairwell below them that they were now moving into the city itself.

A signal to be ready to fight if needed.

All the torches were immediately doused. Anticipation shivered through the darkness, swords rang as they were drawn, and then Lira pushed the door open slowly, slid through the gap, then stilled, ready to move if attacked.

The hall beyond was dim, the greenish light coming from the river-facing residences. Ivy crawled over the stone floor and walls and the sound of the rushing ravine river roared in the distance. No guards were posted. She straightened, then opened the door fully, waving the all clear.

Lira and Caverlock stood aside as their warriors filed through, Tarion and Fari taking point on making sure the way ahead was clear. Once everyone was inside, they re-locked the door and replaced the bars. If all went well, they wouldn't need to come back this way, and they wanted to keep any questing razak out.

Tarion—flashing in and out of existence as he scouted ahead—got them all the way up another two levels without needing to emerge from the interior hallways into any external areas of the city.

Eventually they moved up a long set of steps and emerged into the sunlit courtyard at the western side of the Seven's hall. There they halted while Tarion and Caverlock went ahead to deal with the guards posted on the building's side entrance—this one Lira was familiar with from the night the anonymous Rotherburnian telepath had sneaked her into the building.

Lira took the opportunity to find Rani. "You know what to do?"

"Wait until Lucinda is contained, then unleash the full force of my telepathy to find your mysterious telepath friend." Rani grinned. He was young, eager, almost trembling with the anticipation of his first ever battle. "But if I move too soon and tip Lucinda to what's going on, you'll murder me in horrible Darkmage fashion."

"Damn straight." Lira held his gaze. "This is serious, Rani."

"I know. I'll do what you need, I promise." His expression sobered. "My range might not be very powerful, but I'm good at this, Lira. I'll find your telepath and tell you whether we can trust them, and I'll be right."

She gave him a smile. "All right, then."

A soft whistle from the direction Caverlock had gone in had them moving again. When Lira followed the strike team around the corner, the red-uniformed guards were unconscious, gagged, and firmly bound. She helped Caverlock and Tarion move them into a nearby garden, then followed the others inside.

The strike team divided, as practised. Caverlock and half the force peeled left to circle around the other side of the building, while Lira and Fari led the other half to the right. Two more guards had to be dealt with as they moved, quickly now, down a long corridor running parallel to the audience hall.

A door set into the wall opened into the dim space between the wall of the audience hall and the long banners hanging down from its ceiling. Lira remembered clocking these banners the first time she'd been in this hall, the distance they sat from the wall, the ridiculously large hiding place they offered—a vulnerability she'd filed away in the back of her mind the way she'd learned on the streets of Dirinan. One she could exploit if she ever needed to.

The murmur of multiple voices came from the top of the room, where the council would be sitting, sounding soft and relaxed. The light shining through the tiny cracks between each banner held the golden glow of morning sunlight coming from the windows high above.

Good, the Seven were still gathered.

When nobody came running or called the alarm, Lira gestured to the warriors lined up behind her and then slipped into the room, back pressed against the wall. She inched along it, staying hidden behind the tapestries. Fari and the rest followed, one by one quietly slipping into the hall.

Anticipation heated her blood, and she had to spare a moment's concentration to keep her magic from leaking out again and betraying their presence with its violet glow.

Lira, back pressed to the wall to avoid touching the banners, travelled as far as she could towards the top of the hall, stopping when she reached the final tapestry. Stilling, she peered around it. Two guards stood at the bottom of the steps leading up to the dais. Both looked bored, and neither were paying much attention to their surroundings. Directly across from her, Lira could just make out faint shadow in the gaps between those tapestries; Caverlock and his team.

Nobody inside seemed aware anything was awry yet—the tenor of voices from the Seven hadn't changed in pitch or volume, and the guards didn't shift from their bored stance. Risking another look, Lira angled her head until she could see the dais. The Seven sat in their chairs around a table in the middle of the dais; its surface scattered with papers, mugs, and plates of food.

A moment later Lira spotted movement directly across from her. Caverlock had reached his spot. He gave her the hand signal they'd agreed on.

They were ready.

She glanced over her shoulder, met Fari's reassuring gaze, then lifted a hand, making a sharp gesture. The movement swept down the line of waiting warriors. Simultaneously, they all stepped out from behind the tapestries, dust clouding the air as the cloth was pushed aside. Lira's gaze went straight to the gathered Seven, searching out Lucinda.

She knew almost immediately that something was wrong.

The hall was entirely empty of all but the two guards and the Seven. No clerks or servants hovered near the meeting area. It wasn't that, though, that tipped her off.

It was the utter lack of surprise on Lucinda's face. Or exhibited by any of the other Seven. Ignoring the dread sliding through her stomach, Lira walked forward, boots rapping against the floor, a single hand gesture telling everyone else to hold their position.

Lucinda rose gracefully from her chair and walked to the edge of the dais, where the steps began. "Lira, how pleasant to see you again."

A chill went through her as suspicion became certainty. The Seventh had expected Lira. At this time. In this place. She'd simply been waiting for her to appear. Not only that, but none of the other Seven said anything, not even Burgen. They were so far under her influence now that Lucinda was in full control of this show.

For them to have known that level of detail … had Lira been wrong about Lorin? The thought flitted through her mind, quickly dismissed. Questions later. Right now, she had to focus everything on overcoming whatever came next.

"I can't return those sentiments, I'm afraid." Lira filled her voice with confidence. "I'm here to kill you. Once I've done that, my army is here to ensure the rest of your Seven agree to cease any thoughts of invading our home."

"*Your* army? So Athira's message was true. You succeeded in the task I set you?"

Lira stilled, not sure how to reply. She'd always known that it was going to become obvious to Lucinda as soon as she saw Caverlock among the warriors that Lira hadn't done what she'd pretended to, but by this point it should have been too late to matter. Yet something about the woman's manner made it seem like she already...

Lucinda stepped closer. "Or are you and Alyx Egalion secretly working together to make me think that you've taken control of the Mage Council while you send a strike force here to kill me?"

Lira said nothing. How could she possibly have known?

Lorin had died before he could send any kind of message, and Lira was sure he hadn't suspected Lira before that. Athira had similarly been prevented from sending any messages. Could it be that Lucinda was simply a flawless actress in pretending not to be surprised? Was *she* stalling while she figured out how to respond to Lira's attack?

"Very good. Impressive even," Lucinda murmured. "There's not a trace of shock on your face. You see, you did a good job taking out my spies. I never expected you to find out about Lorin, and killing the Magor-lier in front of the entire council, well … that took guts. Athira was utterly convinced by your charade. I hadn't expected that level of creative planning from you."

Lira shrugged casually. "It was what you asked me to do, no? I told you I would."

Lucinda cocked her head. "I almost feel sorry for you. You fight so hard, so persistently, so determinedly. And yet you fail to recognise that you have a fatal weakness that ensures that you will *always* fail." She let out a breath. "I even warned you about it. Multiple times."

Lira had had enough. She'd been anticipated, but that didn't mean everything was lost. "Caverlock, go!"

But there was nothing. No sound of movement. No crisp calling of orders.

Lira spun around, dread crawling up her spine. Every single member of the strike team was frozen to the spot, unable to move. And just as she turned, the double doors at the end of the hall opened, admitting brown- and red-jacketed soldiers. They moved, quick and disciplined, into the large space, each one taking up a position behind a member of the strike team, placing a knife at their throats.

"I can hold a room paralysed like this very easily," Lucinda said conversationally. "And for as long as I need, so don't get any ideas in your head about waiting for me to get too tired. If any of them so much as twitch, however, my soldiers have orders to kill them."

Fear unfurled through her at the realisation Lucinda could do the same to her at any moment. Instinctively, she summoned her magic, but Lucinda was faster. Lira found herself frozen in place, unable to move anything from the neck down.

"I told you she was your greatest enemy," Lucinda murmured, voice rich with nauseating triumph. "And you refused to listen."

Lira's gaze unconsciously followed Lucinda's as the woman glanced over her shoulder. Ahrin appeared from the shadows at the top of the hall, long coat swirling around her ankles, gaze surveying the room in satisfaction as she said to Lucinda, "I did as you asked. Now, you agreed she would be mine."

"I did." Lucinda stepped away, that cold glee lighting up her face as she regarded Lira. "I always doubted you'd succeed in doing what I asked, but I was even more confident that my Darkhand would choose whoever gave her more power. When you decided to hand over all your power to the council, when you *could* have destroyed them instead, well of course she returned to me. And now ... well, who is there to stop me from taking everything?"

# CHAPTER 43

Lira stared at Ahrin as she approached, Lucinda's words twining through her mind and heart, all the woman's warnings flooding back. The ones Lira had dismissed over and over. Her chest clenched so tightly her breath came in shallow gasps.

"Think about it." Lucinda was almost *purring* now. "How much of your plan here today was actually *yours*, and how much my Darkhand's?"

"Don't you see, Lira," Ahrin murmured, coming to a stop before her. Her expression was calm, that flat killing look in her eyes. "It was always going to come down to this. I told you that you should have taken the power we both deserved, but you didn't listen."

"You can try and kill me." The words rasped out of her, but they lacked any strength. She felt as if her soul had been ripped out of her body and crushed against the floor.

Lucinda had been right. She'd always been right. Lira was never going to win, no matter what she did. The despair of that realisation would have brought her to her knees if the Seventh's magic wasn't holding her frozen.

Lucinda's gaze lingered on her for a moment longer, then she turned to look at the Seven. "Thank you for your help in laying my trap, but things are now in hand. Why don't you go and board the ship and ensure the captain is ready for departure on the evening tide? I'd like to make sure we're in Carhall just at the right moment."

Lira was reeling—from Ahrin's betrayal, to Lucinda's comprehensive victory—but still, she stiffened at those words. "What takes you to Carhall?"

Lucinda said nothing, merely watched as the Seven rose and filed away. Burgen shot a regretful glance over his shoulder, but Adellin looked smug, almost as triumphant as the Seventh. It was hard to tell what the others truly thought.

"I'm going to enjoy this." Lucinda's voice drew Lira's attention back to her. The woman's gaze was riveted on the despair that was no doubt written all over Lira's face. "Not to mention the fact that your little army will get to watch you die before I kill them. Imagine dying without any hope. What a beautiful thing to observe."

A spark of anger flared then, strong enough that Lira snarled at her. "How long exactly can you hold so many people? Because if you let me loose, your pet Darkhand is not going to kill me quickly."

Lucinda smiled, then released Lira from her hold. Relief flooded through her so strongly the woman's words sounded almost distant. "I can hold the room long enough to savour the sight of her killing you." There wasn't a trace of doubt in the Seventh's voice. Nor did she look weary. "What made you think, after so many failures, that you could beat me, Lira Astor?"

Lira held her gaze, kept hold of her determination, her will, that undying thing inside her that would never go away. "Because you are beatable."

Lucinda laughed, genuinely amused. "Even if you had succeeded here today, taken over the Seven, killed me even. You *still* would have lost. You and your council are in the midst of being wiped out. Their destruction is already coming and there's no stopping it now, no matter what you do."

Lira stilled. Lucinda's counterattack, the one that involved whatever was in the package that had been delivered to Dirinan. Did it have something to do with the Seven travelling to Carhall? Could she push the Seventh to tell them about it if she feigned shock and ignorance? "What are you talking about?"

"You'll never know, and you'll never need to, because you'll soon be dead."

Lira turned back to Ahrin. "*Why?*"

Ahrin shrugged. "It's not personal, it never has been. Lucinda can give me the power I want."

"So everything between us was just a pretence?" Lira swallowed, knowing she was stalling, but having no choice. She didn't want this fight. If she died here, Tarion would die too. And Fari. And she wanted more than anything else for them to live. She was the one who'd brought them here. They'd trusted her, and she'd failed them.

Ahrin frowned. "I'm honestly disappointed that you believed me so readily. I taught you better than that. I even told you to your face that it was impossible for me to feel genuine emotions, that I'd never known how. Lord Anler told you in detail what was done to us."

"I told you. I believed you because I love you, because I chose to," Lira said.

"And like *I* said, you're a fool. Your grandfather would be ashamed." Ahrin's face hardened. "Now stop stalling. If you don't want to fight, I can just kill you and be done with it."

Lira closed her eyes, took a deep, steadying breath. And in those seconds, she gathered every part of herself that *was* the Darkmage. She pushed out anything else.

When she opened her eyes, she looked at her enemy.

Something rippled over Ahrin's face, something unreadable, and then she smiled that cold predator's smile of hers. "Knives or magic?"

"Both." Lira lifted a hand, wrapped Ahrin in telekinetic magic, and sent her flying down the hall. The Darkhand used her own magic to stop her flight and drop to the ground lightly.

"Weak," she snarled, then sent two quick concussion bursts flying through the space between them.

Lira dropped to her stomach, winced as they exploded over her head and squeezed her chest in a vice-like grip, then rolled to her feet and set Ahrin's coat alight. It burst into white flame, but Ahrin shrugged it off.

"You're not even trying," she snapped, visibly irritated.

She came at Lira with her knives then. Lira drew her uncle's staff, spun it through the air, and knocked away both of Ahrin's slashes. It felt good in her hands. Right. Like she was invincible with it.

But that was a false confidence … a straight-up battle with weapons was a foolish situation to get into with a trained Hunter. Lira was more than capable with a staff, but she was no match for Ahrin's fighting skill. Magic was where she had the edge.

She had to use it or she'd die quickly.

The *only* path open to her now was to prolong her death long enough that Lucinda grew tired and Caverlock and the Taliath were able to free themselves from her hold. She had enough faith in their strength of will to know that it was possible.

Gasping aloud, she snatched both knives from Ahrin's hands with telekinesis and sent them flying out of reach, then swung her staff at the Darkhand's head.

Ahrin swayed, only just avoiding the blow, then used her own magic to try and yank the staff from Lira's hands. Lira stopped her with insulting ease.

They paused, circling each other. Ahrin drew more knives.

"You're still not trying," Ahrin taunted, breathing faster now, midnight blue eyes alight. "You know I'm going to kill you if you don't kill me first."

She lunged, moving so fast that Lira couldn't react in time. A knife sliced down her arm as she desperately twisted away, stumbling and dropping to the floor. Furious, she shoved Ahrin away with her magic, giving herself time to get to her feet. She called her staff back to her hand, swung it in a series of fast, strong blows. Tried her best to keep Ahrin far enough away to stop her using her knives.

Ahrin ducked aside from each one, dancing, taunting, then drew another knife from her belt and came at Lira. She could do nothing but back desperately away from the flurry of too-fast attacks, her staff only managing to block a handful. Ahrin's footwork was sublime, her speed a match for Lira's agility; like Tarion, she *danced* rather than fought.

Lira was forced inexorably backwards, pain burning down her arm. Her blood dripped to the floor, and with it, her anger rose. With a roar, she lifted both arms and ripped the blades from Ahrin's hands again, pummelling her with so much magic she couldn't counter it.

The Darkhand flew backward, landed hard on the floor, so hard it took a few seconds for her to scramble lightly to her feet. "That's more like it," she said in satisfaction.

Then she came at Lira, lithe and swift, drawing another knife—her last one. Lira lifted her staff, focused her mind, and again they battled. Ahrin's fighting ability was far superior, but Lira's skill with her telekinesis was unparalleled. Each time Ahrin got through her guard, Lira's magic nudged the blade aside before it could touch her.

Their breathing came faster, the flurry of blows a blur, feet moving back and forth across the marble floor. Lira's face curled in a snarl, the magic lighting up her blood, speeding her moves, giving her strength and confidence and power.

But Ahrin would win.

She was too fast. Too skilled. Slowly, she pushed Lira back towards the stairs leading up to the dais where Lucinda stood, expression alight with sickening triumph. And then Lira stumbled, twisting awkwardly to avoid a lightning-fast slash and slipping on where her blood had earlier dripped to the floor.

Lira's back hit the unyielding surface of the floor, her breath escaping in a grunt. Ahrin was on her before she could react, straddling Lira, knife driving down towards her heart.

Lira grabbed hold of Ahrin's wrist with both hands, desperately holding her back, the blade bare inches from her heart. Ahrin was strong, but Lira augmented her strength with magic, and they strained against each other for what seemed an interminable period.

Gasping for air, strength waning, Lira met Ahrin's midnight blue gaze.

And she stilled.

Her mind flashed back to that first night in the alley in Dirinan. Three dead bodies and a bloodied eight-year-old girl crossing the dirty snow towards her. Offering a coat and a home and a *life*. Offering belonging. Protection. Acceptance.

Then, only months earlier, Lucinda's taunting words. '*You and the Darkhand could be a true challenge to my mastery, but her mercenary disregard for anything but her own interests, and your complete inability to trust, means that will never happen.*'

And Lira knew in that moment how Lucinda could be beaten. It had been so simple, all this time. So easy. Lucinda herself had been the one to give Lira the answer.

Ahrin had to choose to care, to love. And Lira had to learn to trust.

So she did.

Lira took a large, gasping breath, still holding Ahrin's gaze, and she chose ... not to love Ahrin, but to *trust* her. Fully, implicitly, unconditionally. To trust that Ahrin had already made the choice to care.

Then she smiled, and she stopped trying to hold Ahrin back.

Ahrin didn't hesitate. She drove the knife down, buried it to its hilt. Pain flashed bright and hot through Lira. A scream of pain escaped her as Ahrin withdrew the blade and stood in one graceful movement. She looked up and to the side, presumably where Lucinda stood. "It's done."

Lira gasped on the floor, agony threatening to cut off her awareness, the sudden blood loss making her dizzy. She fought hard to hold to consciousness.

Then Lucinda came into view, stepping up beside Ahrin, more triumph in her hooded gaze. "You were right," she said to Ahrin. "She couldn't bring herself to really try to kill you."

"You were wrong," Lira gasped, grunting in pain, feeling hot blood soaking through the cloth of her tunic, beginning to trickle down her left side. But not much. Not enough to threaten her life. A laugh bubbled out of her. She wasn't dead, and after a clean strike from a Hunter she should be ... which could only mean ...

"What?" Lucinda frowned, shifting closer to hear.

"Ahrin was never my greatest enemy." She smiled, despite the pain and increasing weakness. "She was yours."

Lucinda was still frowning as Ahrin stepped up behind her, wrapped one arm round her neck, and drove her knife into the woman's side, angled up towards her heart.

A single killing strike.

Lucinda's eyes flew wide. She coughed. Blood trickled from her mouth. And then she swayed and dropped to the floor in a crumpled heap. Her eyes glazed; her chest stopped moving.

The Seventh was dead.

# CHAPTER 44

"YANZI!" Ahrin bellowed, a roar of command sweeping through the hall.

The main doors slammed open, and a multitude of figures streamed through the gap, howling and whooping. They were tattooed and weaponed and wearing torn clothes and ragged boots, and they were the most beautiful sight Lira had ever seen. Caverlock's strike team, now freed from Lucinda's magic, turned on their captors. The Revel Kings joined mages and Taliath in subduing Lucinda's soldiers and mages.

Lira tried to sit up, grunted in pain, and immediately swayed as dizziness swept over her. Ahrin was kneeling beside her in the next second, one arm supporting her back. "Careful! I didn't hit anything important but you're still bleeding everywhere," she snapped.

"I can't believe you stabbed me," she joked, biting her lip in pain.

"Are you..." Ahrin swallowed, eyes dark. "You trusted me."

She nodded, let her head fall forward against Ahrin, eyes closed. "I did."

Ahrin spoke quickly, words falling over themselves. "I knew she'd be prepared for you, Lira. I figured if I made it look like I'd played you, she wouldn't see my betrayal coming, because she was always so convinced I resented you."

She shifted away, lifting her uninjured arm to frame Ahrin's cheek in her hand, feeling the tears welling in her eyes and unable to stop them. "Thank you. For being someone I could trust."

Ahrin swallowed, eyes going dark, her forehead pressing against Lira's. "Thank you. For being someone to make me *feel*. To show me what joy is."

Her Darkhand was too still, too rigid, so Lira chuckled and pulled away a little. "I won't pretend that for a moment there I wasn't completely and utterly devastated, but I eventually realised I was being an idiot ever believing Lucinda about you."

"Took you long enough," Ahrin grumbled. "Though at least it made a convincing show. You should have used your fire on me. I have no counter to that."

"That would have meant killing you." Lira said quietly. "I don't have that in me."

Fari and Tarion appeared before Ahrin could respond to that, the healer dropping beside Lira while Tarion hovered anxiously.

"What the rotted hells was all that?" Fari asked at the same time as Tarion demanded, "Are you all right?"

"Ahrin decided to play her own con and not tell us about it." Lira groaned. "Can you please do something about this pain?"

"Did you really need to stab her?" Fari tutted, resting a palm over the wound.

"I hit muscle only, she'll be fine." Ahrin hesitated. "There was another reason I did things this way. It was the only way I could think to find out what Lucinda's backup plan was."

Fari stared at her in realisation. "She told you, didn't she? And it's bad."

Lira didn't like the grim look creeping over the Darkhand's face. "What is it, Ahrin?"

She stood up. "I want to make sure this area is firmly under our control first, that you're safe. Then we can talk."

Tarion nodded. "I'll find the Seven. The faster we get them back here the better."

They both vanished, and Fari scowled, going back to inspecting Lira's wound. "I can't believe you let her stab you. And now we've got some crazy other plan of Lucinda's to deal with while you're injured. How did you know Ahrin was faking?"

"I didn't." Lira hissed as Fari pressed a little too hard. "Careful!"

"You're as insane as she is. Lucky she's right; she only got muscle." Fari closed her eyes in concentration, one palm pressed over the wound, her dark skin soon soaked in Lira's blood. A few minutes later, Lira was able to get to her feet, though her shoulder throbbed unceasingly, and she felt a little woozy from blood loss.

The fighting was over by then. Dashan Caverlock had the mages and Taliath moving like a perfectly orchestrated theatre production to secure the space and herd the defeated Rotherburnian soldiers into a corner.

Their part over, the criminals of Dirinan watched all this in evident entertainment, offering an encouraging whistle every now and then. Yanzi and Ahrin stood huddled near them. Lira limped over, Fari trailing her.

"Lira!" Yanzi brightened. "Pleasure as always."

She smiled. "What brings you to these far distant shores?"

"Boss's orders."

"I knew I'd have to hand over your army to Lucinda as part of the deception," Ahrin said. "So I had Rilvitha bring Yanzi and the Revel Kings after you, to ambush the ambushers, so to speak. They took out all guards on their way in. Nobody is coming to save the Seven."

"Lucinda had nothing on you," Lira said, shaking her head in admiration. "I should have just let you run this thing from the start."

"No," Ahrin said quietly. "This was as much you as it was me. You got us here, Lira."

Dashan strode over, hair ruffled, blood-spattered, and inordinately cheerful. "Tarion found the ship they've all boarded, so I sent him with one of the captains, guarded heavily, to fetch them. As soon as they're back here we'll give them our demands. Nice touch with your cutthroat criminals, Darkhand."

Lira rounded on Ahrin, eyes wide, "He *knew*?"

"I needed him to know what was coming so he wouldn't put up a fight and ruin anything." Ahrin shrugged. "Besides, he's a halfway decent strategist and a telepath can't read his thoughts. I can work with that."

"Stop, you'll make my head too big," Dashan said dryly, gaze lingering on Lira's bloodied tunic. "You up for this, Councillor Astor?"

"Councillor Duneskal," she said quietly. "I don't want my grandfather's name any longer. I choose my uncle's. He's the part of me that I want to be."

Fari reached out, touched her arm, and gave her a little smile. "Just like I thought."

Caverlock beamed. Literally from ear to ear. Lira was in the midst of rolling her eyes when Ahrin spoke again. "No time for celebrations just yet. You still have a problem."

The moment Ahrin said it, Lucinda's words flashed through Lira's mind: *Even if you had succeeded here, you would have lost.* "Ahrin, what did she do?"

Lira knew that Ahrin Vensis genuinely cared absolutely nothing for the Mage Council, its mages, or anyone outside Lira Astor and her crew. So her grim expression as she answered spoke volumes. "The package that Athira carried onto the ship leaving Rotherburn with you? One of Lucinda's people took it from Dirinan to Carhall, and its contents were placed somewhere near Centre Square."

"What were its contents?" Fari asked.

"Razak and nerik eggs."

Caverlock stared at her. "For what possible purpose would she have done that?"

"We all know Lucinda wanted to rule the Mage Council and the kingdoms. Her bargain with Lira was the easiest way of achieving it—if Lira could use her name to gain power it would have been a simple handover with Lira as Lucinda's puppet, as long as Lucinda held me as leverage." Ahrin shrugged. "The nests were a failsafe in the event Lira failed."

"How exactly?" Lira demanded.

Ahrin looked admiring. "When I showed up here, pretending to betray you, it became her perfect endgame. Wait for you all to come, lure you into an ambush, and wipe out the cream of your fighting strength. Then she would travel to Carhall with the Seven—she planned to time her arrival for just *after* the monsters had destroyed every mage in Carhall, including the councillors, because both razak and nerik hunt mage power above all. Then, she would step in, use her paralysis magic to stop the monsters before they started eating the good citizens of Carhall, and hold that threat over King Mastaran's head until he agreed to recognise the Seven as the new Mage Council."

"At which point she would release Lord Anler and all his men, use *you* to re-form the Hunters, and deploy that strength to hold power," Lira breathed. The woman's mind had been a marvel. "She basically found a way to succeed where the Darkmage failed."

"Hold on, how exactly was she going to do that?" Caverlock jumped in then, looking incredulous. "Those nests are of no use to Lucinda unless she can control their hatching somehow. Not to mention, even if she could control it, what threat do a bunch of baby monsters really pose?"

Ahrin's mouth thinned. "Lucinda sent off a message the moment I arrived here and she finalised her plans. That message has reached Carhall by now. She had a way of triggering the hatching of those nests, General Caverlock, and if I were you, I'd assume that's exactly what she's done."

Fari frowned. "Even if that's true, who would she have sent the message to? Lira took out all her key people."

"Lira took out the people who were spying on *her*," Ahrin pointed out. "Lucinda was in Shivasa for years. She's been planning this for years. It's why she went there in the first place. Who knows who else she has there, in place, ready to move at her word?"

Caverlock cleared this throat. "What you're saying is that right now there are probably numerous baby nerik and razak crawling around underneath Centre Square in Carhall, and at some point, they're going to get big enough to start hunting and eating mages?"

Ahrin nodded. "Upwards of a hundred is my guess. Rather counterintuitively, the monster eggs are small. I've seen them before. And I'm betting the babies grow big enough right around the time Lucinda planned to arrive in Carhall."

Caverlock sighed. "And without Lucinda there and able to use her magic to freeze the monsters..."

Ahrin shrugged. "Carhall is in a spot of trouble."

Lira touched her arm. "How long have we got?"

"You heard the woman. The Seven's ship is ready for departure. I know because I was supposed to be going with her." Ahrin paused. "She planned to be in Carhall in ten days. She was very specific about that. That makes me think the creatures will probably reach maturity around the nine-day mark."

Fari frowned. "Hang on—are you telling us that those things can grow from babies to those monstrous creatures, or at least big enough to pose a threat to the number of mages in Carhall, within a couple of *weeks*?"

Ahrin cocked her head. "Why else would she be so particular about when she arrived?"

Caverlock began pacing. "That makes things simple. We have to get back to Carhall and destroy the baby monsters before they mature."

"We can do better than that." Ahrin nodded at the mages around them. "You brought a telepath, I'm guessing? They can contact Egalion or Lord-Mage A'ndreas as soon as they're in range from the ship, warn them. Then—"

"General!" Rani came running up, eyes wide with excitement as they locked on Caverlock. "I've got her!"

"The telepath?" Lira asked quickly.

They all turned as Rani pointed to where three Taliath and a mage were shepherding the Seven back into the room, led by Tarion. He watched them closely, one hand on the hilt of *Darksong*.

"One of the Seven?" Lira wasn't surprised. "Which one?"

"Me." Nessin, the Sixth, stepped forward. "There's no further need for anonymity."

Caverlock snarled. "Tell us everything you know about Lucinda's plans in Carhall, right now!"

"Da, what's going on?" Tarion looked concerned. Fari went over to him, drew him aside and starting murmuring. Even as Lira glanced away to return her attention to the Seven, he was turning deathly pale at her news.

"Why should we tell you anything?" Adellin spoke, bristling. "You've just forced your way in here, murdered our Seventh, and—"

"Adellin, enough!" This from Burgen, who looked older and wearier since the last time Lira had seen him. "We're done, and if you can't see that, you're a fool of an idiot. Lucinda has burned us all along with her. All we can hope for now is mercy."

"You get nothing unless you tell us everything you know about Carhall," Caverlock said evenly.

"We don't know the full details of what she planned," Nessin said, regret written all over her face. "No more than the Darkhand. I am sorry."

"Can you tell us how long it takes for a razak or nerik to mature enough to start hunting and feeding?" Lira asked.

Nessin let out an uncertain breath. "Both creatures were literally created from magic so they don't develop like humans or other animals. We've tried studying them over the decades, and from what we've pieced together, they grow rapidly once hatched, usually reaching adult size, or maturity, within three to four weeks. Once they reach maturity, they start hunting blood, and we think that's when they begin to sense magic. If they don't feed within a few days, they die."

"Three to four weeks? That doesn't fit with Lucinda's timeline. Why be so insistent on being in Carhall in ten days?" Lira demanded. "They won't be mature for at least a week after that."

"I don't know." Nessin hesitated.

"What *do* you know?" Ahrin took a threatening step towards her, hand cradling a knife.

"I don't *know* anything, but I got the sense ... it was Lucinda's arrival in Carhall that would somehow trigger their eruption."

"How?"

"I don't know. I swear I don't. But when Dasta was alive, we did some experiments with him. He was able to control not only adult razak, but nestlings too. Maybe Lucinda's paralysis magic could control them somehow ... she was always very secretive about the extent of her abilities."

"She's telling the truth," Rani confirmed, sweat beading on his brow. "Her mind and thoughts are open to me."

Lira ran a hand through her hair in frustration. None of Nessin's responses gave her the answers they needed.

"That might be good news?" Fari ventured. "Maybe without Lucinda being there, they won't mature as fast."

"They'll still reach maturity at some point within the next few weeks," Nessin said. "If you want to save your city, you need to find them before that happens."

Caverlock raked the Seven with a single glance of disgust, then spun around, clapped his hands, and launched into a parade ground bellow. "CHANGE OF PLAN. EVERYONE DOWN TO THE JETTIES NOW. No dawdling. GO!"

"Before you go!" Nessin's voice pitched above the sudden chaos of sound. "There is one thing we can offer you as recompense."

"I don't have time for lingering so make it fast," Caverlock snapped.

Nessin came down the steps. "If you'll come with me? I promise I'm not wasting your time."

"Her intentions are genuine." Rani confirmed at a questioning glance from Lira. "She wants to help—she's afraid and she thinks this will be the only way to win mercy."

"Lira, you, Tarion, and Vensis are with me," Caverlock said quickly. "Fari, you take control of the strike force, get them all aboard boats, patch up anyone who needs it. We'll meet you down there."

"Aye, captain!" She saluted, moved off.

Ahrin waved Yanzi over. "Take the crew and get yourselves on Rilvitha's ship. Caverlock and the mages will travel with Ropin. I'll meet you down there."

"Boss." He nodded and began calling orders to his crew.

Nessin led them out of the hall and through a series of thoroughfares mostly empty of people. As they headed down a narrow set of steps, Ahrin and Caverlock shared a glance.

"We're heading in the direction of the cells where Lucinda held us," Ahrin explained to them in a murmur.

"Feels just like home," Caverlock muttered as they entered a low-ceilinged corridor with cells on either side.

Nessin tossed them a regretful glance. "What will you do with us?"

"We have other priorities right now, thanks to you lot," Caverlock said brusquely. "But don't think we'll forget what you tried to do … what you *helped* Lucinda do."

Nessin paled but forged on. "Without the Seventh, our people will die sooner rather than later. The monsters encroach farther into the city every month, and our mage strength is dwindling. Do what you wish with the Seven, but our people are innocent."

"So are the residents of Carhall," Caverlock said grimly. "So forgive me if I prioritise my people first."

Nessin didn't say anything further, leading them in silence all the way down the hall and through the door at the other end. Ahrin drew a second knife. Both Caverlock and his son's hands went to the hilts of their swords. Lira readied her magic.

But there was no ambush waiting on the other side, just a small foyer where a single, red-uniformed guard sat at a table reading. On the other side was a barred cell larger than those they'd just walked past, furnished with a narrow cot, table and chair, and a couple of lanterns.

Inside that cell was Tarrick Tylender.

Caverlock let out an inarticulate sound of joy and leaped forward, crossing the space in two strides. "Tarrick!"

"Dash!" The Magor-lier's voice was rusty and cracked from disuse. A tangled beard grew almost down to his waist, and his dark skin had the pallor of someone who'd been without sunlight too long. His eyes were wide with stunned shock and disbelief. "*Lira?*"

"Let him out at once!" Caverlock's voice rang with command and the guard practically fell out of her chair in a scramble to go and unlock the cell door.

Tylender's gaze shifted from Lira to Nessin. "What is going on?"

"So much," Lira drawled, hiding her surprise at the sight of a man she'd been convinced was dead. "But it's rather a long story, and we have a bit of a time imperative."

"She's right." Dashan engulfed Tylender in a bone-crushing hug, then stepped away. "Can you walk? We have to move."

"Yes, but not much more than that." Tylender's eyes darkened, the pain in them something Lira instantly recognised as matching her own. "It's been a long time since I've had freedom of movement."

Lira stood aside as Dashan and Tarion took up a position on either side of Tylender and he made his slow way out of the room. Tarion stepped in to give the man a brief hug too, tears in his hazel eyes. Nessin took the lead back the way they'd come.

Ahrin caught Lira's wrist as she went to follow them out. Lira smiled before she could say anything. "I know you don't care about the people in Carhall, and you have no interest in risking yourself to save them. That's okay. I'll come find you when it's all done."

"You don't care about them either," Ahrin pointed out.

Lira shrugged. "I'm not entirely unmoved by their plight. Besides, Garan is in Carhall. I care about *him* very much. Not to mention Tarion and Fari will be going there too. I'm going to make sure they survive."

Ahrin's gaze narrowed in accusation. "You just want an excuse to use your magic and put yourself in ridiculous amounts of danger."

Lira grinned. "That too."

Ahrin leaned down, kissed her. "Count me in."

"Really? Because I think if you come, we might be able to really do something."

"I don't think I'm needed for that. But yes, I'll come with you. I'm not averse to a bit of risky fighting either." Ahrin went to walk away, then stopped. "But also ... the Hunters are in Carhall."

Lira smiled.

"I'm not—"

"Taking orders from me or Caverlock." Lira burst into a chuckle. "That goes without saying."

"Good. Let's go slay some monsters. Hopefully for the last time."

# CHAPTER 45

Lira stood at the prow of Ropin's ship, feet spaced apart for balance, eyes closed, sunk deep in her magic. It filled the water around them, pushing it against the ship from behind. A soft violet glow shone from her hands and forearms where they rested easy at her sides. The healing stab wound in her shoulder throbbed constantly, but Lira let the thrill of being so deeply buried in her magic soothe it away.

Balanced on the roof of the deckhouse, one of the council mages—a man named Skot who had weather ability—filled the sails with wind.

Together they sent Ropin's ship rocketing northeast towards Tarnor, increasing the top speed it was capable of at full sail. Wood creaked and groaned at the unfamiliar stressors being placed on it, sails snapping sharply in the breeze. Ropin was calm at the wheel, the only sign of his deep concentration the slight furrow between his brows. One wrong move at this speed and the ship could hit a swell at the wrong angle and break apart.

A half step behind Lira, at her left side, stood her Darkhand. Though she didn't move, her entire aura was watchful. Fari stood on Lira's other side, one hand on her shoulder, draining her fatigue.

They'd been going like this for a full day, and the sun was lowering towards the horizon. Lira was reaching that level of weariness where she wasn't sure which way was up or down.

"Vensis!" Caverlock's booming voice was a welcome distraction. She opened her eyes and turned around. It was an effort to shift some of her focus away from the magic, and Fari mumbled a complaint at her shoulder.

Ahrin spun, one eyebrow raised.

His long strides brought him over quickly, Tarion with him, and Rani scrambling to keep up. Tylender lagged behind, still too pale and gaunt, but there was a light in his dark eyes that told Lira that freedom was already beginning to work its own healing magic.

"We can't reach Alyx or Dawn," Caverlock said without preamble. "Rani has been trying since we left Rotherburn but no luck so far."

"Explain what that means," Ahrin said.

"Most likely that they're out of range," Caverlock said. "Rani can just barely reach Temari and Karonan from here ... enough to get a telepath's attention and make a strong enough link to communicate. But—"

"It would have been lucky if I could," Rani ventured. "There aren't any telepath students studying at Temari right now."

Ahrin's gaze shifted to Rani. "Will you be able to reach Carhall from Tarnor? That's where Egalion and A'ndreas will be."

"Maybe. But..." He shifted uncomfortably.

"So help me, Caverlock, if the boy doesn't—"

Tylender spoke then, voice deep and already losing some of its rasp. "Carhall is a difficult place for any telepath to reach a particular individual. Even Dawn finds it hard. There are so many mage minds, and the farther the distance the harder it is to begin with. Alyx is immune to magic, so she must let a telepath in before communication can happen. It's doubtful Rani will be able to reach her. And he's never met Dawn, so it will be difficult for him to find her mind."

"But he *can* find another telepath mage there?" Ahrin snapped. "After all, he just found Nessin for us. Don't tell me the headquarters of the Mage Council won't have at least *one* telepath present."

Again, Tylender was unruffled. "Telepathy is a rare ability. Outside Rani, Alyx, and Dawn, there are only two other telepath council mages."

Rani cleared his throat. "Last I heard, Iya was in Samatia as part of the search for Lira. I don't know where Dari was sent, but he was searching too."

"The far north of the continent," Ahrin said flatly. "Extremely unhelpful."

Rani straightened his shoulders. "I will be able to do it. We just have to get me closer to Carhall."

"What about reaching out to a non-telepath?" Lira asked. "Like Nessin contacted me back in Rotherburn."

"The problem is finding the right person ... a random citizen is unlikely to believe a strange voice in their head is real, let alone a crazy story about monsters attacking Carhall. I'd have to search until I found a person that would not only listen, but be able to do something about it," Rani explained.

Ahrin gave Caverlock a sharp look. "If he's useless to us right now, then why are we having this conversation? Lira needs to concentrate."

Dashan grinned. "You really are to the point. We're having this conversation because you and I are in charge of this little rescue mission, Vensis, and I was seeking your views on the best way to approach things if we can't warn anybody in Carhall before we get there. I like to be prepared for all eventualities."

Ahrin's eyes narrowed, shifting from Caverlock to Tylender. "You're willing to have me in charge?"

"Dash has filled me in on everything that happened," Tylender said. "You are no friend to the council, Vensis, but I understand that if it weren't for you, we'd be sailing idly back home only to arrive in a city destroyed by monsters, with thousands dead. Given the current stakes, I accept whatever help you are willing to offer."

Caverlock shrugged. "I'm not one to ignore what's right in front of me. You're as good a tactician as I am, if not better."

She regarded him for a moment. "I like you, Caverlock."

"I've yet to meet anyone who doesn't." He winked. "So?"

"Lucinda planned to be in Carhall within ten days. She doesn't leave things to chance, so I'm going to assume she'd arranged it so the monsters would erupt just before her arrival, especially if Nessin was right about her presence being the trigger." Ahrin spoke quickly, precisely. "We'll shave at least a day off that travelling time if we keep pushing. If Carhall isn't warned before we get there, that gives us a day, two at the most, to search a very large area for those growing monsters. I'd rate our chances of success as slim to none."

"Won't Lira be able so sense them?" Fari asked, sounding weary.

"We don't know," Ahrin answered. "It's possible she won't be able to sense them until they've matured."

"My thoughts exactly," Caverlock said on a sigh. "Even if Carhall knew *now*, a few days isn't enough time to search such a large area. Rani—there's a militia barracks in Tarnor, and I know the commander in charge. We're old friends. If you can find his mind, then I can help you convince him that you're real and he can get a warning via messenger bird to Carhall. That should beat us there by a couple of days at least."

Rani wilted but said gamely, "Tarnor is large, and finding one mind … I can't guarantee it, but I'll do my best."

"Good." Ahrin cocked her head in thought. "The only other thing we can do is get there faster ourselves."

"I'm trying," Lira said through gritted teeth, feeling the need to join the conversation.

Ahrin nodded. "Keep trying. Fari, let Lira work alone for a bit. We need you helping Rani here. The sooner he finds this militia commander the better."

Lira gave Ahrin an aggrieved glance, which she ignored. "That's an order, Dirsk."

Fari shot Lira an apologetic look, then removed her hand and went over to the young telepath. "Come on then," she said to him cheerfully. "I assume you'll be more comfortable in your cabin? Neither of us will be getting any sleep for a while."

He swallowed, nodded, and trailed after her.

"Will your ragged bunch of criminals be coming with us to Carhall?" Dashan enquired. Rilvitha's ship had already fallen behind hours earlier.

Ahrin shook her head. "No. They're going straight back to Dirinan."

"Then I won't include them in our planning. Tarion and I have been talking over the best approach once we're on land." Caverlock looked at Ahrin. "You happy with us continuing to do that?"

Ahrin nodded. "I'll make sure our three mages don't keel over."

"Excellent division of labour." Dashan grinned at them both, then left them to it, long legs carrying him away quickly.

"I thought you loved me," Lira muttered, already feeling the extra drain on her magic now that Fari had gone.

"I thought you wanted to be a hero and save Carhall." Ahrin waved a hand. "So suck it up, dearest, and get us there as fast as you can."

They were roughly a day out from the Tregayan coast when Rani finally found the commander of the militia barracks at Tarnor. He, Fari, and Caverlock huddled together in Rani's cabin before all three emerged, the two mages pale with exhaustion. Rani was swaying on his feet.

"I managed to convince him who we were, thanks to an old incident featuring a bar, two glasses of ale, and some spiders," Caverlock told Lira and Ahrin with a wink. "Commander Yeserin is sending a message to Alyx in Carhall as we speak. He'll also use his authority to have horses and supplies ready for us when we arrive, not to mention he's preparing almost every soldier at his command to travel with us."

Ahrin and Lira exchanged a look. By the time a message reached Carhall ... well, there was nothing more they could do about that. Caverlock merely nodded at them before turning to Rani. "Good work, now go and get some rest. Fari, you up to giving Lira a final push?"

"I can do that."

"No." Lira shook her head. "Go and help Skot instead. If he can keep that wind going, it makes what I need to do much easier."

"I'm not going to have much left to help anyone soon," Fari warned them.

"Do your best."

Ahrin waited until Fari had gone before muttering, "If you keel over on me, Astor..."

Lira snorted, gritted her teeth against the exhaustion weighing her down. "You're the one who told me to suck it up. I'll be fine."

In less than a day, they were dropping anchor outside Tarnor just as dawn lit up the horizon. By then, Fari, Skot, and Lira were tottering wrecks, suffering from magic overuse and barely able to stay on their feet. Rani had managed some rest but was still bleary eyed.

Commander Yeserin waited for them at the docks, briefing Caverlock on the status of horses and supplies. "You can ride out as soon as you're up to it. My men are already mounted and waiting outside the city—you'll have a hundred soldiers and ten scouts at your back."

Caverlock glanced at the sky. "Good. News from Carhall?"

"None. Councillor Egalion should be getting my message right about now, if all went well and at least one of the three messenger birds I sent made it through." He paused. "I took the liberty of sending messages to the two barracks closest to Carhall and requested that they ride for the city for an unplanned training exercise with my men. That way you'll have extra backup but nobody will panic."

"Thanks, Yeserin." Caverlock shook his hand. "Excellent work."

"I wish we were working together again under better circumstances, Caverlock. Is there any more I can do?"

"No. Now it's up to us and luck." Caverlock turned to the mages. "We can wait a couple hours here, give you some time to rest, or do you think you can manage riding immediately?"

"I'm fine," Lira said instantly.

"Me too." Fari crossed her arms.

Skot scrubbed at his face, as if to keep himself awake. "Don't think I can ride alone, but happy to ride double with Amal or Yoori, whoever has the strongest horse."

"I might have to ride double too," Rani said faintly. "But it's either that or you leave me behind. There's no time to waste."

"They will all ride double," Ahrin snapped the order. "We might need their magic in Carhall so it's imperative they rest on the ride. Let's go."

Despite the situation, Caverlock grinned. "I really do like her efficiency."

# CHAPTER 46

The ride across Tregaya from Tarnor to Carhall passed mostly in a blur for Lira. Laid out by the exhaustion of magic overuse, not to mention her still-healing wound, she rode with Ahrin, the Darkhand guiding the horse while Lira slept curled up against her front. Fari rode with Tarion, who kept a close eye on them both.

By the end of the crossing, she and Fari had recovered enough to be functional. The entire strike force was weary after a straight four-day ride barely leaving the saddle, but all were determined and focused.

When the high walls of Carhall loomed in the distance, it was a clear, sunny morning. The blue sky above the city was cloudless, with no trace of swooping nerik, and the roads winding towards the city were busy with the usual amount of traffic.

"They haven't matured yet, then," Ahrin observed.

"I'm not surprised," Lira murmured.

"You're wearing your thinking frown." Ahrin glanced down at her.

Lira nodded, her head resting against Ahrin's shoulder, eyes half closed against the bright sun. "It's like you said, Lucinda doesn't leave things to chance. How did she organise to have the creatures hatch on command so that they'd be close enough to maturity by the time she arrived? And I know she was powerful ... but upwards of a hundred monsters? Was her paralysis magic really strong enough to contain that many at once?"

"Does it matter at this point who her person in Carhall was? It's too late to stop it, and we have no time to go looking for those answers."

*Person in Carhall.*

Blinding realisation flashed through Lira, and she sat up straight, turning her head to look at Ahrin. "Athira!"

At Lira's sudden movement, Tarion brought his horse in closer, concern on his face. Fari stirred in front of him, eyes opening from a doze. "Everything okay?" Tarion asked.

Lira ignored them, watching Ahrin's gaze narrow in thought, her quick mind catching on fast. "Athira didn't need to be on board the ship from Rotherburn to smuggle the eggs—any one of the crew could have done that. And she didn't need to come with us to spy, because you knew she was a spy and Lucinda already had Lorin in your inner circle."

"So why send Athira with us?" Lira frowned. "Ahrin, do you know why they kept her instead of sending her back like the rest of us after our kidnapping?"

"Lucinda never told me exactly, but I do know that Jora considered the early results of the experiments on her promising. He was quite energised about it, more so than the rest of you. Enough that they were willing to take the risk of keeping the child of such important mages a prisoner."

Tarion looked between them. "Did Athira talk about having any extra abilities, apart from an increase in the strength of her amplification ability?"

"No, but now we know she was mentally conditioned," Lira said. "If the experiments gave her extra abilities, she probably wouldn't have been able to tell us."

"Amplification..." Tarion murmured. "Could it be she was a failsafe for Lucinda? For her paralysis magic to be able to hold back so many creatures, maybe she was going to rely on Athira to bolster her strength."

*Of course.* Lira berated herself for not seeing it sooner.

"That makes a lot of sense," Fari said.

"It does, but if that was Athira's only purpose, why send her with you? Why not keep her in Rotherburn and just bring her along when Lucinda travelled to Carhall?" Ahrin asked. "For someone who kept everything so locked down and carefully planned, that would have been the least risky move."

"She's the trigger," Lira said. It was the obvious answer. "Either she has another ability, or it has something to do with her amplification power. Athira must have been the recipient of the message Lucinda sent, and she has somehow triggered the hatching of the nests."

A brief silence fell, then Fari spoke, "And that makes even more sense because ... Athira is in Carhall right now, isn't she?"

Lira thought back to the room in the gambling hall, the relief on Athira's face when she'd asked Dawn to take her to Carhall. They'd assumed Athira had been glad to finally be going home ... but no. The relief had been because her mental conditioning had wanted her to be in Carhall.

"If this is true, it also means she knows exactly where the baby monsters are!" Tarion said, gaze snapping to Lira's.

Lira lurched backward into Ahrin's chest as the Darkhand set her heels to her horse and sent him galloping along the column of riders to join Caverlock at the front. In response to his raised eyebrows, she merely snapped, "Let's move this along."

Not protesting, Caverlock lifted a hand, brought it sharply down, and the entire column moved into a swift canter towards the city gates.

A noticeably larger presence of militia was posted at the western city gates as they rode in, and mingling with the crowds in the streets too. Caverlock led them straight through to Centre Square. The orderly rows of militia trailing them caused a few raised eyebrows and surprised looks, but nobody looked worried.

Centre Square was empty of any but those wearing the green of the militia or blue of a council mage. By the time they'd ridden across the massive open space and dismounted at the base of the steps leading up to the Town Hall, Egalion and Garan appeared, striding out the front doors. Caverlock dismissed the strike team to get what rest they could before they were needed again, and Lira and the others joined his wife and Garan.

Egalion gave a cry of delight at the sight of Tylender and almost bowled him over with the force of her hug. They clung to each other for a long time, tears streaking both their faces.

Everyone else gave them a moment, but eventually Caverlock cleared his throat. "You've closed the square?" he asked his wife.

She nodded and stepped away from Tylender but kept a hand on his arm, as if not wanting to lose the contact so quickly. "And emptied all the surrounding buildings. It seemed the safest option, the best we could do without causing widespread panic. Even so, we're getting a lot of questions." Together, they began ascending the steps. "We got your news three days ago and immediately instituted a search, but so far nothing. Every building lining this square, including Town Hall, has been swept clean from top to bottom. No eggs, no baby monsters."

From the top of the steps, Lira swept her gaze around the open space. The walls of Centre Square weren't high, nothing that would stop a razak, let along the nerik, from flooding out into the rest of the city and gorging themselves on its citizens.

"Where's Athira?" Ahrin asked.

Egalion frowned. "What has that—?"

"Mama, please, is Athira still here?" Tarion asked urgently.

"Yes, she's with the Hunters, spending time working with Dawn and the healers."

"Can you have her brought to us, as quickly as possible?" he asked.

By now, they'd reached the council chamber. It was empty of councillors for the moment, and they all dropped wearily into seats around the table. Having read the expression on her son's face, Egalion spoke to one of the warrior guards at the door, asking him to have Athira brought to them as soon as possible.

"There's worse news than not finding anything yet." Egalion looked grim.

Caverlock cursed under his breath. "Don't tell me. King Mastaran, Cayr, and Leader Astohar are still here too?"

Egalion nodded, the frustration spilling out of her. "Mastaran is honourable to a fault. He says he won't flee a city filled with thousands of his people if they can't leave either—and no, a mass evacuation is too risky ... worst case scenario? The monsters reach maturity while the entire population is trying to flee. Cayr wants to stand with Tregaya, and Astohar seems to think this whole thing is his fault because he's done a poor job of dealing with discontent in Shivasa, so he won't abandon Carhall either."

"A group of utter fools," Ahrin said with disgust. "What do they think is going to happen to their countries if they all die here?"

"She's right," Lira spoke up when everyone turned to look incredulously at the Darkhand.

Dashan grimaced. "At least tell me Jenna came with Cayr?"

"She did." Egalion nodded. "Not that she's been able to talk any sense into him. The only silver lining is that the Zandian emperor was still on his way to Carhall, so we've been able to contact his mage guards and turn the delegation around."

Tarion turned to Lira. "Can you sense anything?"

She shook her head in disappointment. "I'll keep trying, but I have a sinking feeling that I won't feel them until they've matured."

Tylender spoke into the silence. "Is it possible that Lucinda's message never got here, that the recipient never received it and the things *haven't* hatched yet?"

"Anything is possible," Ahrin said dryly. "But if I were you, I wouldn't want to bank the lives of everyone in this city on it."

Caverlock waved a hand. "The Darkhand is right, we proceed on the assumption those things are crawling around somewhere and about to flood the square en masse to hunt down every mage they can sense."

"What do you advise, Dash?" Egalion asked him. Nobody at the table seemed bothered by her deference to him. Not even Ahrin. Lira's mouth quirked in a smile—had her Darkhand finally come across someone she respected enough to follow?

Caverlock didn't hesitate. "You and I will concentrate on the protection of the city and our monarchs if the worst happens. I propose we have them bunker down in the militia barracks in the city—it's the most defensible building we have on hand. Vensis does have a point; magic help us if Lucinda manages to posthumously destabilise our entire continent in one go." He took a breath, turned. "Lira, can we ask you and your Darkhand to coordinate finding and destroying the creatures?"

Silence fell. Egalion didn't protest. She merely looked at Lira with an eyebrow raised expectantly.

Lira glanced at Ahrin, who nodded, then turned to the others. "We can do that, but I need my people, including Tarion and Fari. You'll put as many militia soldiers as you don't need to protect the monarchs at Ahrin's disposal."

"Done," Caverlock said crisply.

Garan leaned over the table, a smile turning up the corners of his mouth. "I'm with you too, Lira. The combat patrol that never was, right?"

Lira grinned at him and nodded.

"Now where in rotted hells is Athira?" Ahrin demanded.

Almost as if summoned, the doors swung open, revealing the mage Egalion had sent to bring Athira. "Councillor, I'm sorry but we can't find her."

Lira leaned over to Tarion. "Find your aunt, now!"

He nodded and teleported from the room.

"What do you mean, you can't find her?" Egalion asked.

"She's not in her quarters, nor in the healing centre. I asked the healers. Nobody has seen her since yesterday."

"You weren't watching her?" Ahrin snapped.

"She's not a prisoner," Egalion snapped back. "And Dawn has been making good progress with her."

Rotted hells. "We'll find her," Lira said. "I suspect she has something to do with the monsters." She gave a quick run through of her theory.

Caverlock nodded. "Go, do what you need to. Alyx and I will get the monarchs and councillors safely to the militia barracks, make sure they've got enough protection around them, and then we'll meet you back here." He held their gazes. "If the worst happens, our one and only goal is holding those creatures inside Centre Square. Under no circumstances can we let them get free into the city."

Quick nods around the table—nobody disagreed with that.

"Aunt Alyx, I propose we send any mages whose abilities won't be of use against razak to stay with the monarchs and councillors," Garan suggested. "The rest we'll gather here in the council building ready to deploy. Given Lucinda's timeline, those monsters could literally start pouring through the doors at any moment."

A little shiver ran down Lira's spine—he was right. They might not have much time left.

"Do it." Egalion nodded.

Everyone rose to their feet, wearily pushing chairs back. They paused when Tarion flashed back into sight with Dawn A'ndreas.

"Go," Lira told them. "Do what you need to do. We'll stay in touch."

"You need my help?" Dawn asked Lira, eyes tracking everyone else as they began filing out of the room.

"I assume you know what's coming?"

"Alyx told me, yes."

"Athira is missing. We think she might have something to do with the razak and nerik reaching maturity." Lira gave her a quick run-through of their suspicions. "I know you've been helping with her healing, but is it possible that she could still be acting on conditioned orders?"

"We've made some positive progress with undoing her mental conditioning, but it was soundly done and over a long period of time," Dawn said. "It was also more complex than what was done to your Hunters. There are parts of her mind still blank to me. So the answer to your question is very much yes."

Rotted carcasses. Lira had been hoping for a different answer. "Can you find her mind? You can do it faster than us wandering around aimlessly searching. If we can get Athira, we might be able to have her lead us to the creatures before they mature."

Dawn smiled, looking relieved at being able to do something to help. "I absolutely can."

Ahrin drew Lira aside while Dawn closed her eyes and took a deep, focusing breath, Tarion hovering protectively over his aunt. "What about our Hunters? I trust them more than the Tregayan militia, and they're in as much danger here as everyone else. We might need them before this is done."

Lira hesitated, then nodded. "Let's talk to Shiasta."

The healing centre in Carhall was a sunlit building only a block away from Centre Square and taking up almost a full block itself. A mixture of mage and human healers worked there.

"They're staying in a dormitory at the militia city barracks." A friendly clerk told them when they showed up. "Because there are so many, they come in here in small groups on a rotating basis. You're lucky—Shiasta is here this morning."

Ahrin and Lira followed the directions the clerk gave them, finding Shiasta and several other Hunters in a larger room on the second floor. They were seated in a circle, eyes closed, while a man wearing a blue council robe spoke softly. Another man stood outside the circle, paying close attention.

"I'm sorry to interrupt," Lira said when the opening of the door drew their attention. "We wouldn't have unless it was important."

"Lady Astor." A wide smile crossed the Hunter's face as he rose to his feet in one lithe movement. The others broke out into smiles at seeing her too.

"It's good to see you, Shiasta. Can we talk to you?"

"I..." He hesitated. "I don't have to, do I?"

Something clenched tightly in Lira relaxed at those words. These mage healers were truly helping him. "No, you don't. It's up to you."

He nodded, clearly adjusting to that, but then he said quietly, "I'd like to, though."

Ahrin waved Shiasta out the door, and Lira followed, but not without a small nod of gratitude in the direction of the healers.

"Something is wrong, Lady Astor, Commander Vensis?" Shiasta asked as they gathered in the hall outside.

"Just Lira, now," she said gently.

He merely nodded.

"The city is in danger," she explained, then told him everything they knew.

"As soon as we find Athira, we'll do our best to get to the monsters before they mature and forestall an attack," Ahrin told him. "But if we're too late—"

"You'll need help to protect the citizens of Carhall and kill the creatures," Shiasta cut her off, suddenly firm and assertive. "I will gather the Hunters at once. Is the Tregayan militia willing to give us weapons?"

"This isn't an order, Shiasta." It was Ahrin who spoke, before Lira could.

Those words spilled into a silence. Shiasta's head bowed for a moment, as if he were thinking something over, working through a problem. When he spoke, it was slow, halting. "You sent us here so that we would learn what freedom is," he said. "We are often still confused. It has been hard. But ... while I admittedly feel an impulse that I cannot explain to follow your wishes, it no longer binds me." His head came up, a light in his eyes. "I would like to help protect the people in this place that have been helping us so selflessly."

Ahrin cleared her throat. "Let's go and offer the other Hunters the same choice."

"They will make the same decision," Shiasta said softly. "Shiven lords created us as elite weapons to be used and disposed of at their whim. We would like a chance to use what they made us into for something better."

"You have nothing to prove," Lira said softly. "But I hear what you're saying." It resonated with her so powerfully that it had taken a moment for her to be able to speak. Hadn't she wanted the exact same thing?

"Then lead the way, Lira, Ahrin." A smile curled at Shiasta's mouth as he sounded out their names with an evident mix of discomfort and joy. "And let's go hunt some monsters together."

# CHAPTER 47

Dawn's voice speared into Lira's head just as they filed out of the militia barracks with every single one of the Hunters that had once been hers to command. *"We've found her. She's in Centre Square."*

"Centre Square, now!" Lira shouted, loud enough for them all to hear.

A breeze whipped up as they ran through the streets, ignoring the looks of surprise and concern thrown their way. It was early afternoon and the main thoroughfares were busy. There were so many people in this city. Such easy prey for monsters like the razak and nerik.

At least Egalion had had the forethought to clear Centre Square and the buildings lining it. If Lira was confident of nothing else, it was that Lucinda had designed her plan for the monsters to emerge there and take out the entirety of the council's mage strength first.

Lira spotted Athira immediately as they came through the eastern gate, standing with Dawn, Tarion, Garan, and Fari near the centre. Her boots and breeches were muddy, blonde hair tangled, as if she hadn't bathed or changed in a while. "Shiasta, would you wait here?" she asked him.

He nodded, and the Hunters formed neat rows, assuming that eerie stillness that had been drilled into them since birth. Lira and Ahrin jogged over to join the group, Lira's gaze catching movement at the steps of the Town Hall as they did—Egalion and Caverlock heading their way.

"I don't know what you're talking about," Athira was saying as Lira and Ahrin came to a halt. Her face was white, there were dark shadows under her eyes, and her hands trembled where they hung at her sides. All signs of the weariness that came from magic use.

"Where have you been, Athira?" Dawn asked gently. "Nobody has seen you in almost two days."

Athira shook her head. Swallowed. "I don't know."

"Where did you get that mud on your boots and pants?" Lira asked, pressing forward. As she did, she caught a familiar waft of something rotting. Her stomach sank as realisation flashed through her.

They'd put the eggs in the sewers underneath Centre Square.

Lira shared a quick glance with Ahrin—the Darkhand gave a quick nod; she'd picked up the scent too. Athira's attention jerked to Lira, and something in her eyes shifted, turned blank. "The Darkhand is here. She said she would be."

Lira was vaguely aware of Ahrin stepping away, walking to join Caverlock and Egalion, Tarion, Fari, and Garan trailing her. "Yes, Ahrin is here." Lira stepped closer to her cousin. "*Who* said she would be here? Lucinda?"

Athira hesitated. "It's time. The message said to start it. Now the Darkhand is here too, they'll come—is the Seventh ready? She said she might need my help."

A chill shuddered through Lira, realisation making her stomach sink to her toes. "Is Ahrin's presence a trigger, Athira?" she asked carefully. "Please, talk to me. Tell me what you know."

But Athira had drifted off, eyes sliding closed. A look of peace settled over her features. At her side, her fingers twitched.

"Is she using her magic?" Lira snapped at Dawn.

"Maybe." The telepath stepped closed to Athira, reached out to touch her arm. "It's hard to tell. I've healed some parts of her conditioning, but the rest of her mind is a maze."

"How much does she understand of what's happening?"

"She knows what Lucinda did to her, and she's been actively helping me and the healers work on her. Before you arrived just now, I told her your theory. She was horrified but didn't seem to know anything about it. Her conscious mind might not be aware of what she has been ordered to do—from what I can tell, the techniques Anler was using focused on the mind's subconscious."

"Rotted..." Lira stared wildly around, wishing she had some damned Hunter medallions with her. Swearing aloud, she shook Athira's arm. The woman merely swayed on her feet, eyes remaining closed, an expression of focus on her face.

"Her mind isn't responding to me either," Dawn said, jaw tight with effort.

Lira slapped Athira across the face, hard as she could. "Athira, stop!"

The woman reeled, then her eyes blinked open and she gave a little shake. "What happened?"

"You were using your magic. Why?" Lira searched her face.

"I ... you didn't kill me," Athira said abruptly. "When you captured me in Dirinan."

"I had no reason to kill you. You can't be blamed for what Lucinda did, what she made you do." Lira paused. "Athira, what were you doing just now?"

"I don't know. I don't remember." Her eyes had gone dark, and her shoulders were rigid. Lira's questions were brushing up against her conditioning. "I'm sorry. I don't know."

"Will you let Dawn into your thoughts, please?"

Athira gave a jerky nod, her gaze turning back towards the telepath. Dawn gave Athira a reassuring smile, then reached out to take gentle hold of her hand, eyes closing in concentration.

While the telepath worked, Lira waved the others over. Caverlock had left them, crossing the square at a run towards Town Hall.

"Our knowledge of the Carhall sewer system is hazy at best," Egalion explained. "But there are entrances into the basements of all these buildings. Some of them will be large enough to fit razak and nerik. Dash has gone to gather the militia and Taliath and send guards to set watch at the entrances we know about."

"Get your mages out here as well," Lira said. Instinct was weighing on her, warning her of approaching danger. Urging her to run. "I'm not sure we have much time."

Egalion gave Garan a quick look and he nodded, turning and running after his uncle. He'd only just left when Dawn let out a gasping breath and stepped away from Athira. "It's no good. I can't breach the conditioned parts of her mind, not without causing damage that can't be fixed."

"You want to save one girl's mind over the thousands of people who will be slaughtered if we don't stop these creatures?" Ahrin's sharp voice snapped out.

"We'll figure out another way," Egalion said firmly.

"There *is* no other way," Ahrin insisted. "Athira has clearly been in the sewers. Those things are coming, soon, and we need to get to them first. Do you want to save the people in this city or not?"

"Ahrin is right. Athira has been using her magic," Lira pointed out. "Look how tired she is. I don't think we've got time to figure out another way."

"She is your cousin, Lira," Tarion said quietly.

"I don't *want* to hurt her, Tarion," she snapped. "But is she really more important than everyone else in Carhall?"

"There's no guarantee it would work anyway," Dawn said. "Even if I push my way through the blocks, I can't be certain the knowledge I need will be there. It could collapse with her mind."

"Try," Ahrin said coldly.

"It's all right," Athira said then, sounding more like herself, still pale but determined. "I don't know what's going on. My mind is ... so many pieces. But if I can help, I want to."

Rotted carcasses. Lira couldn't help but think back to that night on Shadowfall Island. Athira refusing to escape so that she could stay behind and help spy on Underground. Risking her life to do so. And now she was offering to do it again, even though she didn't properly understand what was going on.

"We'll keep searching," Egalion said eventually. "And hope we find the creatures before they mature."

Lira shook her head. It was too late for that.

She could force this, push them to pry the information out of Athira's mind. Ahrin gave her a pointed look, understanding the power Lira had. Movement in her peripheral vision drew her attention to the Town Hall steps, where long rows of militia filed out, splitting at the base of the steps to line the square. Blue-cloaked mages appeared too, one or two at a time, coalescing in a loose group at the base of the steps. She looked to the opposite side of the square, where her Hunters stood, armed and ready. Men and women that could get hurt and die if the creatures erupted.

She turned back to Egalion. "I disagree. I don't want to hurt Athira, but it's the only course of action open to us, and we need to take it. If you want my help and that of my Hunters defending your city, then you'll get what you can from Athira's mind."

"Lira's right," Fari said. "It's unpalatable, but necessary."

Athira spoke again, stronger this time. "Lord-Mage A'ndreas, please. Do what you need to do. I accept the risks."

Just as the words came out of Athira's mouth, hanging in the air like a death knell, Lira felt the first faint prickle of heat in her head.

Then another.

And another.

Then, in the space of heartbeats, they erupted in her brain, so many that it felt like her head was on fire. She let out a gasping breath, swaying forwards.

Ahrin was there to catch her before she fell. "Lira?"

"Too late." She gasped, then her eyes rolled back in her head and she blacked out.

# CHAPTER 48

Lira groaned, aware of nothing but the fire in her skull. A moment later, Ahrin's voice sounded in her ear. "We need you to tell us where they are, Lira. I know it's overwhelming, but try to focus on my voice. On me."

She did her best, narrowing her focus on the sound of Ahrin's cool voice, the sensation of the Darkhand's fingers tangled with hers.

"That's right," Ahrin kept talking, her cool voice a balm to the unbearable heat in her brain. "Focus on me. We need you to tell us where the creatures are coming from so we can try and stop them before they emerge into the square."

Lira tried, but it was so hard to string a thought together, to do any more than simply listen to Ahrin's words. There was shouting nearby—Caverlock's voice, she thought, calling out orders? Egalion was speaking too, and then she thought she heard Fari.

"Just me, beloved, focus on my words," Ahrin murmured. "You can do this."

Lira began to breathe. In and out. She fought to relax, to adjust to the fire swarming across her brain. Slowly but surely, she drew the threads of her attention together. "Underneath Town Hall," she murmured. "And the Hub. Prison too. Converging on us, I think, but they're pretty far below."

"Good." Ahrin squeezed her hand. "Now open your eyes."

She did, looked straight into Ahrin's midnight blue gaze. She steadied herself there, compartmentalised the storm in her brain, and she came back to the present. The moment Ahrin could see that Lira was centred, she spun away, calm and magnificent. "The creatures are underneath Town Hall, the prison, and the Hub, and they're heading this way."

"How long?" Egalion demanded.

"I can't..." Lira winced. "They're deep, I think. Not in the next few minutes, but less than a half hour. I'm not certain ... it's too much for me to get a proper read, too overwhelming."

Dawn looked around, as calm as the others. "So maybe ten to fifteen minutes to figure out how to hold them all here once they erupt so they don't start feeding on the city."

There was a moment's silence, then Tarion's head flashed up. "It's simple. They hunger for mage blood above all, and they can sense magic. We can draw them all in here by using our magic."

"I'm talking to Garan right now." Egalion's eyes were half closed. "Telling him to have the mages open up all entrances between the basements and the square on their way out, and closing any others, giving them a clear path straight to us."

"That won't hold all of the nerik," Ahrin said. "But it's a good start. We need the militia archers lining the edges of the square. They can try to stop any nerik flying over—"

"Already done." Caverlock arrived, breath quick from running. "Tarion, can you take Athira to safety where Mastaran and the others are locked down? Dawn, you should go too ... you can be a line of communication between us if things go badly; we'll warn you if you need to run."

Everyone glanced towards Athira. At some point she had crumpled to the ground, out cold. Fari hovered over her. "I put her to sleep," the healer explained, standing. "Just to make sure she couldn't do anything else with her magic. She's okay."

Ahrin turned her attention to Dawn. "Once you're safe, Lord-Mage, contact every mage you can. Nobody is to use magic outside Centre Square. Not a single drop of it. The razak should stay here as long as they don't sense magic anywhere else."

"Done." Dawn immediately closed her eyes, sinking into her magic. Tarion stepped up beside her, and they both flashed out of sight. A heartbeat later, Tarion reappeared, and he gently picked up Athira before vanishing again. When he returned, he reported, "Everyone's safe in the barracks. They'll be fine as long as we hold the creatures here."

All gazes swung to Garan as he came running over to re-join them, cheeks flushed. "All mages whose magic abilities are ineffective against razak are stationed with the monarchs, along with half the Taliath we could gather," he reported. "Those who can still be of use are out here—six warrior mages and seven Taliath. They'll join the militia along the walls to help hold the nerik. Aunt Alyx, Rani is with them and will keep his mind open to you so that you can maintain communication."

Fari lifted a hand. "Nobody else is mildly concerned about being the bait for hundreds of deadly monsters?"

Garan flashed her a smile. "We got this."

"What we 'got' is the world's most powerful mage," Lira pointed out dryly. A mage who could also breach the monsters' immunity ... that thought brought an idea. Her eyes narrowed in thought as she chased it down.

Caverlock stared up at the sky. "Lira, how long do we have?"

She winced as she used a tendril of magic to re-engage. The maturing of the creatures had caused her ability to surge earlier, but it seemed to be settling now, becoming a more bearable sensation in her head. When she concentrated, she was able to sense more nuance in their presence. "They're closing in. Maybe five minutes." She swore, urgency filling her voice. "Some are meandering, though, heading in a different direction, under the walls. We need to start using magic to draw them here."

Caverlock ran over to the militia commander hovering nearby to relay his orders. Egalion closed her eyes, presumably to order Rani to get the mages to start using their magic. Garan employed telekinesis, sending his staff swooping through the air. Tarion started randomly flashing in and out of sight. Ahrin summoned a bright scarlet concussive burst, allowing it to spin in her palm.

Lira allowed enough of her magic to escape to light her hands and forearms in a violet glow, then gestured at Egalion, drawing her a few paces away from the huddle.

"Something wrong?" The mage councillor followed without hesitation, keeping her voice low.

"There aren't enough of us to keep all the nerik contained to Centre Square," she said bluntly. "The archers will stop a few, but their eyes are damnably difficult to hit, especially in the dark, which it will be once razak are swarming all over the place."

"What do you suggest?"

"It's going to have to be you, Egalion. You can fly, and the nerik aren't immune to your magic." Lira paused. "I know what I'm asking of you."

"You want me to leave the five of you down here alone to face a horde of razak?" Egalion snorted. "Not happening."

"We're not alone. We have my Hunters," Lira pointed out. "Not to mention all five of us have fought razak multiple times before. You will have, by far, the most dangerous job."

Egalion's gaze drifted skyward. Still, she hesitated.

"How about we make a deal, you and I?" Lira suggested. "You destroy the nerik before they can start eating random citizens of Carhall, and I'll stop the razak from breaking out of Centre Square."

"And if doing that means you need to risk your life over-using the magic that can breach their immunity?" Egalion asked quietly.

"A deal's a deal."

Egalion offered her hand. "Accepted, Lira Astor."

Even as she spoke, a sudden chill racked Lira's frame.

The temperature was dropping.

Egalion's voice, magically enhanced, rang out across the square so that all the soldiers and mages could hear it. "Dashan, you've got command of the Taliath and militia. Your job is to surround the square and stop anything that tries to leave. The rest of us will remain in the centre as a beacon to draw them in."

Caverlock drew his wife in close, murmured something in her ear that made her smile and nod. He spoke with Tarion next, hugged his son tightly, then jogged off, drawing *Heartfire* from its sheath as he did so. Egalion's gaze lingered on him for a few more moments, then she turned to their son. "Be safe."

"You too, Mama." He hugged her fiercely.

Egalion levelled a single glance at Lira, and they exchanged a nod, before the most powerful mage in the world soared into the sky. That left Lira and her Darkhand standing there with Fari, Tarion, and Garan.

Garan flashed his charming grin. "First outing for the combat patrol that never was?"

Lira cast a worried gaze at Fari, who gave her a murderous look. "Don't you dare suggest I go and cower inside the militia barracks. If one of you gets hurt in the middle of the fight, who else is going to help?"

"We fight together, not alone," Tarion reminded Lira.

Ahrin glanced between them. "I'll lead the Hunters. We'll make sure you don't get overwhelmed."

Lira caught her hand as she went to leave. "Don't you dare die on me, Ahrin Vensis."

Ahrin flashed her wicked smile. "I don't do dying, Astor."

It was then they heard the first rattle echo through the afternoon.

# CHAPTER 49

Deep, biting cold swept slowly over Centre Square, icy tendrils creeping through clothing and brushing like needles against their skin. Everyone's breath frosted. On the heels of the first rattle came another, from the opposite direction, and then another. And another.

And then the ear-splitting screech of the nerik rang out.

Lira and her friends stood together in the middle of Centre Square. Ahrin and the Hunters surrounded them in a loose protective circle. Her heart gave a solid thump as she saw the first razak emerge from inside Town Hall, seething down the steps. More followed, many more, *too many more*.

And with them came inky black darkness, oozing across the wide-open space until it seemed like night was falling hours too early. Glass smashed in one of the Hub's windows, and a nerik flew out of it, wings spread as it soared high into the sky. Several followed, more windows smashing open. Others came padding out of the doors that had been left open, wings immediately spreading to take flight. Their screams were hungry.

Caverlock's voice sounded in a crisp order and arrows hissed into the sky. None brought a nerik down. The first boom of Alyx Egalion's concussive magic sent green light slicing through the darkness, giving the defenders heart.

But as the boom faded away, it was replaced by a frenzied, angry rattling. And more hungry screeching as the nerik converged on Egalion and her magic. Within moments, the razak were on them.

They *seethed* across the square, making straight for the mages at the centre of it. A handful broke left or right, towards the walls, and they were quickly engaged by the Taliath and militia. Cries of fear and surprise sounded, mixing with the infernal rattling. Nobody had ever fought creatures like this before.

There were so many that their inky darkness obscured everything from sight, and as they came even closer, the walls of Centre Square faded from sight behind a wall of writhing, scaled, limbs and fiery silver eyes.

A snarl sounded, close, and Lira spun, magic surging.

Only to see Tarion's tall form grow even taller, shoulders broadening, long claws snapping out from his knuckles, inky scales sliding over his skin. A chaotic copper glow flashed from his eyes and another low snarl rumbled in his throat as he drew *Darksong* from its sheath. The blade whispered its eager anticipation as it was set free.

Lira took a deep breath, summoned her magic, and wreathed the first creature to reach her protective cordon of Hunters in violet-edged white flame.

It screamed.

And then the rest were on them.

The Hunters couldn't stop all the razak from reaching Lira and her friends, only slow them down, and the outer layer was quickly overwhelmed. Several of the creatures joined together into a larger monster, looming high over the group, cutting them off from everything but each other.

Lira's world narrowed to the darkness surrounding her and the infernal rattling pounding at her ears. Cario Duneskal's staff swung freely in her hands. Tarion flashed in and out of sight at her side. Garan's bellowing echoed in her ear. Fari stayed shielded between them, stepping quickly as she used her staff where she could. And occasionally a Hunter appeared out of the darkness to cover her back when she was vulnerable.

Utterly engulfed by the monsters, there was no way to know how the rest of the battle was going, whether they were managing to keep the razak in the square, whether Egalion was succeeding in keeping the nerik in the skies directly above.

It certainly didn't feel like they were winning. It felt like they were barely holding back an inexorable tide.

Lira swung her staff over and over, lit razak limbs alight with flame when they got too close to her or one of the others, moved unceasingly to avoid being hit. Her skin became slicked with sweat despite the cold. Breath rasped in and out of her lungs. Magic thrummed alive in her blood, hot and thrilling.

But they kept coming. No matter how hard she fought, how quickly she moved, how much magic she employed. There were so many of them.

She began to slow down. Saw Garan stumble and almost fall, only Tarion's quick move saving his chest from being ripped open. If they kept going as they were, they would lose. The razak would kill them, and then there would be nothing holding them in this square.

They needed a moment to breathe, to take stock.

Lira took a deep, steadying breath, drew upon a risky amount of magic, and let it out of her with a roar. Flame erupted to life, engulfing everything within fifty paces of them. Razak screamed, the flames catching and spreading before they could separate themselves quickly enough.

It gave them a fleeting moment of space. The darkness drew back enough that everyone came into sight. Ahrin was no more than two strides from Lira. Lira saw the bodies next, Hunters who'd died protecting them. Keeping them alive so their magic could keep drawing in the monsters.

The sight made her want to scream. The desire to burn everything roared through her.

A concussive boom roared out above and Lira looked up. Green light flashed, briefly illuminating a sky that seemed full of nerik, even as a dead carcass plummeted to the ground mere metres away.

Egalion couldn't survive that many, surely? She was already achieving the impossible, keeping them all in the sky above Centre Square, and staying alive.

"Lira?" Tarion's voice was laced with the angry violence of the monster as he pointed.

Their plan *was* working. The razak in the square weren't trying to leave; they were coalescing around the middle of it, seeking the magic they could sense in Lira and her friends. But there were so many. Instinct warned that they weren't going to be able to prevent themselves being overwhelmed by the sheer number of monsters.

Lira searched out Ahrin with her gaze, knowing she would have made the same read. "What do we do?"

"Stop using magic, fight our way free of the square, and save ourselves," the Darkhand replied instantly. She was covered in razak ichor, but unharmed, eyes bright with bloodlust. "Or keep fighting and die before we can kill all the razak."

"I'm staying," Tarion growled, gaze on his mother, high above them, fighting with clear desperation. Flying magic took enormous amounts of energy ... surely she wasn't going to last much longer.

"Me too," Garan added.

"And me." Fari hefted her staff.

Lira Astor was no hero. She'd always known that, deep in her bones. But she wasn't Shakar Astor either. Nor was she Rawlin Duneskal, who was nowhere to be found when his home city was under attack.

Her legacy wasn't just the Darkmage's, or her father's. It was that of a mother who'd done everything she could to protect the little daughter she'd loved more than anything. It was that of a man who'd been the most skilled telekinetic mage of his time, who'd freely given his life to save a friend he loved. A man who'd managed to become clever and funny and loyal even when his family hadn't wanted him. Lira wasn't sure she'd ever be that. Not a hero like Cario.

But she *was* Lira. Someone who found it easy to be ruthless when necessary, who loved the reckless thrill of pitting herself against the worst odds and challenging them to beat her. Someone who didn't much care about what was right but would stand by those she cared for if they needed it. She was also someone who would weaponise her relentless determination without hesitation to make sure she didn't lose those she loved.

So ... if Tarion, and Garan, and Fari were staying, then so was she.

"All right, then, we stay." She glanced at Ahrin. "You go, take the Hunters to safety."

"They choose to stay if you do," Ahrin said simply. "As do I."

"In that case, I have an idea." Lira looked at Tarion. "Can you bring me Athira?"

He opened his mouth, as if to question why, but almost as quickly closed again before vanishing from sight. There was no time for questions.

The razak closed in again before Tarion could return. In those moments without his help, the fighting became desperate. Lira and the others were barely able to avoid getting killed, let alone able to land any blows themselves. Ahrin brought her Hunters in closer, doing her best to help them.

The moment Tarion reappeared, Athira in his arms, still unconscious, Lira shouted to her Darkhand. "Can you keep them off us, just for a few moments?"

Ahrin flicked her a glance. "No longer than that."

"As long as you can." Lira gave her a little smile, knowing what she was asking, but trusting her Darkhand to come through.

Ahrin's wicked smile flashed in return, and then she was turning, knives raised, calling orders to her Hunters. They closed in around the small group of mages, fighting in seamless formation to hold the razak off from where Lira, Fari, Tarion and Garan hovered around Athira's prone body.

"What's the plan?" Garan cast a worried gaze at the razak so close, Hunters fighting desperately to hold them back. Already, as he looked, one of the Hunters fell, blood spraying.

Lira forced her gaze away from them, pushing the worry and grief from her thoughts. "Fari, I need you to wake her up."

"I'm trying," she said through gritted teeth. "I can't ... something is holding her under. I was trying to stop her from using her magic earlier, so I put her in a pretty deep sleep."

"Try again." Lira held her gaze. "You can do it."

"Lira, I think the conditioning might have damaged her mind," Fari said patiently. "I'm not a telepath."

"No, you're a healer. Lucinda didn't account for the fact that Athira was being helped by Dawn and mage healers for days before the monsters hatched. Some of the conditioning has already been undone, Fari. You need to wake her up. I have faith in you."

"We all do, Councillor Dirsk," Garan said, resting a hand on her shoulder.

Tarion let loose a spine-tingling snarl. Lira assumed it was his version of encouragement.

Without any further argument, Fari placed her hand back on Athira's forehead. The infernal rattling of the razak filled the air around them as they waited, tense, restless. Hunters danced and whirled around them, beautiful and deadly, but also falling.

One staggered and Lira watched, her heart clenching ferociously, as blood sprayed from his chest. He staggered and fell to the ground. Another Hunter immediately stepped into the gap, but it was a losing battle.

"Lira, you've got seconds at most!" Ahrin bellowed through the darkness.

Her gaze returned to Fari. The woman's jaw was clenched, shoulders stiff. Garan shifted from foot to foot, gaze darting around them, while Tarion stood still, growling softly, the entirety of his focus on Fari.

Then Athira's eyes blinked open.

Lira immediately dropped to her knees beside her, heedless now of the razak and the screams and the fighting surged around them. "Athira, can you hear me?"

The woman nodded, wincing as she pushed herself upwards, still orienting herself. "What happened?"

"No time for explanations. Right now, I need your help."

Athira blanched as she took in the razak so close, heard their rattling, saw the dire situation they were in.

"Athira?" Lira sought her gaze. "Will you help me?"

"Lira!" Fari's voice cut in. "If you're thinking what I *think* you're thinking, you can't. There are too many. You'll kill yourself."

"Nah." Lira's smile widened as she kept her gaze on Athira's and held out her hand. "We Duneskals are made of sterner stuff than that. Right, cousin?"

A matching smile flickered over Athira's wan face, and without hesitation, she reached out to take Lira's hand.

"Lira, no!" Ahrin's voice was as close to panicked as she'd ever heard it.

But Lira was already gone. She was diving into her magic, Athira's amplification widening her senses, replacing her lost reserves.

This was what she lived for.

Gathering it all together, Lira *roared* with the new strength of her magic, bringing to bear the years and years of effort she'd devoted to honing her focus and using that focus to control the magic roaring through her.

"Everything you can give me, Athira," she murmured, and almost immediately felt the answering surge of strength.

The world exploded into violet flame.

Razak screamed, the echoes of it spreading wider as Lira set them all alight, moving steadily from one to another to another. And as her power drained, she kept going, grimly forcing herself through the exhaustion, allowing the magic to burn through her, bright and hot and heady.

When she swayed, her mind forcing her body past its limits, a pair of hands settled on her shoulders, holding her steady, and when her breathing began to falter, another hand slid into her free one, sending her a jolt of magical healing strength.

And Lira kept going, pushing through, refusing to give up.

Until they were all dead.

And then, instead of stopping, she opened her eyes, still looking straight into Athira's. They were dazed, dark with exhaustion like Lira's own must be. Bright green light flashed as another concussive boom echoed out, though it sounded weaker than the previous ones.

"Can you?" she rasped.

Athira glanced upwards, came back, nodded. Their grip tightened.

Lira's eyes closed again, and she reached out farther, into the sky. And she started killing nerik. Her magic changed form a hot thrill to a rasping burn as she drained her reserves and kept going, determined to kill as many as she could.

Athira didn't stop sending her power, and Fari kept feeding her strength. Garan never let go of his hold on her and none of them tried to stop her.

And some part of her could *feel* Ahrin, the Darkhand's steady gaze watching only her, Tarion and Shiasta and his Hunters doing the same, willing to lay down their lives to keep her safe if she asked it of them. Giving her their heart and their strength.

One by one, the nerik died. And one more after that. And just one more. Lira's breath whistled, she sagged completely in Garan's hold, and her magic finally began to die. Even then, she forced out every bit she could gather.

Until it was gone.

When Lira opened her eyes, her vision was blurry, and she felt strange, like she couldn't quite catch her breath. Her heart pounded oddly in her chest, faltering, skipping the occasional beat.

The darkness had gone, replaced with a bright, sunny afternoon shining over the square. Hunter bodies lay scattered around, the marble ground soaked with blood and ichor, but amidst all that were ashes. They drifted through the air and covered the ground. She could taste them on her tongue.

"I don't feel...," she mumbled.

Garan caught her before she hit the ground, his alarmed voice ringing out just in time for Tarion to catch Fari as she similarly collapsed. Athira had slumped into unconsciousness, her eyes closed, hands limp against the ground. Running feet sounded, but everything felt distant, strange. Blurred.

"Get Egalion here now or I start killing people," Ahrin roared, and it was the last thing Lira heard before she passed out.

Lira woke to Alyx Egalion's green gaze hovering over her. She looked tired, drained, but relieved to see Lira wake. "That was close, Astor. You'll need a better healer than me, and soon, but I've managed to keep you breathing for the moment."

"I held up my end," she muttered. "Fari? Athira?"

"Not as bad off as you. Garan is monitoring them while Tarion fetches the other healers."

"Ahrin?"

"Right here." The Darkhand's voice sounded in her ear and Lira realised that her head was cradled in the woman's lap. "What have I told you about your addiction to danger?"

Lira managed a grin. "Saved everyone, didn't I?"

"Almost killed yourself is what you did," Ahrin grumbled.

"I don't ..." The weakness came over her again. "Not..."

Egalion's palm pressed over her eyes. "Sleep now. We've got you. You're safe with us."

And for the first time in her life, Lira *believed* she was safe in the council's hands.

So she slept.

# CHAPTER 50

L ira stepped out onto the balcony, taking a deep breath of salty ocean air and soaking up the warm sunshine on her face. It was rare that days were so pleasant in Dirinan. Gulls swooped over the ships in the harbour, adding their calls to the music of the morning's activity on the docks. She felt loose and comfortable, rested and fully healed. Her staff hung down her back ... her *uncle's* staff.

"Dressed already?" Ahrin came padding out behind her, wearing only a satin robe that provided tantalising glimpses of bare skin. Her gaze took in Lira's clothes, the pack at her feet.

Lira's stomach flipped lazily, and she smiled. "You were still sleeping when I woke."

Ahrin stopped at the railing, close enough that their arms pressed together. "So?"

"What?" Lira leaned into the touch, resting her head on Ahrin's shoulder.

"We didn't get much chance to talk when you got in last night, and I haven't seen you since I left after the battle of Carhall. Everything settled?"

"Almost. Tylender has resumed his position as Magor-lier. I gave up the Duneskal seat—after helping Garan and Fari push through some promising changes to council rules." Her mouth quirked in a smile. "Tylender himself is taking up the council position in Karonan, at least for a little while. I think eventually the post will be Fari's. For now, though, he wants to impress upon the Shiven how seriously the council takes their grievances."

"How wonderfully boring," Ahrin said. "And Athira and the Hunters?"

Lira gave her a look. "Athira will be fine with time and healing. But don't be sneaky. I know you're in contact with the Hunters. I'm guessing some are already on their way here."

"Working for me is an attractive proposition," Ahrin said airily.

Lira huffed an amused breath. "They're doing well. Some have finished the program the healers set for them. All of them are going to complete it."

"Glad to hear it. Now, give it to me. What do *you* want to do next?" Ahrin asked.

"Right now, I'd like to kiss you." Lira smiled again and lifted her head to press her mouth to Ahrin's.

Ahrin eventually pulled away but kept one hand settled loosely against Lira's hip as she fixed her with a raised eyebrow. "Spill it, Astor. What's next for you? A seat on the council? Magor-lier? Head of Temari Hall?"

Lira snorted. Ahrin knew very well Lira wanted none of those things. "Then what?"

"The council have put together a team to go back to Rotherburn and destroy the razak once and for all. Thanks to Garan and Fari, the council have agreed that if we do that, Rotherburn won't have any need to think of invasion now or in the future. We can resume trade, embassies, all that stuff that prevents war."

"Not only that, but they'll be incredibly grateful to the council for a very long time," Ahrin pointed out. "Any threat they might pose to this continent will be completely nullified."

"Exactly," Lira paused, and then said quietly, "I'd really like to go with them."

"Seriously?" Ahrin regarded her in astonishment. "Did the battle of Carhall turn you into a nauseatingly altruistic hero mage?"

"Do you see me wearing council blue?" Lira lifted an eyebrow. "I really don't care two figs for the people of Rotherburn, *or* for keeping

Tregaya and Shivasa safe when it comes down to it. And I have no further interest, at *all*, in the Mage Council."

Ahrin huffed in annoyance. "Are you really going to make me drag the reasons out of you?"

A little smile toyed at Lira's mouth, and she turned to face Ahrin fully. "Going back to Rotherburn will be dangerous and daunting, and I'll be able to use my magic. My ability to sense the razak will be an enormous help. It will be fun, Ahrin." She shrugged. "Besides, Tarion needs a friend right now. He's a little heartbroken with Sesha betrothed to the Zandian emperor's favourite son."

Ahrin shook her head, a wry smile tugging at her mouth. "Look at you. Shakar Astor's heir making doe-eyed friends with Egalion's spawn. He'd be turning in his grave."

"Good!" Lira laughed, then sobered. "It's nice not to be alone anymore. And Tar and Garan accept that I don't want to save the world like they do."

Ahrin reached out, drew her close, wrapping her arms around her. "I don't want to go back to Rotherburn and hunt monsters in dark caves. I want to stay here and run my crew. I want to expand it. I want to run the whole of Dirinan. I have some other ideas too—alliances with crews in other ports."

"Then that's exactly what you should do."

She scowled. "Just like that?"

"Just like that. I'll be gone a few months, a year at the most, and then I'll come back here." Lira smirked. "And you'll wait for me, pining and counting the days."

She scowled. "I'll do nothing of the sort."

Lira held her gaze. "Do you remember when you asked me, back in Rotherburn, what I wanted when it was all over, after I'd killed Lucinda and gotten my revenge?"

"I do. You said it was all blank, that you couldn't *see* a future."

"It's still pretty unclear." She shrugged. "But I'm realising that's not a bad thing. My life is mine now, Ahrin. I can do whatever I want with it. For now, that's going to Rotherburn and risking my neck to kill some monsters with my friends. And after that's done … well, who knows? That's true freedom. The freedom I've always wanted."

Ahrin shifted closer, hands framing Lira's jaw. "And whatever you choose to do, wherever it takes you, know that you have a place with me always, Lira."

"And you with me, Ahrin."

"Hey, Lira, you're late!" They pulled apart at the sound of Tarion's voice calling up from below.

Garan and Fari stood with him, grinning from ear to ear. Garan waved and called out, "Hello Darkhand! A pleasure as always."

"Tarion has learned to speak at audible volume now?" Ahrin rolled her eyes. "Wonders will never cease. Lira, are you seriously leaving me right this moment? You only just got here."

"I am." Lira wrapped her arms tightly around Ahrin. "But I can't wait to come back and see you running Dirinan."

"You'd better … come back I mean."

"I will miss you fiercely, Ahrin Vensis. And I hope just as fiercely that you will be here when I return."

"You know I will," she said gruffly, then tugged her in for a long kiss.

Fari's voice called up now. "We're going to miss the tide. You know how Ropin gets about that."

Lira grinned at Ahrin, leaned up to give her a final kiss, then slung her pack over her shoulder and swung over the railing to land lightly in the street below. When she glanced back up, Ahrin had already disappeared inside. She grinned. Definitely not one for sappy partings, her girl.

"No chance of her coming along?" Fari asked mournfully as they set off down the street.

"She's mine," Lira said lightly. "Hands off."

"It's not that, it's just that she's much scarier than you. One look at that killing expression she has and the razak will spontaneously keel over."

"Can't help but agree with that," Garan said airily. "If only we had the Darkhand with us, we'd have those razak cleared out in three months."

"That sounds suspiciously like a challenge," Lira said, her smile widening as three figures who'd been waiting farther along the street came to join them. Shiasta, Therob, and Renia wore similar clothing to Tarion and carried swords at their hips and knives attached to various body parts.

"You're sure about this?" she asked them.

"You said we're free now, Lira," Shiasta pointed out. "So you can stop asking every ten seconds if we're sure."

"He has a point," Garan chuckled.

"I like killing monsters," Therob said, a touch of glee in his voice that hinted at real emotion.

"I just like to fight, I love the dance of it, but I don't want to hurt people," Renia said.

"We're sure," Shiasta repeated, in what approached a long-suffering tone. They were learning, her Hunters.

Lira accepted that, giving the three of them another smile before speeding up to fall into step with Tarion, who walked ahead, shoulders a little slumped.

He brightened at her appearance. "I'm so glad you're coming with us."

"How are you?" she asked, searching his gaze.

"That's good," he said approvingly. "It almost sounded like you sincerely care about my emotional state."

She snorted. "Don't be horrible."

"I'm grieving and sad, but that will pass with time." He nudged her shoulder. "I'm looking forward to monster hunting with you, Lira Duneskal."

Ropin's ship rocked at anchor as Lira and her companions traversed the gangplank and dropped down to the deck. The captain was at the wheel, two of his children sitting at his feet, pouring over an old map and compass. His youngest was in his arms, father and son wearing matching eye-patches as they pointed in the direction the ship would be travelling.

The mage warriors and Taliath coming along stood huddled in loose groups along the railing, staring out at the ocean and chatting. There were Rionnan Bluecoats too, a handful of militia scouts, and even a unit of fearsome Zandian Leopards. King Cayr Llancarvan had done a masterful job getting them all there to bolster the Mage Council strike force.

Lira headed belowdecks to drop her pack and staff on her bunk before returning to the deck to find the last of their group alighting from his carriage below. Messy hair flapping in the stiff breeze, Master Finn A'ndreas was almost vibrating with eagerness as he crossed the gangplank. "Lira." He gave her a brisk nod. "Good to see you."

A healer of his powerful skill would be an asset on this mission, but the man's enthusiasm for going to the place he'd been researching for decades was the true reason for his joining them. Not to mention how much help he could be to what remained of the Seven with his limitless font of knowledge and patience. She returned his nod. "A'ndreas, welcome aboard."

"Uncle Finn!" Garan and Tarion reappeared on deck, crowding around their uncle and offering to show him where he was sleeping.

Lira watched them with a smile, then tipped her head up and took a deep breath of the salty, seaweed-edged, air, soaking in the glorious morning sun.

The ship rocked under her, anchor clanging as it landed on the deck. Ropin gave the final call to his crew to depart.

A sharp whistle had her opening her eyes, staring in astonishment at the handsome, gangly Zandian leaping onto the gangplank just before it was pulled away from the dock. "Don't leave without me!"

"Yanzi." She couldn't stop the grin spreading over her face. "What in rotted hells are you doing?"

"Coming with you," he said, dropping his pack to the deck and lifting a hand of greeting in Ropin's direction.

"Since when?"

"Boss's orders." He winked. "I'm to scout out the Rotherburnian criminal element, look for expansion opportunities."

She couldn't help but laugh as he came to stand beside her at the railing, one arm settling loosely around her shoulders. Behind them, Shiasta and Therob were debating with Tarion about whether swords or daggers were more effective against nerik. Finn A'ndreas peppered Fari with questions about what razak wounds looked like. Garan and Ropin erupted into laughter over some joke Garan had made. Meanwhile, Lira and Yanzi stood and watched Dirinan harbour recede from sight, quiet and content to simply be together.

Crew and family.

Lira Duneskal was finally home.

## THE DOCK CITY CHRONICLE

Want to delve further into the world of *Heir to the Darkmage?*

By signing up to Lisa's monthly newsletter, *The Dock City Chronicle,* you'll get some free exclusive content: a deleted prologue froom Book 1, *Heir to the Darkmage.*

You'll also get exclusive access to lots of subscriber-only special content, updates on Lisa's books, her writing process, the books she's reading, and more!

**Sign up for *the Chronicle* and enter the adventure today...**

ALSO BY LISA CASSIDY

**The Mage Chronicles**

DarkSkull Hall

Taliath

Darkmage

Heartfire

**Heir to the Darkmage**

Heir to the Darkmage

Mark of the Huntress

Whisper of the Darksong

Rise of the Shadowcouncil

**A Tale of Stars and Shadow**

A Tale of Stars and Shadow

A Prince of Song and Shade

A King of Masks and Magic

A Duet of Sword and Song

## CONSIDER A REVIEW?

*'Your words are as important to an author as an author's words are to you'*

Hello,

I really hope you enjoyed this story. If you did, I would be genuinely thrilled if you would take the time to leave an **honest** review on GoodReads or Amazon, or both (it doesn't have to be long - a few words or a single sentence is absolutely fine!).

Reviews can be absolute game changers for the success and visibility of a book, and by leaving a review you'll help this story reach others. Not to mention you'll also be helping me write more stories.

Thank you so much for reading this book,

Lisa

# MORE ABOUT LISA...

Lisa is a self-published fantasy author by day and book nerd in every other spare moment she has. She's a self-confessed coffee snob (don't try coming near her with any of that instant coffee rubbish) but is willing to accept all other hot drink aficionados, even tea drinkers. She lives in Australia's capital city, Canberra, and like all Australians, is pretty much in constant danger from highly poisonous spiders, crocodiles, sharks, and drop bears, to name a few. As you can see, she is also pro-Oxford comma.

A 2019 SPFBO finalist, and finalist for the 2020 ACT Writers Fiction award, Lisa is the author of the young adult fantasy series *The Mage Chronicles* and *Heir to the Darkmage*, and epic fantasy series *A Tale of Stars and Shadow*. She is currently diving into a brand new series.

As part of her writing journey, Lisa has partnered up with One Girl, a charity working to build a world where all girls have access to quality education. A world where all girls — no matter where they are born or how much money they have — enjoy the same rights and opportunities as boys. A percentage of all Lisa's royalties go to One Girl.

You can follow Lisa on Facebook and Instagram, where she loves to interact with her fans. Lisa also has a Facebook group - Lisa's Writing Cave - where you can jump in and talk about anything and everything relating to books and reading.

If you want to learn more about Lisa and her books, head on over to
Lisa's Website - lisacassidyauthor.com

CPSIA information can be obtained
at www.ICGtesting.com
Printed in the USA
BVHW052008251122
652783BV00004B/38